HOUSE
of
EL

BOOK ONE

written by
CLAUDIA GRAY

illustrated by
ERIC ZAWADZKI

colors by
DEE CUNNIFFE

letters by
DERON BENNETT

BASED ON CHARACTERS CREATED BY
JERRY SIEGEL AND JOE SHUSTER
BY SPECIAL ARRANGEMENT WITH THE JERRY SIEGEL FAMILY

HOUSE of EL

BOOK ONE

THE SHADOW THREAT

JIM CHADWICK Editor
DIEGO LOPEZ Associate Editor
STEVE COOK Design Director – Books
AMIE BROCKWAY-METCALF Publication Design

BOB HARRAS Senior VP – Editor-in-Chief, DC Comics
MICHELE R. WELLS VP & Executive Editor, Young Reader

JIM LEE Publisher & Chief Creative Officer
BOBBIE CHASE VP – Global Publishing Initiatives & Digital Strategy
DON FALLETTI VP – Manufacturing Operations & Workflow Management
LAWRENCE GANEM VP – Talent Services
ALISON GILL Senior VP – Manufacturing & Operations
HANK KANALZ Senior VP – Publishing Strategy & Support Services
DAN MIRON VP – Publishing Operations
NICK J. NAPOLITANO VP – Manufacturing Administration & Design
NANCY SPEARS VP – Sales
JONAH WEILAND VP – Marketing & Creative Services

HOUSE OF EL BOOK ONE: THE SHADOW THREAT

Published by DC Comics. Copyright ©
2020 DC Comics. All Rights Reserved.
All characters, their distinctive likenesses,
and related elements featured in this
publication are trademarks of DC Comics.
The stories, characters, and incidents
featured in this publication are entirely
fictional. DC Comics does not read or
accept unsolicited submissions of ideas,
stories, or artwork.

DC – a WarnerMedia Company.

DC Comics, 2900 West Alameda Ave.,
Burbank, CA 91505

Printed by LSC Communications,
Crawfordsville, IN, USA. 11/27/20.

First Printing.

ISBN: 978-1-4012-9112-9

Library of Congress Cataloging-in-Publication Data

Names: Gray, Claudia, writer. | Zawadzki, Eric, illustrator. | Cunniffe,
  Dee, colourist. | Bennett, Deron, letterer.
Title: The shadow threat / written by Claudia Gray ; illustrated by Eric
  Zawadzki ; colors by Dee Cunniffe ; letters by Deron Bennett.
Description: Burbank, CA : DC Comics, [2021] | Series: House of El ; book 1
  | Audience: Ages 13+ | Audience: Grades 10-12 | Summary: "Zahn is one of
  Krypton's elites: wealthy, privileged, a future leader. Sera is one of
  Krypton's soldiers: strong, dedicated, fearless. Their rule-bound
  society has ordained that their paths should never cross. But
  groundquakes are shaking the planet's surface. Rebellious uprisings are
  shaking the populace. Krypton's top scientists-Jor-El and Lara-conduct a
  secret experiment that is meant to reform their planet from the cellular
  level up. Zahn and Sera must join forces to investigate the hidden
  dangers truly threatening Krypton. In the process, they form a bond that
  will endure past the end of the world."-- Provided by publisher.
Identifiers: LCCN 2020038528 (print) | LCCN 2020038529 (ebook) | ISBN
  9781401291129 (paperback) | ISBN 9781779508690 (ebook)
Subjects: LCSH: Graphic novels. | CYAC: Graphic novels. | Science fiction.
Classification: LCC PZ7.7.G7315 Sha 2021 (print) | LCC PZ7.7.G7315
  (ebook) | DDC 741.5/973--dc23
LC record available at https://lccn.loc.gov/2020038528
LC ebook record available at https://lccn.loc.gov/2020038529

CHAPTER
ONE

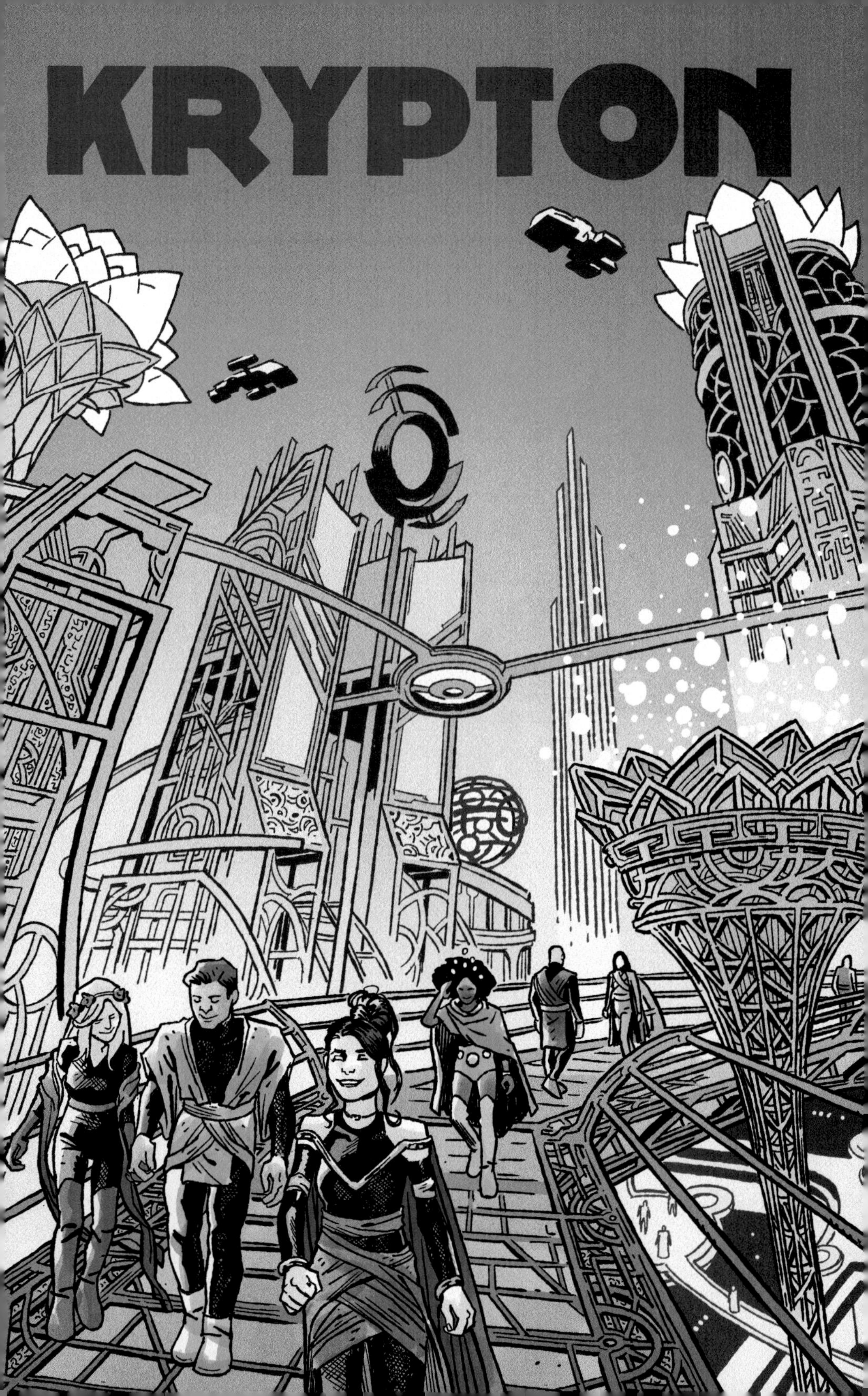
KRYPTON

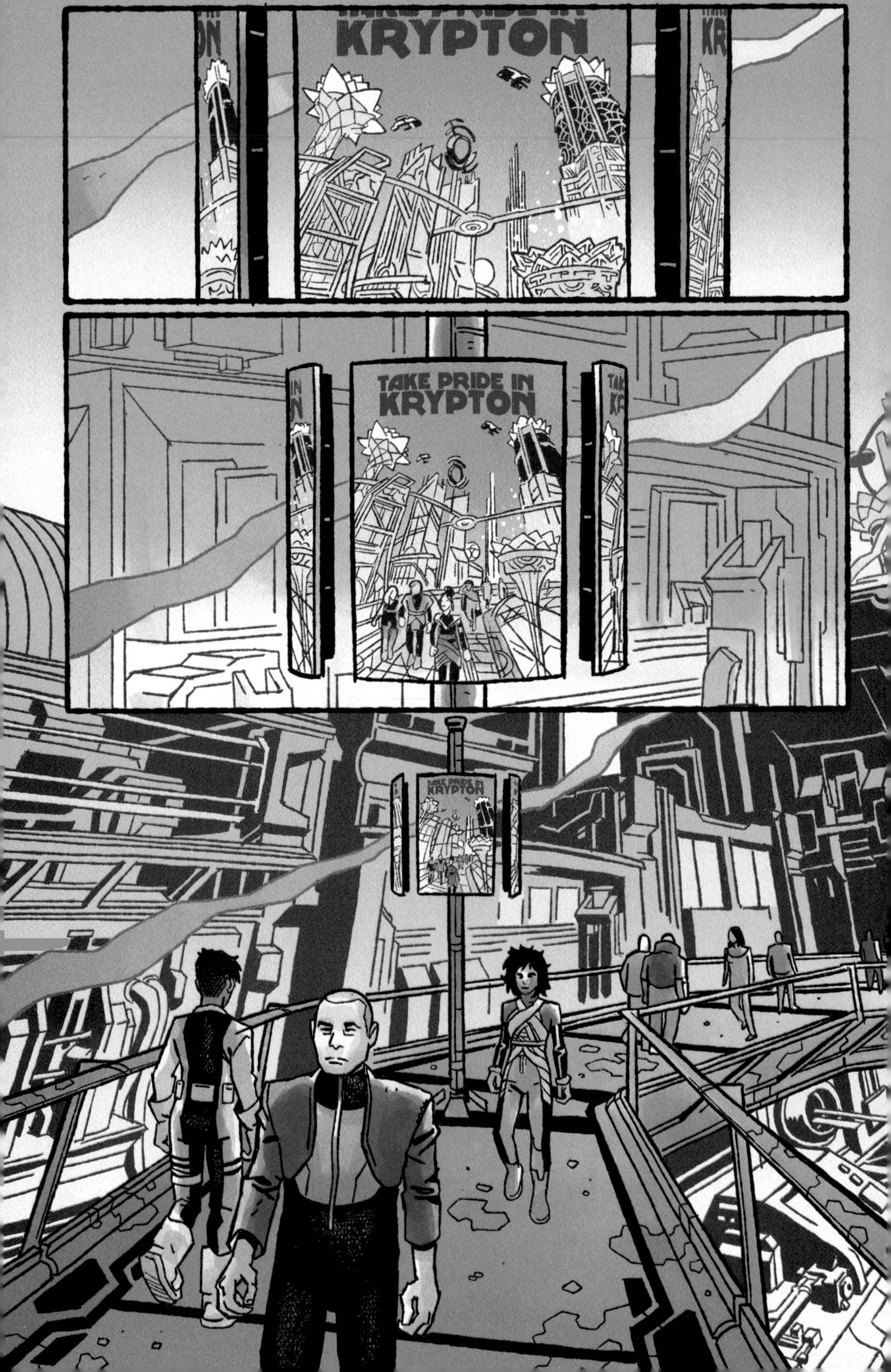
KRYPTON
TAKE PRIDE IN
KRYPTON
TAKE PRIDE IN
KRYPTON

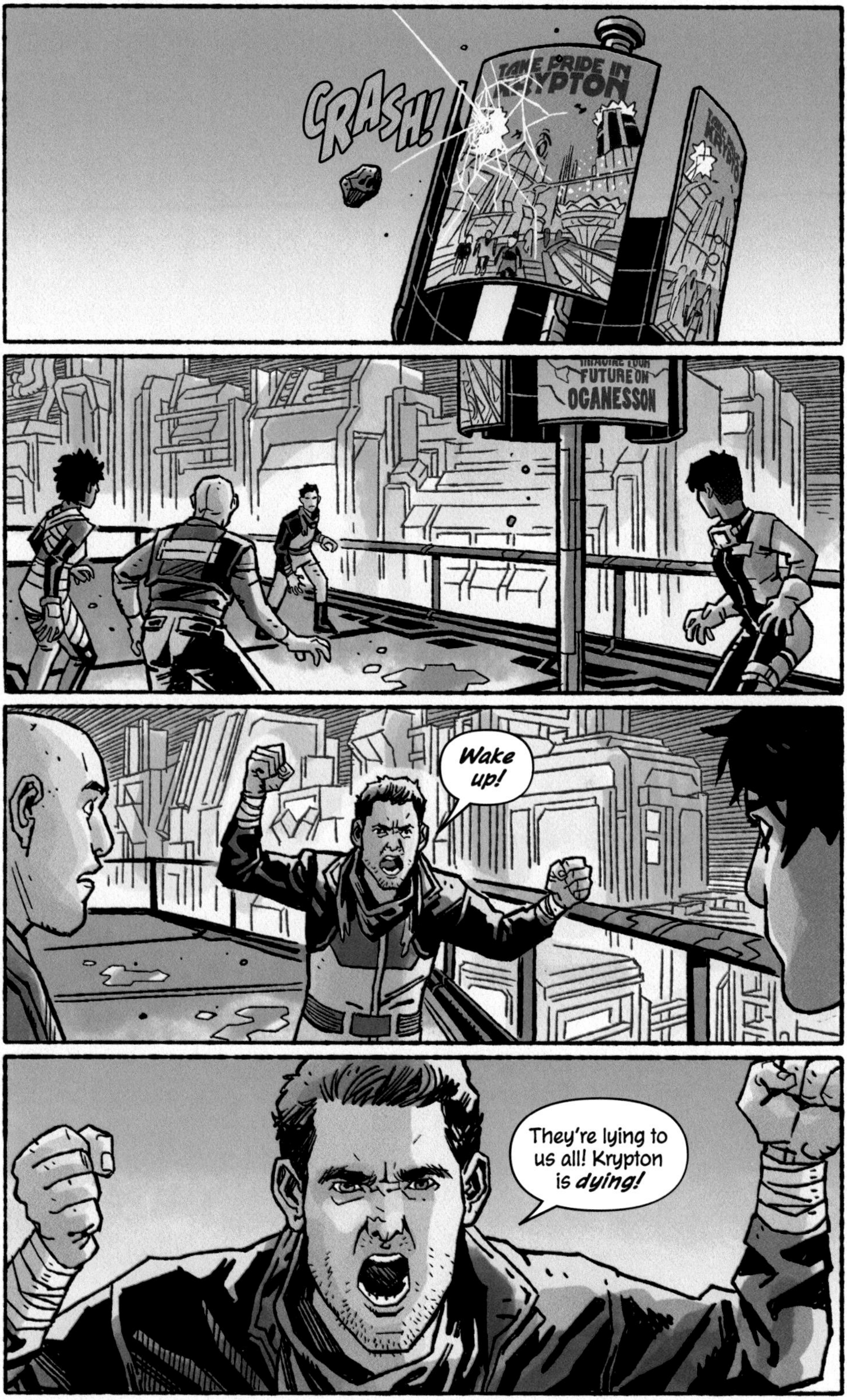

PRIDE IN
CRASH!
FUTURE ON
OCANESSON
Wake up!
They're lying to us all! Krypton is *dying!*

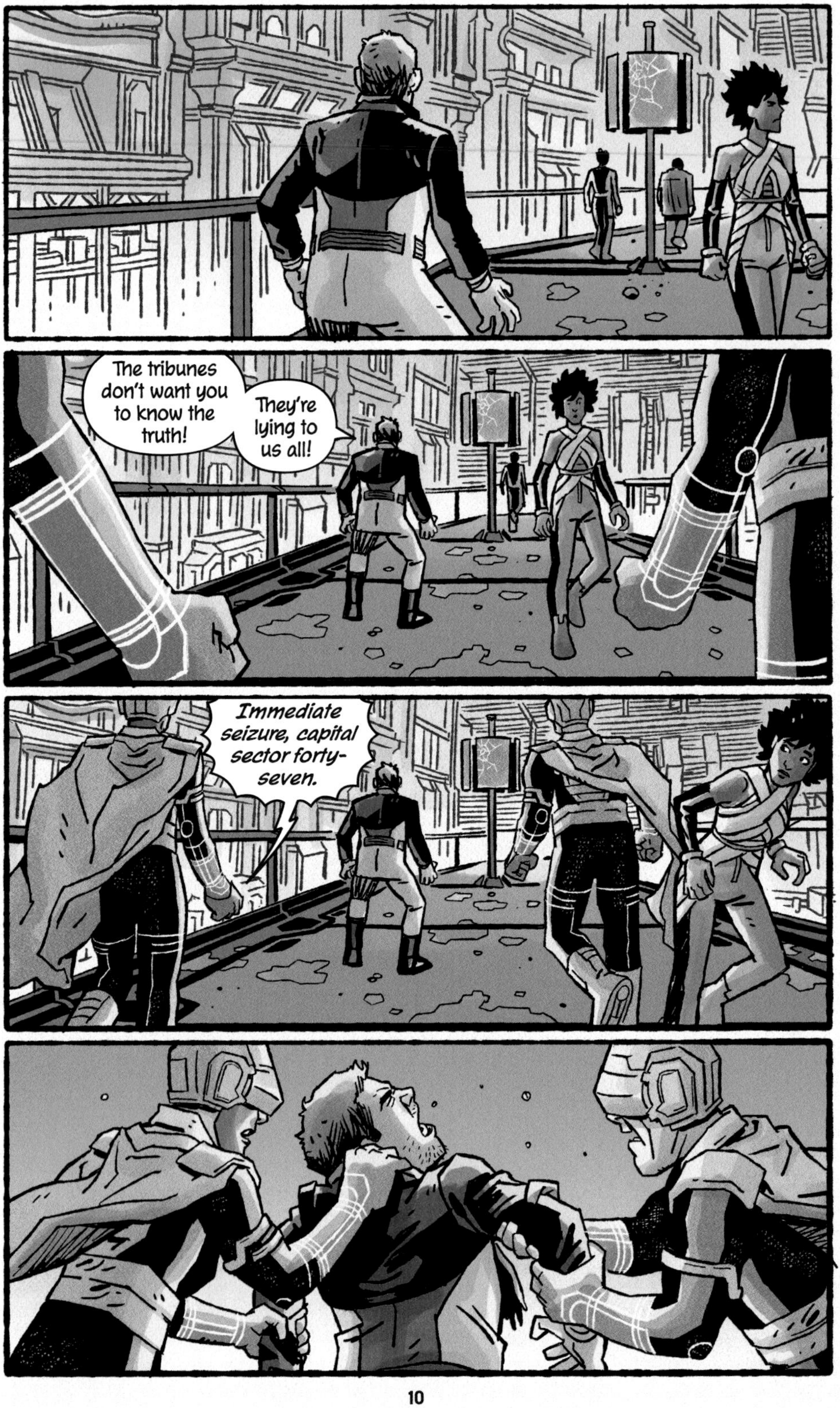
The tribunes don't want you to know the truth!
They're lying to us all!
Immediate seizure, capital sector forty-seven.

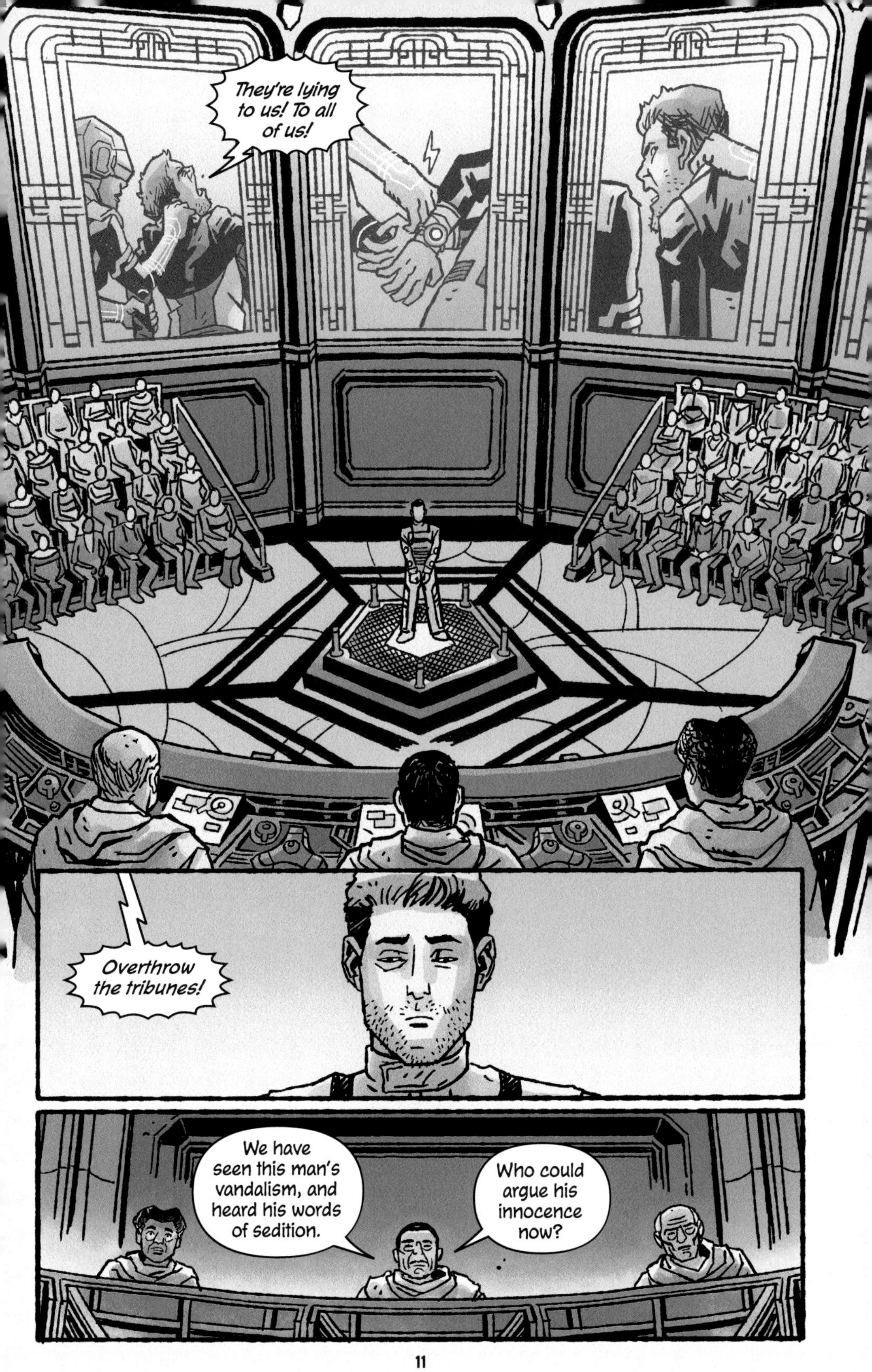
They're lying to us! To all of us!
Overthrow the tribunes!
We have seen this man's vandalism, and heard his words of sedition.
Who could argue his innocence now?

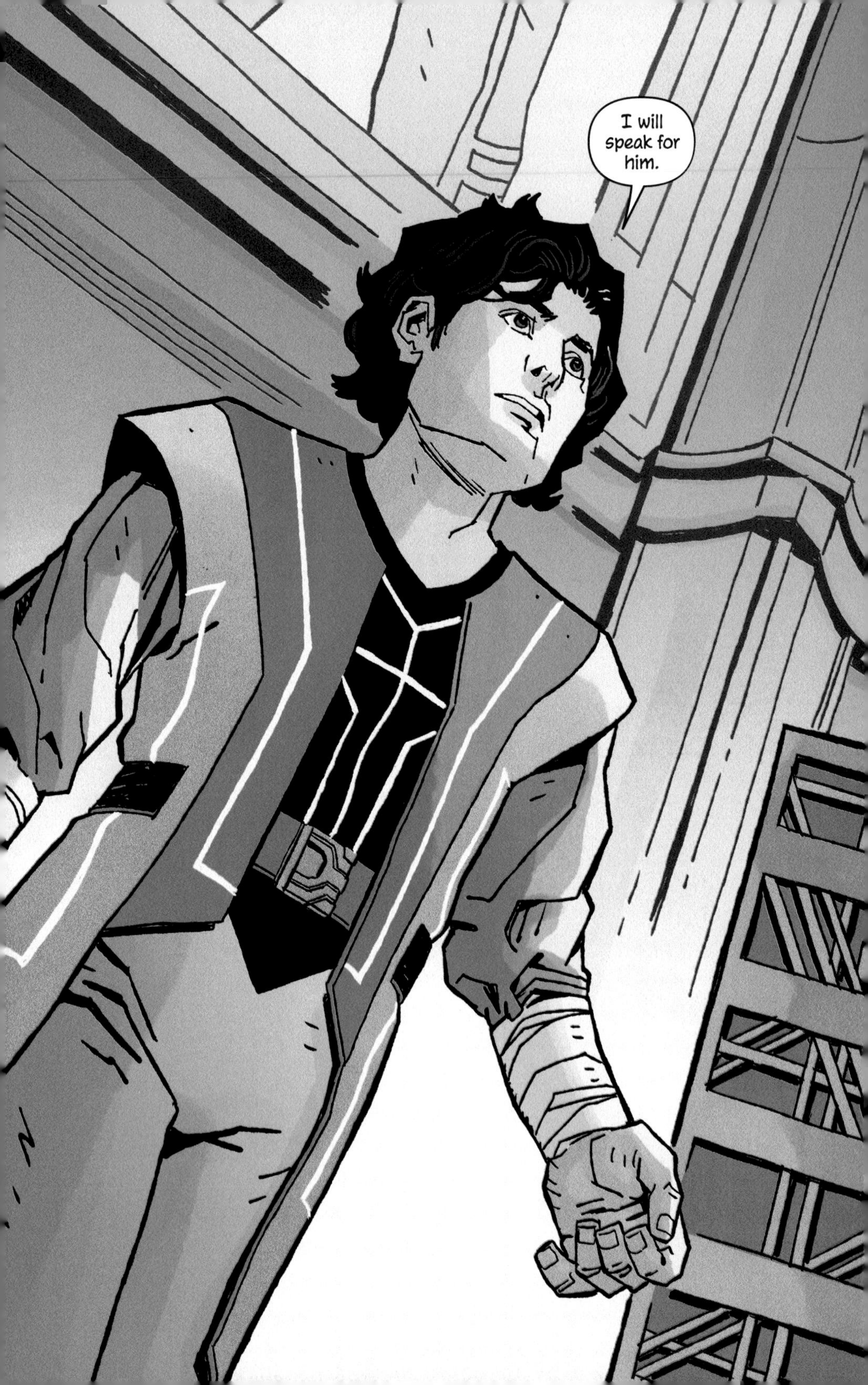
I will speak for him.

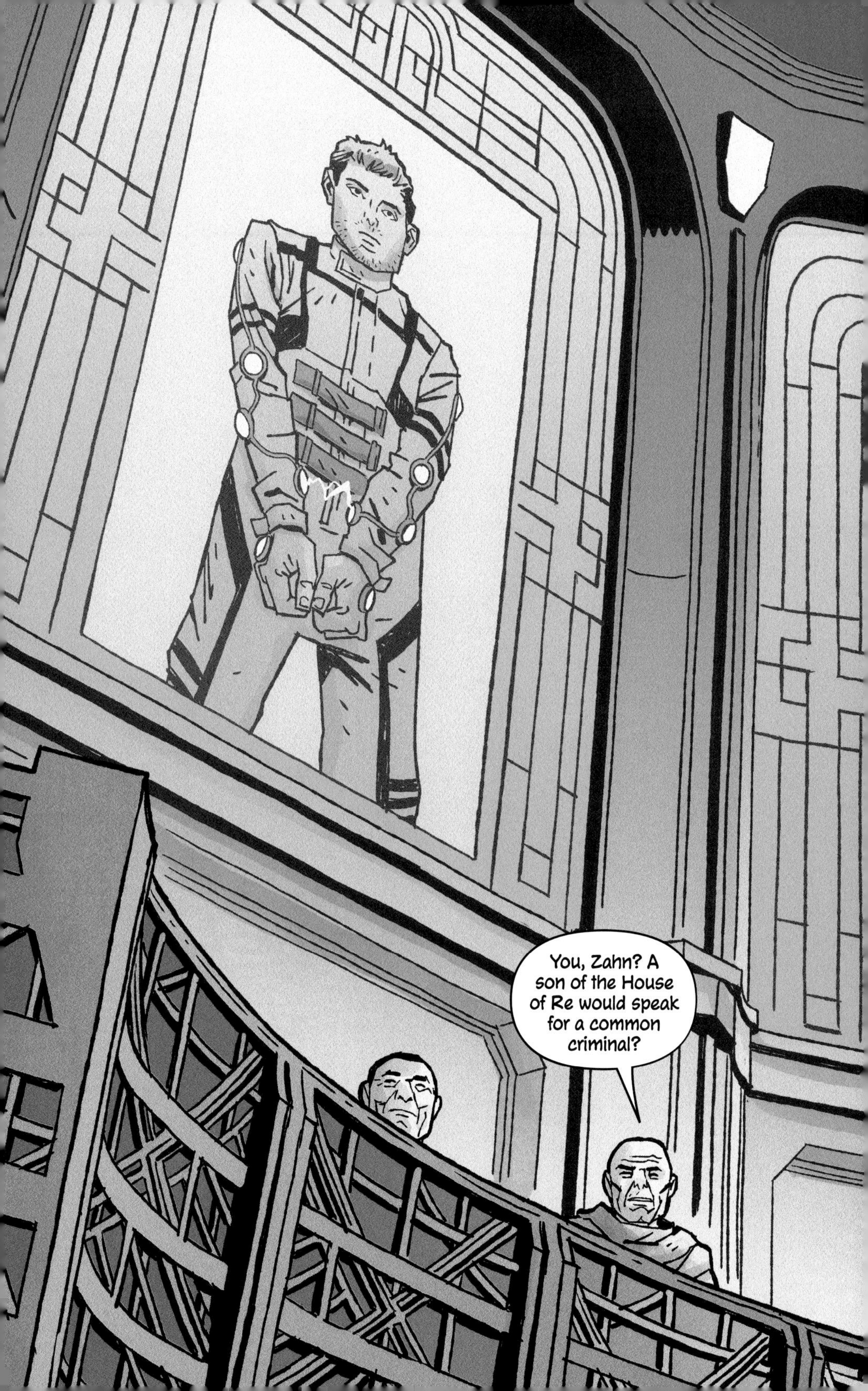
You, Zahn? A son of the House of Re would speak for a common criminal?

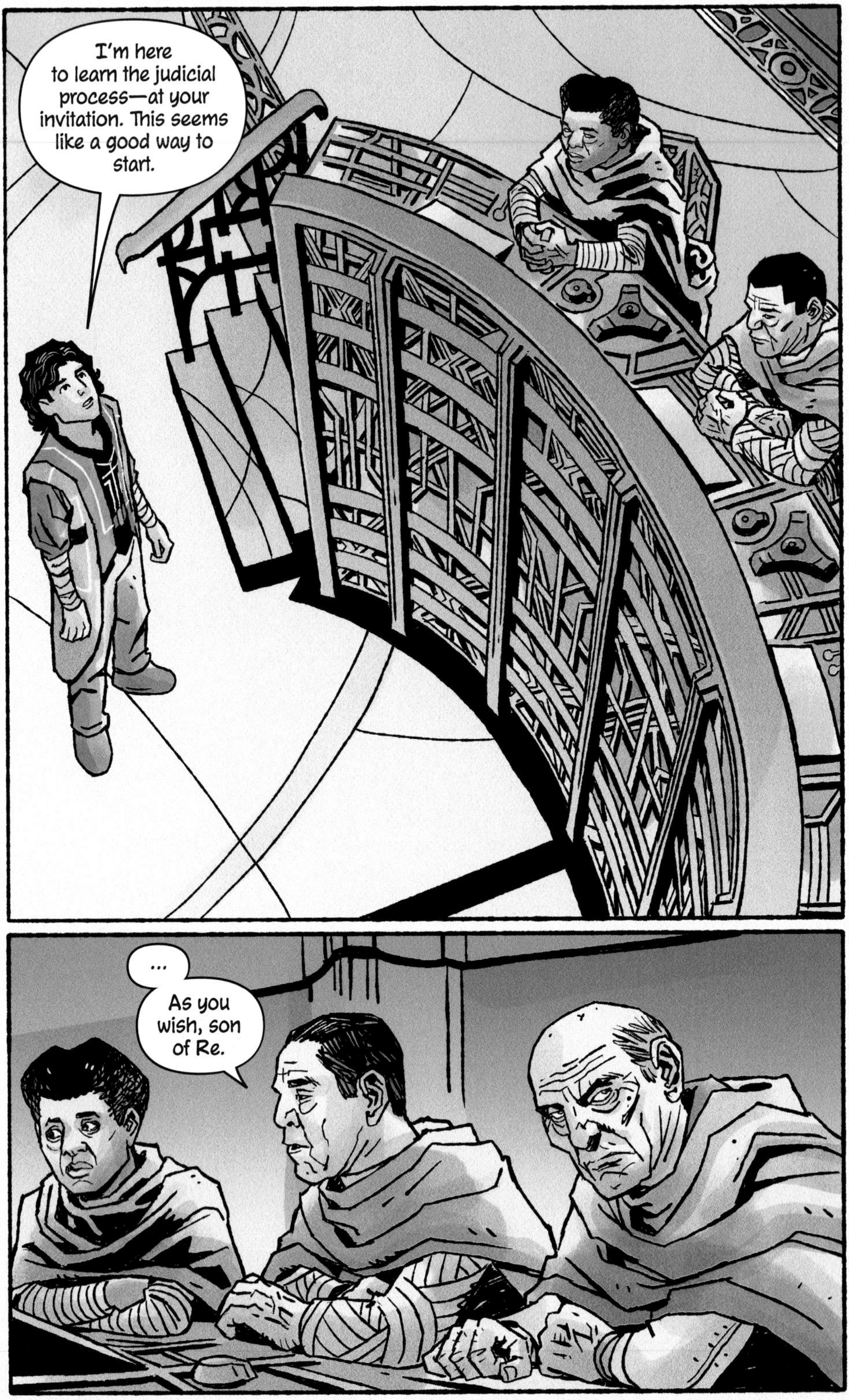
I'm here to learn the judicial process—at your invitation. This seems like a good way to start.
...
As you wish, son of Re.

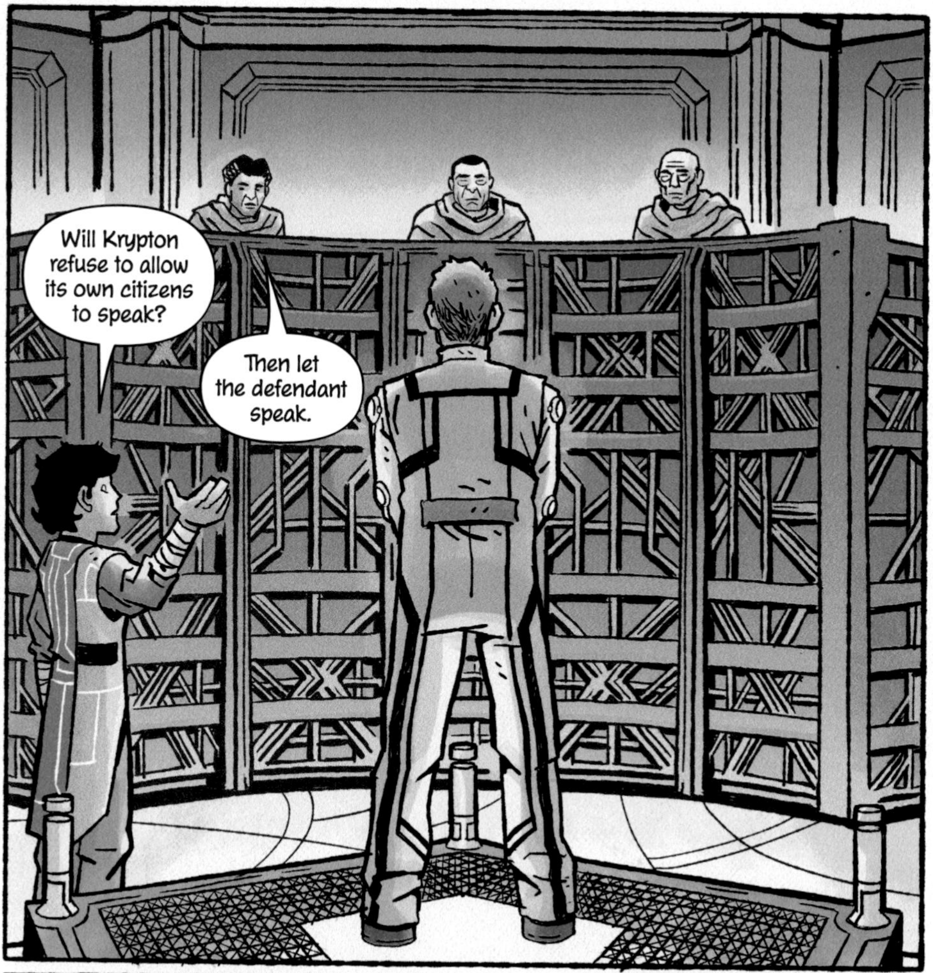
Will Krypton refuse to allow its own citizens to speak?
Then let the defendant speak.

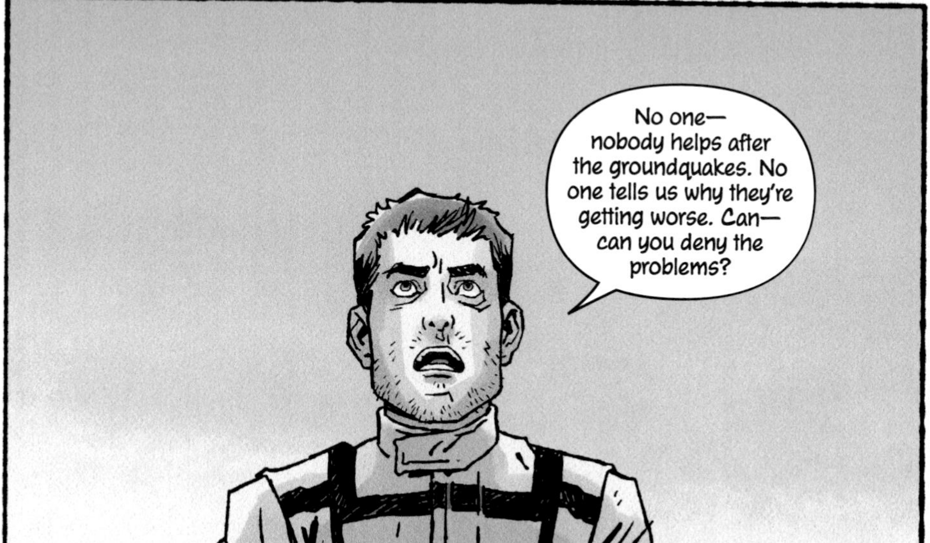
No one— nobody helps after the groundquakes. No one tells us why they're getting worse. Can— can you deny the problems?

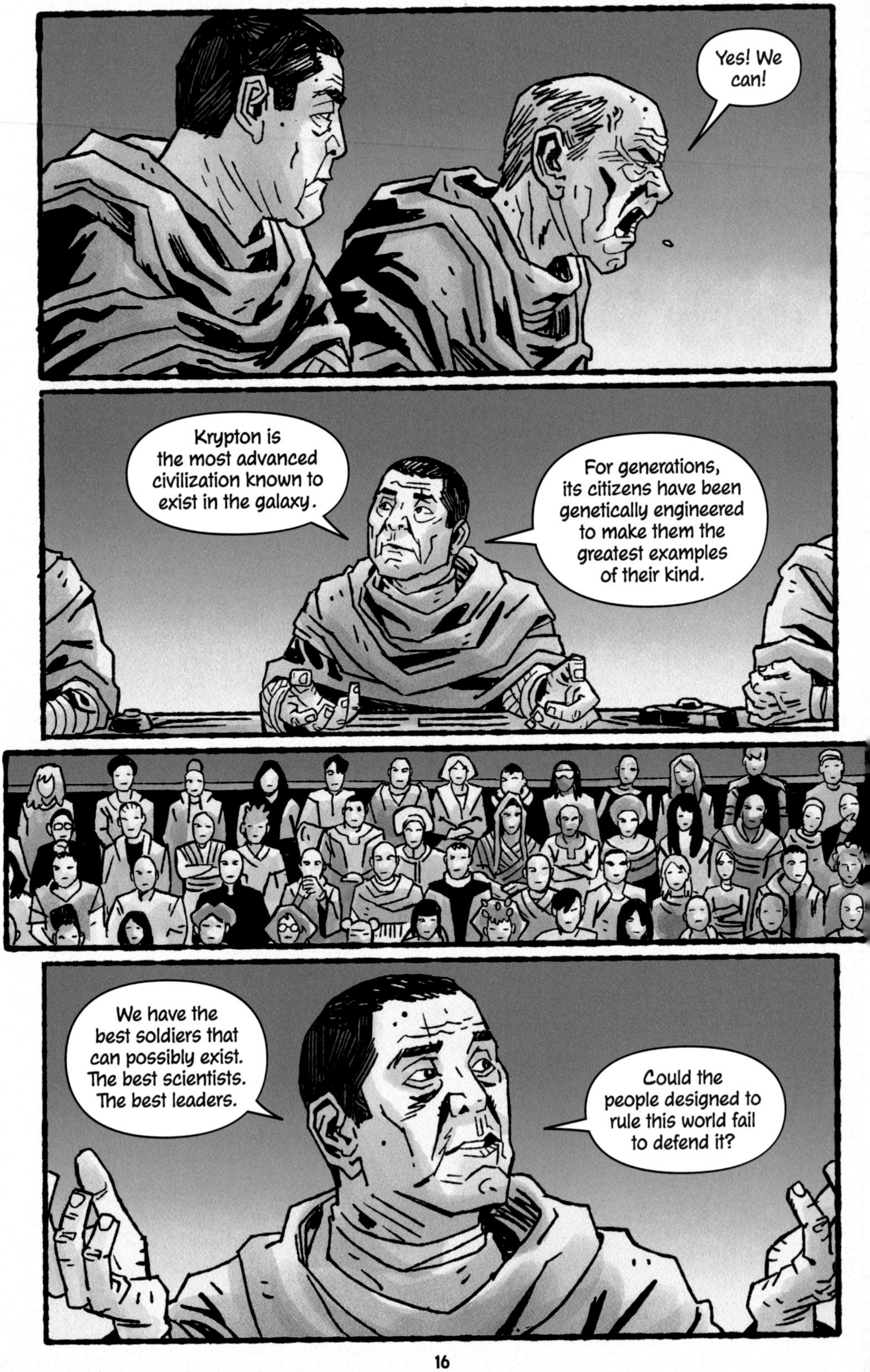
Yes! We can!
Krypton is the most advanced civilization known to exist in the galaxy.
For generations, its citizens have been genetically engineered to make them the greatest examples of their kind.
We have the best soldiers that can possibly exist. The best scientists. The best leaders.
Could the people designed to rule this world fail to defend it?

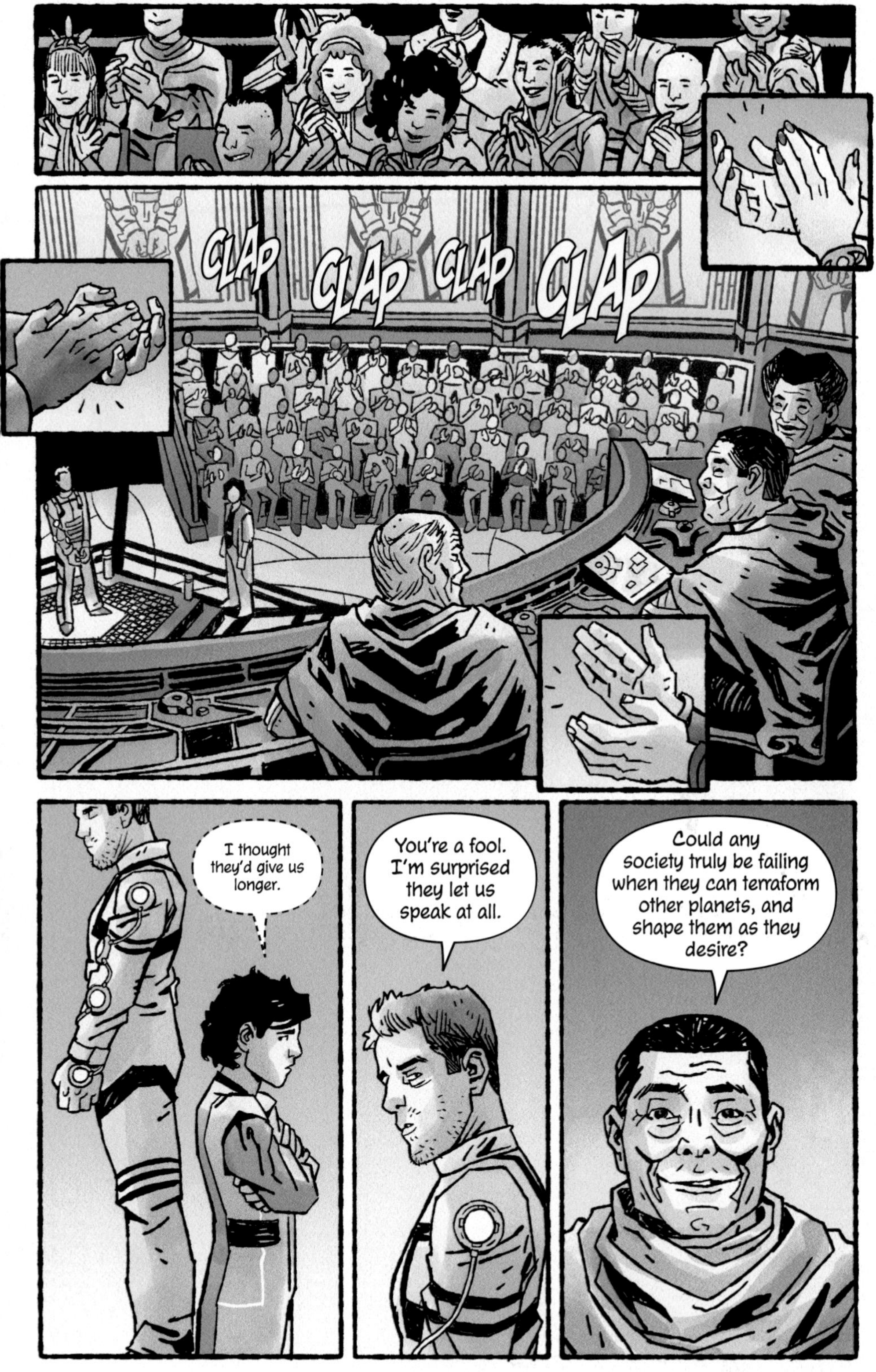
CLAP CLAP CLAP CLAP
I thought they'd give us longer.
You're a fool. I'm surprised they let us speak at all.
Could any society truly be failing when they can terraform other planets, and shape them as they desire?

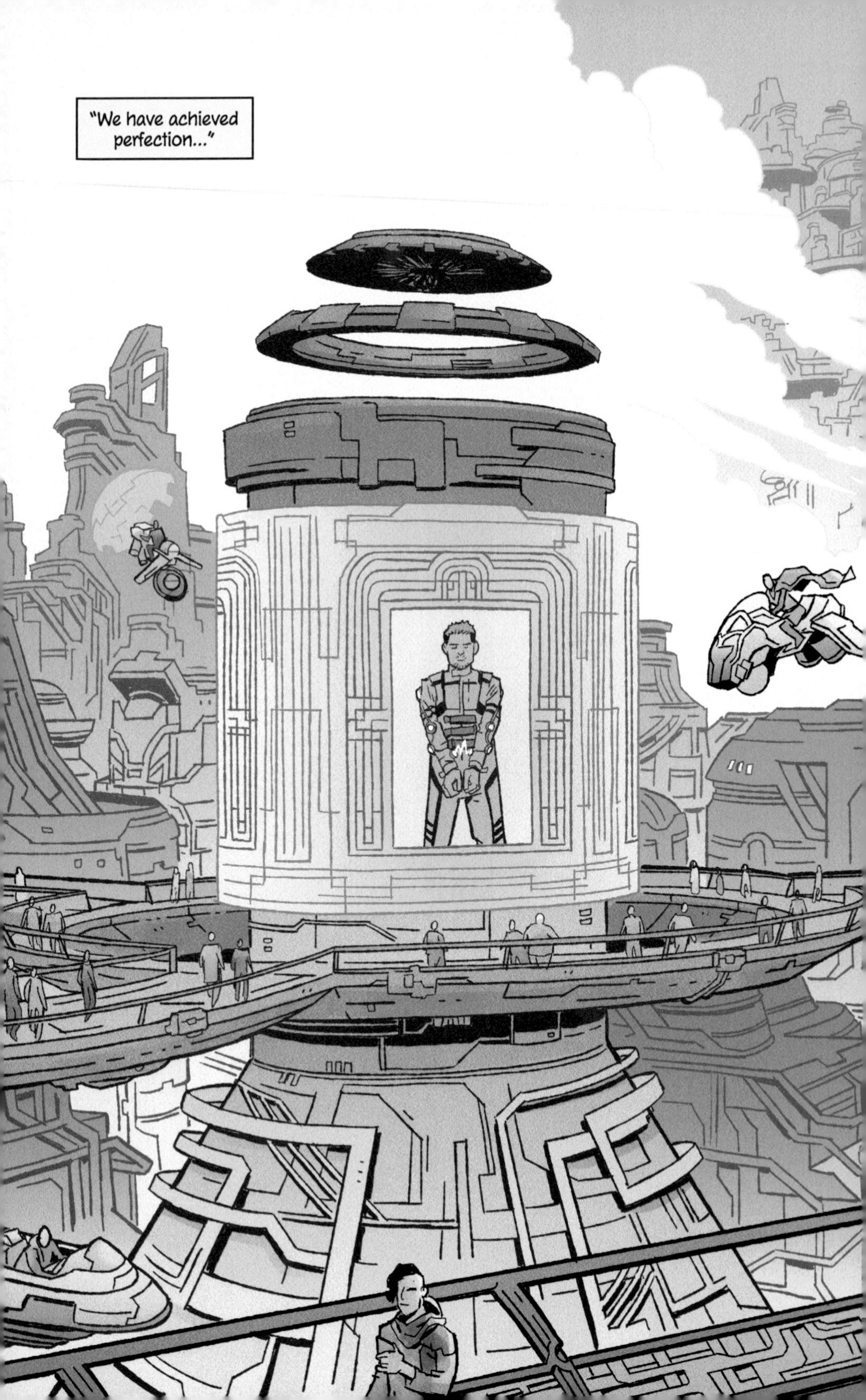
"We have achieved perfection..."

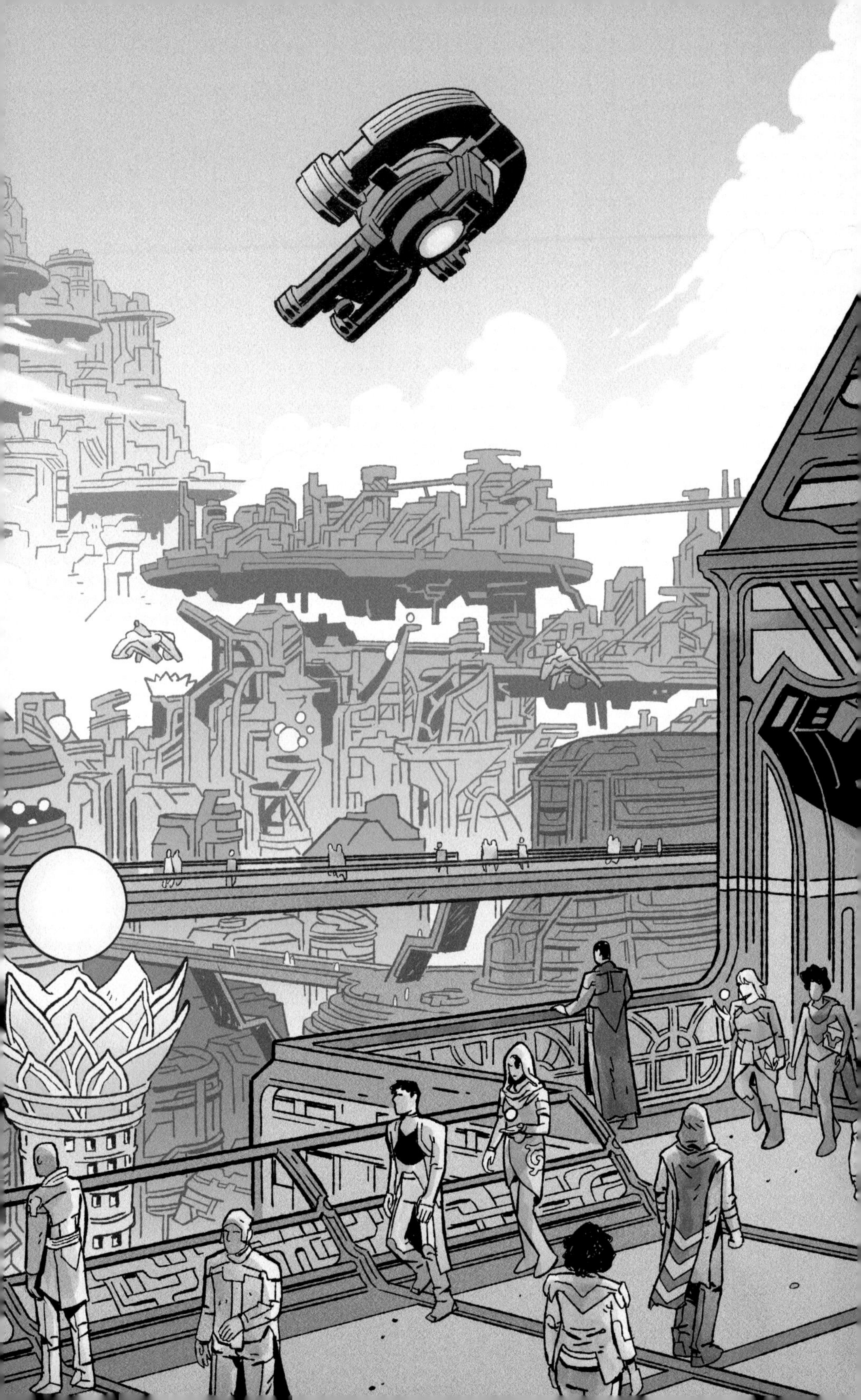

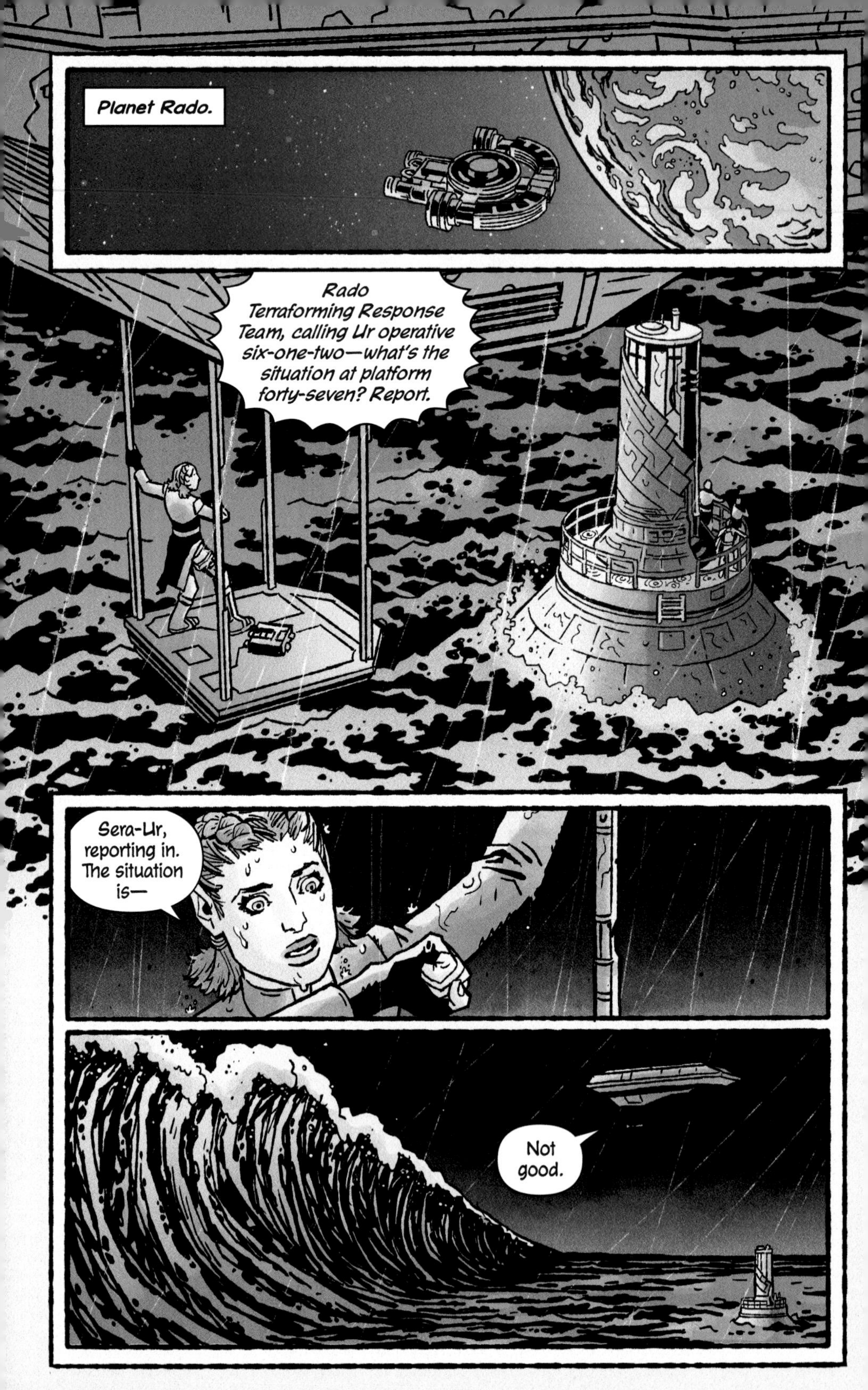
Planet Rado.
Rado Terraforming Response Team, calling Ur operative six-one-two—what's the situation at platform forty-seven? Report.
Sera-Ur, reporting in. The situation is—
Not good.

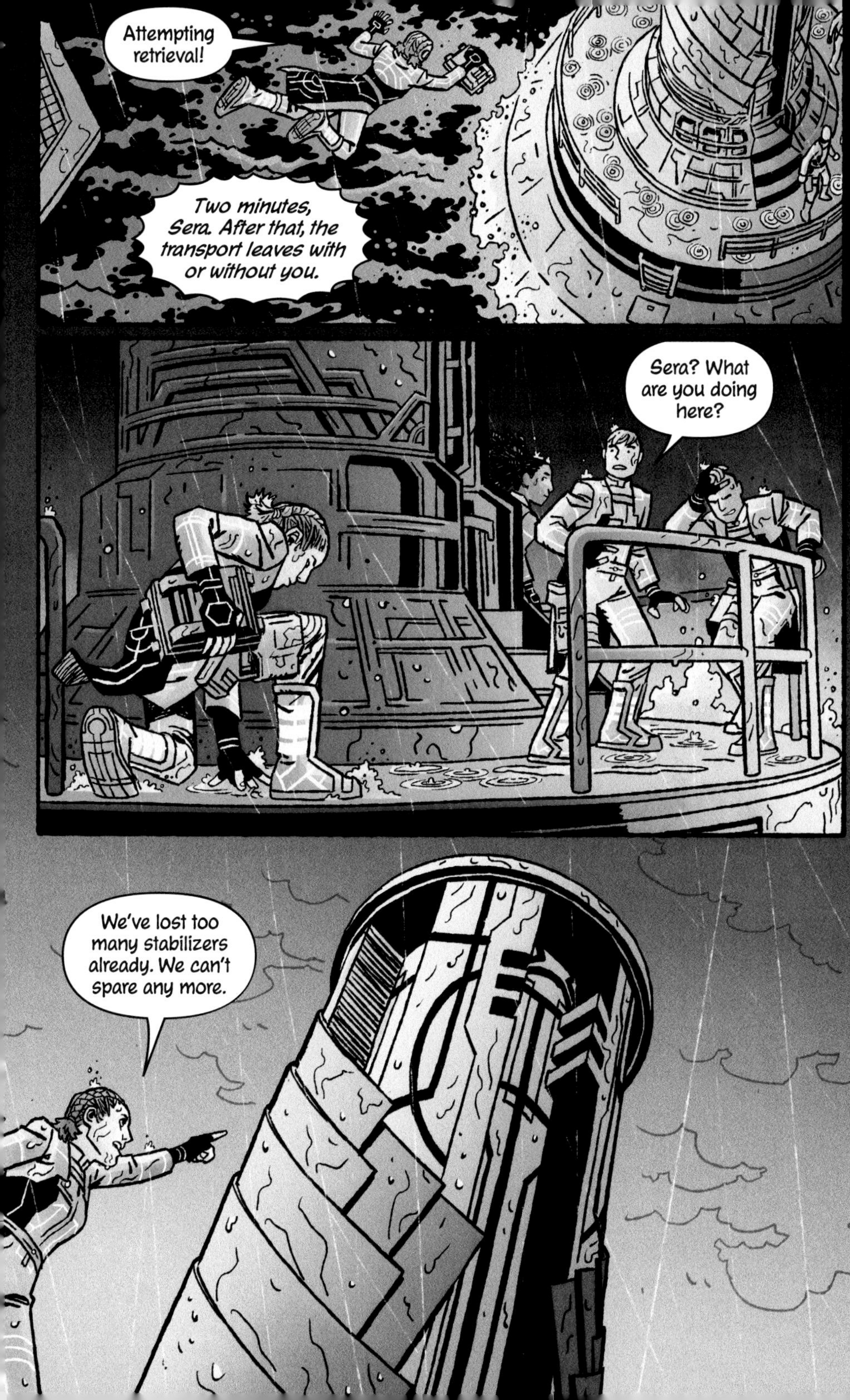
Attempting retrieval!
Two minutes, Sera. After that, the transport leaves with or without you.
Sera? What are you doing here?
We've lost too many stabilizers already. We can't spare any more.

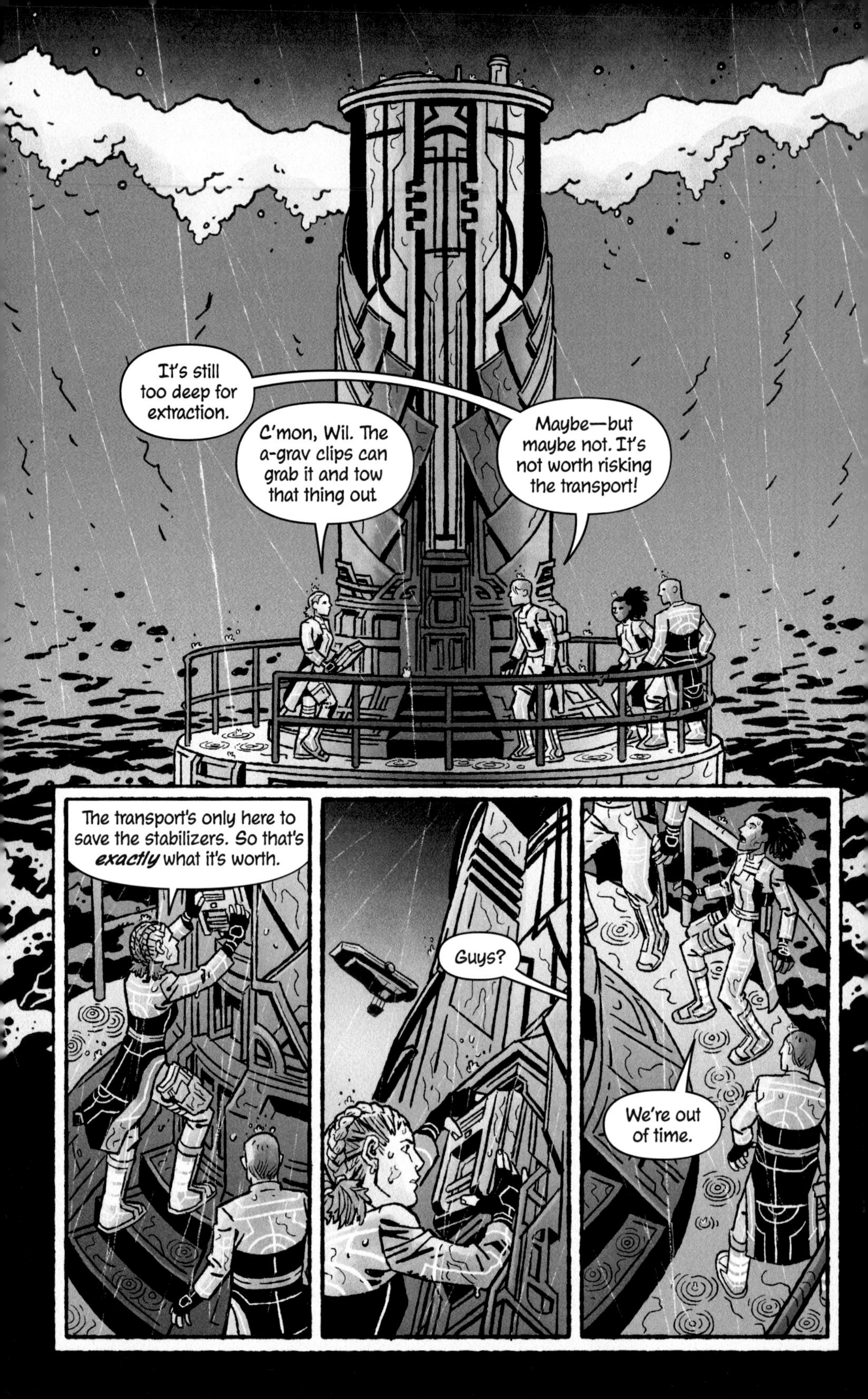
It's still too deep for extraction.
C'mon, Wil. The a-grav clips can grab it and tow that thing out.
Maybe—but maybe not. It's not worth risking the transport!
The transport's only here to save the stabilizers. So that's *exactly* what it's worth.
Guys?
We're out of time.

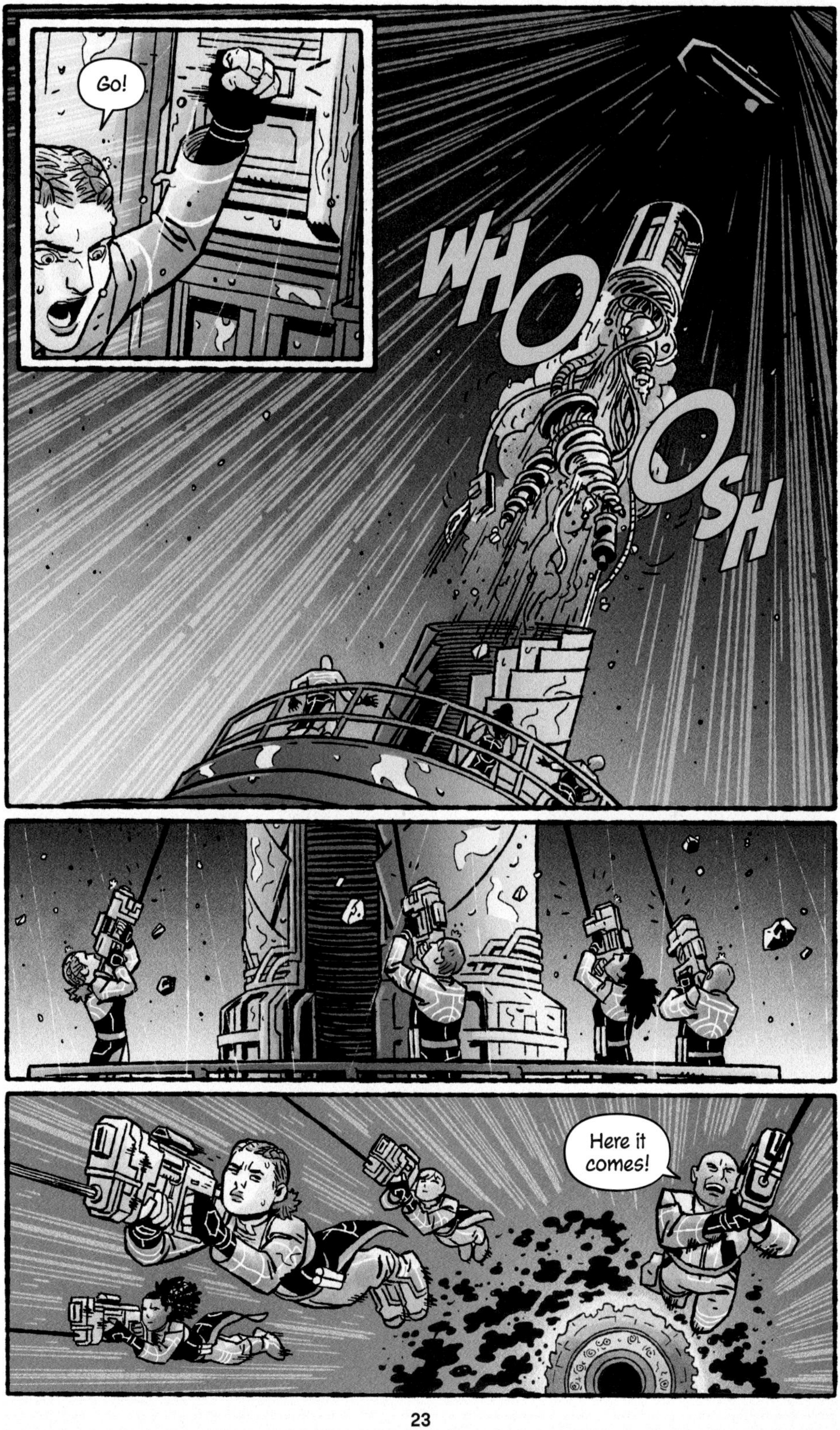
Go!
WHOOOSH
Here it comes!

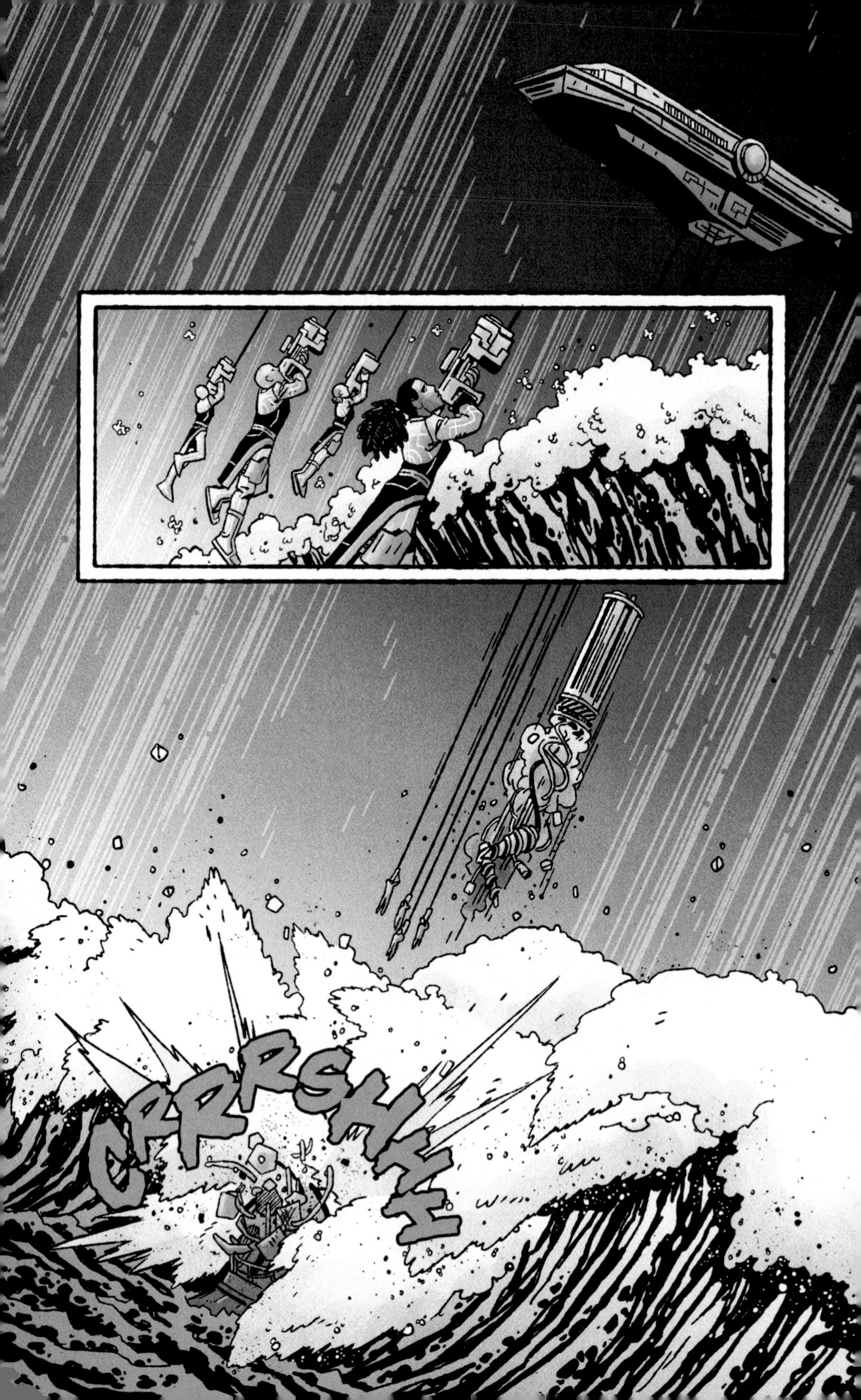
CRRRSHHH

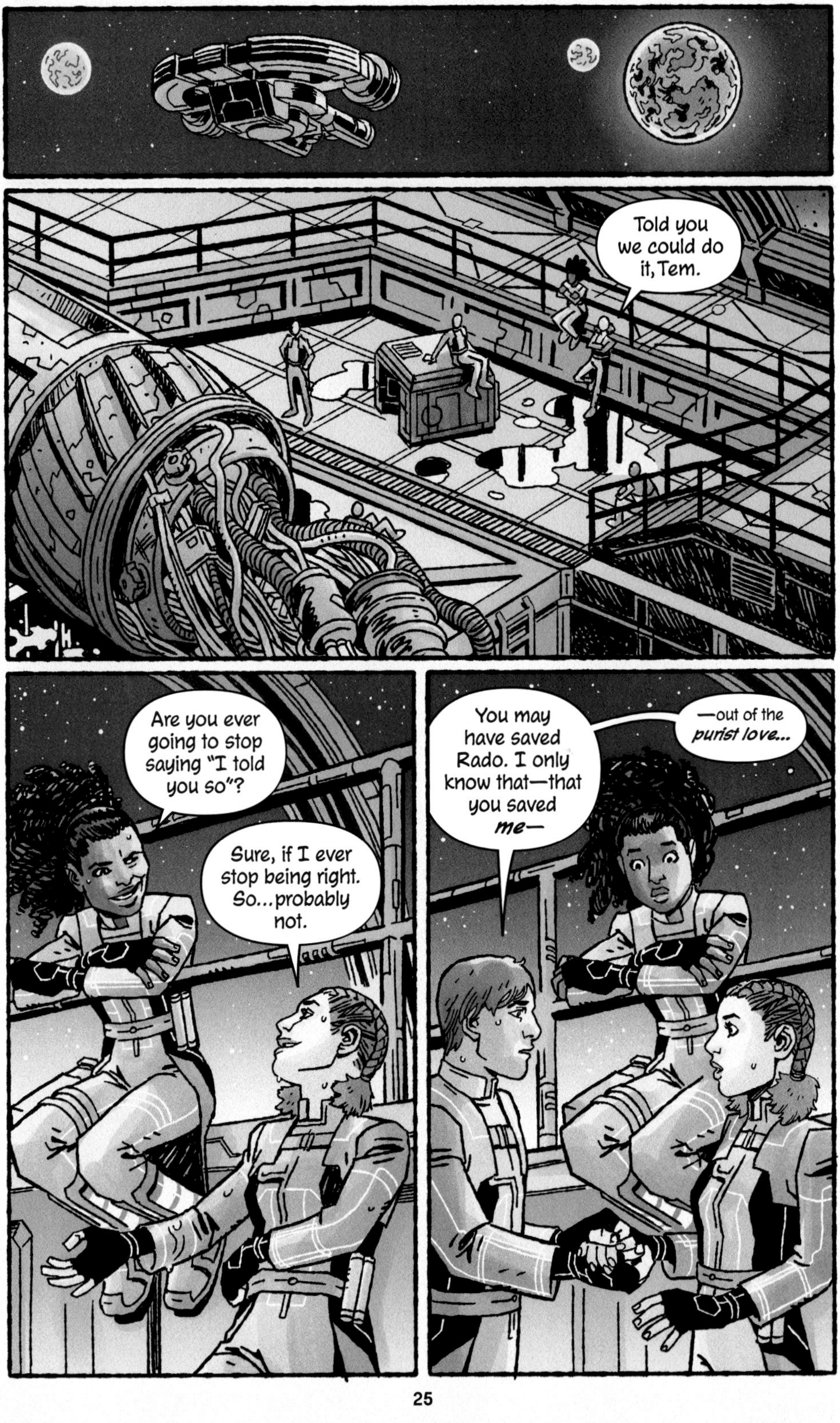
Told you we could do it, Tem.
Are you ever going to stop saying "I told you so"?
Sure, if I ever stop being right. So...probably not.
You may have saved Rado. I only know that—that you saved *me*—
—out of the *purist love...*

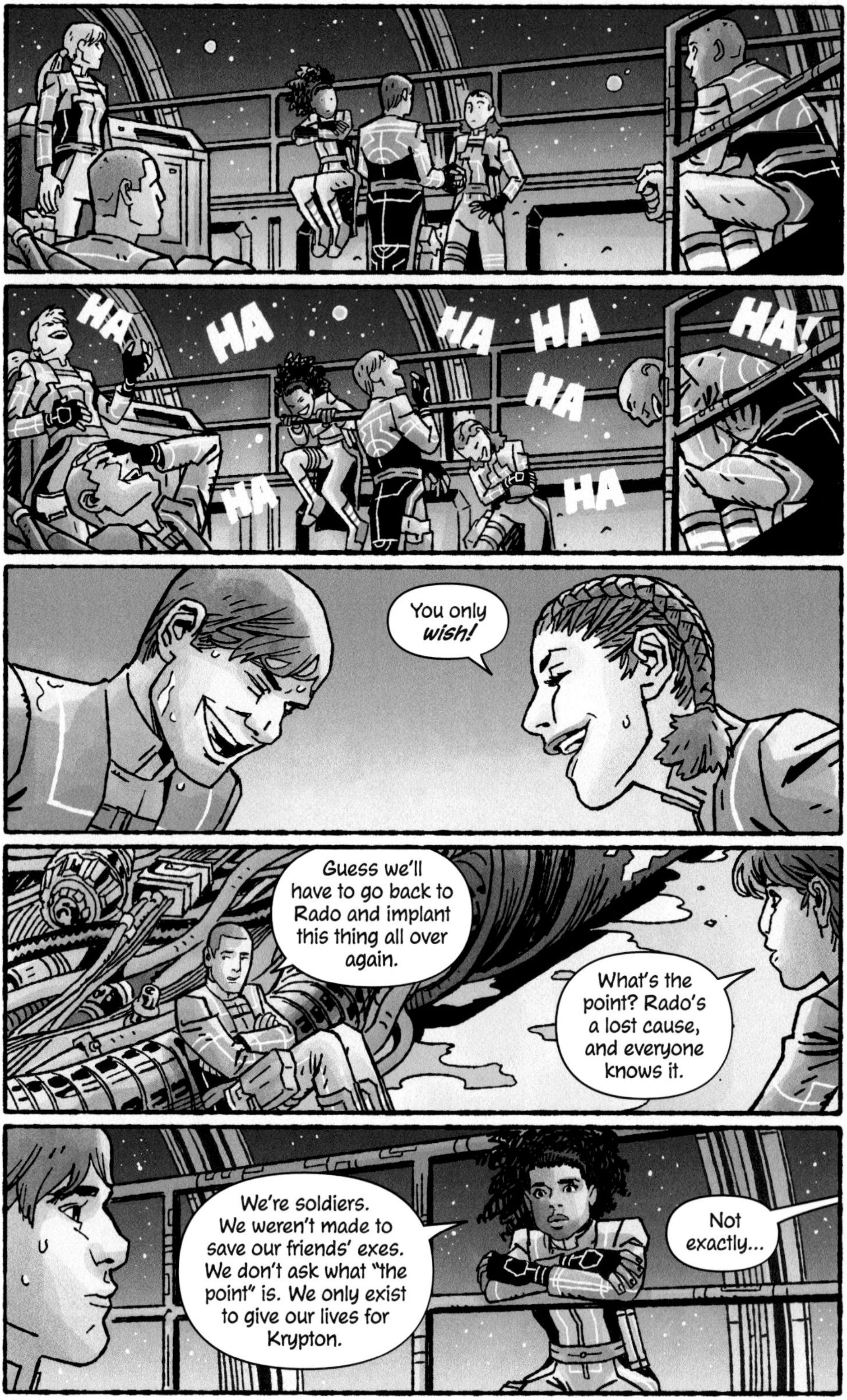
HA
HA
HA
HA
HA
HA!
HA
HA
You only wish!
Guess we'll have to go back to Rado and implant this thing all over again.
What's the point? Rado's a lost cause, and everyone knows it.
We're soldiers. We weren't made to save our friends' exes. We don't ask what "the point" is. We only exist to give our lives for Krypton.
Not exactly...

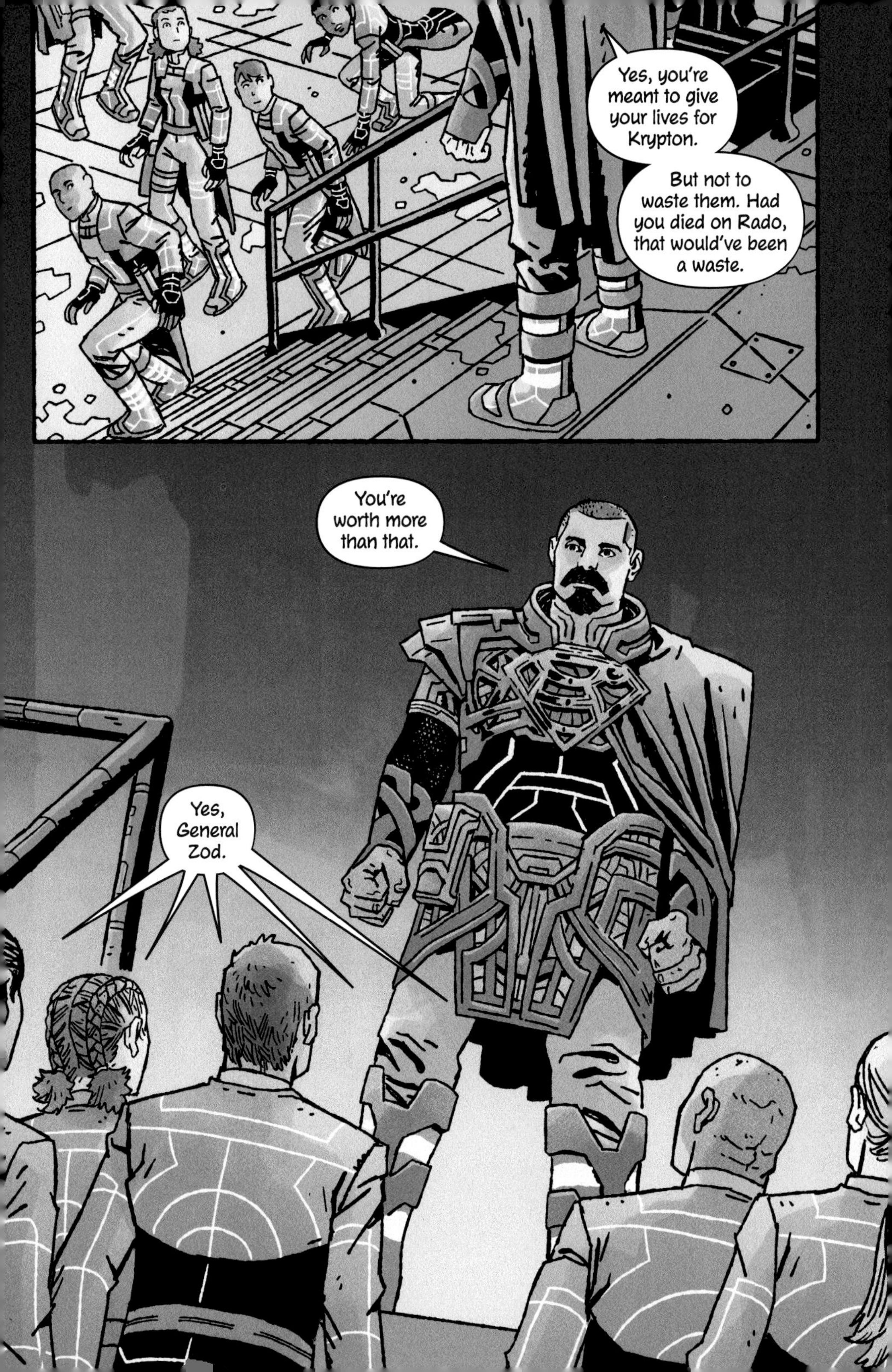
Yes, you're meant to give your lives for Krypton.
But not to waste them. Had you died on Rado, that would've been a waste.
You're worth more than that.
Yes, General Zod.

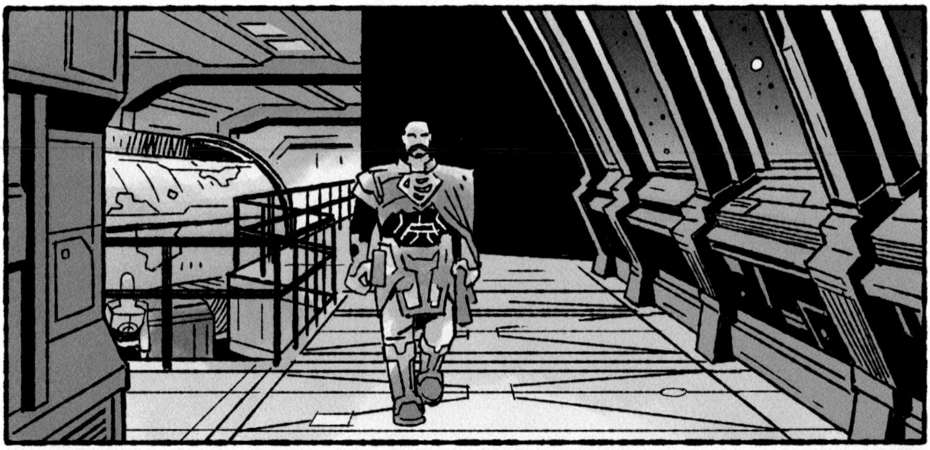

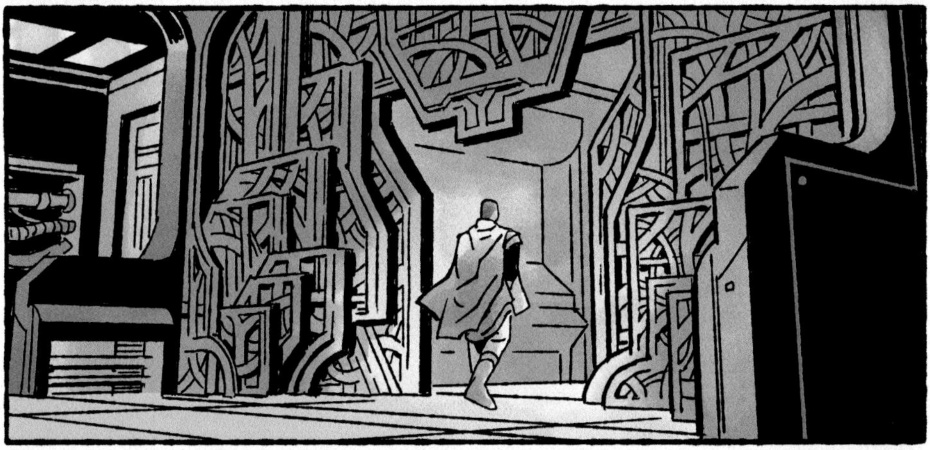

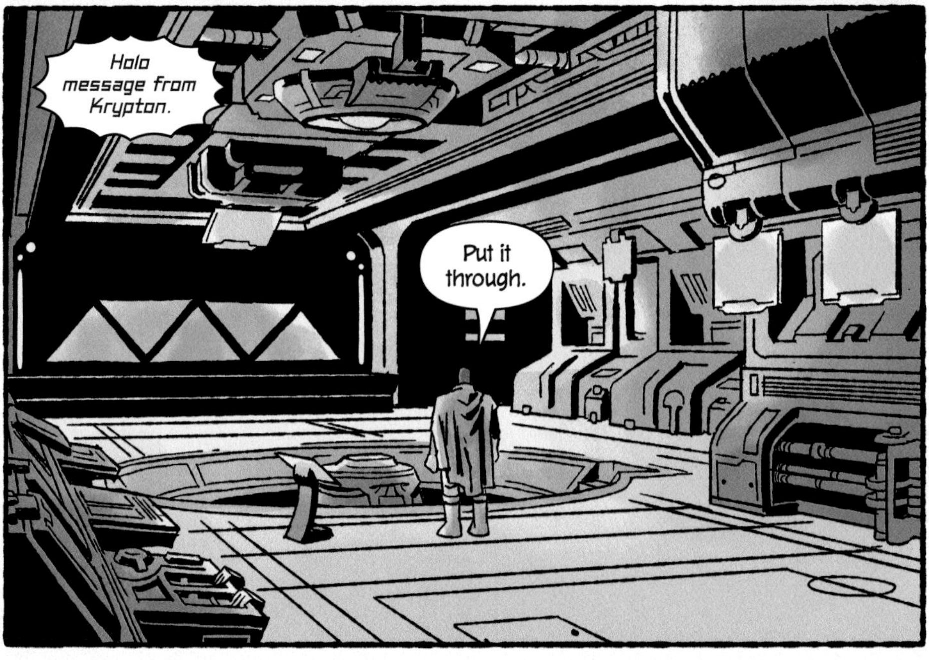
Holo message from Krypton.
Put it through.

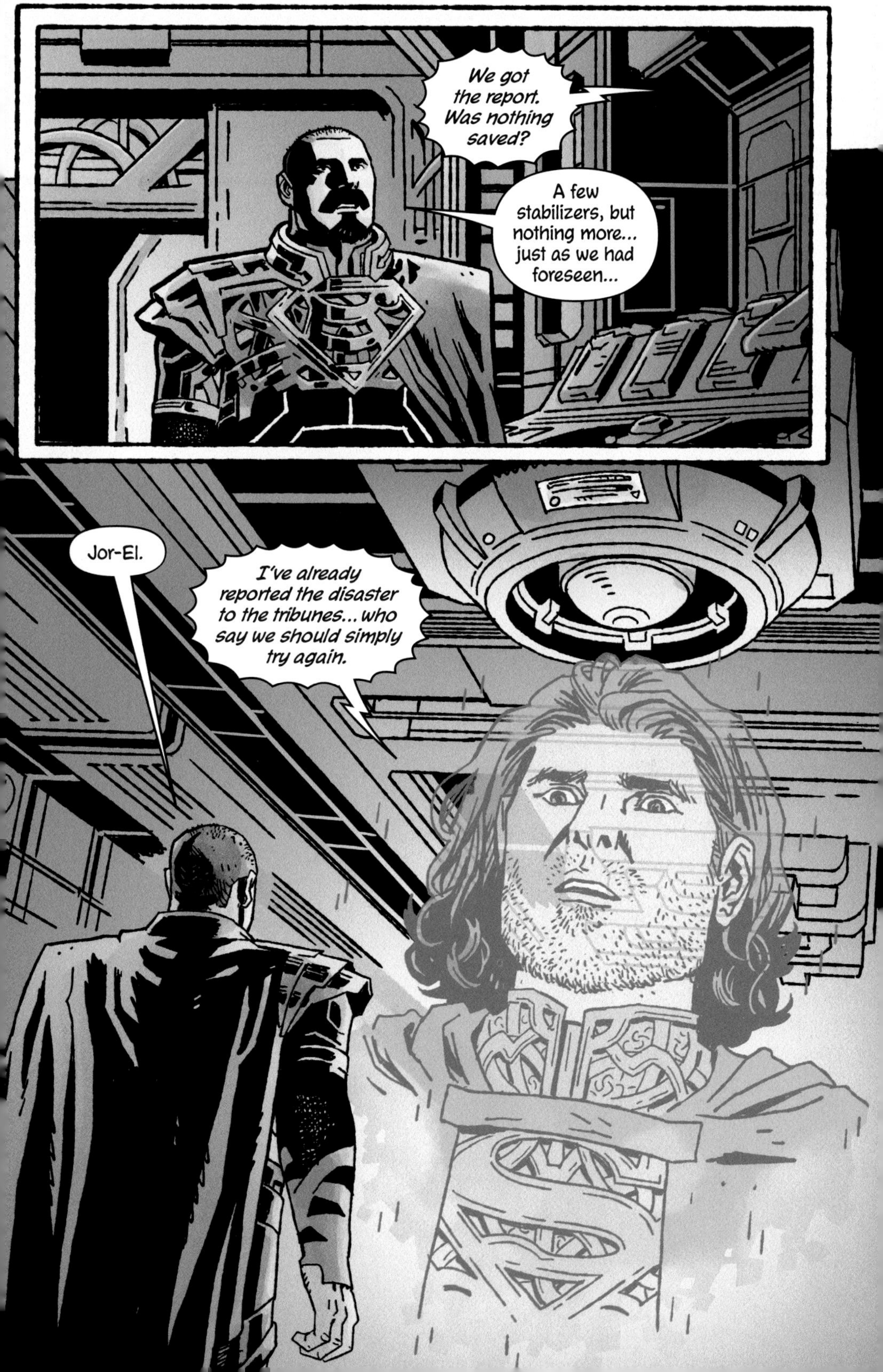
We got the report. Was nothing saved?
A few stabilizers, but nothing more... just as we had foreseen...
Jor-El.
I've already reported the disaster to the tribunes... who say we should simply try again.

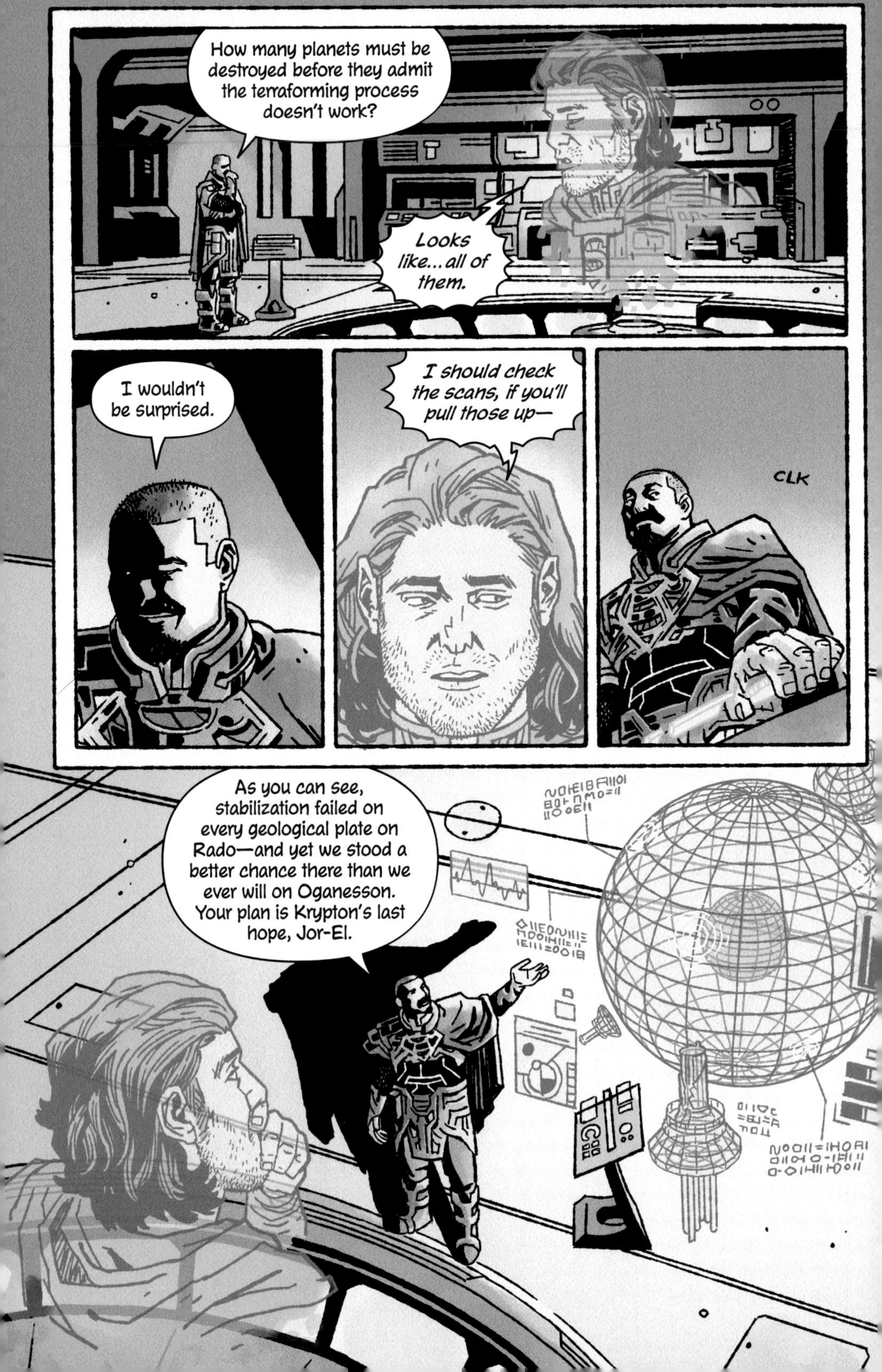
How many planets must be destroyed before they admit the terraforming process doesn't work?
Looks like...all of them.
I wouldn't be surprised.
I should check the scans, if you'll pull those up—
CLK
As you can see, stabilization failed on every geological plate on Rado—and yet we stood a better chance there than we ever will on Oganesson. Your plan is Krypton's last hope, Jor-El.

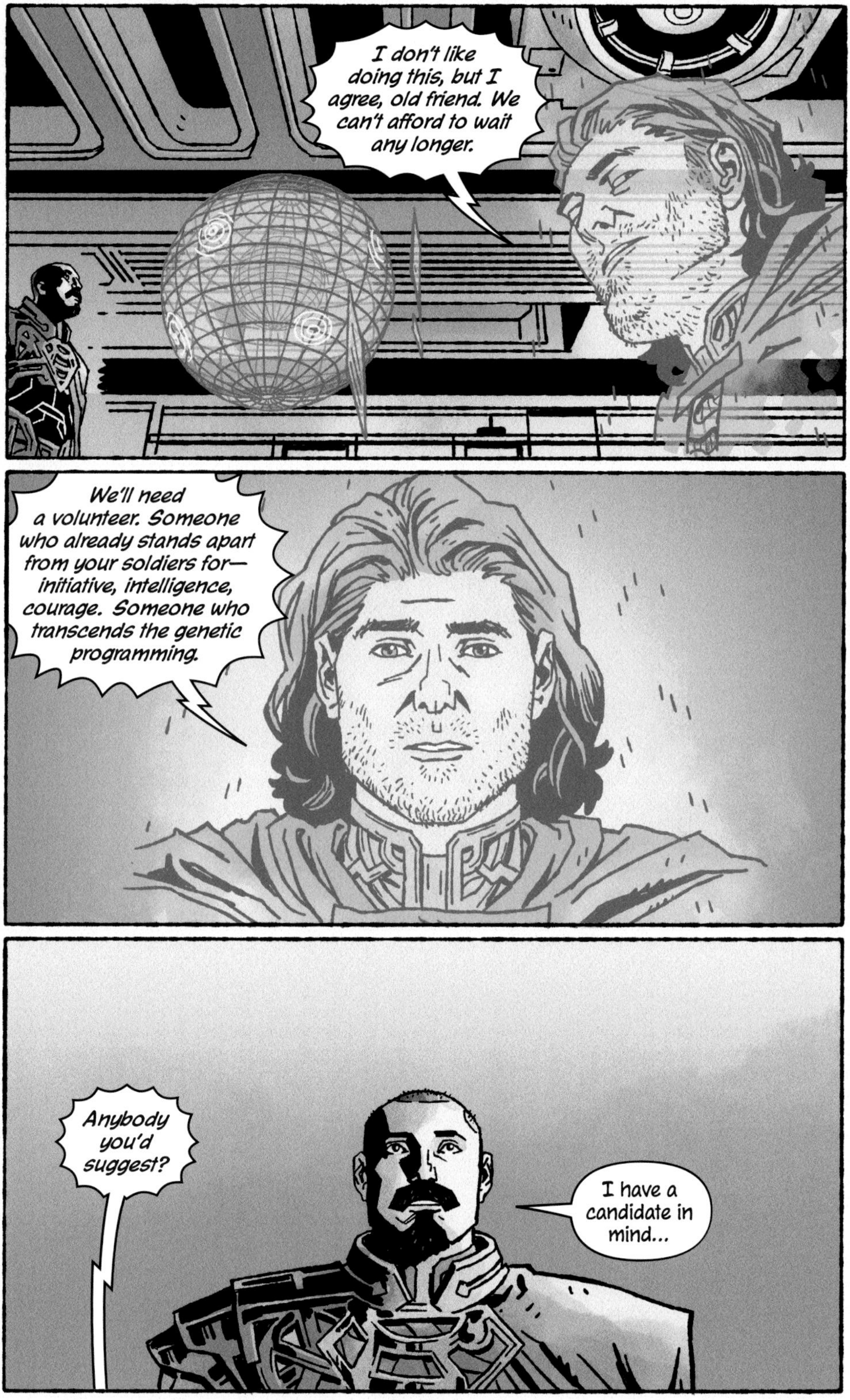
I don't like doing this, but I agree, old friend. We can't afford to wait any longer.
We'll need a volunteer. Someone who already stands apart from your soldiers for—initiative, intelligence, courage. Someone who transcends the genetic programming.
Anybody you'd suggest?
I have a candidate in mind...

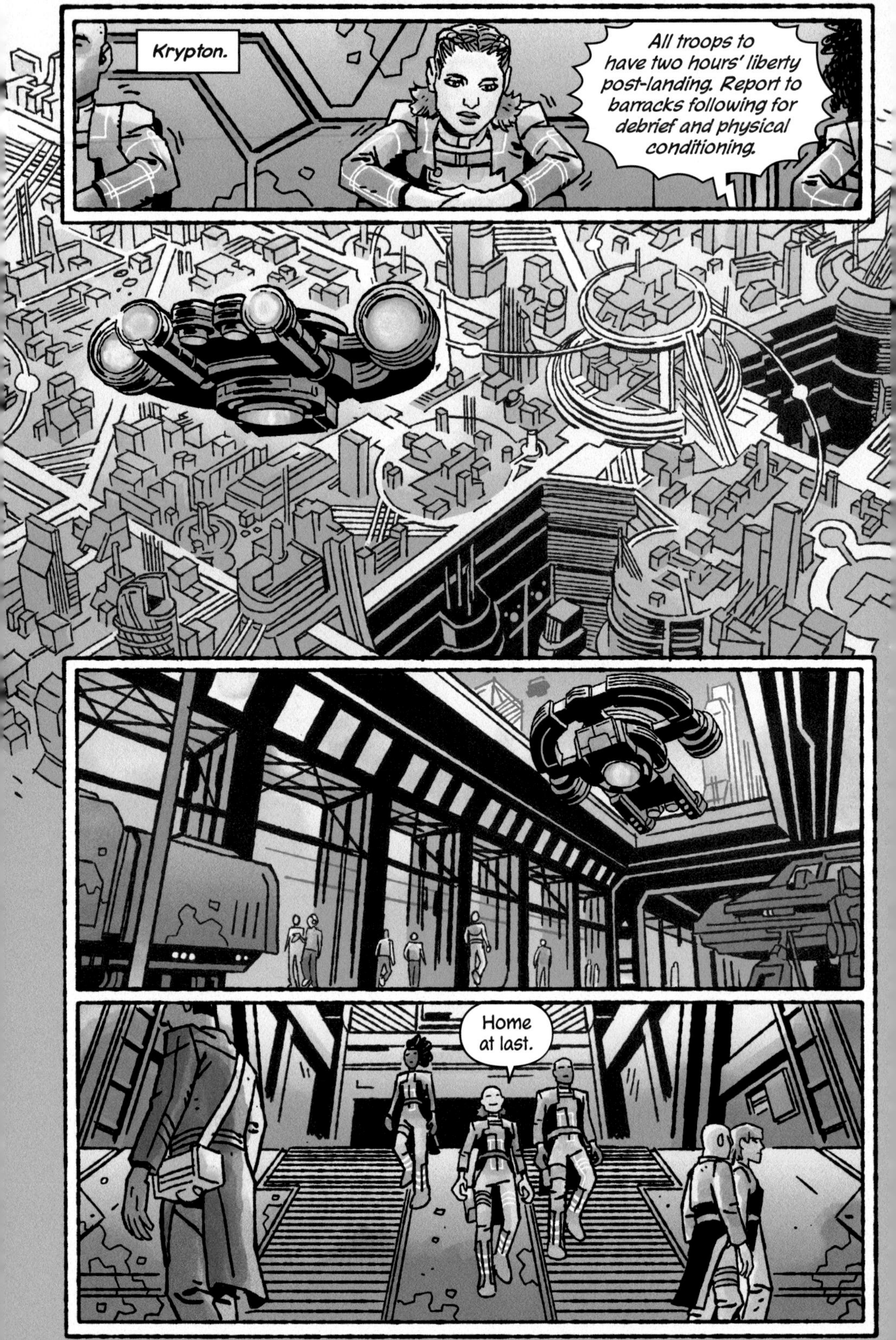

Krypton.
All troops to have two hours' liberty post-landing. Report to barracks following for debrief and physical conditioning.
Home at last.

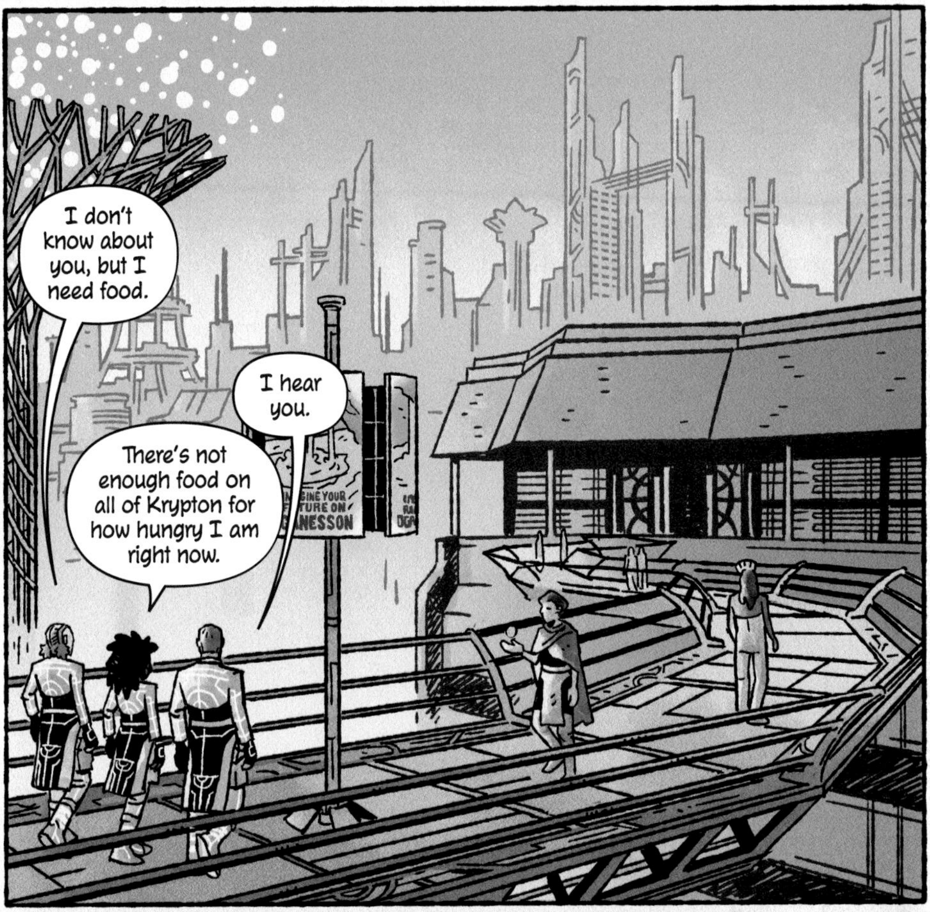
I don't know about you, but I need food.
There's not enough food on all of Krypton for how hungry I am right now.
I hear you.

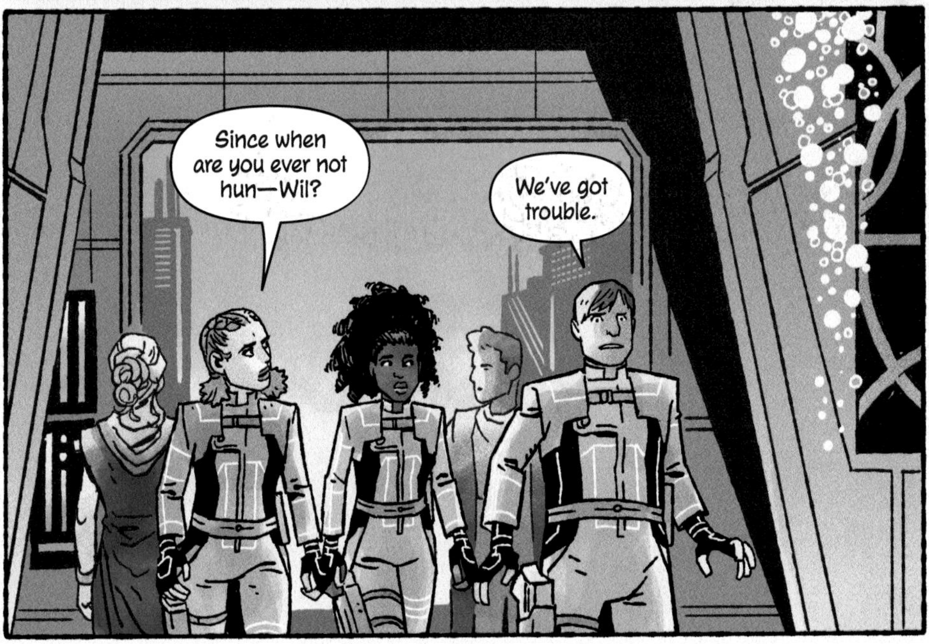
Since when are you ever not hun—Wil?
We've got trouble.

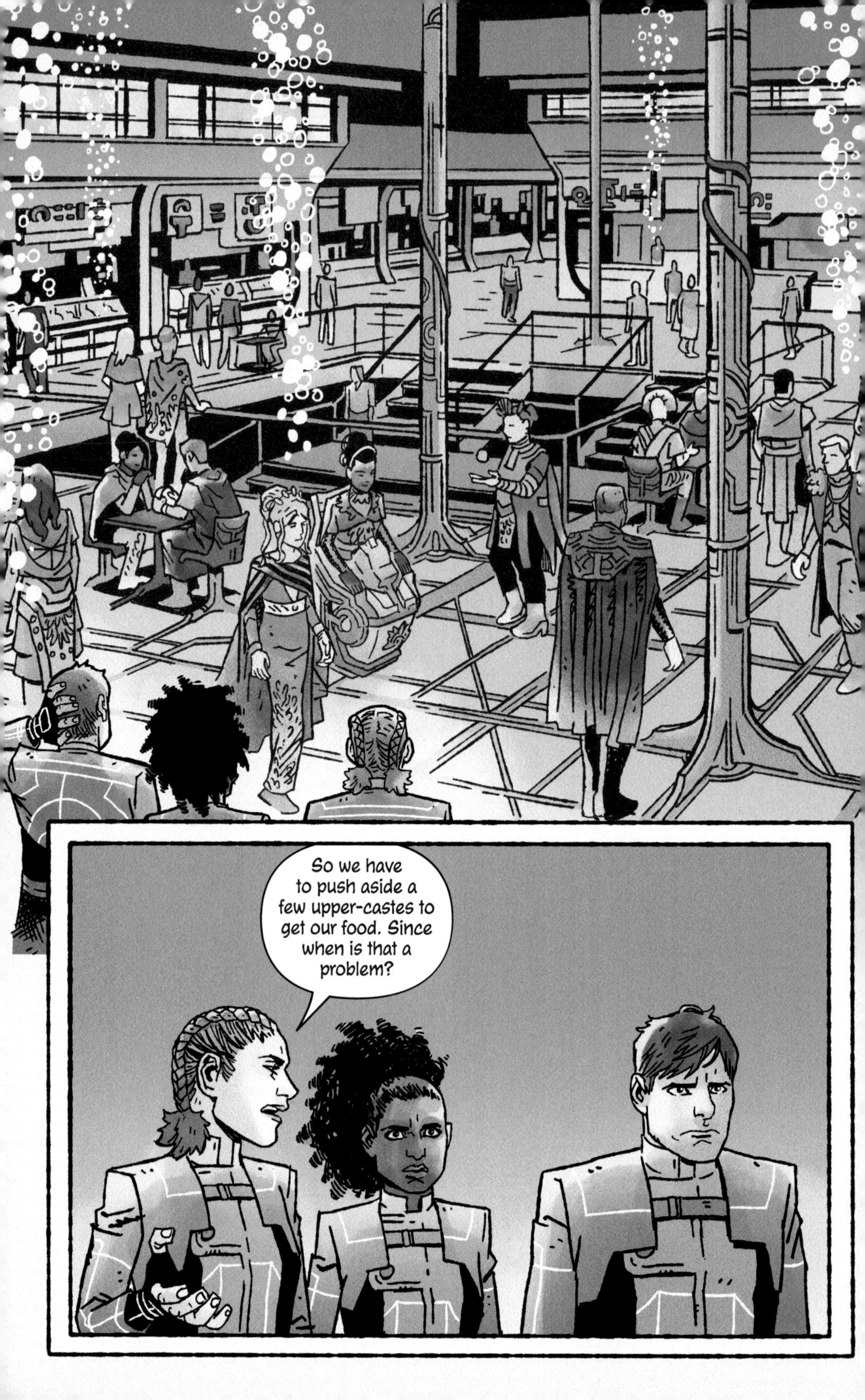
So we have to push aside a few upper-castes to get our food. Since when is that a problem?

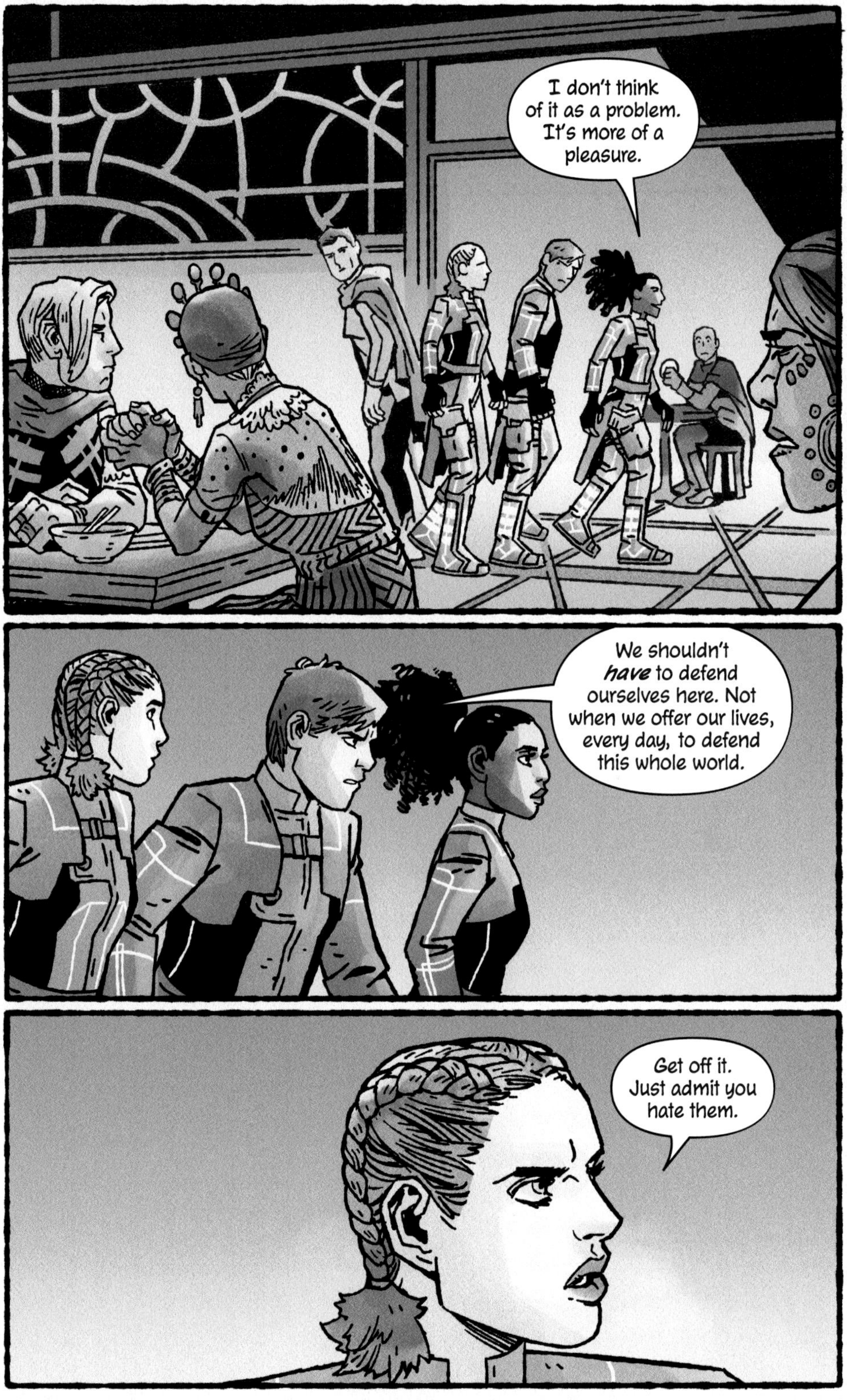

I don't think of it as a problem. It's more of a pleasure.
We shouldn't *have* to defend ourselves here. Not when we offer our lives, every day, to defend this whole world.
Get off it. Just admit you hate them.

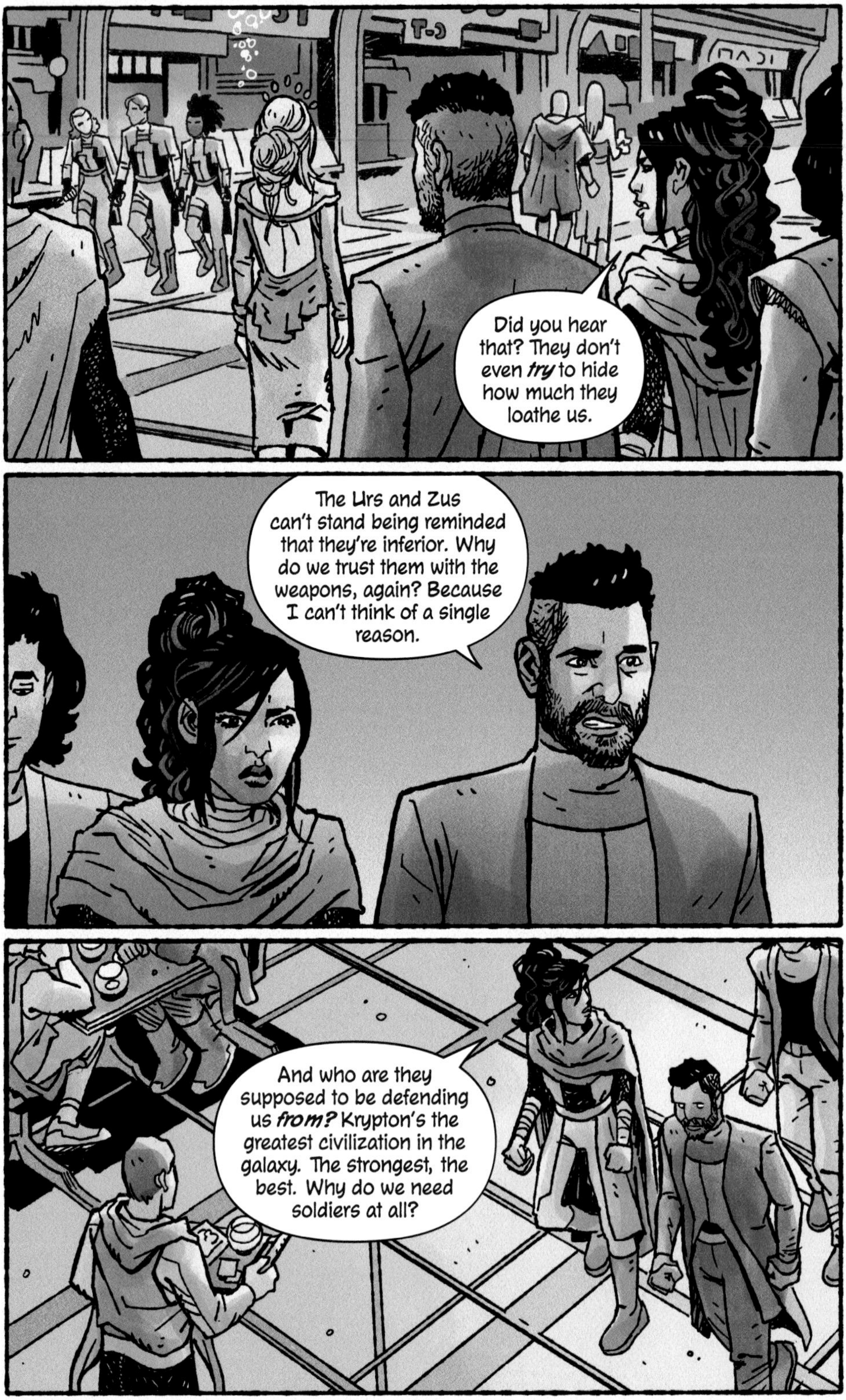
Did you hear that? They don't even *try* to hide how much they loathe us.
The Urs and Zus can't stand being reminded that they're inferior. Why do we trust them with the weapons, again? Because I can't think of a single reason.
And who are they supposed to be defending us *from?* Krypton's the greatest civilization in the galaxy. The strongest, the best. Why do we need soldiers at all?

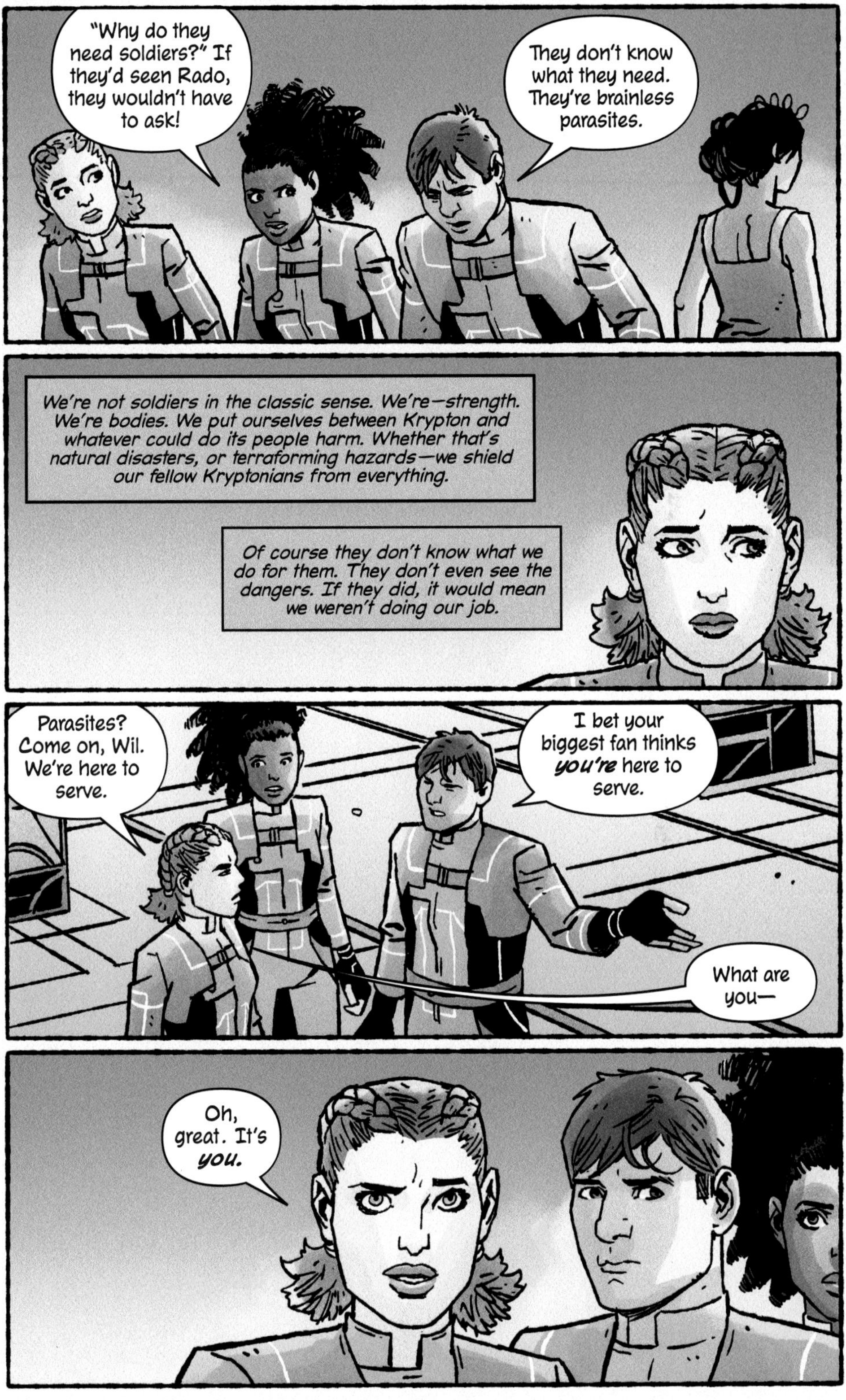
"Why do they need soldiers?" If they'd seen Rado, they wouldn't have to ask!
They don't know what they need. They're brainless parasites.
We're not soldiers in the classic sense. We're—strength. We're bodies. We put ourselves between Krypton and whatever could do its people harm. Whether that's natural disasters, or terraforming hazards—we shield our fellow Kryptonians from everything.
Of course they don't know what we do for them. They don't even see the dangers. If they did, it would mean we weren't doing our job.
Parasites? Come on, Wil. We're here to serve.
I bet your biggest fan thinks *you're* here to serve.
What are you—
Oh, great. It's *you.*

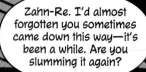

Zahn-Re. I'd almost forgotten you sometimes came down this way—it's been a while. Are you slumming it again?

This place sells the greatest vella leaves on the planet, Sera. I wouldn't call that "slumming it." Just—seeking out the best.

Not as shocking as an Ur with taste.

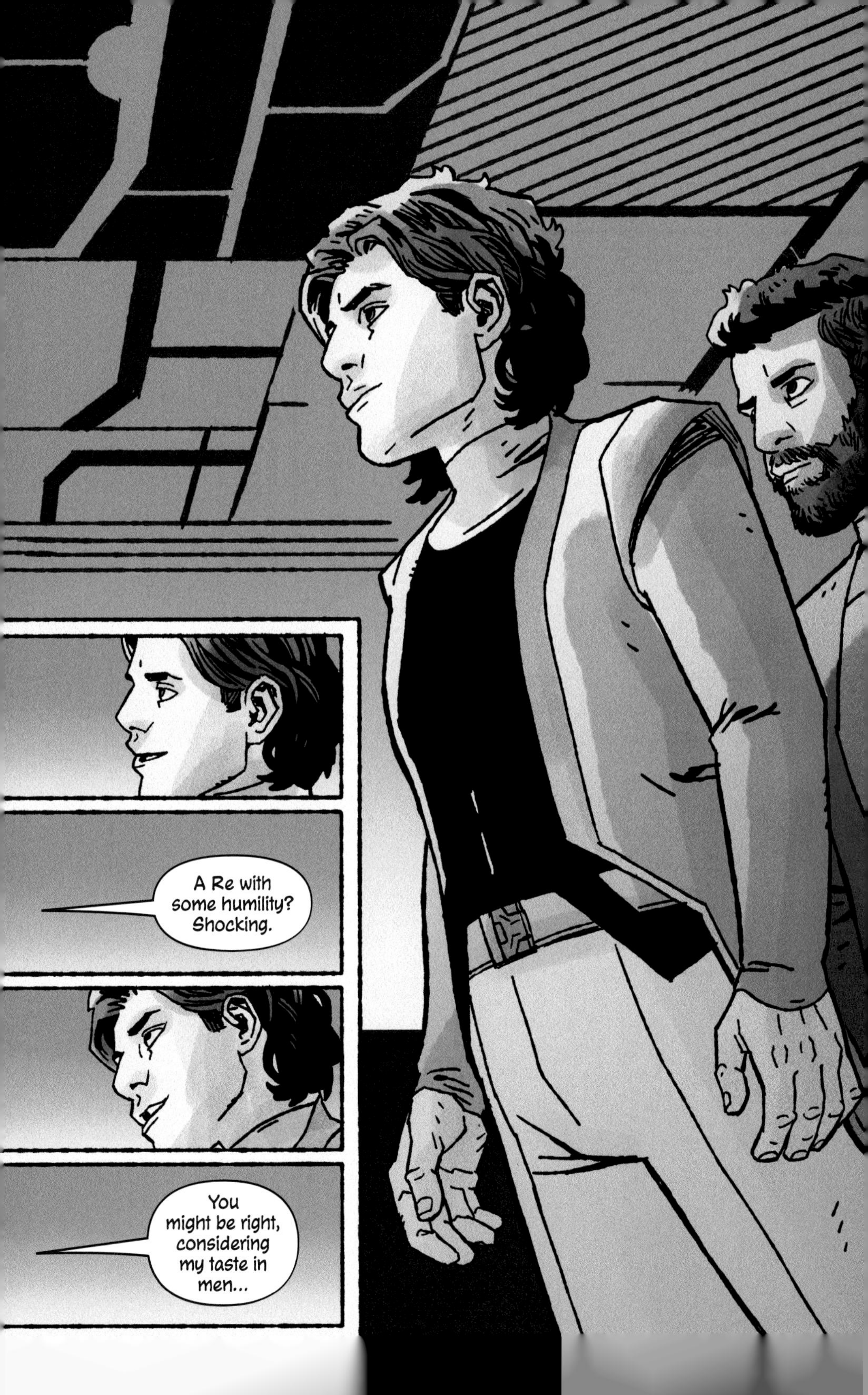
A Re with some humility? Shocking.
You might be right, considering my taste in men...

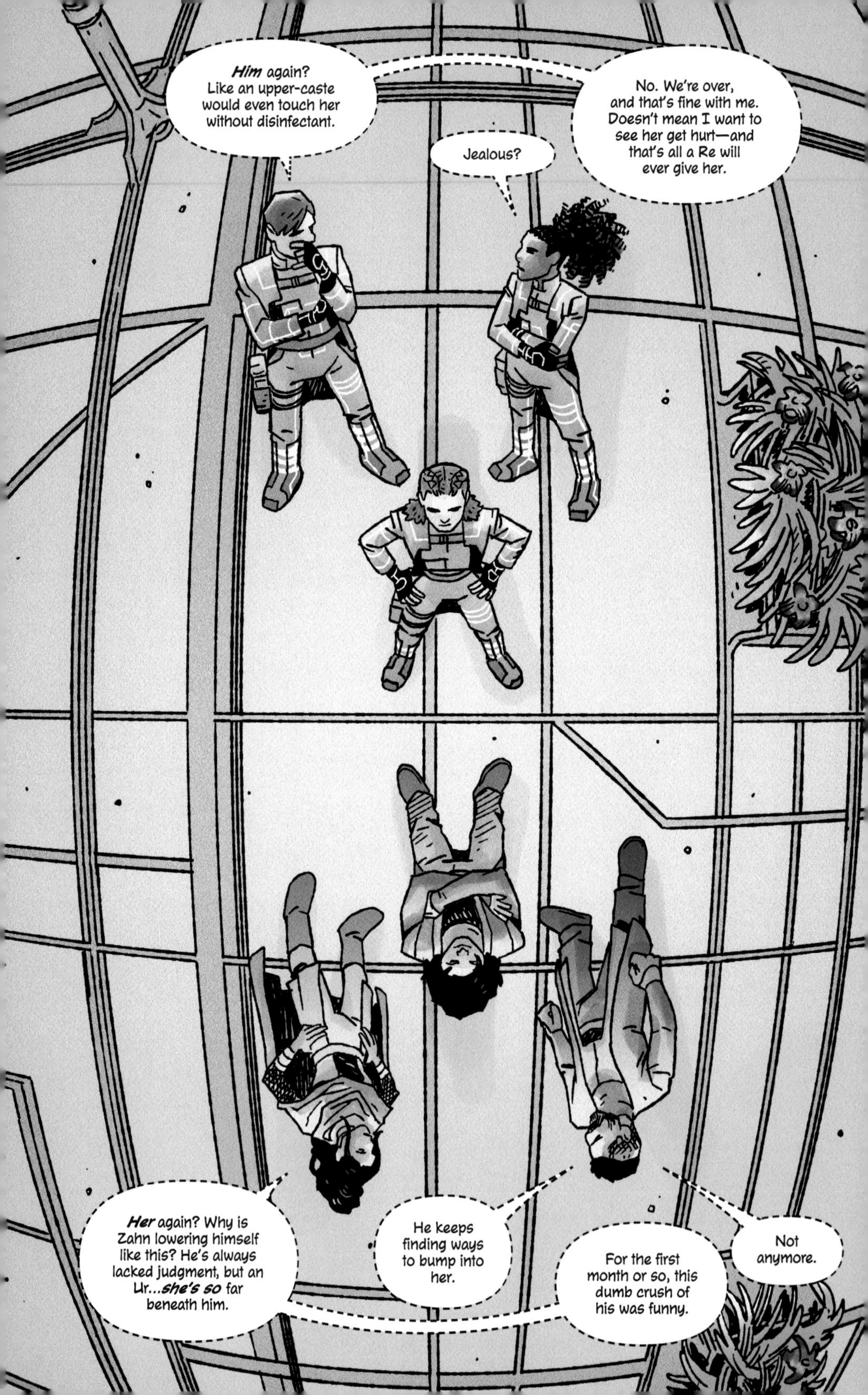

Him again? Like an upper-caste would even touch her without disinfectant.
Jealous?
No. We're over, and that's fine with me. Doesn't mean I want to see her get hurt—and that's all a Re will ever give her.
Her again? Why is Zahn lowering himself like this? He's always lacked judgment, but an Ur...*she's so* far beneath him.
He keeps finding ways to bump into her.
For the first month or so, this dumb crush of his was funny.
Not anymore.

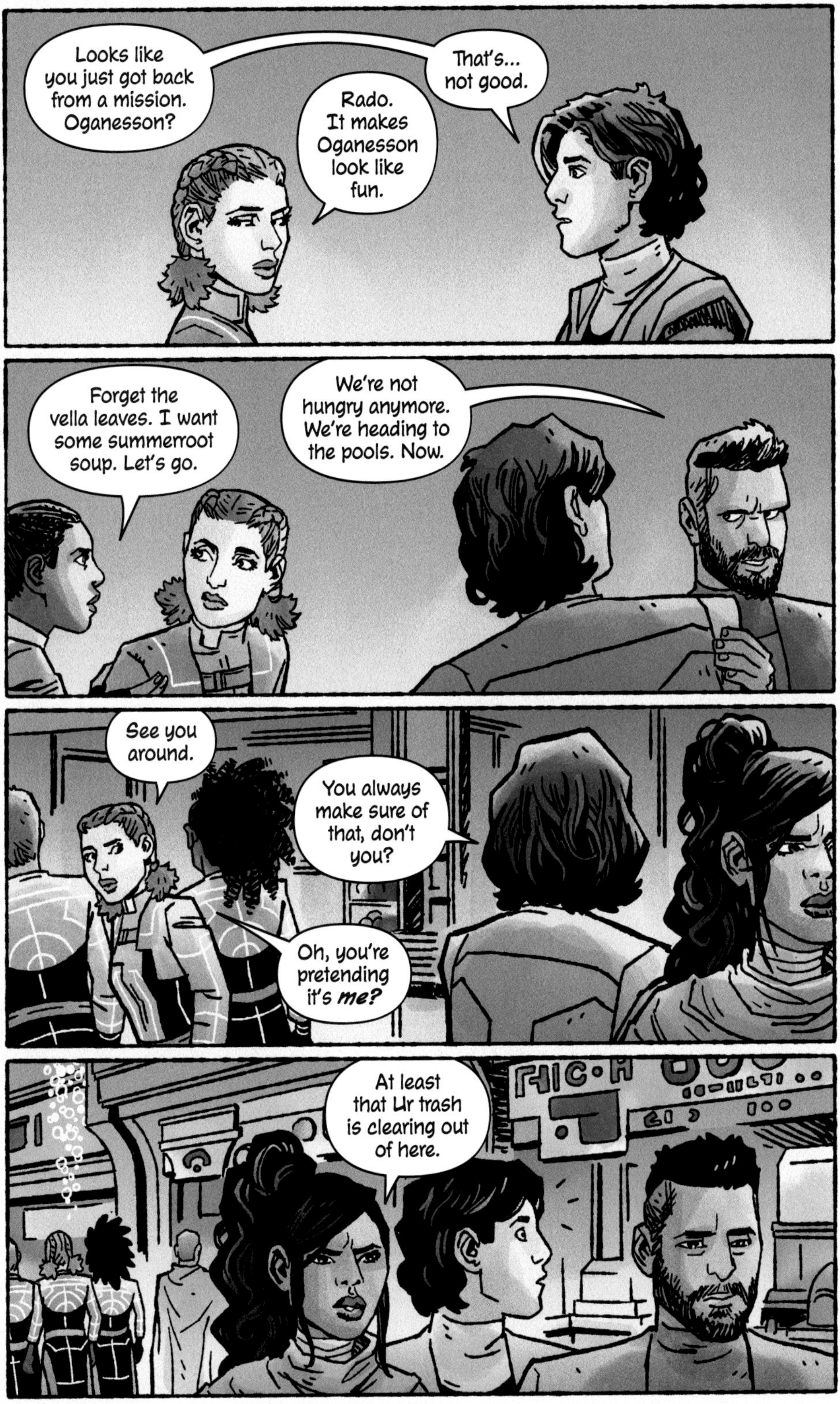
Looks like you just got back from a mission. Oganesson?
Rado. It makes Oganesson look like fun.
That's... not good.
Forget the vella leaves. I want some summerroot soup. Let's go.
We're not hungry anymore. We're heading to the pools. Now.
See you around.
You always make sure of that, don't you?
Oh, you're pretending it's *me?*
At least that Ur trash is clearing out of here.

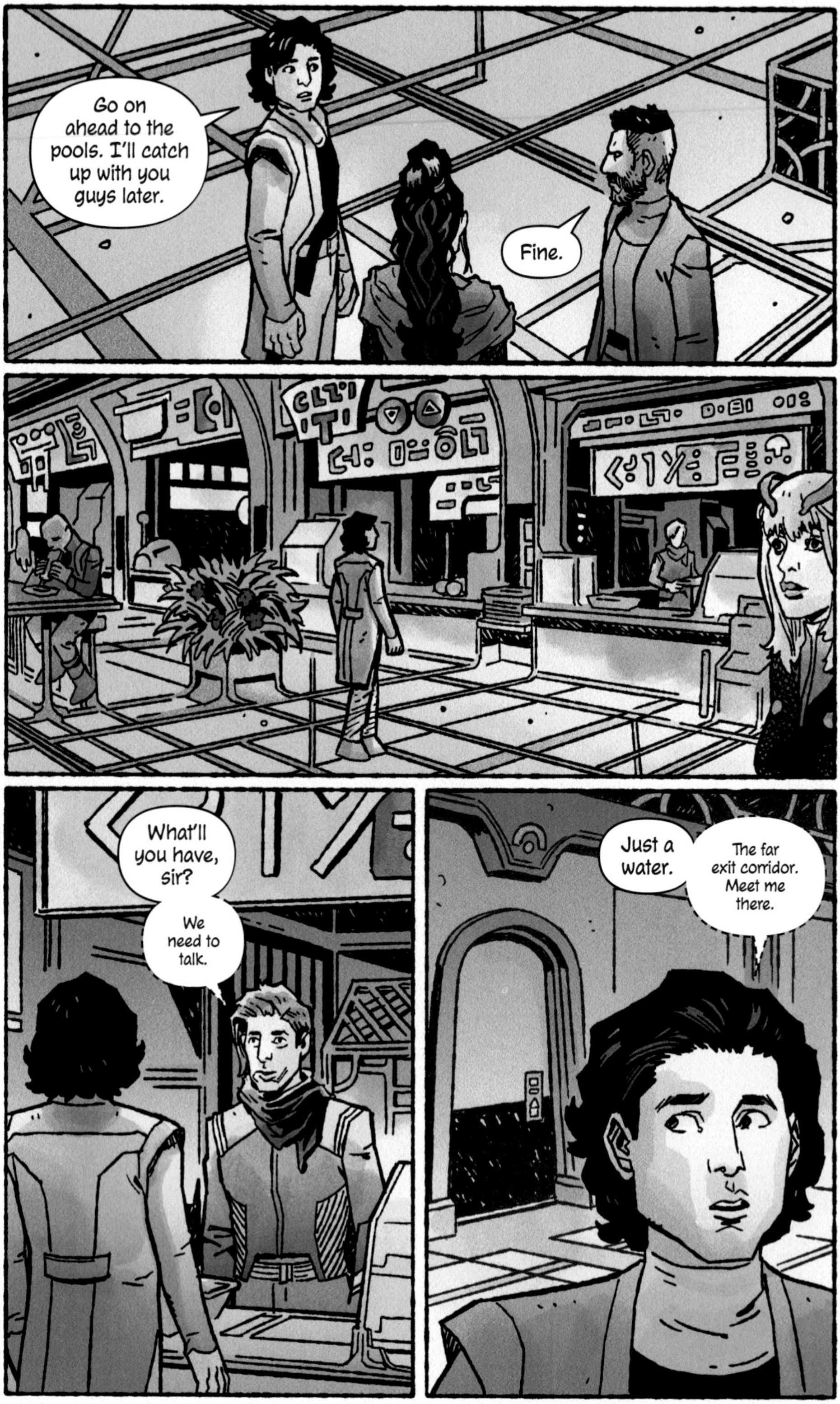
Go on ahead to the pools. I'll catch up with you guys later.
Fine.
What'll you have, sir?
We need to talk.
Just a water.
The far exit corridor. Meet me there.

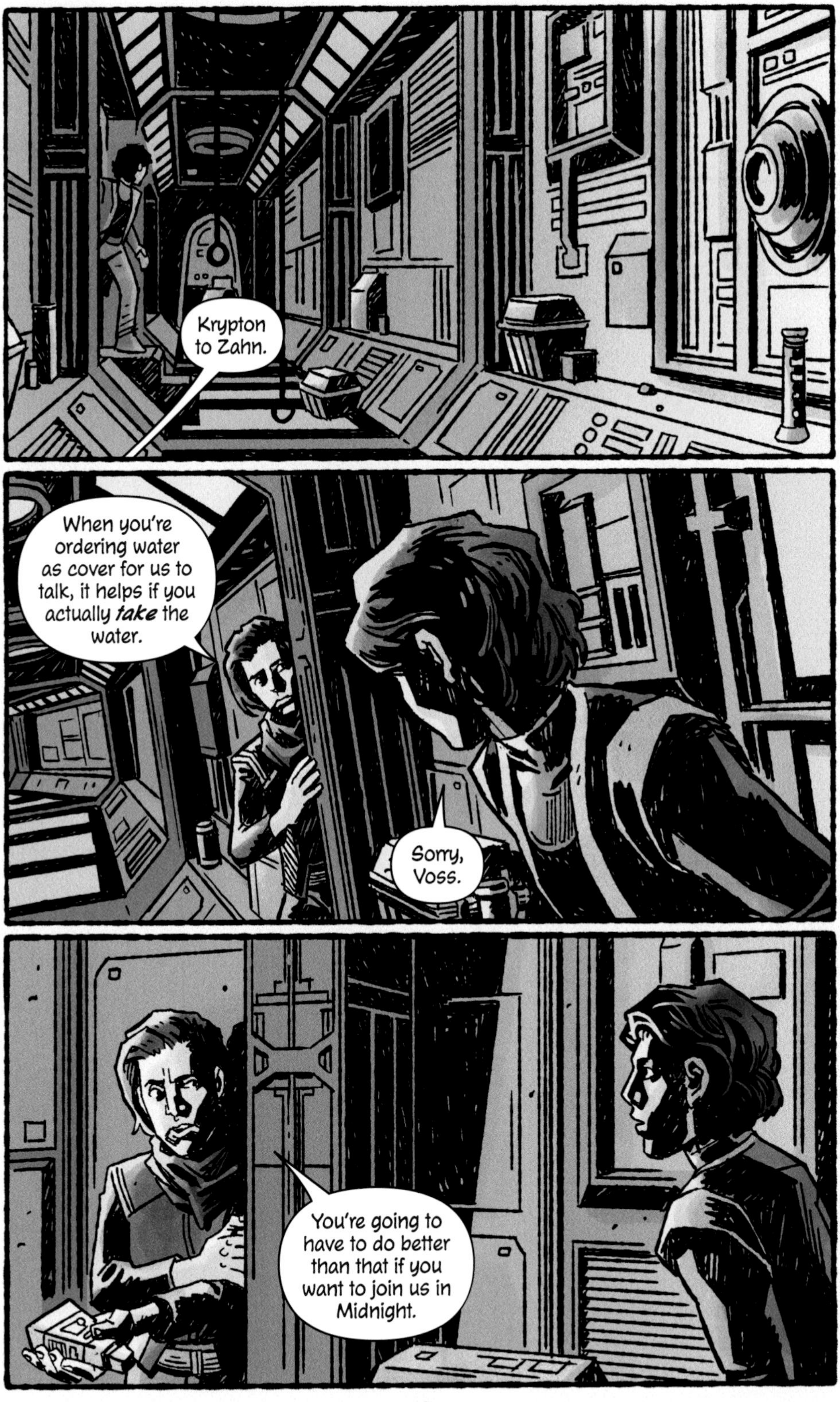
Krypton to Zahn.
When you're ordering water as cover for us to talk, it helps if you actually *take* the water.
Sorry, Voss.
You're going to have to do better than that if you want to join us in Midnight.

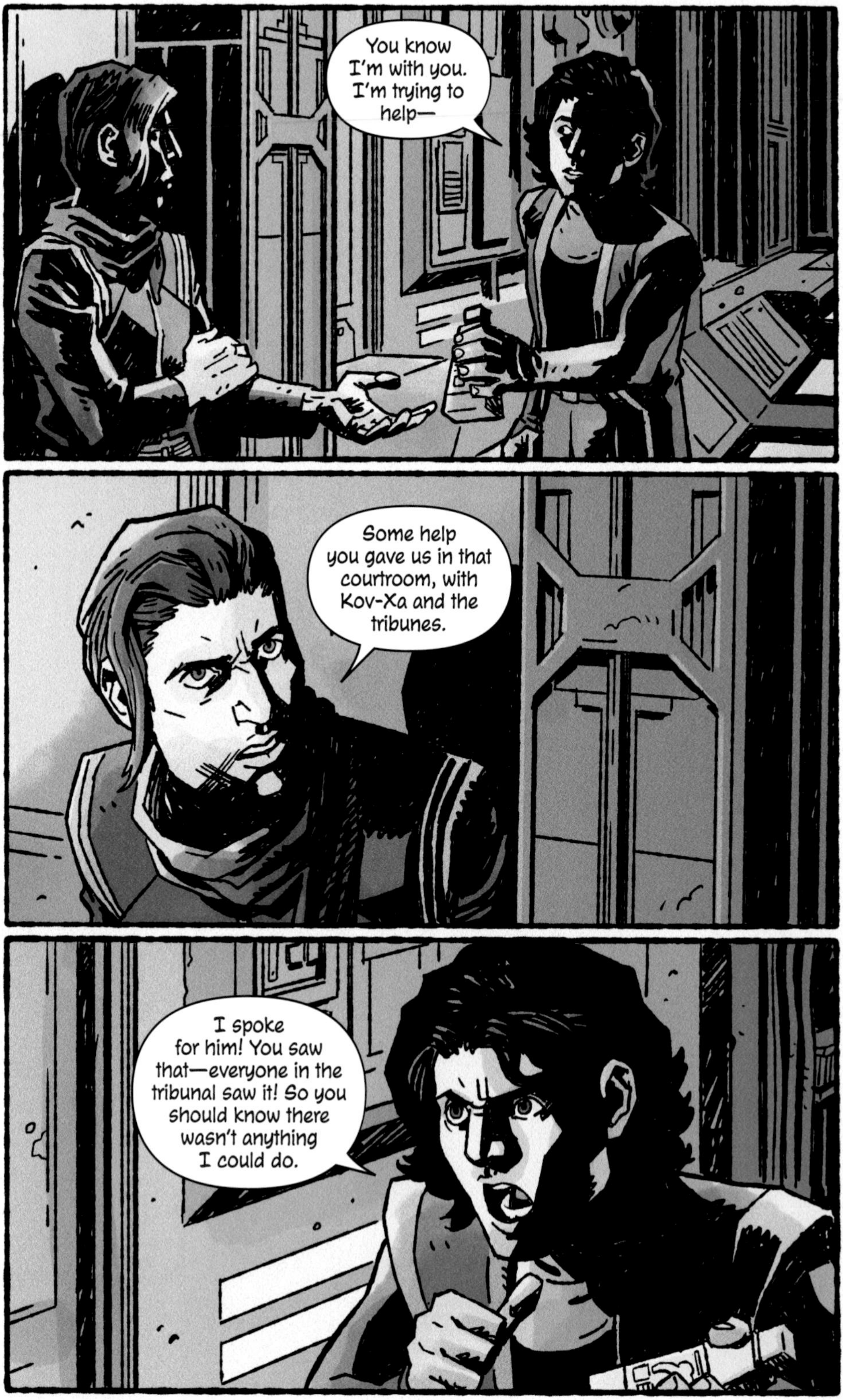
You know I'm with you. I'm trying to help—
Some help you gave us in that courtroom, with Kov-Xa and the tribunes.
I spoke for him! You saw that—everyone in the tribunal saw it! So you should know there wasn't anything I could do.

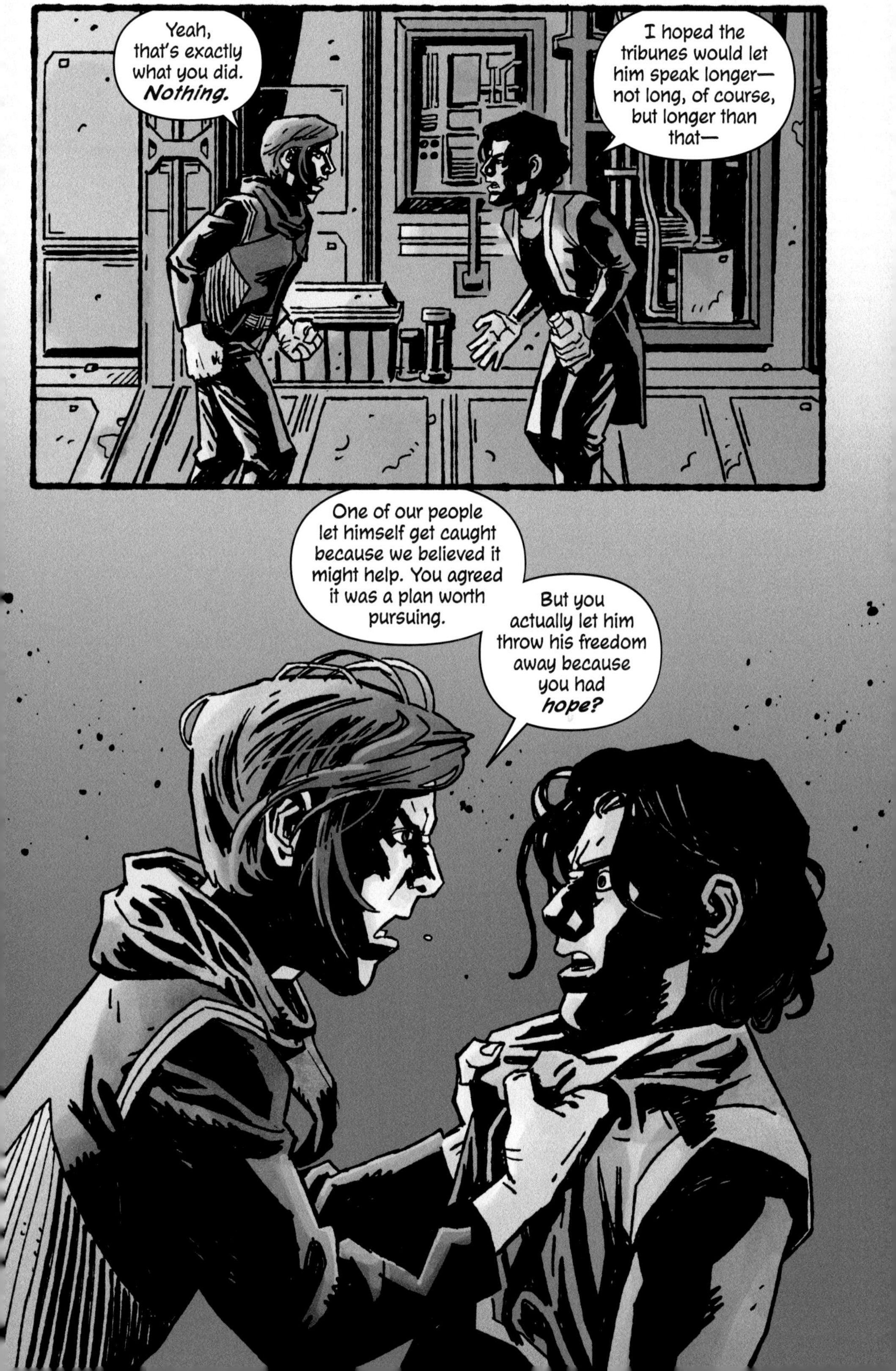
Yeah, that's exactly what you did. ***Nothing.***
I hoped the tribunes would let him speak longer—not long, of course, but longer than that—
One of our people let himself get caught because we believed it might help. You agreed it was a plan worth pursuing.
But you actually let him throw his freedom away because you had ***hope?***

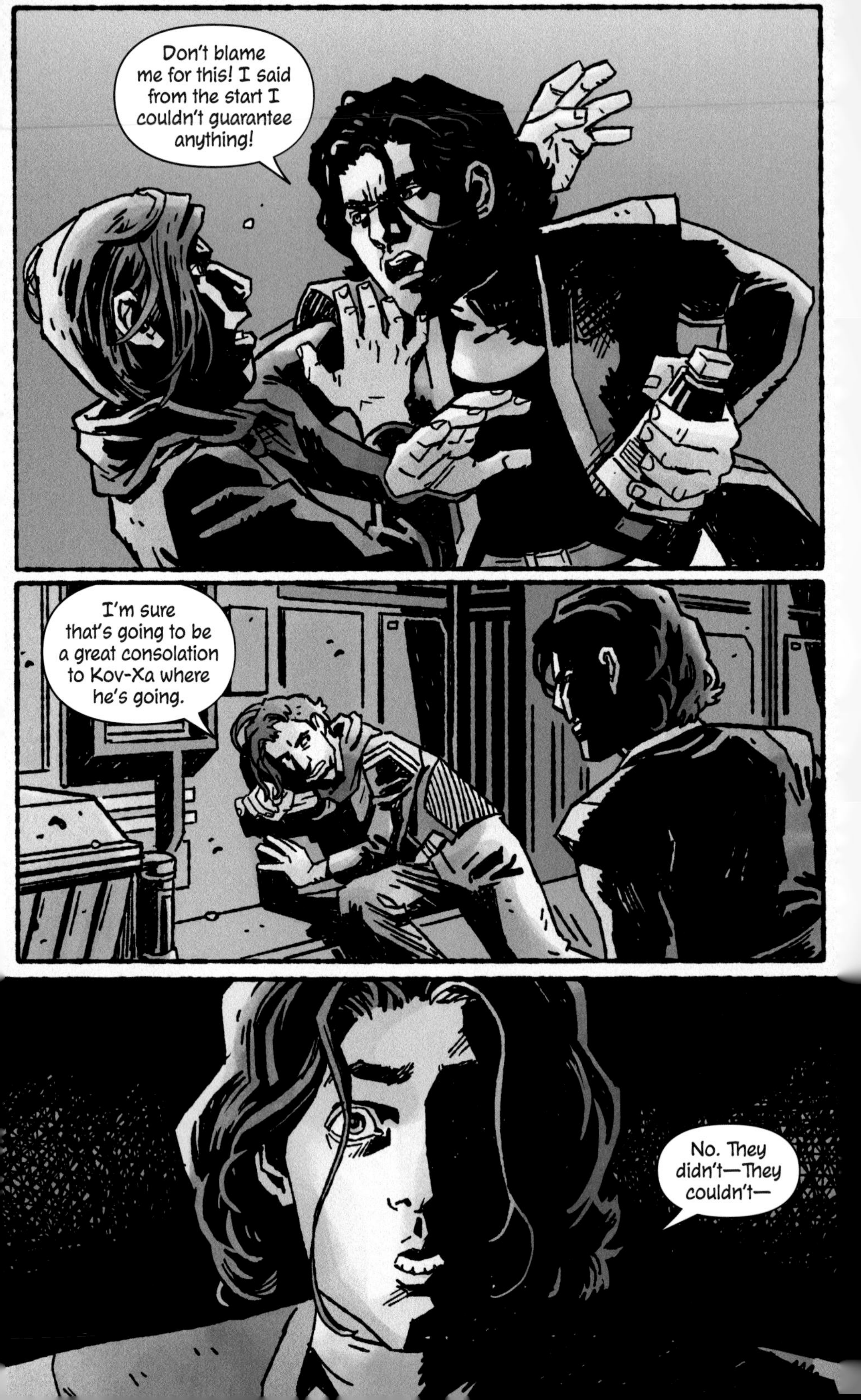
Don't blame me for this! I said from the start I couldn't guarantee anything!
I'm sure that's going to be a great consolation to Kov-Xa where he's going.
No. They didn't—They couldn't—

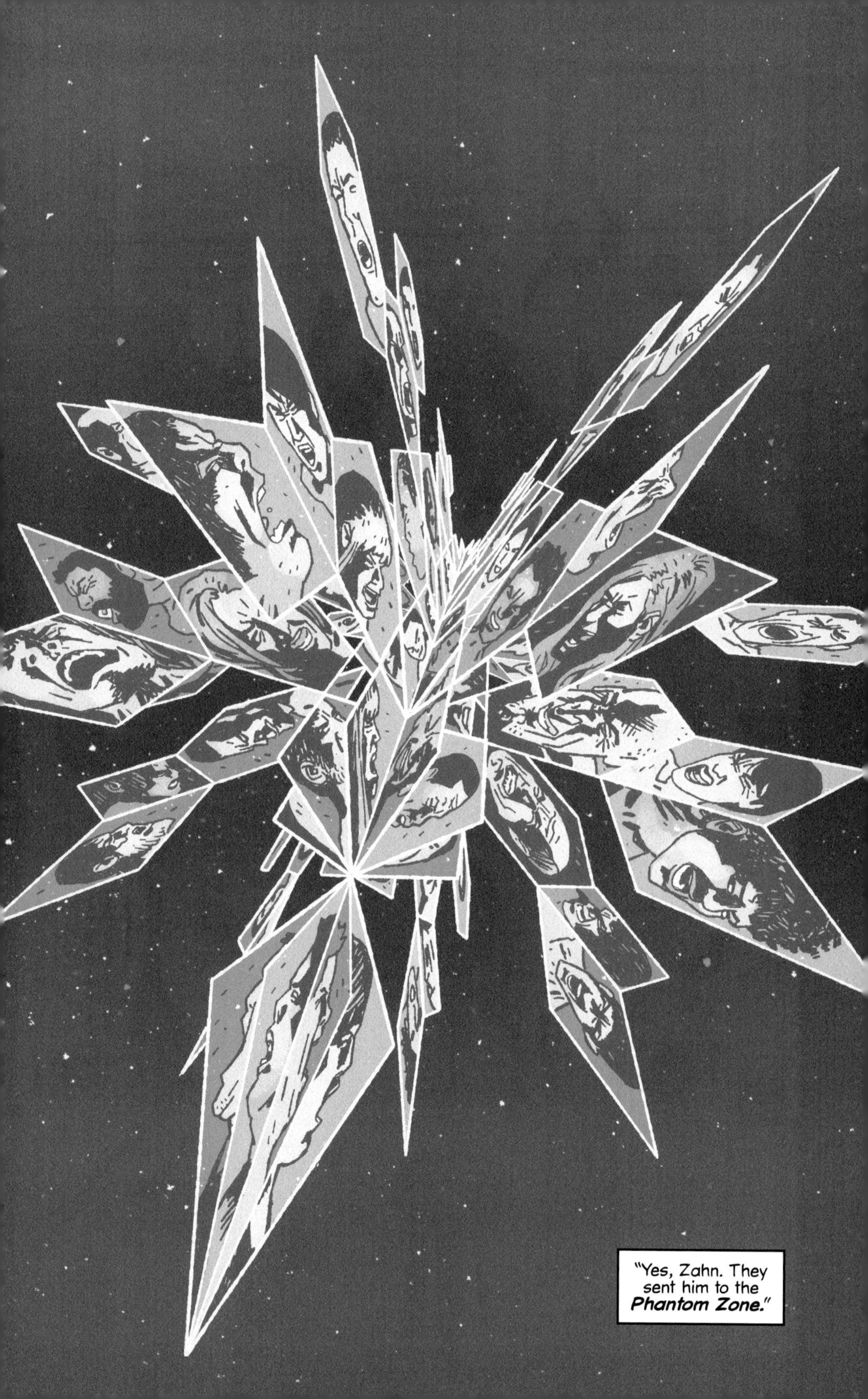
"Yes, Zahn. They sent him to the *Phantom Zone.*"

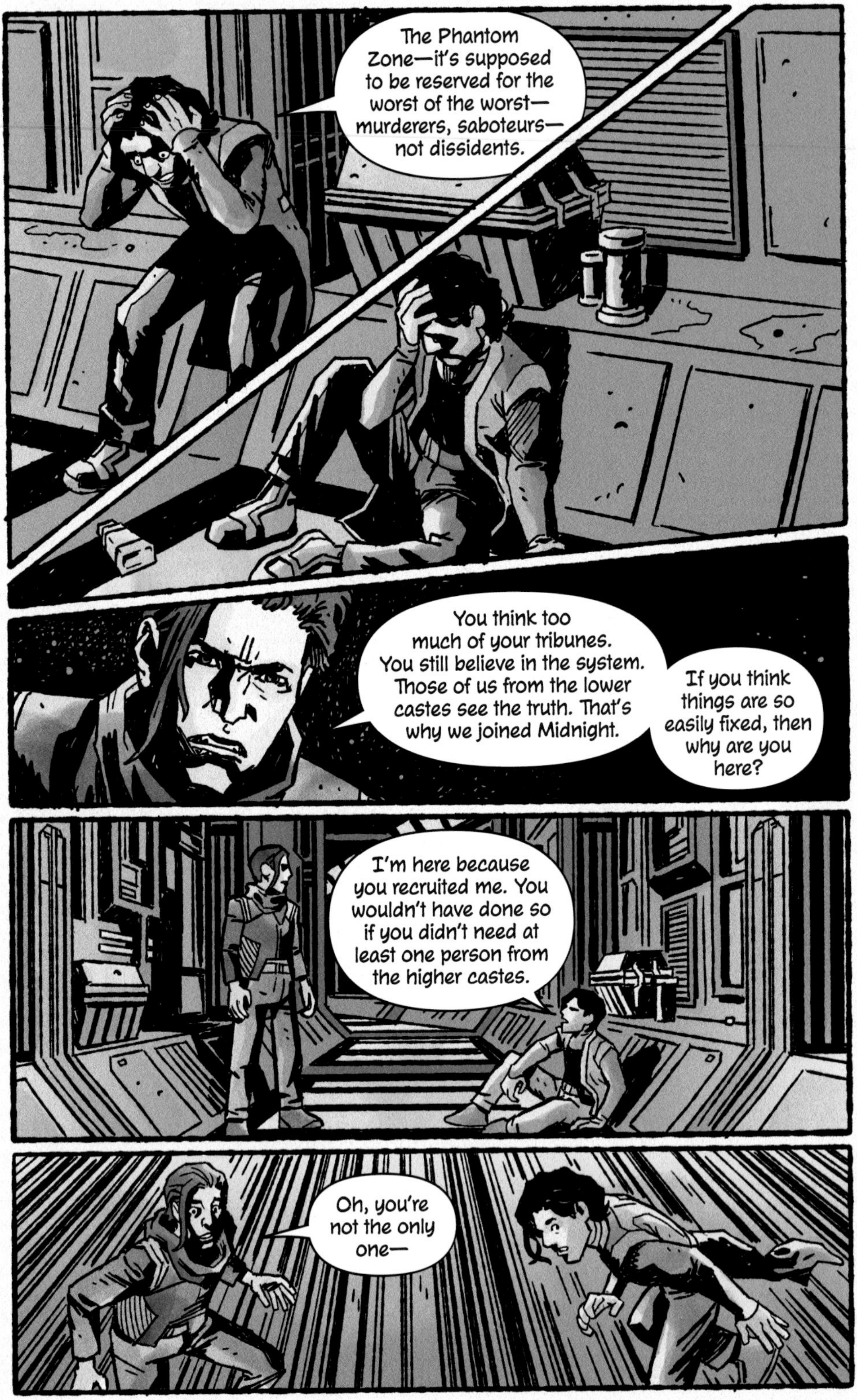
The Phantom Zone—it's supposed to be reserved for the worst of the worst—murderers, saboteurs—not dissidents.
You think too much of your tribunes. You still believe in the system. Those of us from the lower castes see the truth. That's why we joined Midnight.
If you think things are so easily fixed, then why are you here?
I'm here because you recruited me. You wouldn't have done so if you didn't need at least one person from the higher castes.
Oh, you're not the only one—

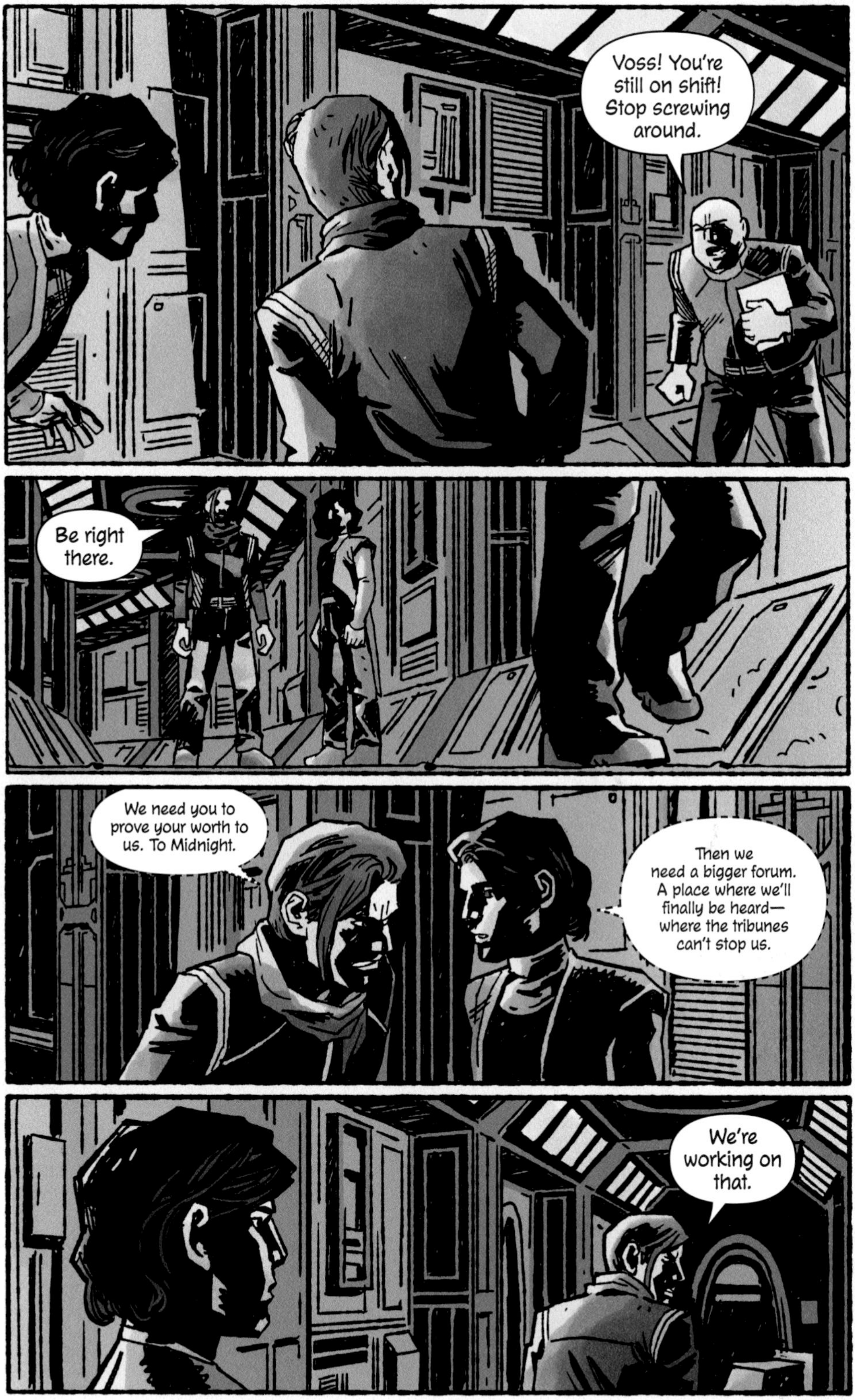
Voss! You're still on shift! Stop screwing around.
Be right there.
We need you to prove your worth to us. To Midnight.
Then we need a bigger forum. A place where we'll finally be heard— where the tribunes can't stop us.
We're working on that.

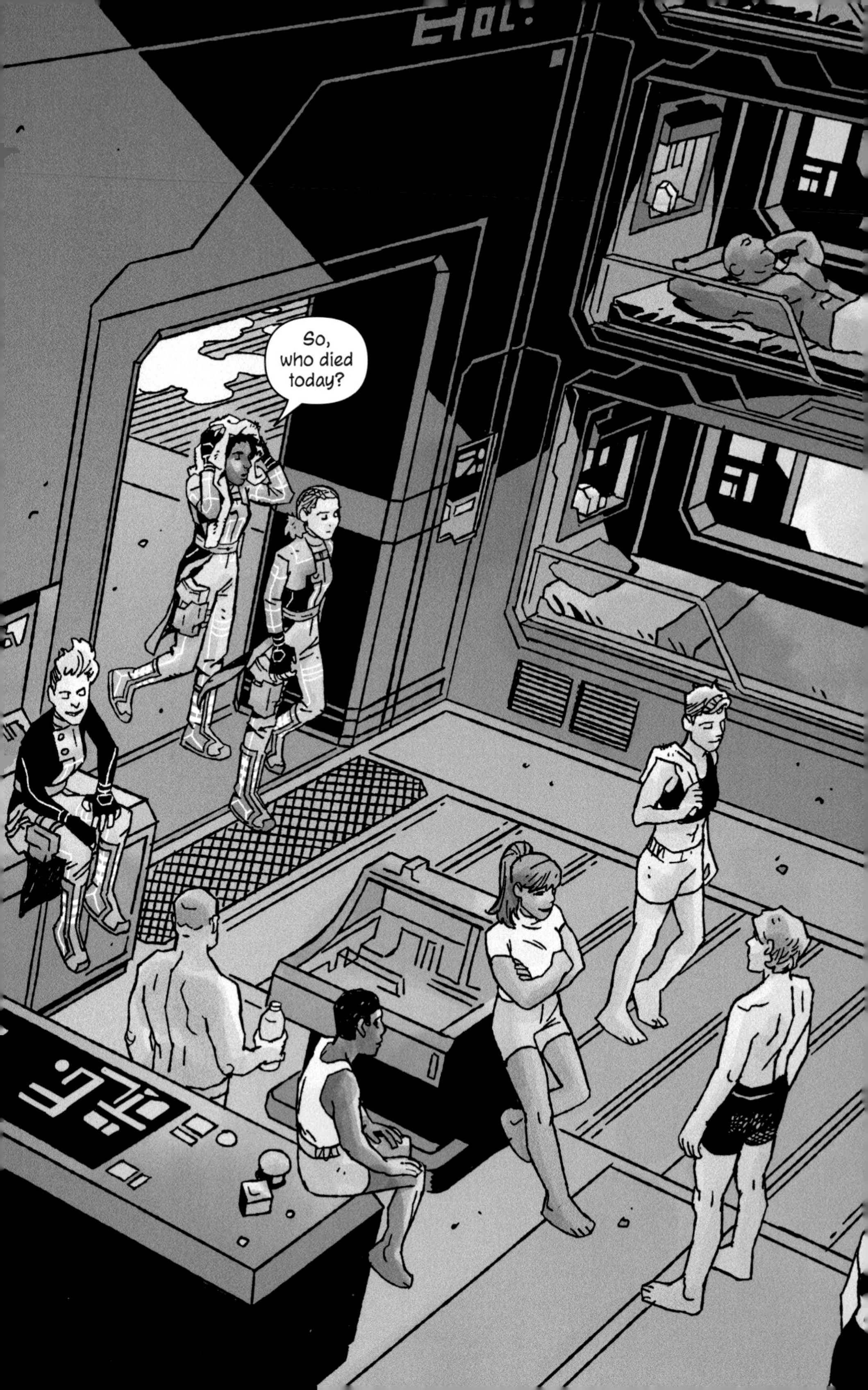
So, who died today?

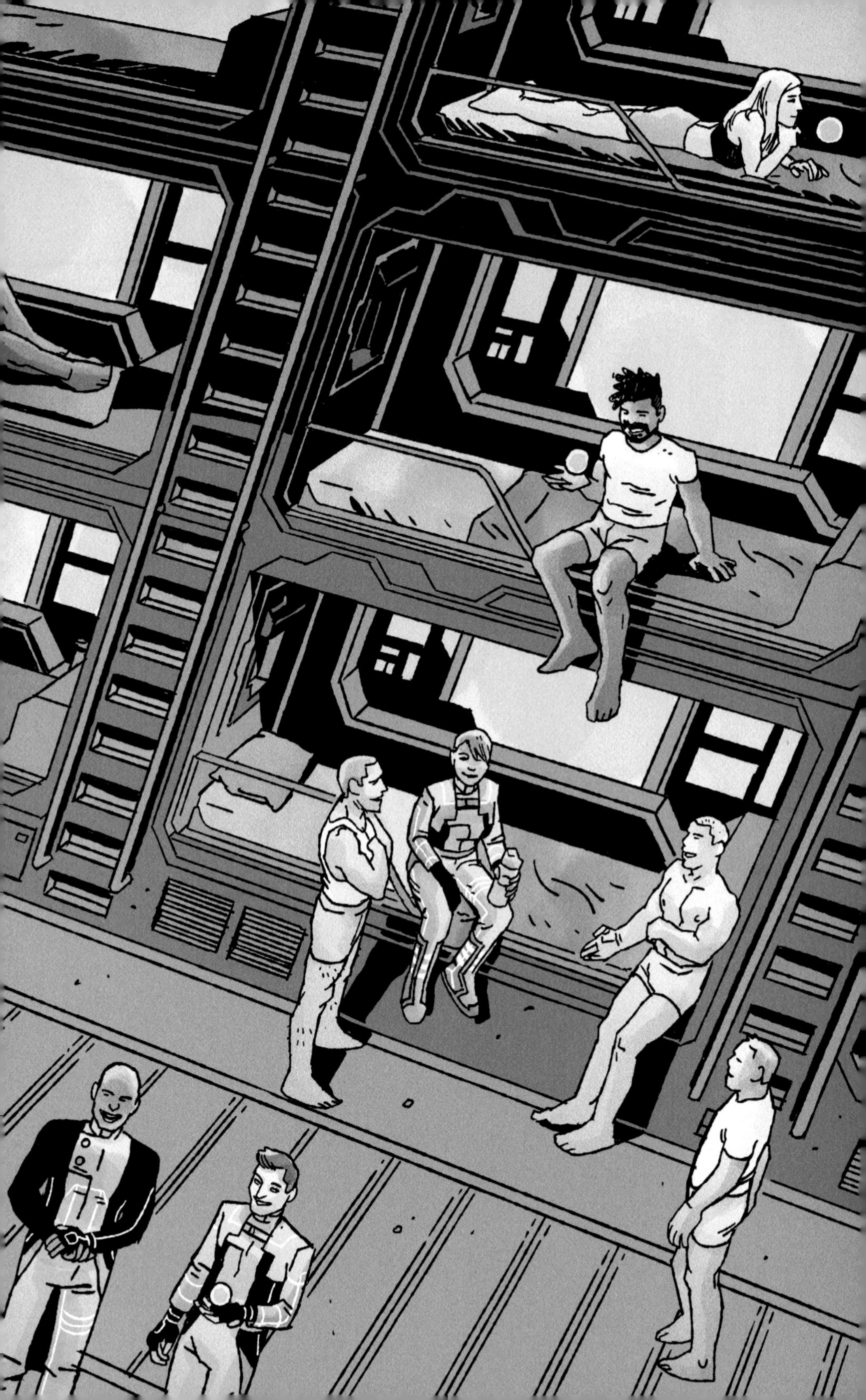

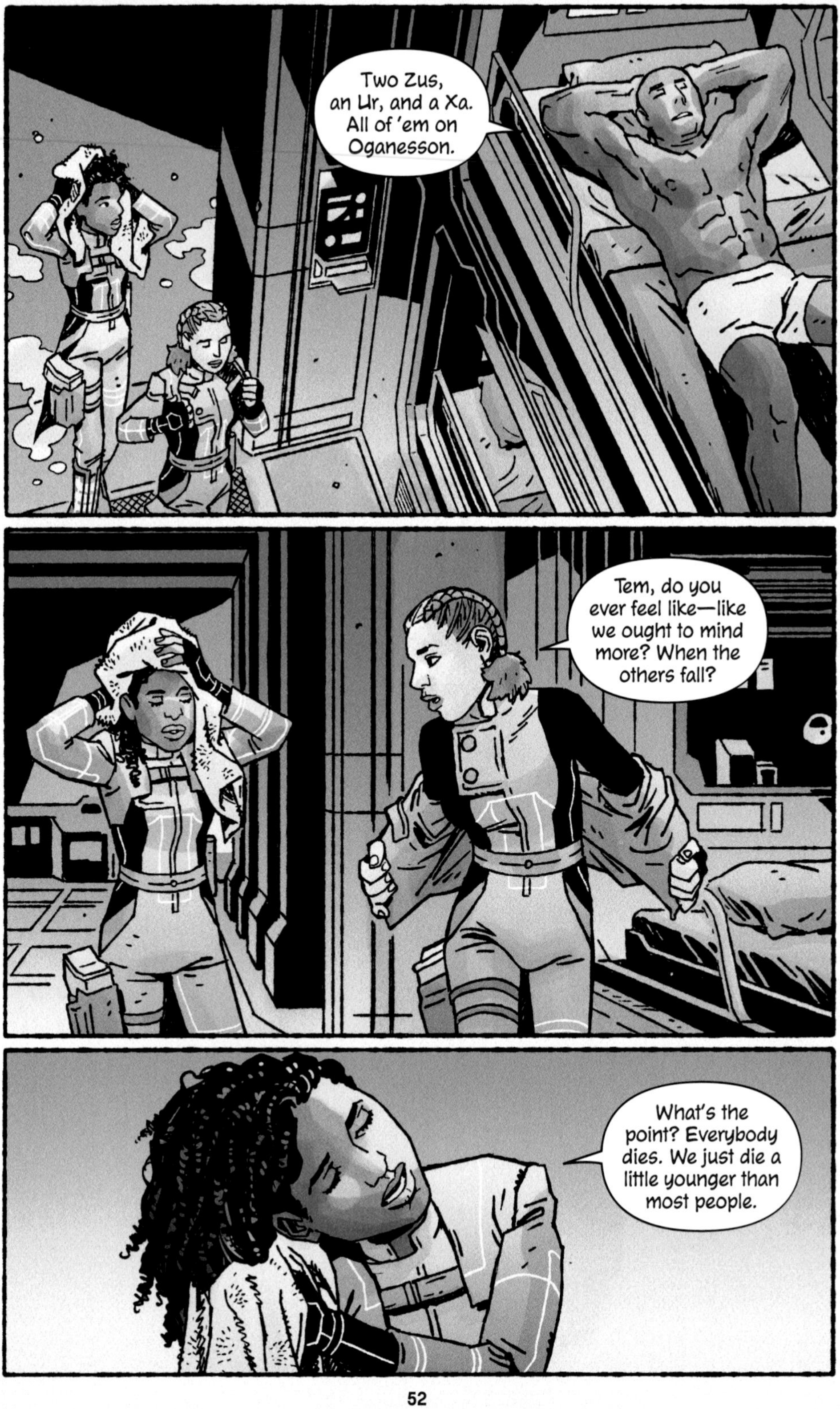
Two Zus, an Ur, and a Xa. All of 'em on Oganesson.
Tem, do you ever feel like—like we ought to mind more? When the others fall?
What's the point? Everybody dies. We just die a little younger than most people.

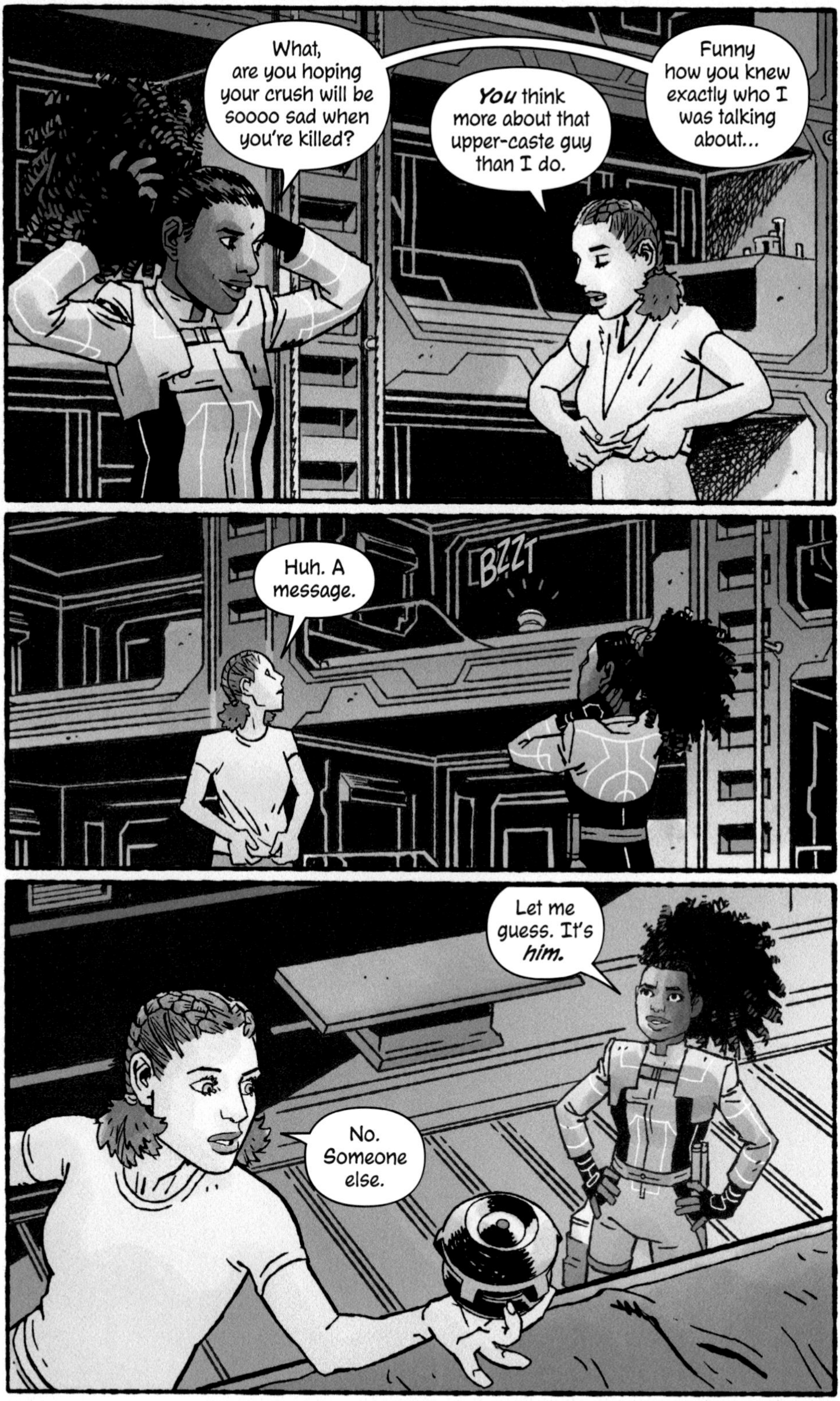
What, are you hoping your crush will be soooo sad when you're killed?
You think more about that upper-caste guy than I do.
Funny how you knew exactly who I was talking about...
Huh. A message.
BZZT
Let me guess. It's *him.*
No. Someone else.

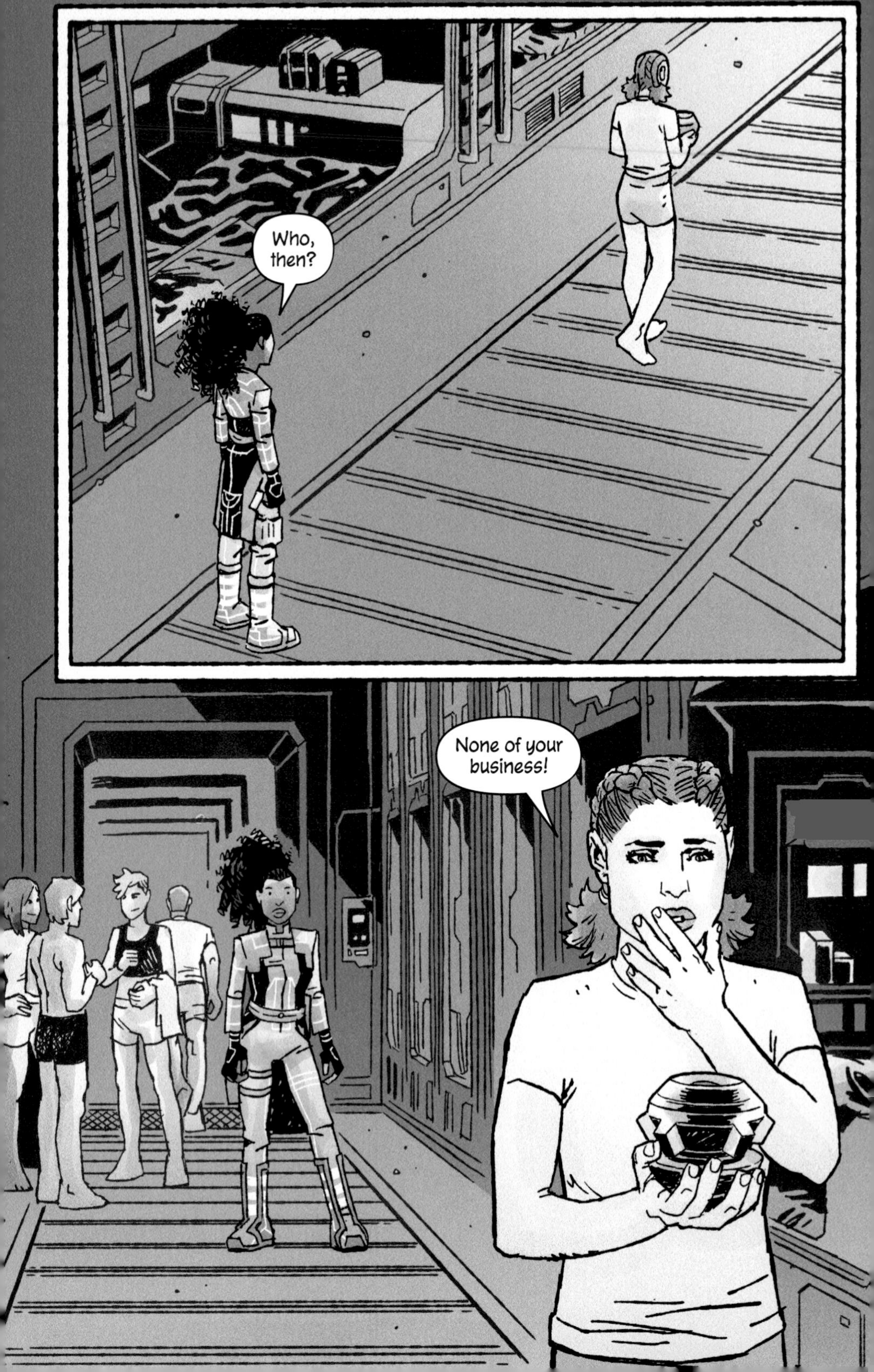
Who, then?
None of your business!

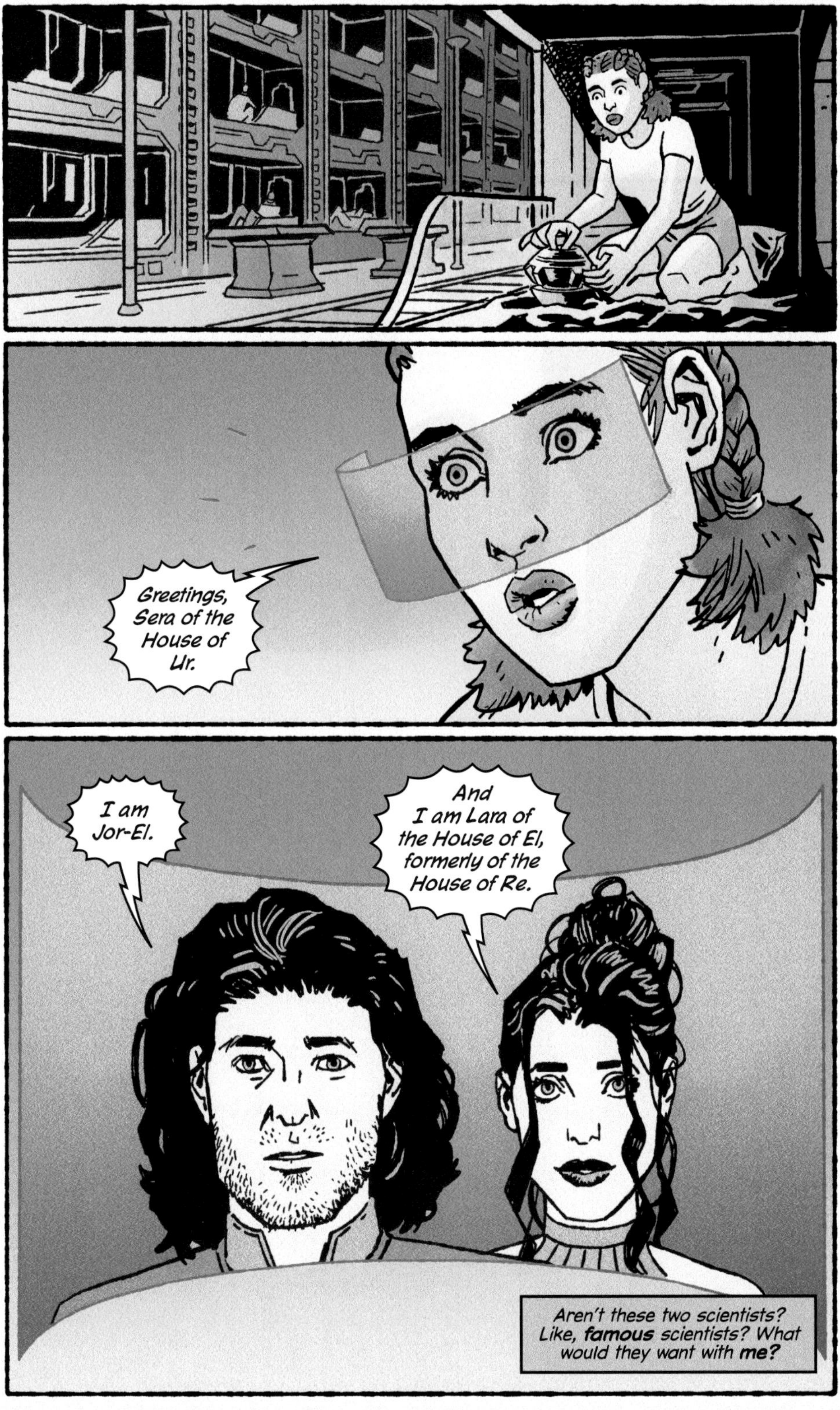
Greetings, Sera of the House of Ur.
I am Jor-El.
And I am Lara of the House of El, formerly of the House of Re.
Aren't these two scientists? Like, **famous** scientists? What would they want with **me?**

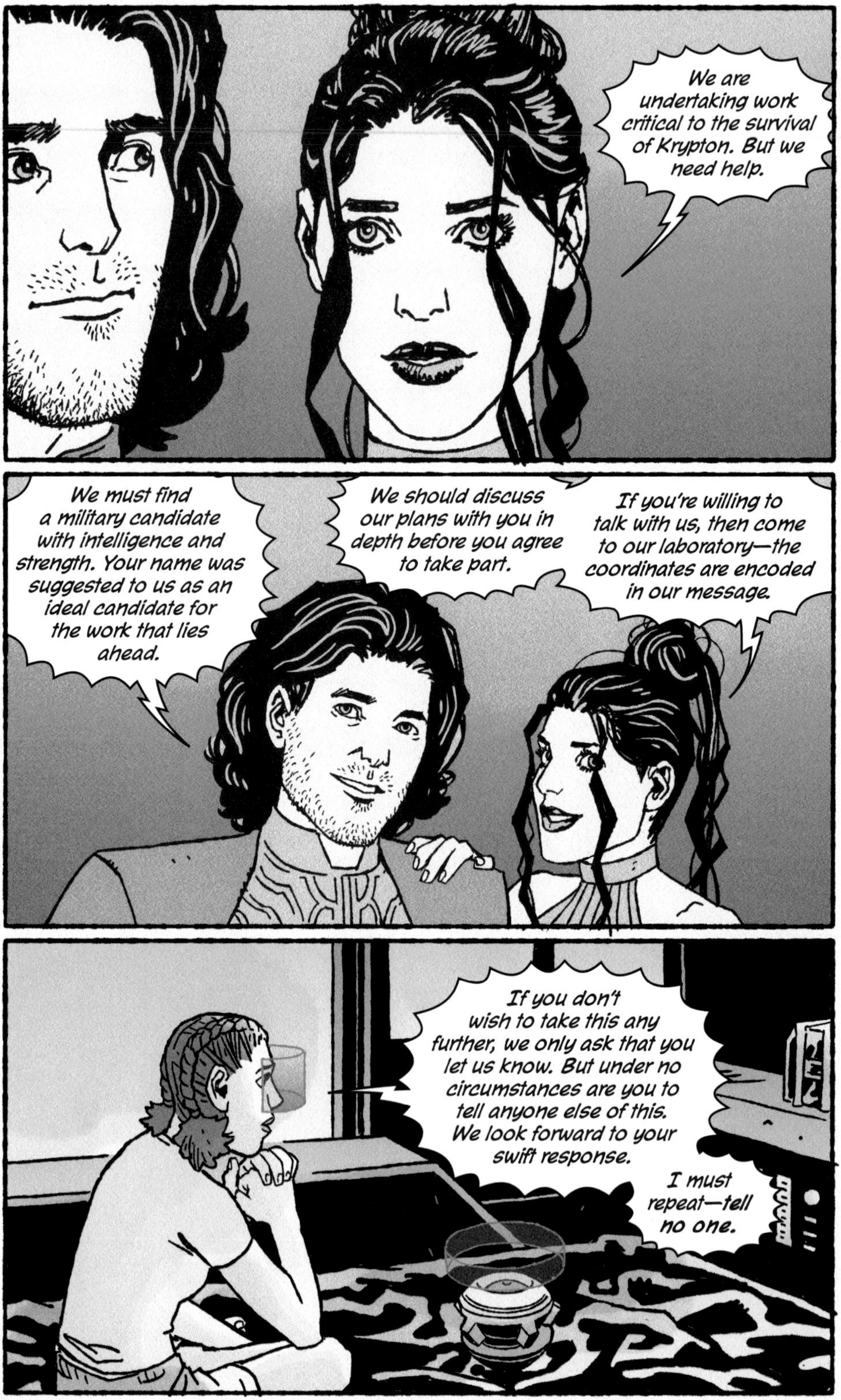
We are undertaking work critical to the survival of Krypton. But we need help.
We must find a military candidate with intelligence and strength. Your name was suggested to us as an ideal candidate for the work that lies ahead.
We should discuss our plans with you in depth before you agree to take part.
If you're willing to talk with us, then come to our laboratory—the coordinates are encoded in our message.
If you don't wish to take this any further, we only ask that you let us know. But under no circumstances are you to tell anyone else of this. We look forward to your swift response.
I must repeat—tell no one.

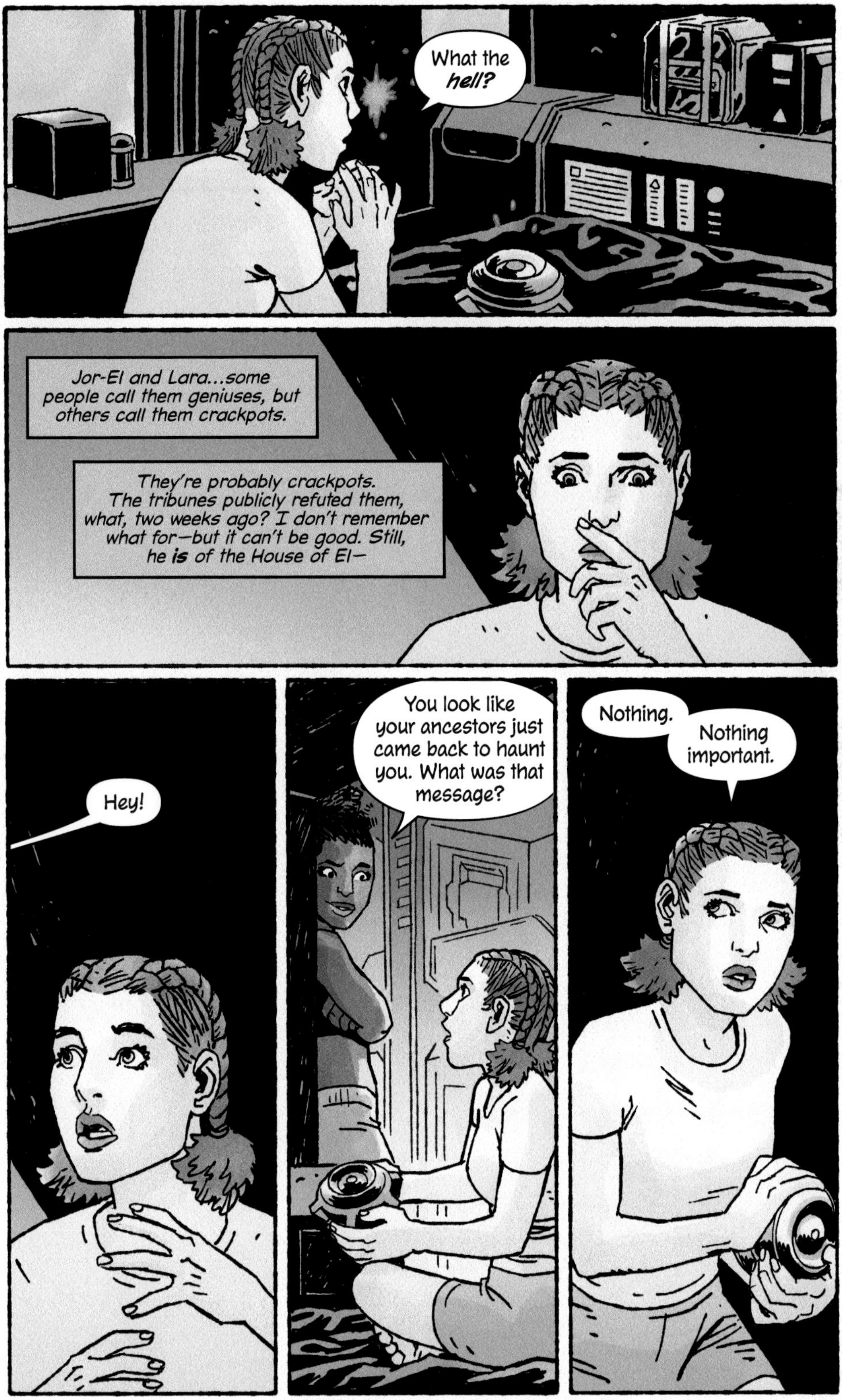
What the *hell?*
Jor-El and Lara...some people call them geniuses, but others call them crackpots.
They're probably crackpots. The tribunes publicly refuted them, what, two weeks ago? I don't remember what for—but it can't be good. Still, he **is** of the House of El—
Hey!
You look like your ancestors just came back to haunt you. What was that message?
Nothing.
Nothing important.

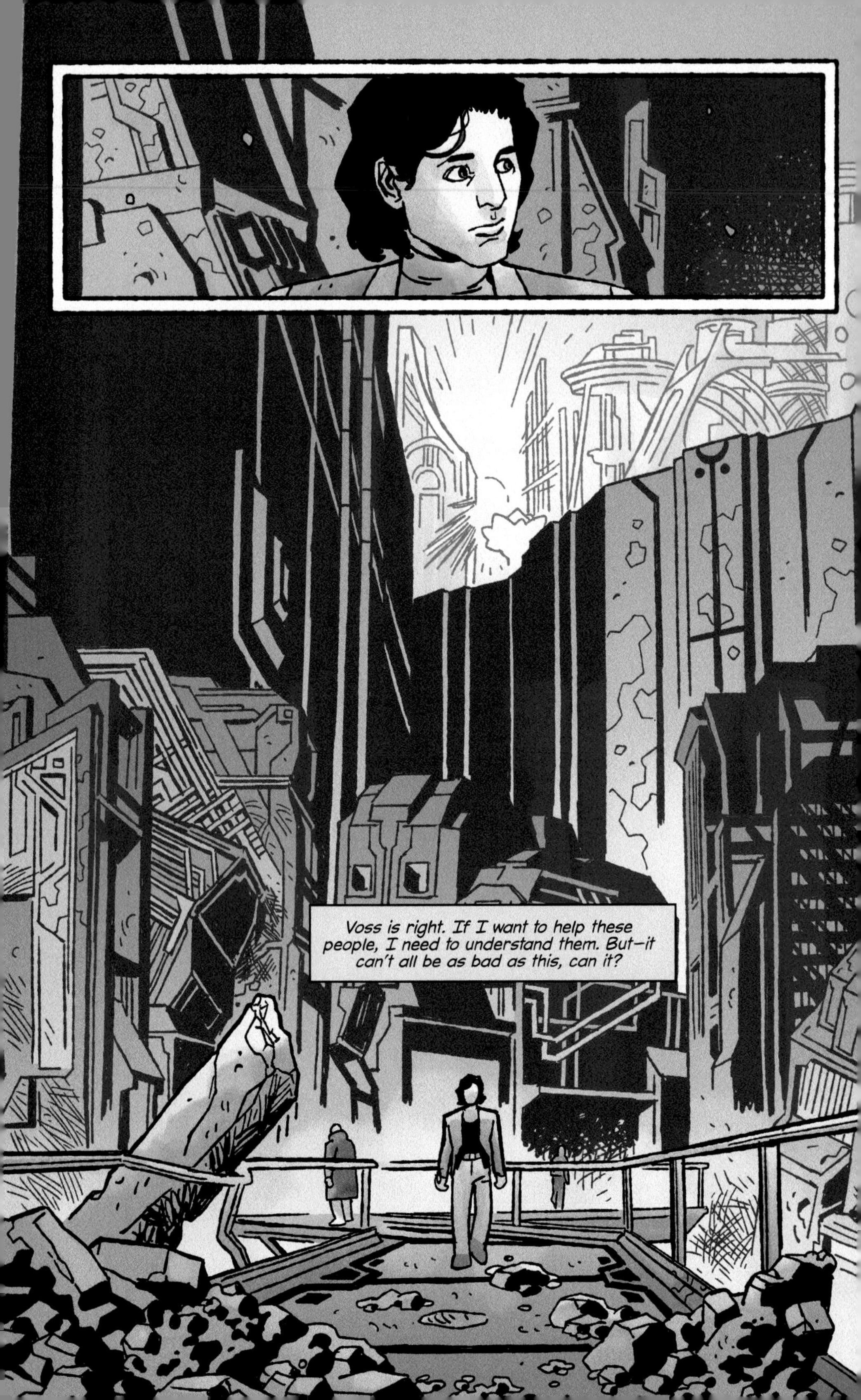
Voss is right. If I want to help these people, I need to understand them. But—it can't all be as bad as this, can it?

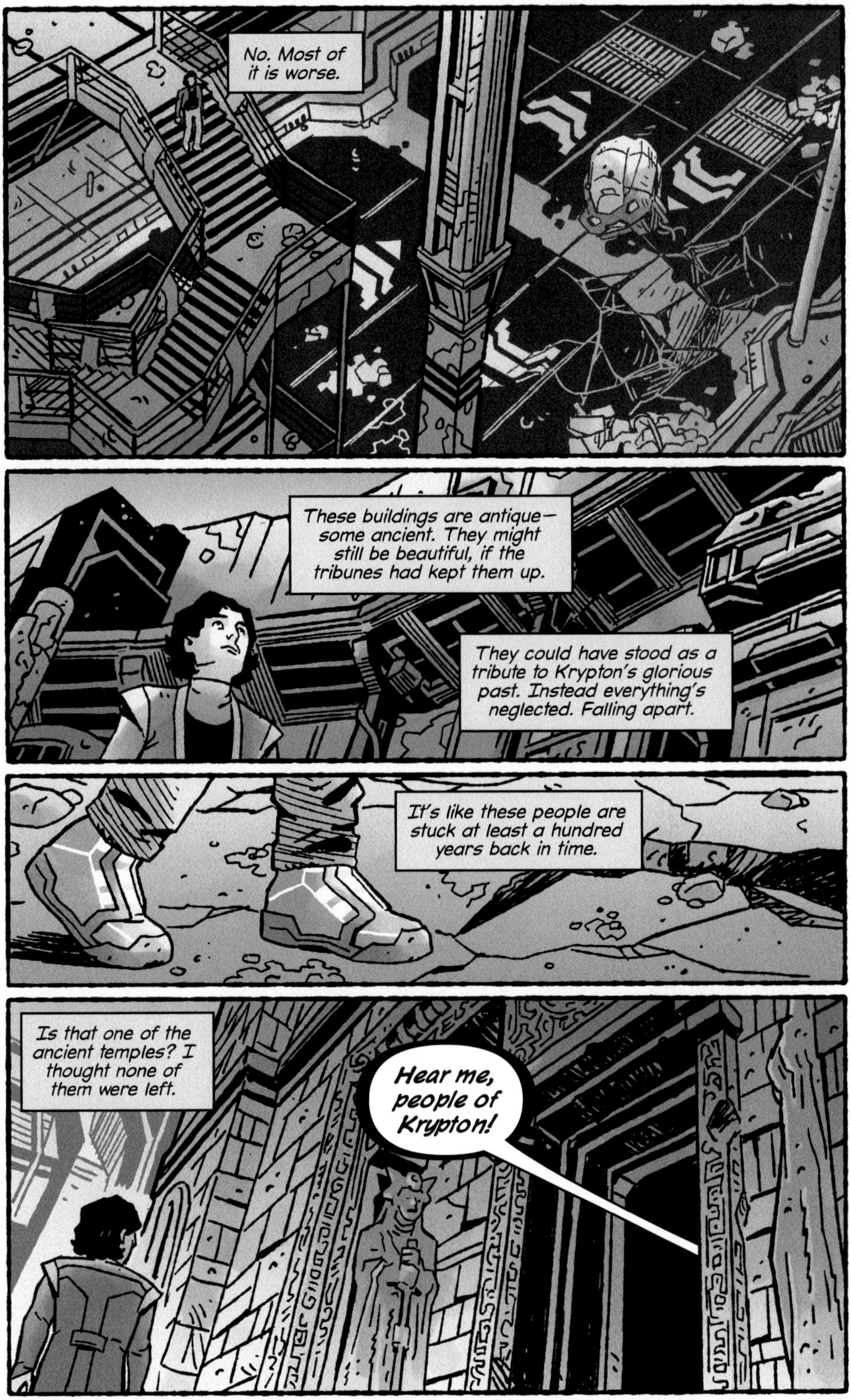
No. Most of it is worse.
These buildings are antique— some ancient. They might still be beautiful, if the tribunes had kept them up.
They could have stood as a tribute to Krypton's glorious past. Instead everything's neglected. Falling apart.
It's like these people are stuck at least a hundred years back in time.
Is that one of the ancient temples? I thought none of them were left.
Hear me, people of Krypton!

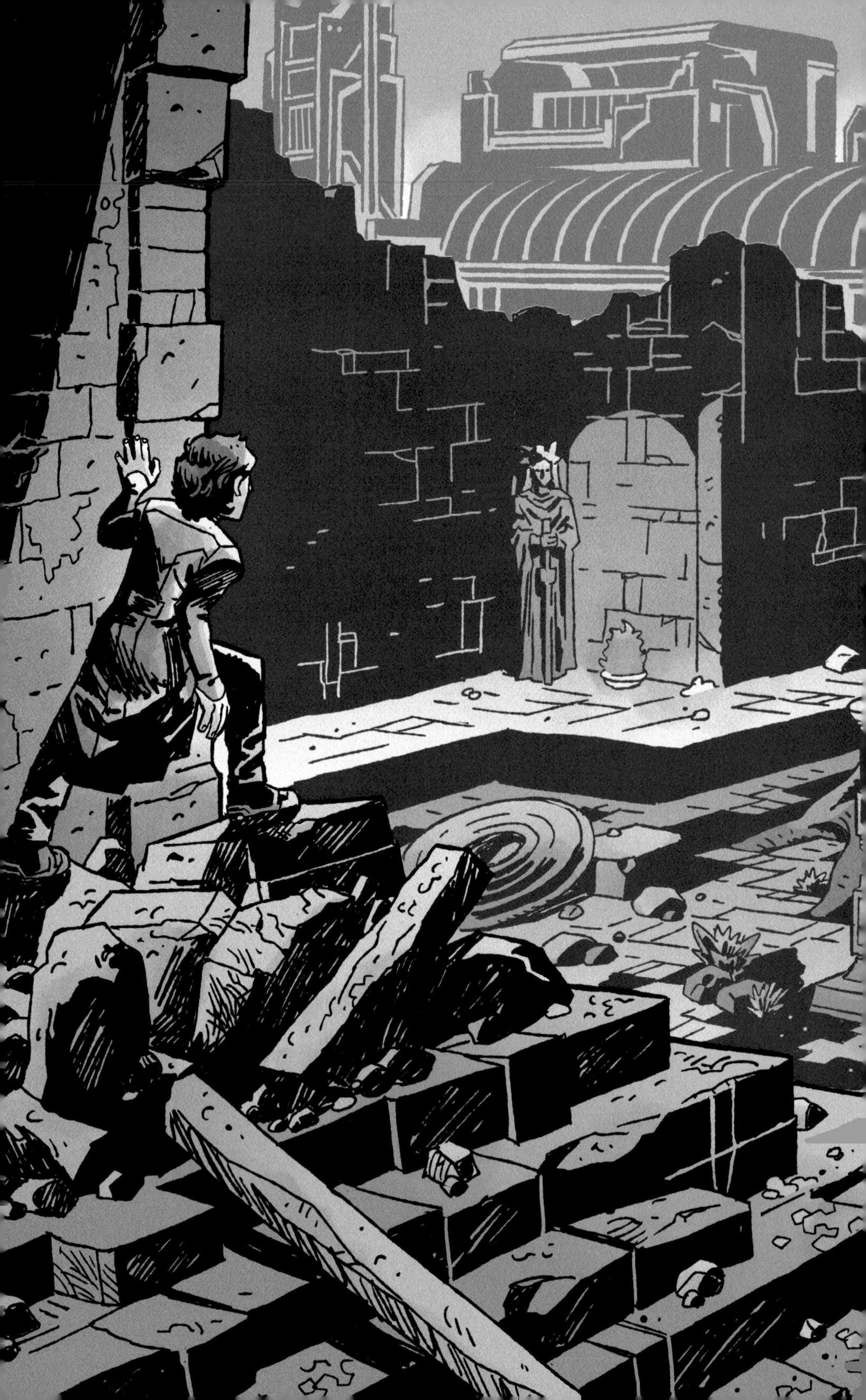

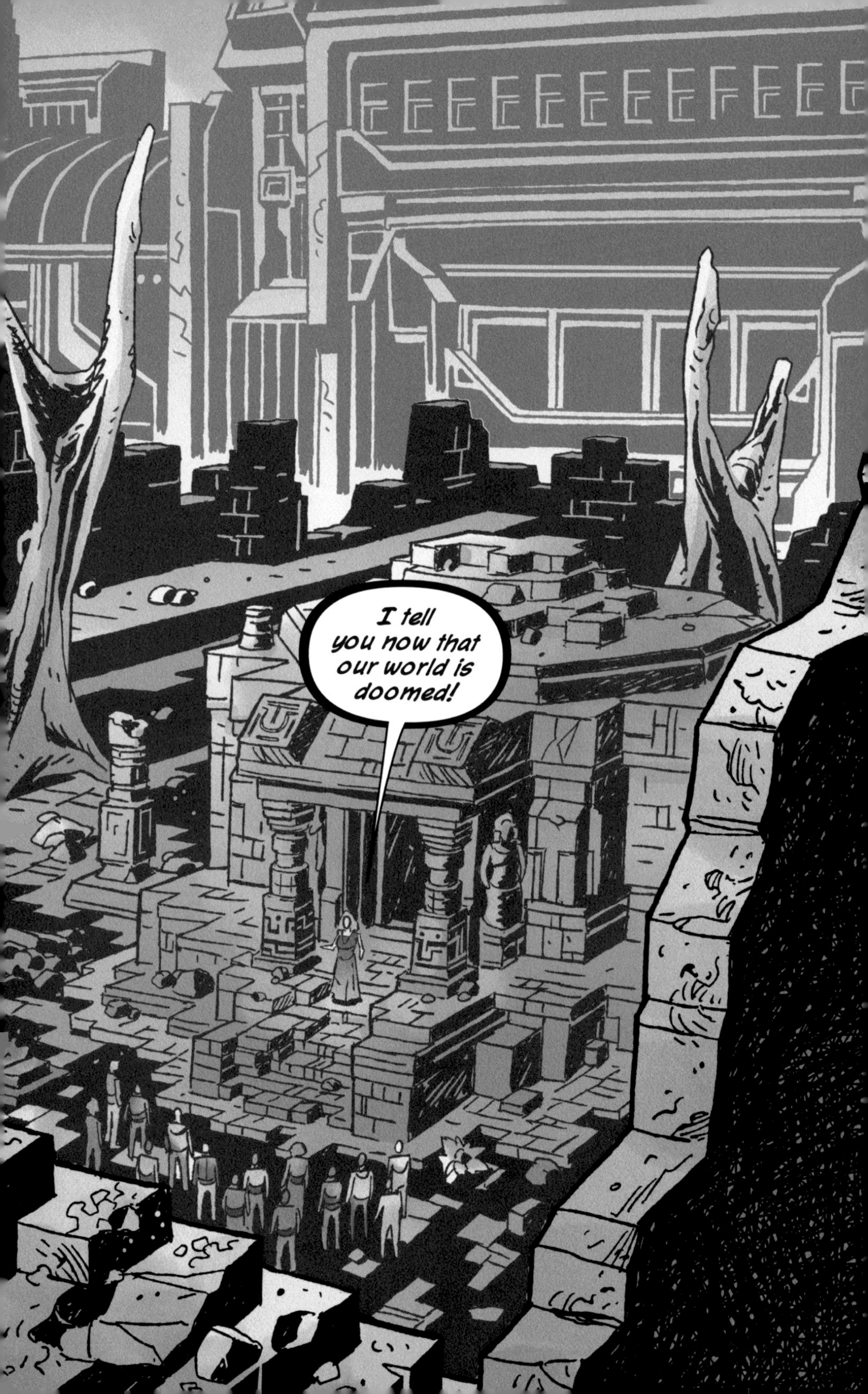
I tell you now that our world is doomed!

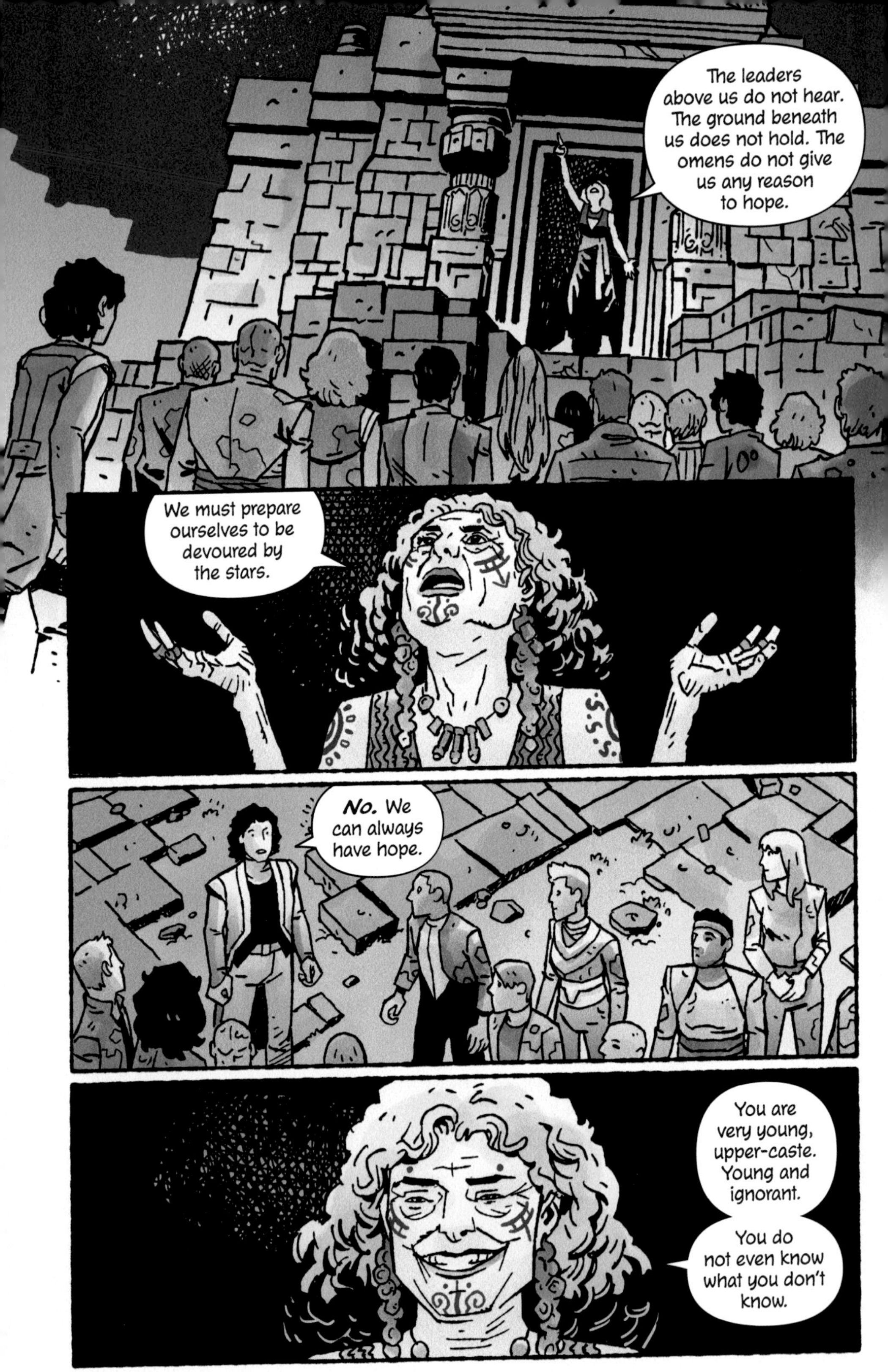
The leaders above us do not hear. The ground beneath us does not hold. The omens do not give us any reason to hope.
We must prepare ourselves to be devoured by the stars.
No. We can always have hope.
You are very young, upper-caste. Young and ignorant.
You do not even know what you don't know.

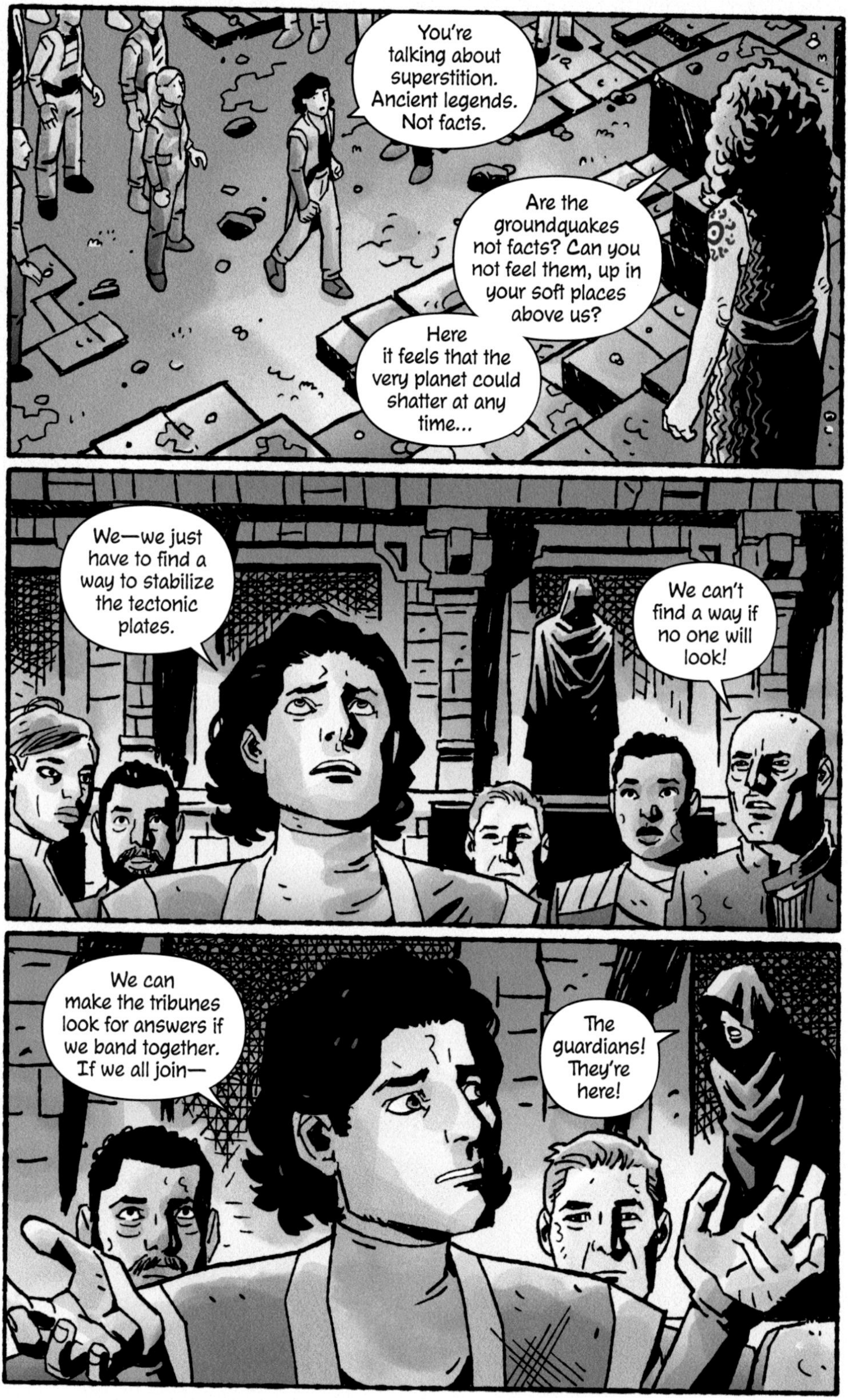
You're talking about superstition. Ancient legends. Not facts.
Are the groundquakes not facts? Can you not feel them, up in your soft places above us?
Here it feels that the very planet could shatter at any time...
We—we just have to find a way to stabilize the tectonic plates.
We can't find a way if no one will look!
We can make the tribunes look for answers if we band together. If we all join—
The guardians! They're here!

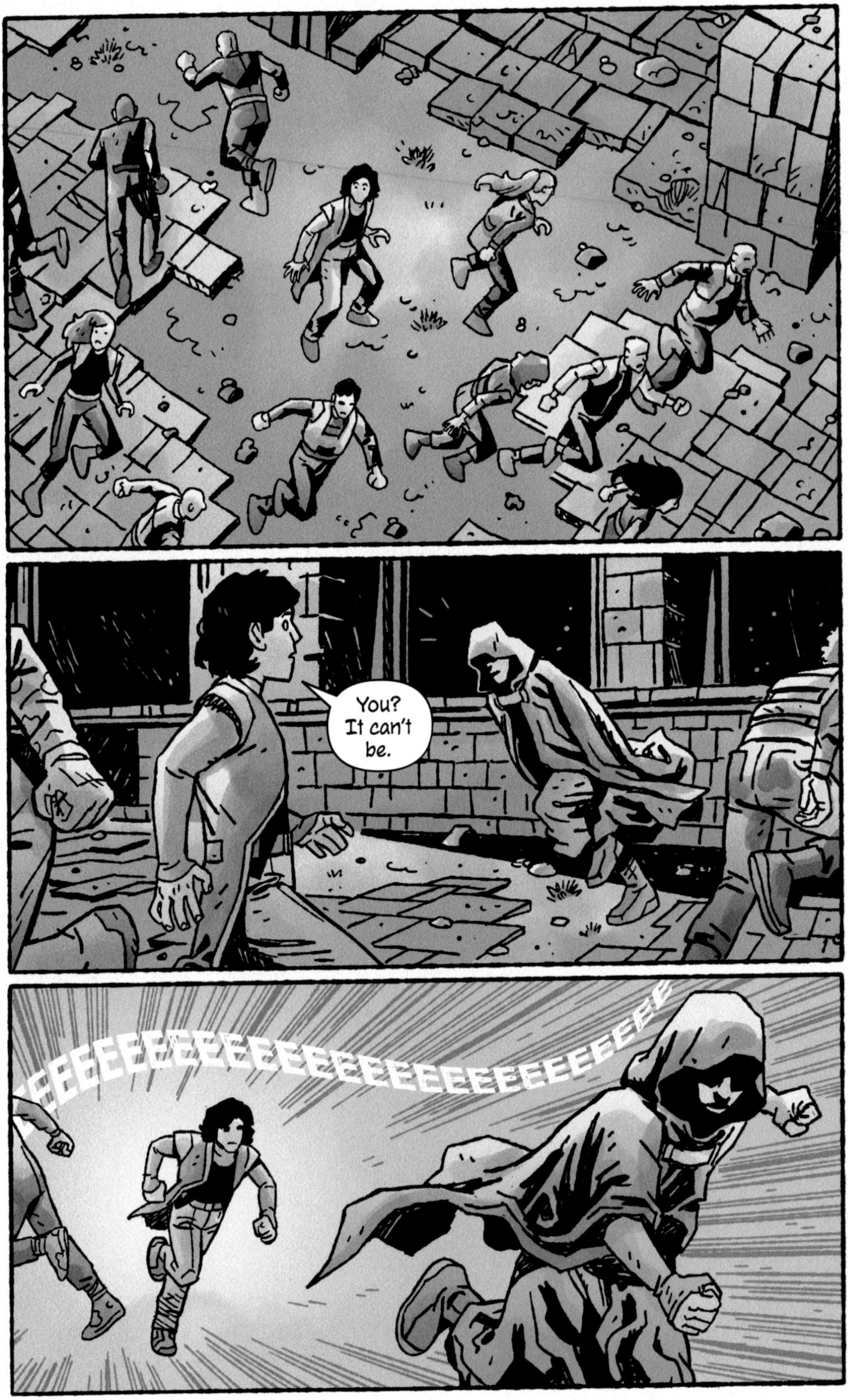
You? It can't be.
EEEEEEEEEEEEEEEEEEEEEEEEEEEEEE

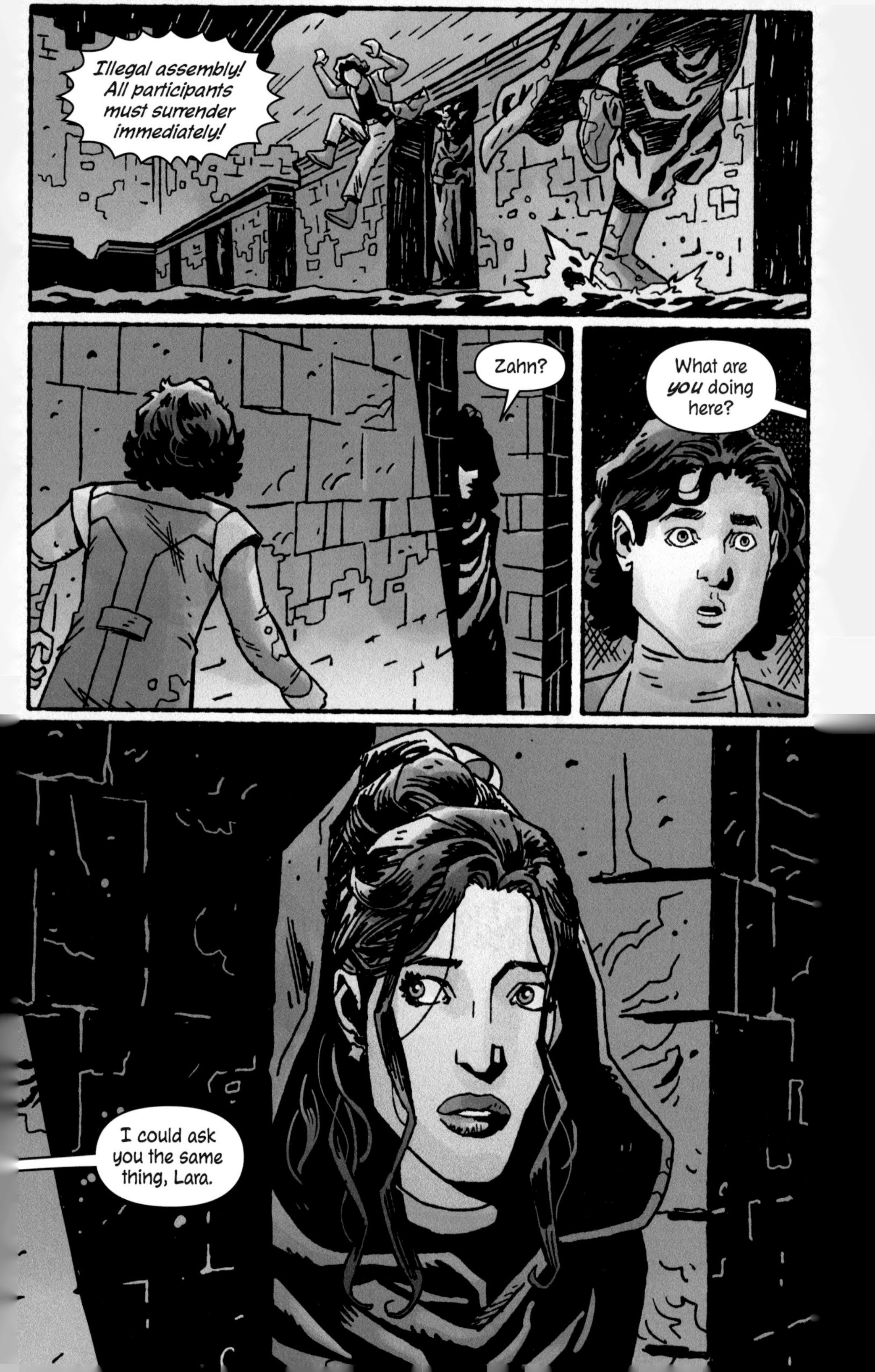
Illegal assembly! All participants must surrender immediately!
Zahn?
What are *you* doing here?
I could ask you the same thing, Lara.

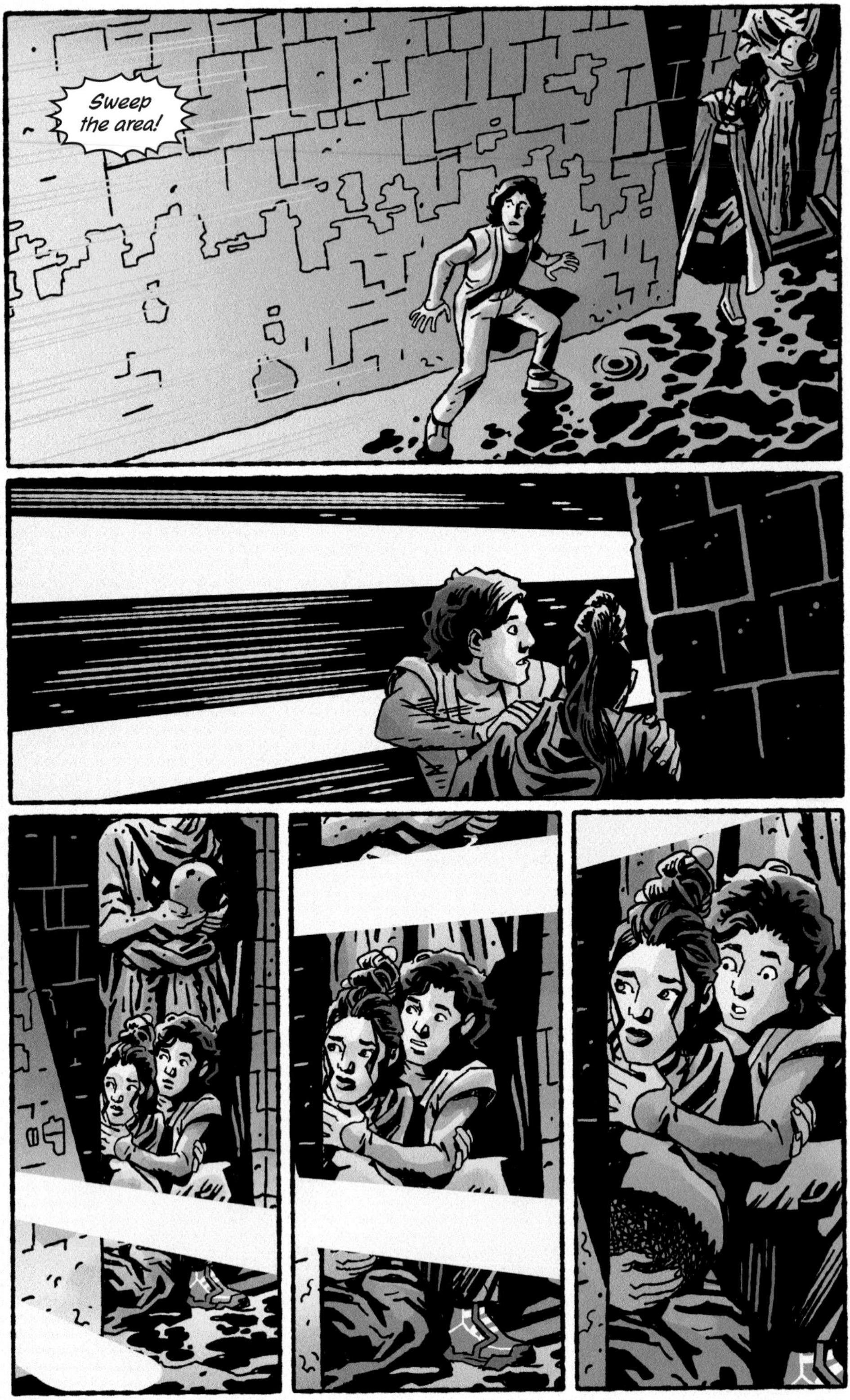
Sweep the area!

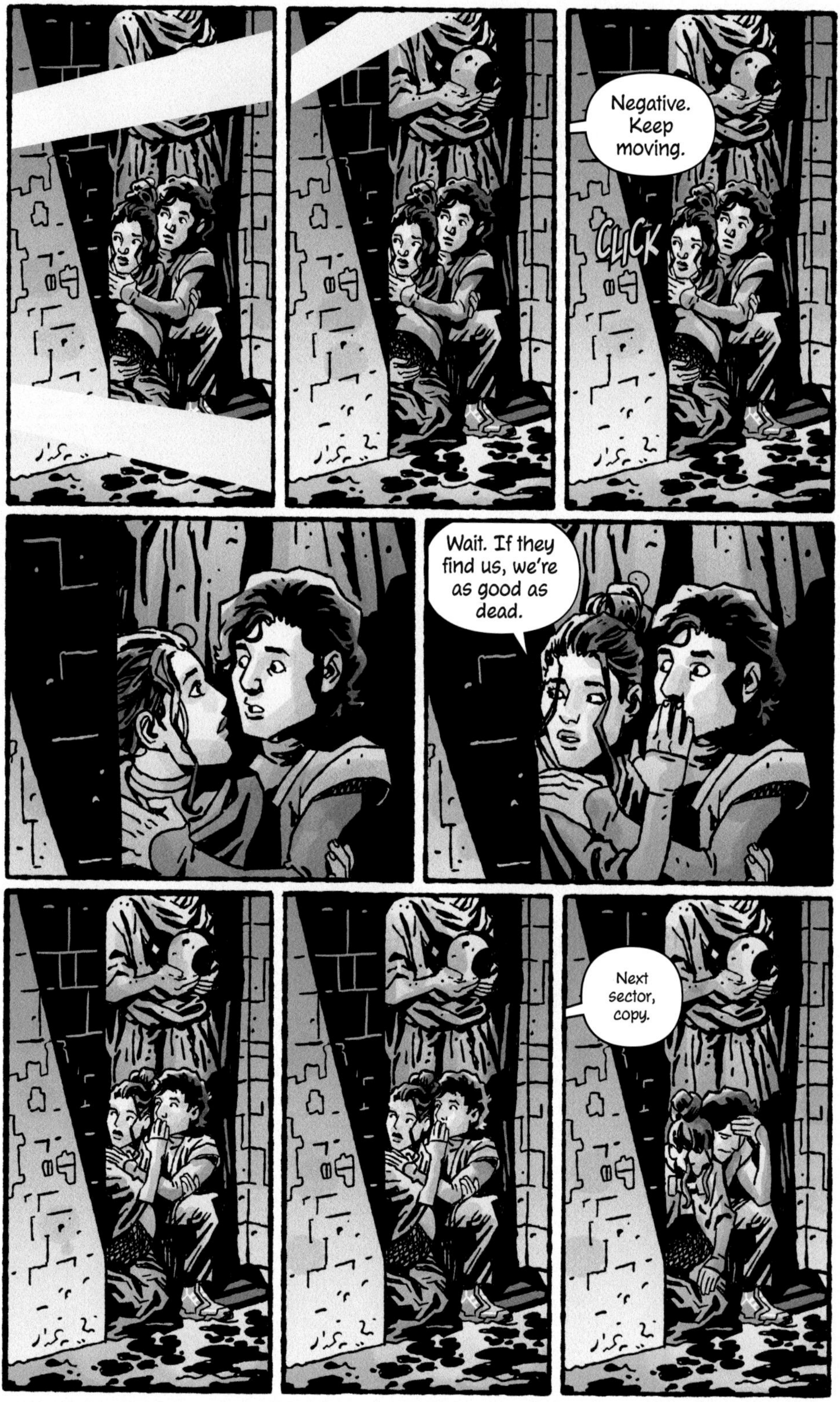
Negative. Keep moving.
CLICK
Wait. If they find us, we're as good as dead.
Next sector, copy.

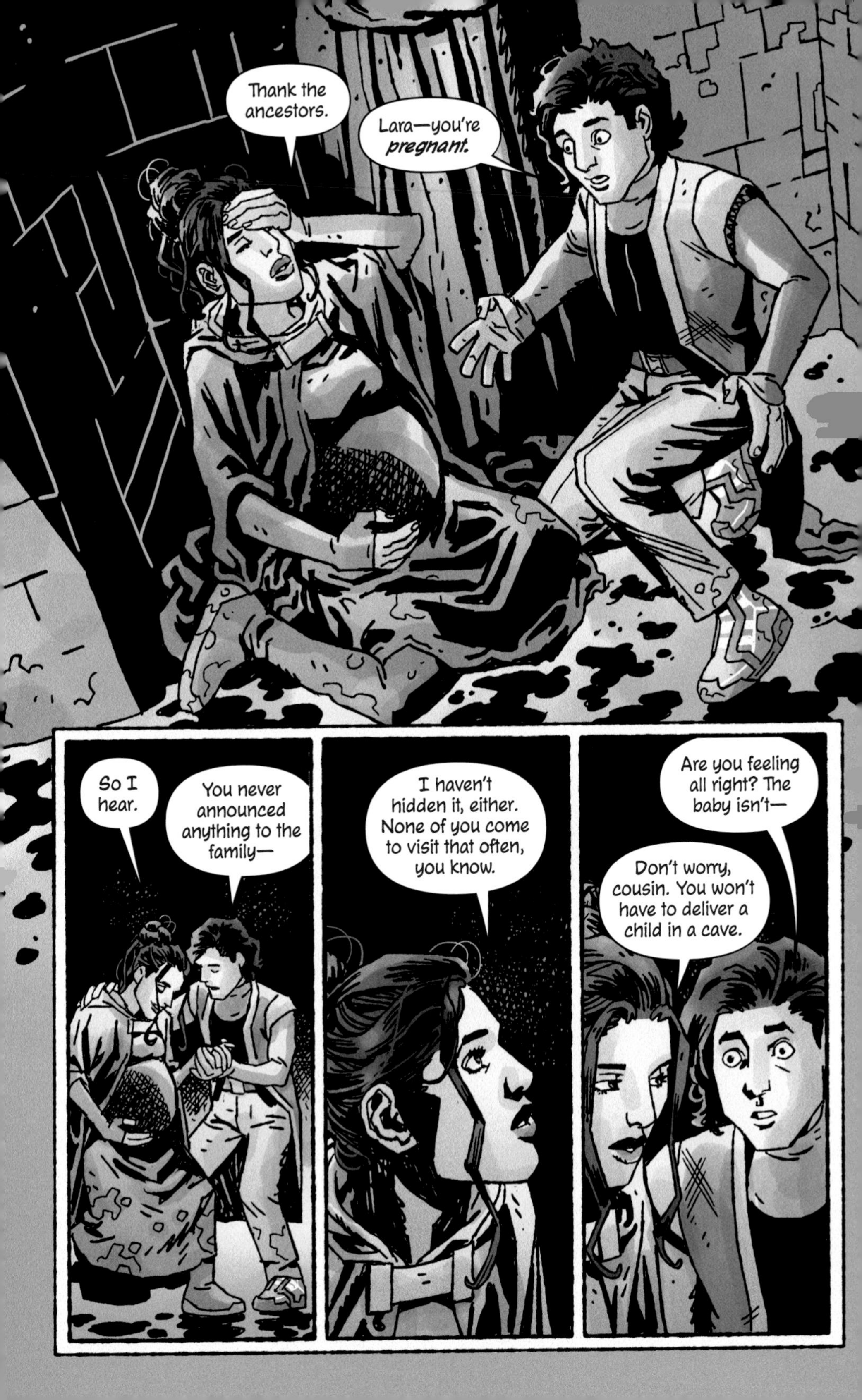
Thank the ancestors.
Lara—you're *pregnant.*
So I hear.
You never announced anything to the family—
I haven't hidden it, either. None of you come to visit that often, you know.
Are you feeling all right? The baby isn't—
Don't worry, cousin. You won't have to deliver a child in a cave.

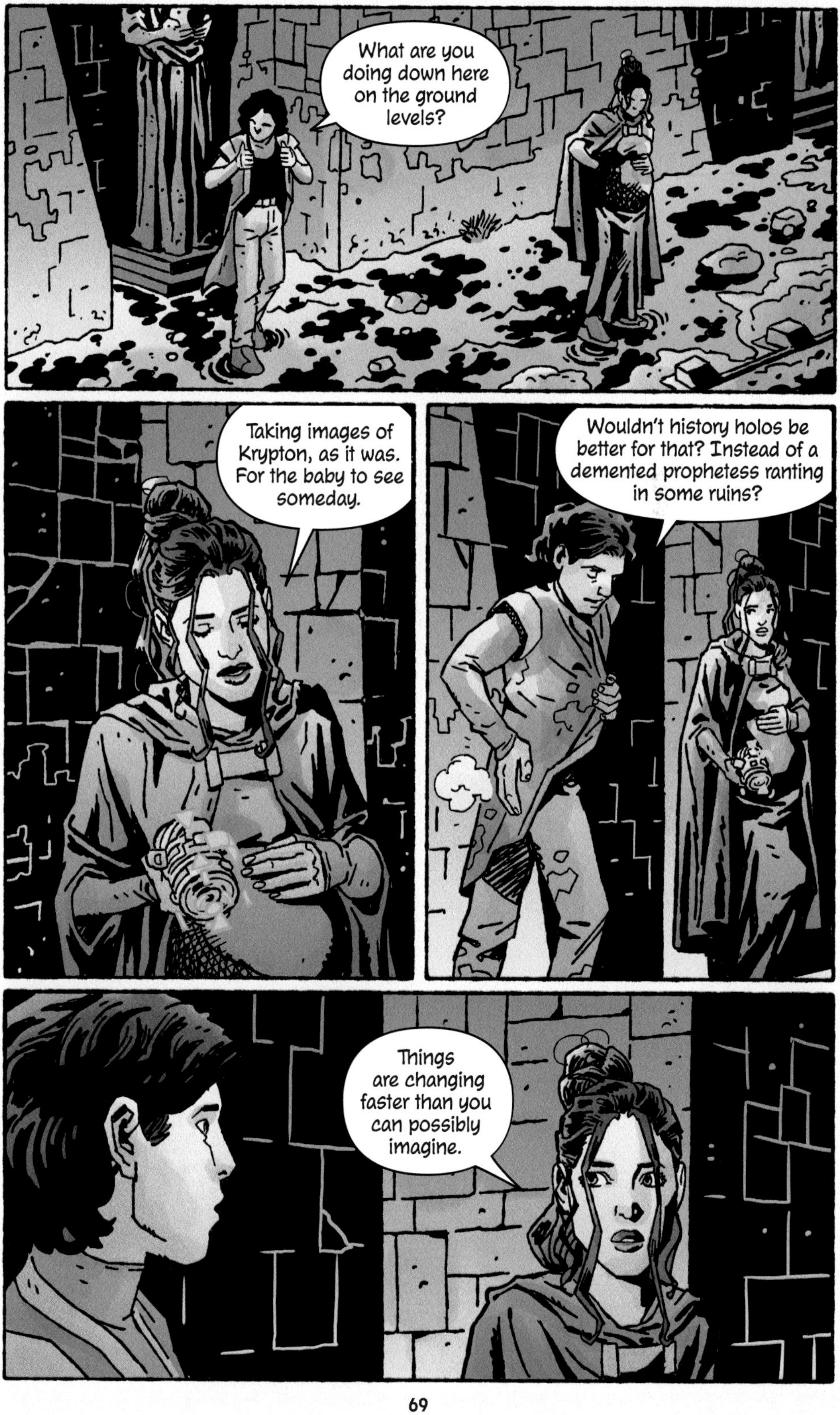
What are you doing down here on the ground levels?
Taking images of Krypton, as it was. For the baby to see someday.
Wouldn't history holos be better for that? Instead of a demented prophetess ranting in some ruins?
Things are changing faster than you can possibly imagine.

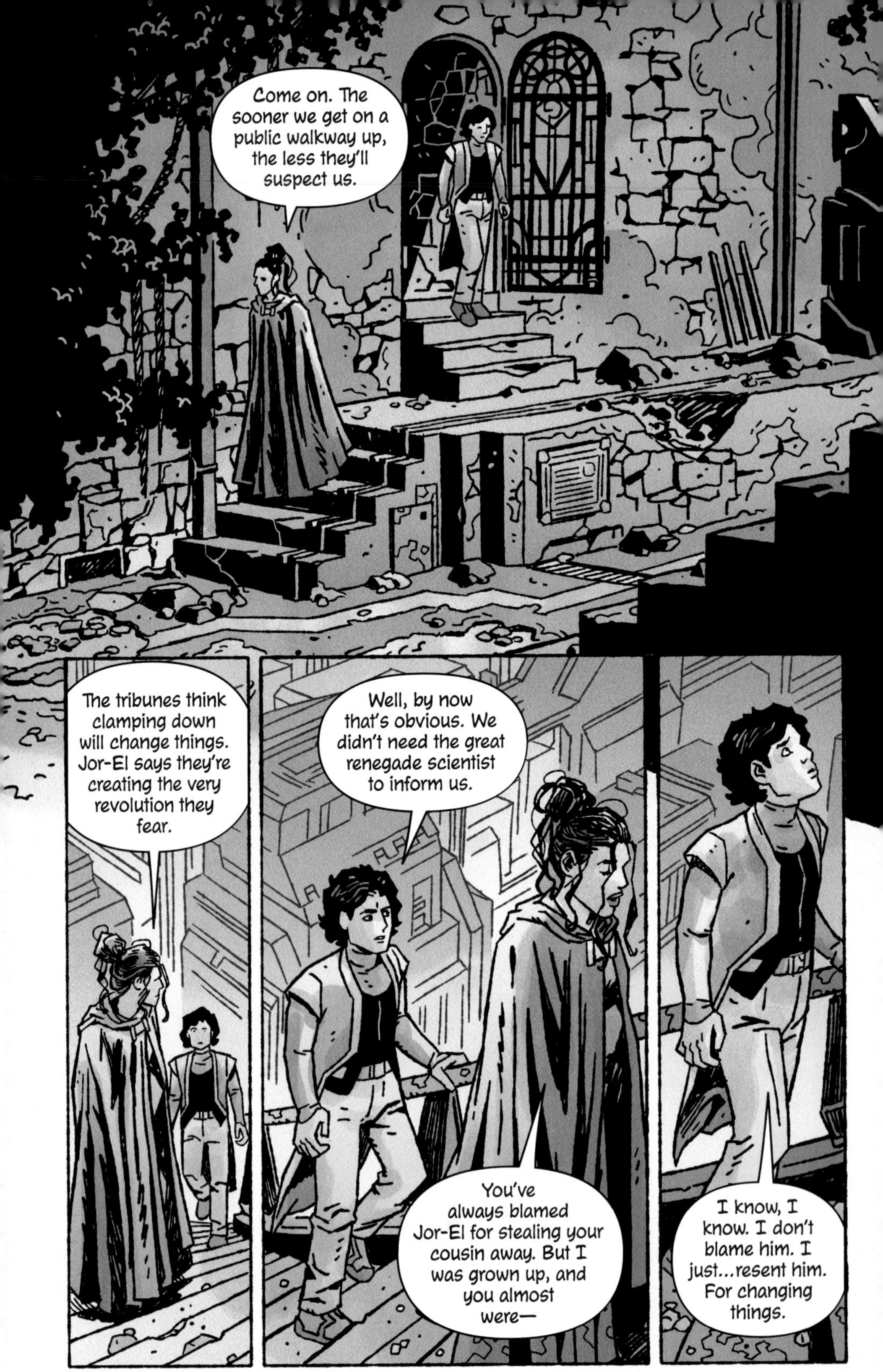
Come on. The sooner we get on a public walkway up, the less they'll suspect us.
The tribunes think clamping down will change things. Jor-El says they're creating the very revolution they fear.
Well, by now that's obvious. We didn't need the great renegade scientist to inform us.
You've always blamed Jor-El for stealing your cousin away. But I was grown up, and you almost were—
I know, I know. I don't blame him. I just...resent him. For changing things.

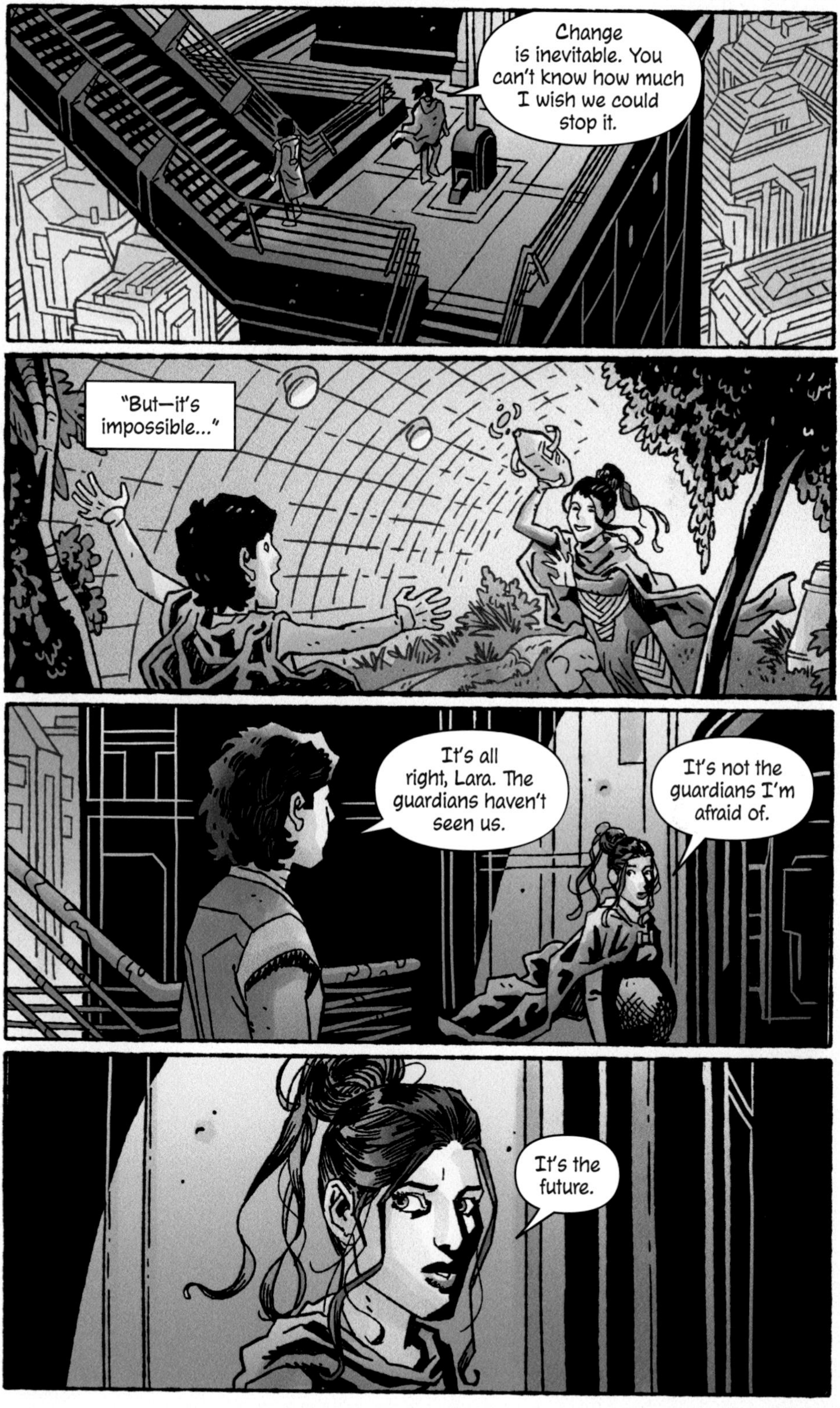
Change is inevitable. You can't know how much I wish we could stop it.
"But—it's impossible..."
It's all right, Lara. The guardians haven't seen us.
It's not the guardians I'm afraid of.
It's the future.

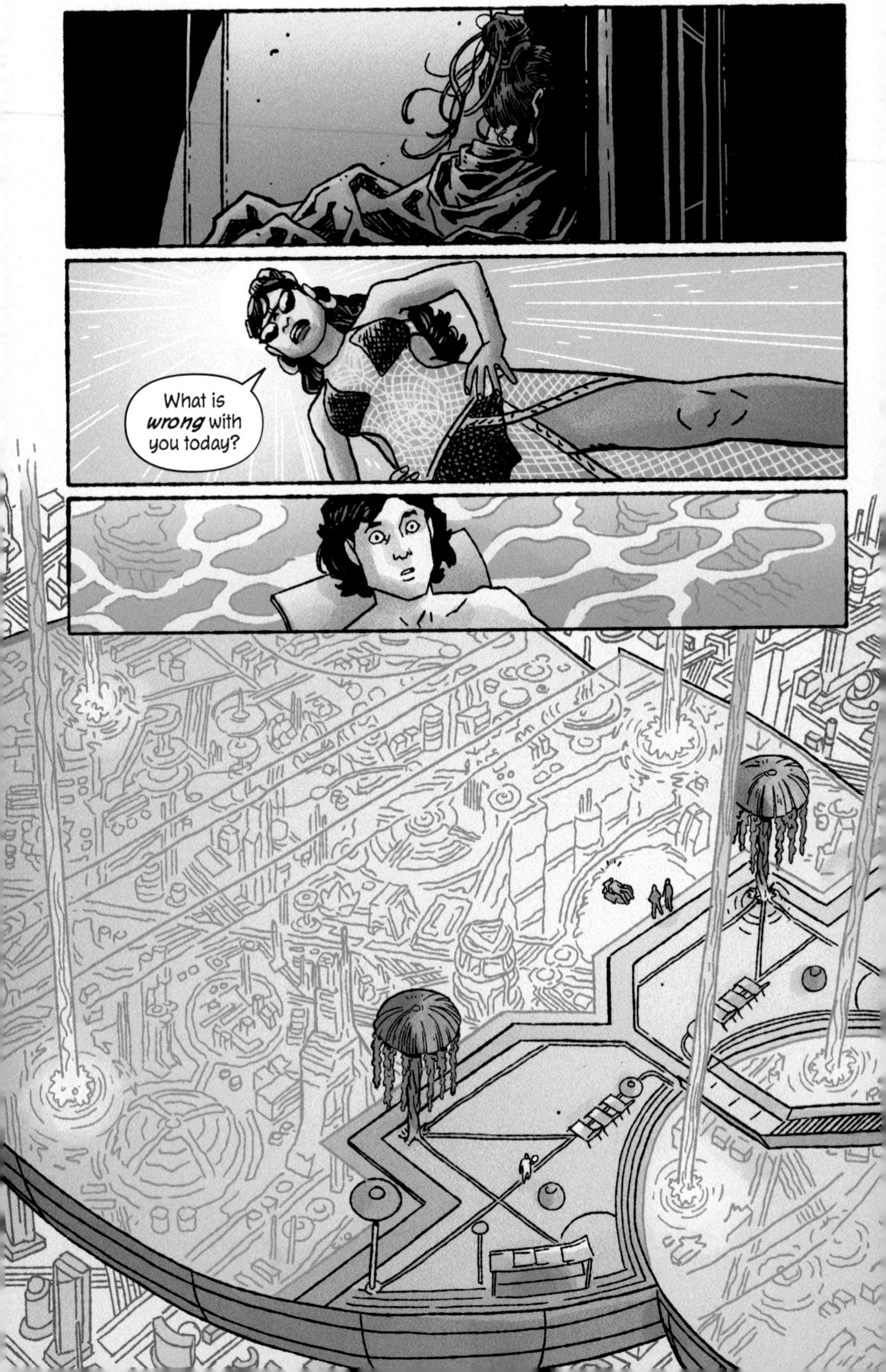
What is *wrong* with you today?

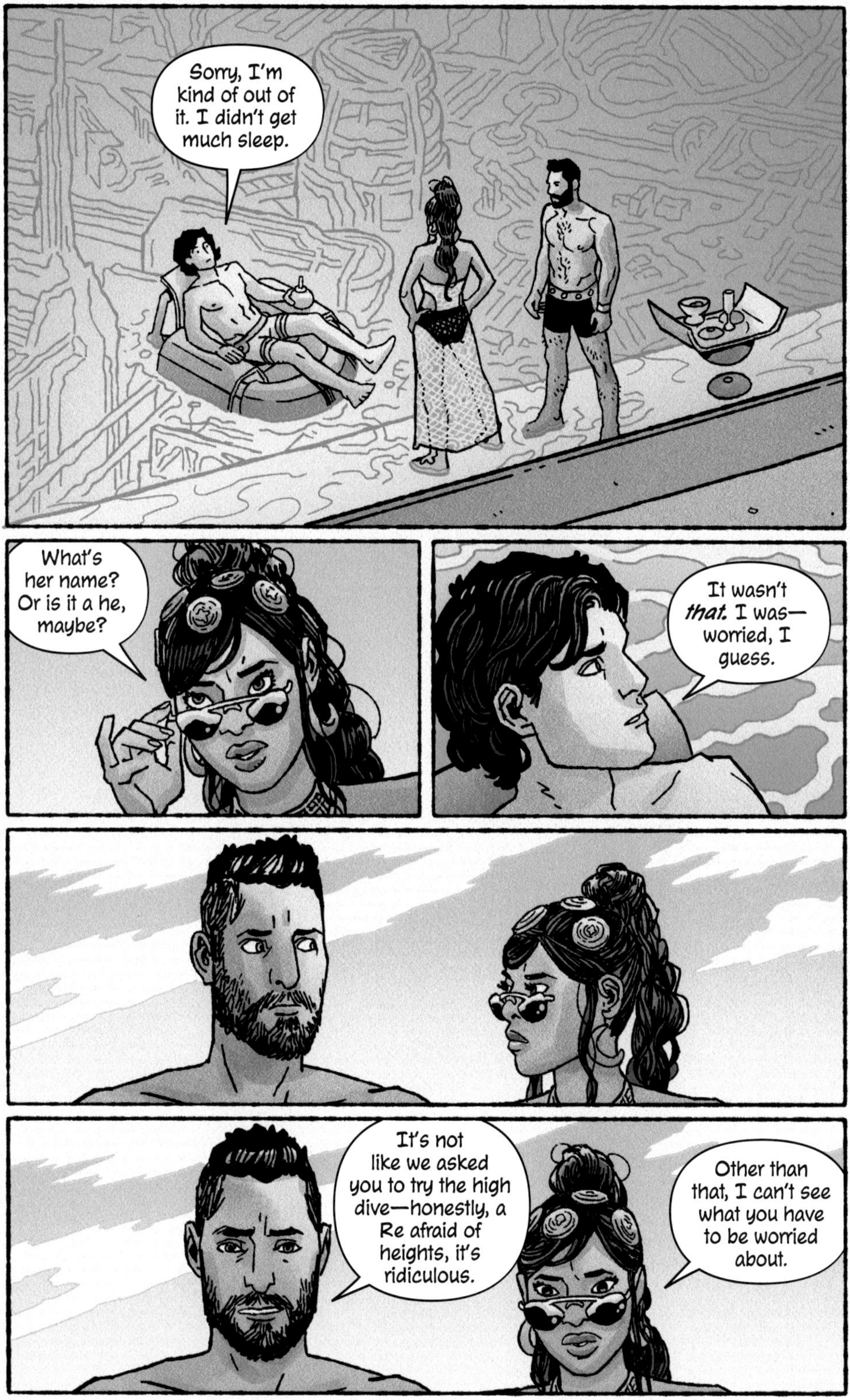
Sorry, I'm kind of out of it. I didn't get much sleep.
What's her name? Or is it a he, maybe?
It wasn't *that.* I was—worried, I guess.
It's not like we asked you to try the high dive—honestly, a Re afraid of heights, it's ridiculous.
Other than that, I can't see what you have to be worried about.

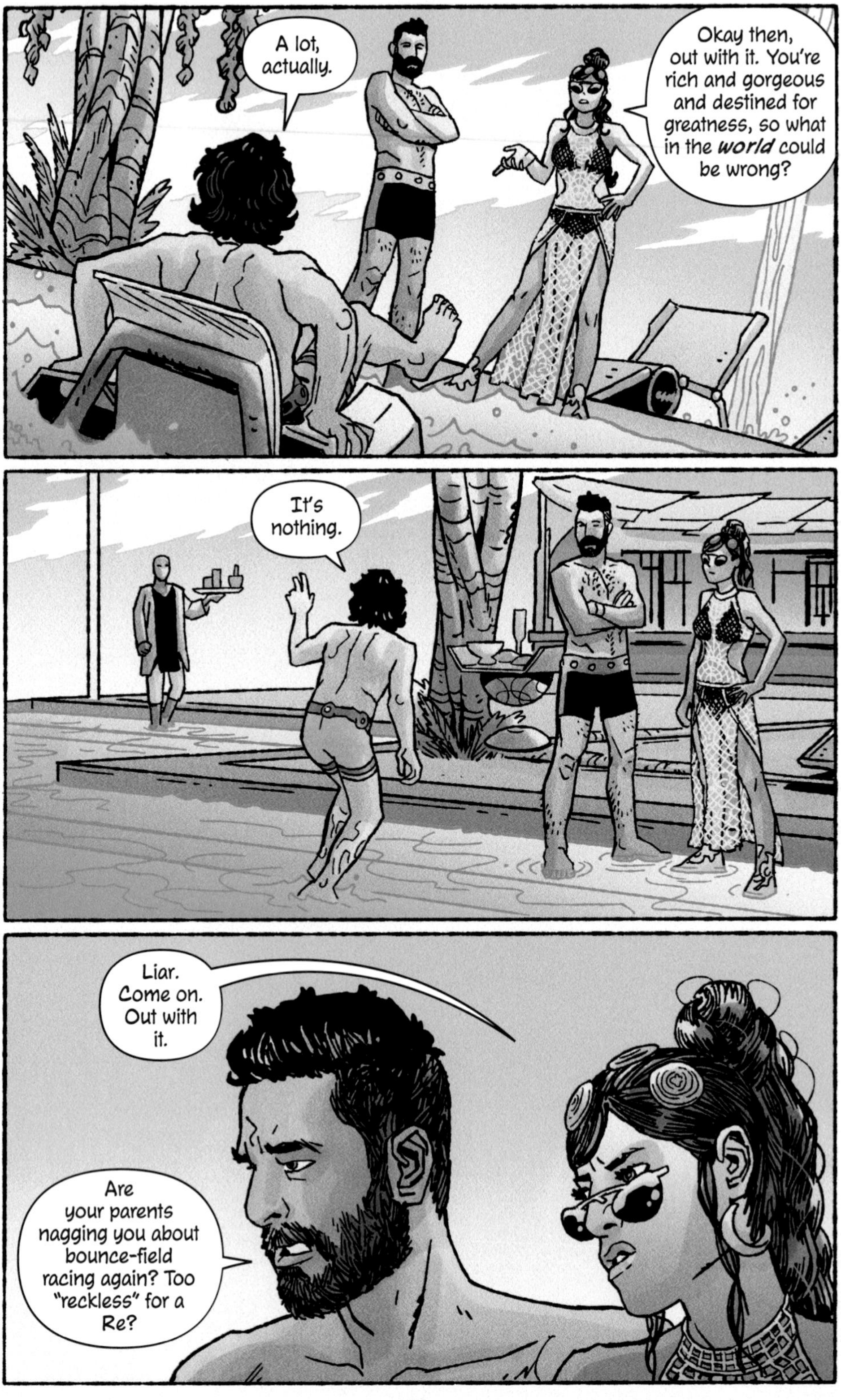
A lot, actually.
Okay then, out with it. You're rich and gorgeous and destined for greatness, so what in the *world* could be wrong?
It's nothing.
Liar. Come on. Out with it.
Are your parents nagging you about bounce-field racing again? Too "reckless" for a Re?

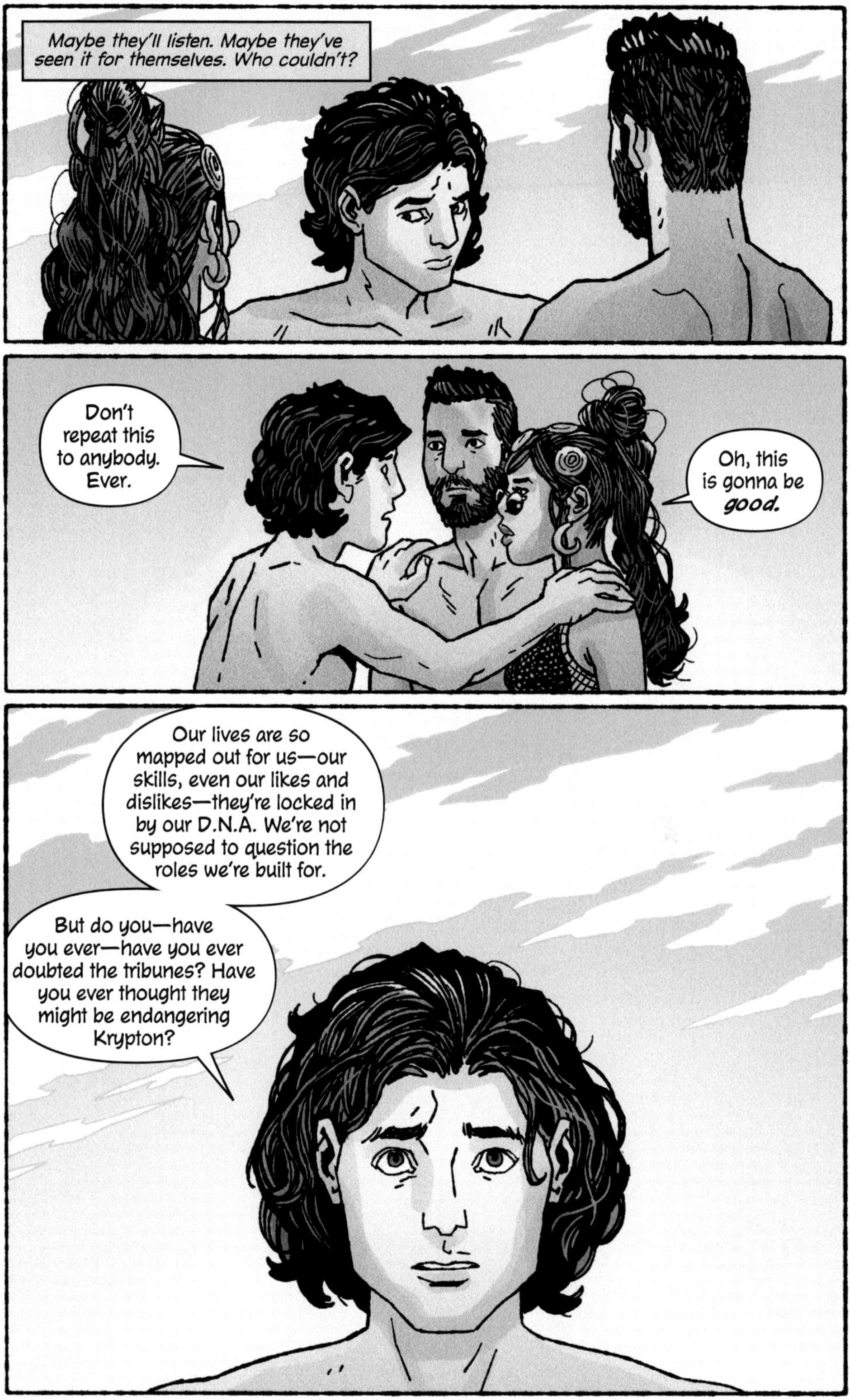
Maybe they'll listen. Maybe they've seen it for themselves. Who couldn't?
Don't repeat this to anybody. Ever.
Oh, this is gonna be *good.*
Our lives are so mapped out for us—our skills, even our likes and dislikes—they're locked in by our D.N.A. We're not supposed to question the roles we're built for.
But do you—have you ever—have you ever doubted the tribunes? Have you ever thought they might be endangering Krypton?

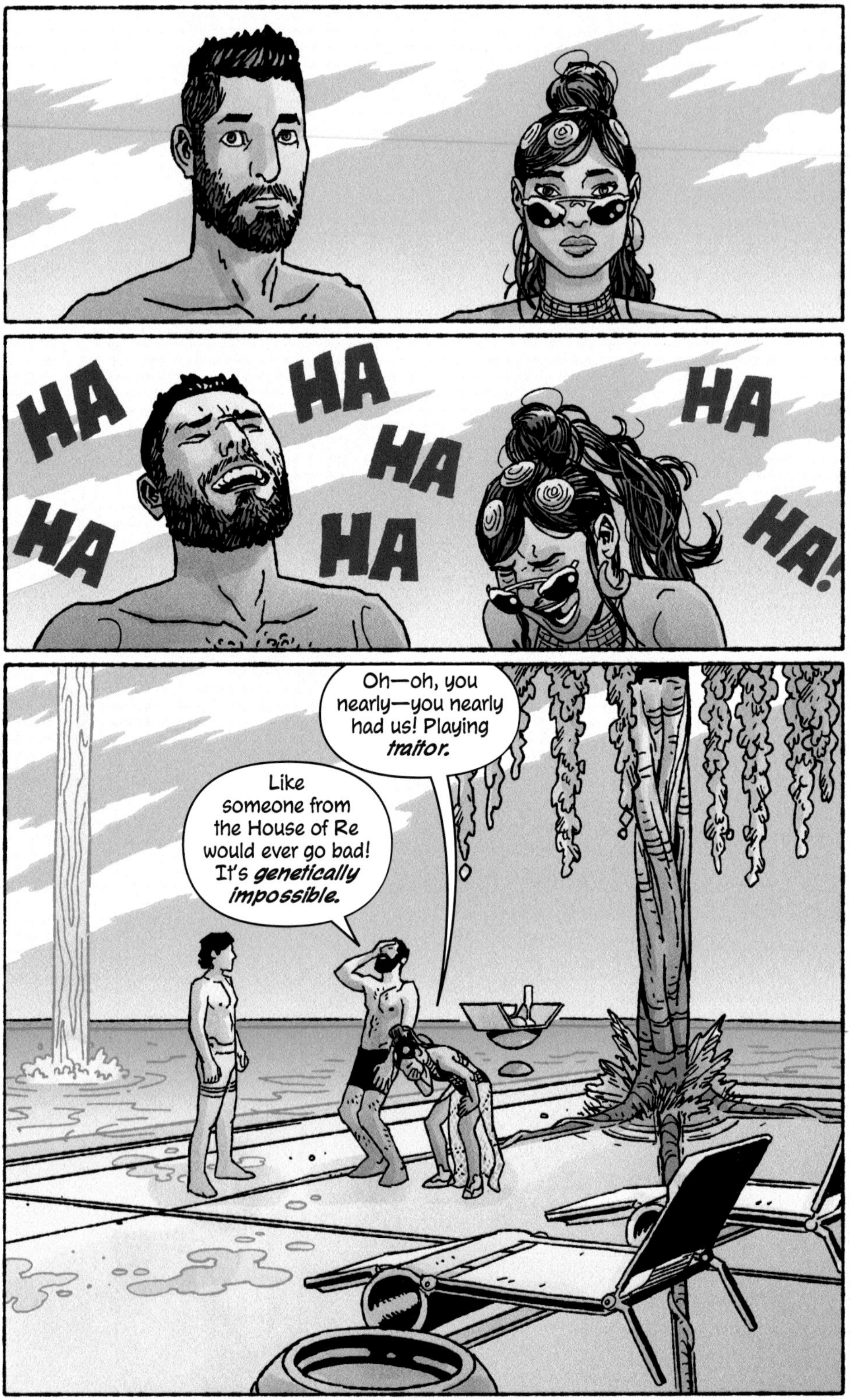
HA
HA
HA
HA
HA
HA
HA!
Oh—oh, you nearly—you nearly had us! Playing *traitor.*
Like someone from the House of Re would ever go bad! It's *genetically impossible.*

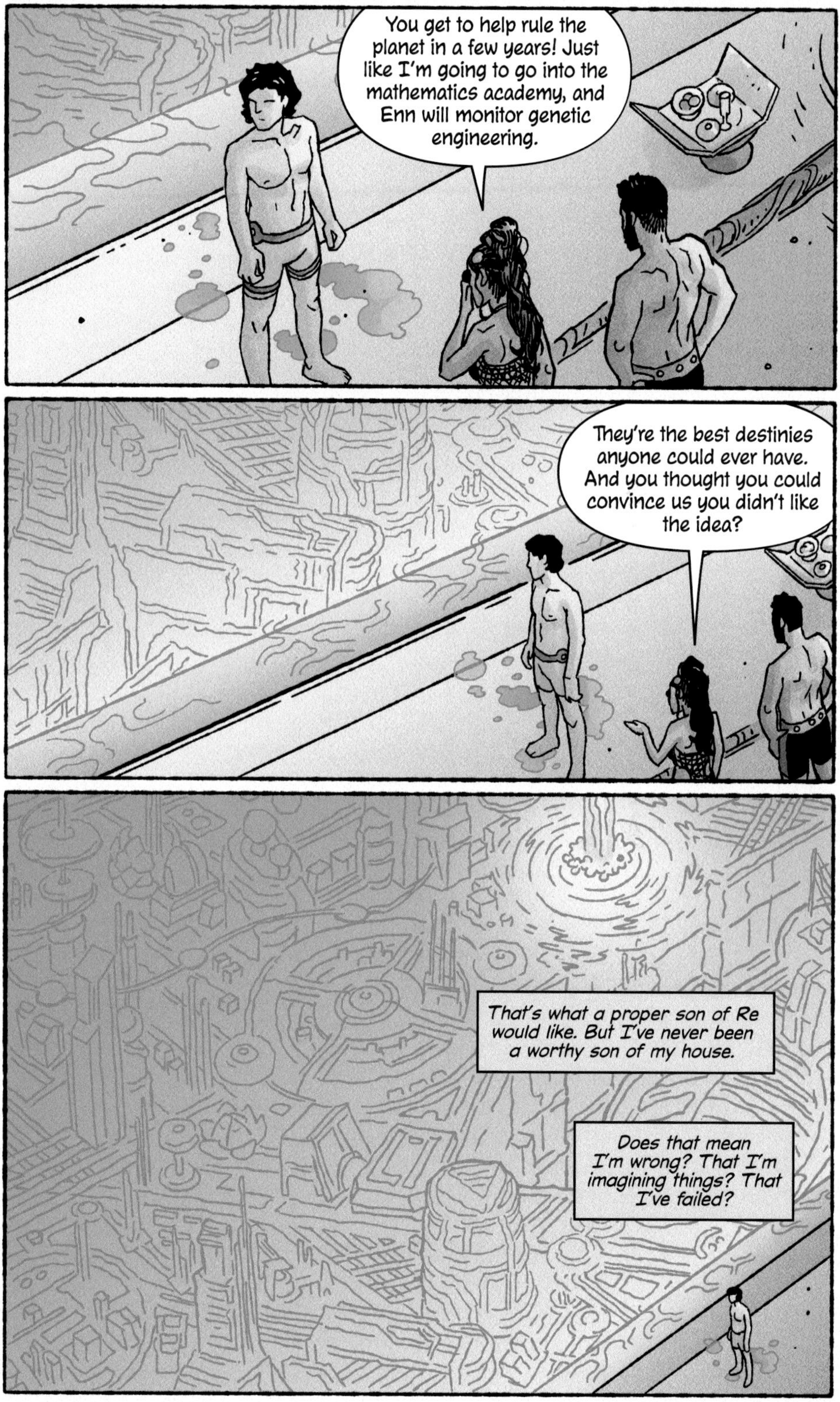
You get to help rule the planet in a few years! Just like I'm going to go into the mathematics academy, and Enn will monitor genetic engineering.
They're the best destinies anyone could ever have. And you thought you could convince us you didn't like the idea?
That's what a proper son of Re would like. But I've never been a worthy son of my house.
Does that mean I'm wrong? That I'm imagining things? That I've failed?

CHAPTER TWO

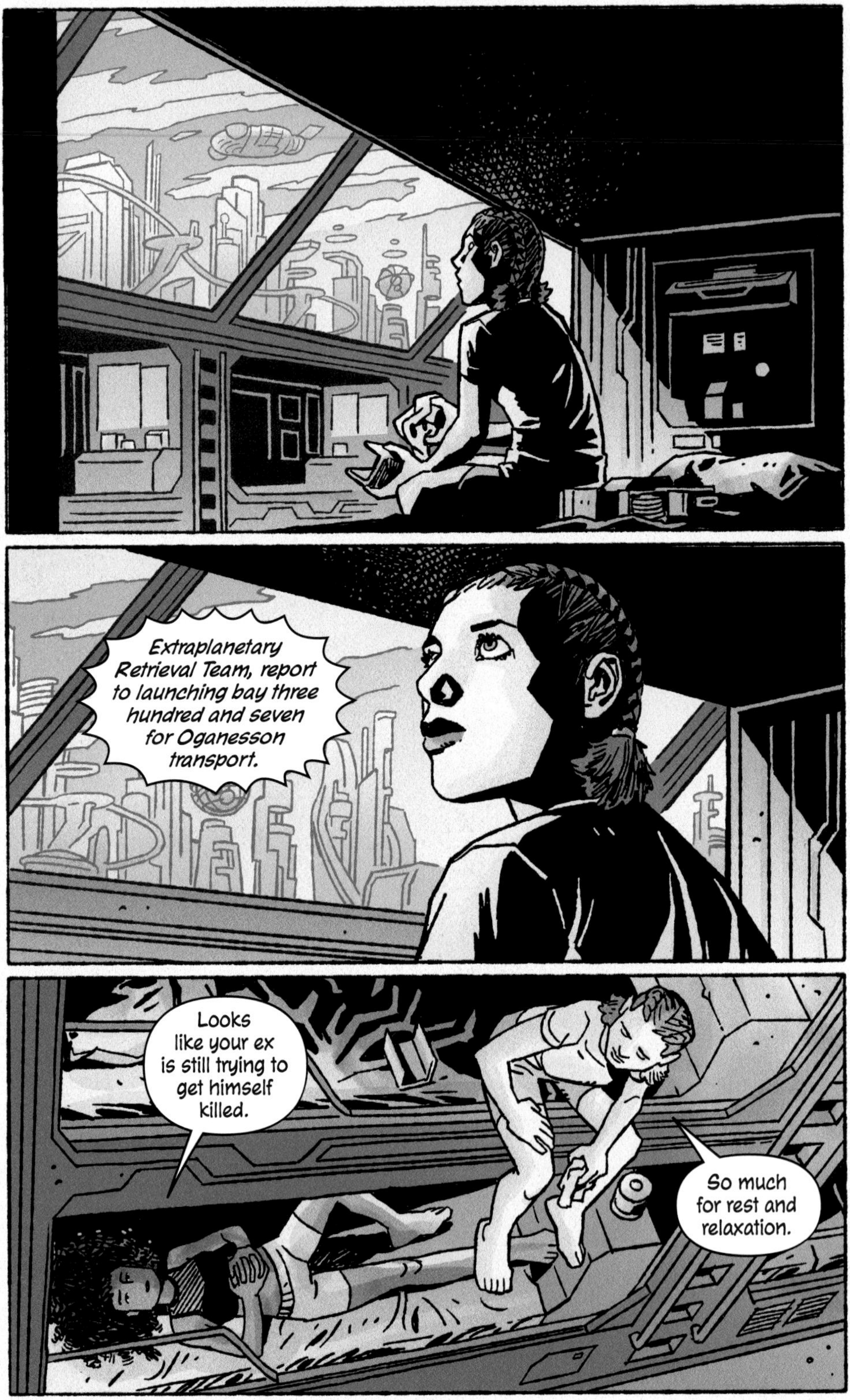
Extraplanetary Retrieval Team, report to launching bay three hundred and seven for Oganesson transport.
Looks like your ex is still trying to get himself killed.
So much for rest and relaxation.

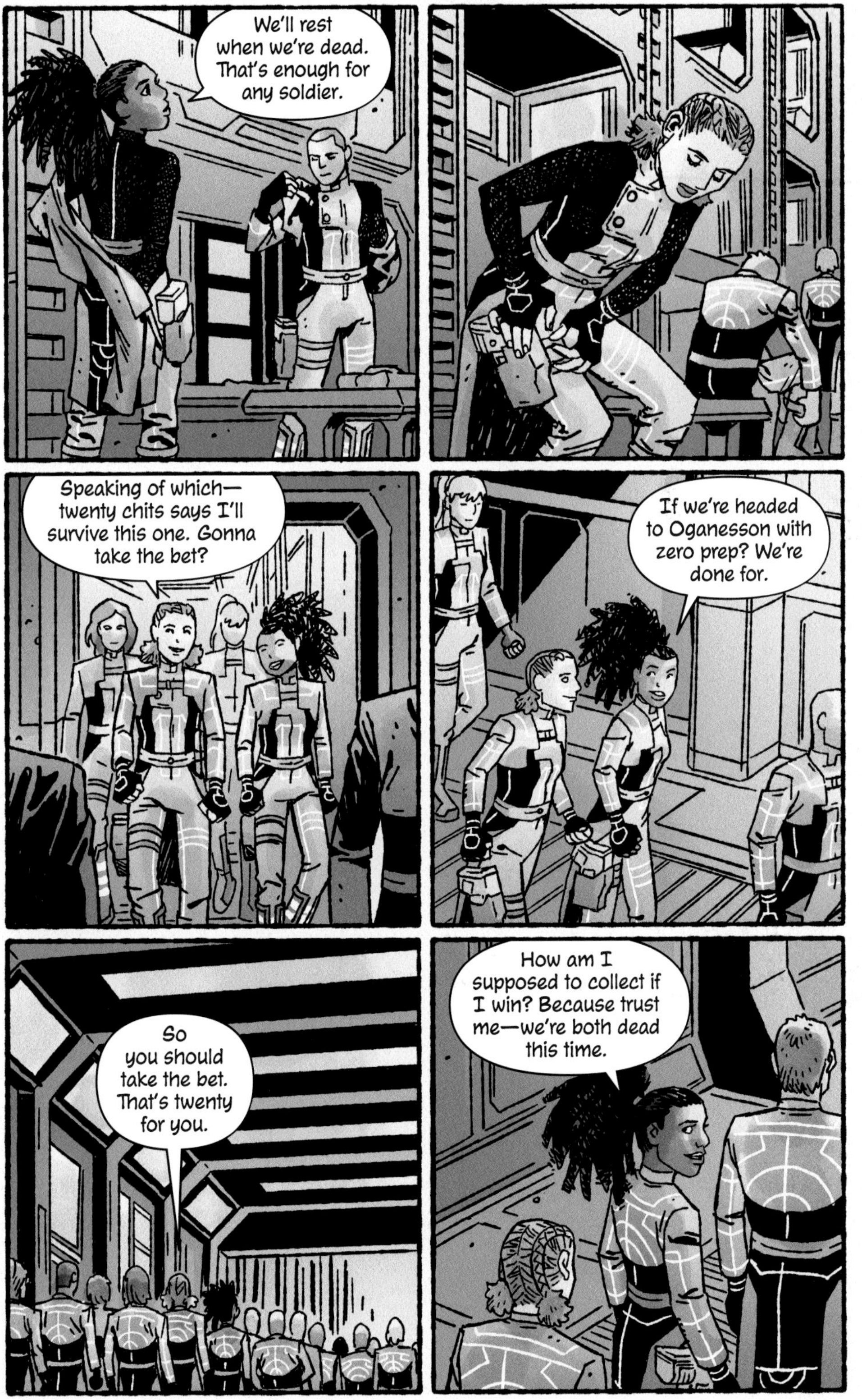
We'll rest when we're dead. That's enough for any soldier.
Speaking of which— twenty chits says I'll survive this one. Gonna take the bet?
If we're headed to Oganesson with zero prep? We're done for.
So you should take the bet. That's twenty for you.
How am I supposed to collect if I win? Because trust me—we're both dead this time.

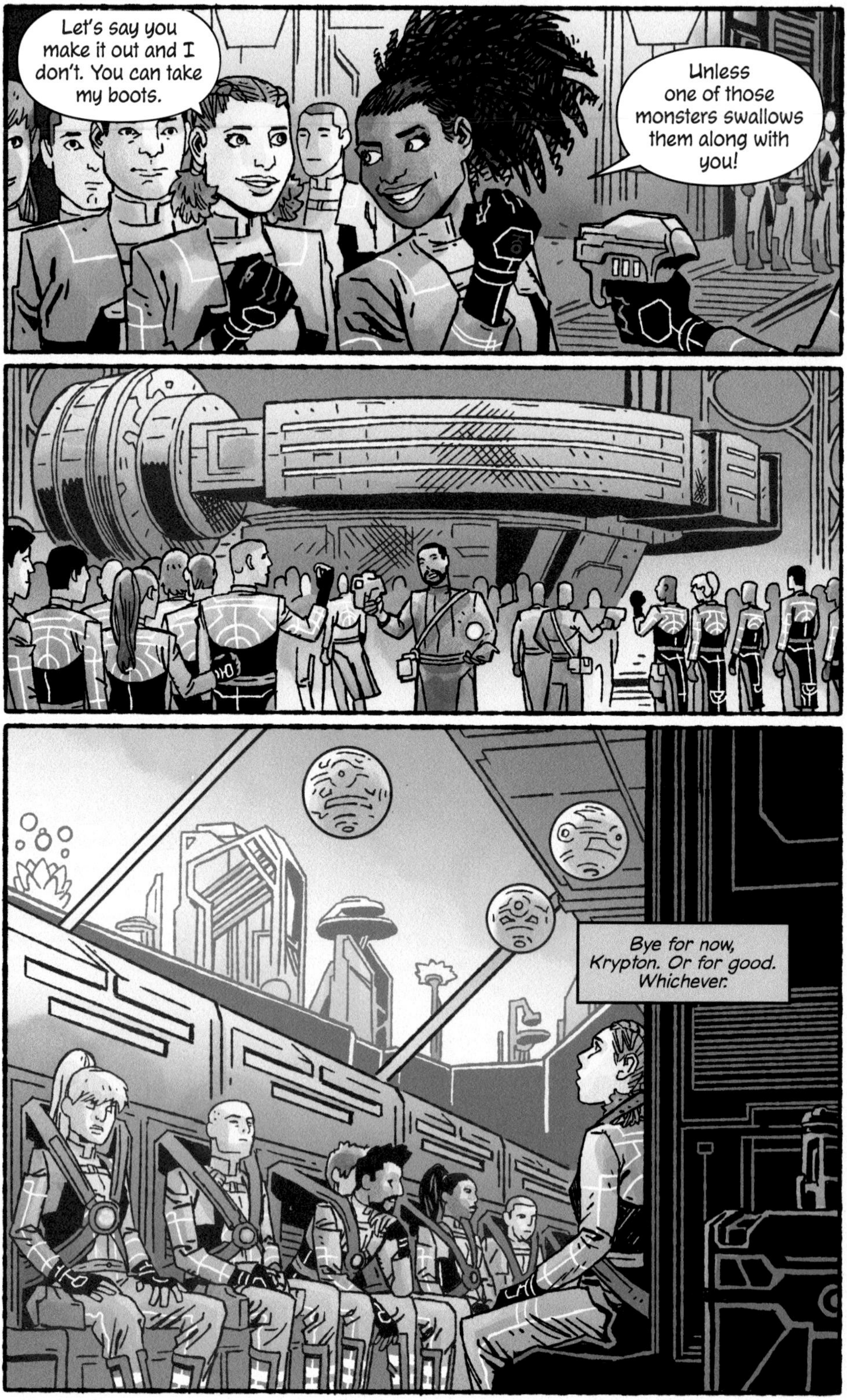
Let's say you make it out and I don't. You can take my boots.
Unless one of those monsters swallows them along with you!
Bye for now, Krypton. Or for good. Whichever.

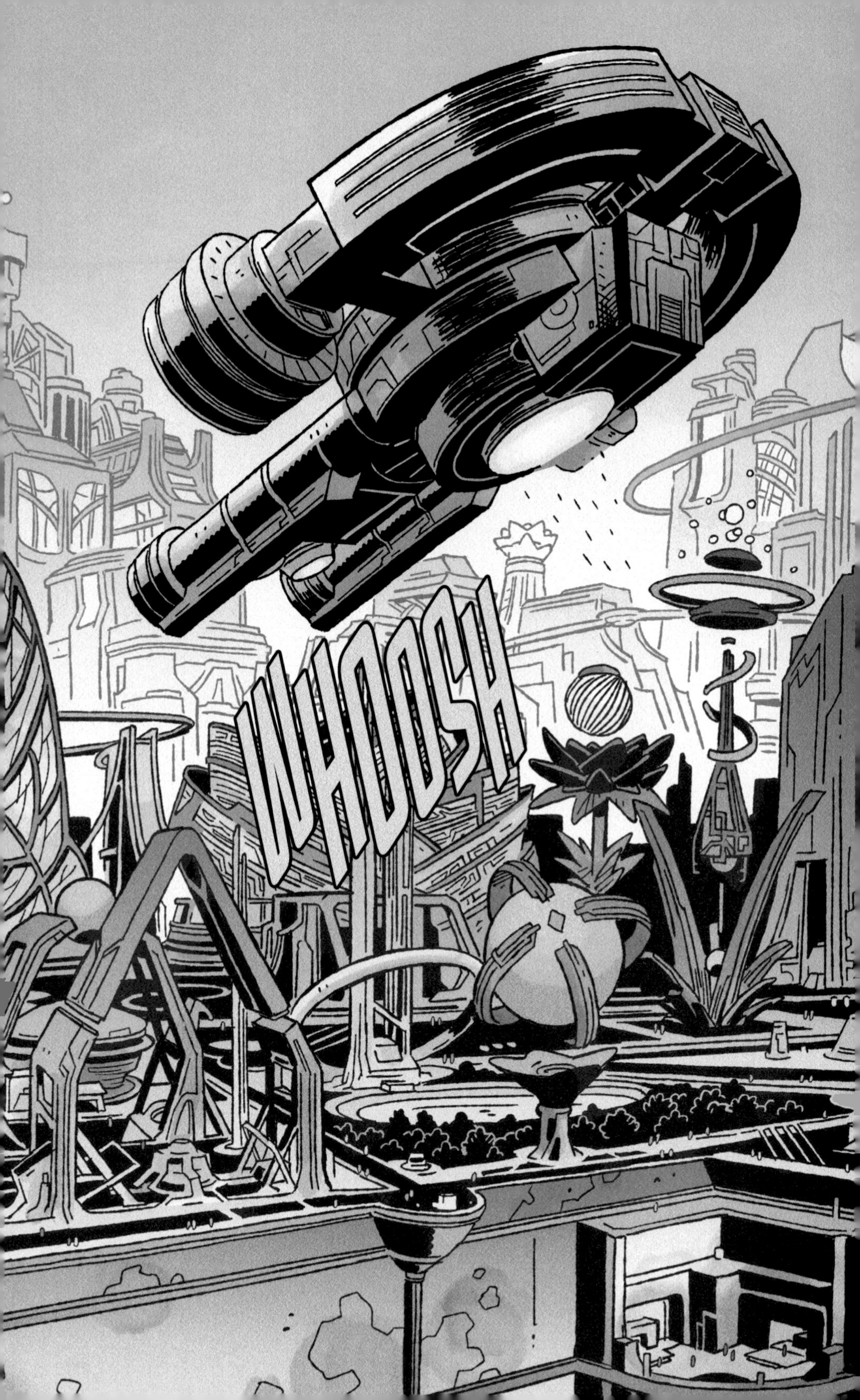
WHOOSH

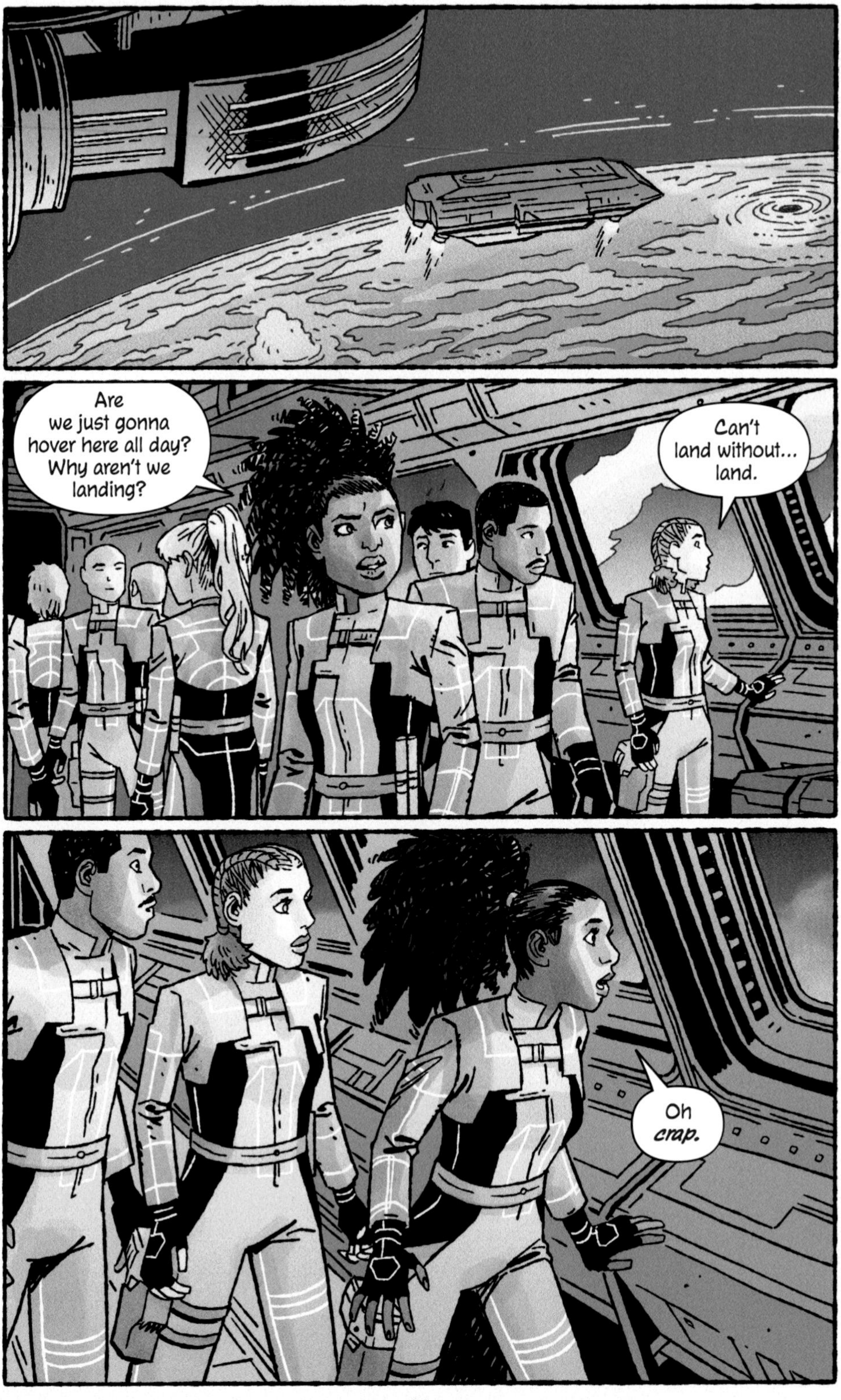
Are we just gonna hover here all day? Why aren't we landing?
Can't land without... land.
Oh *crap.*

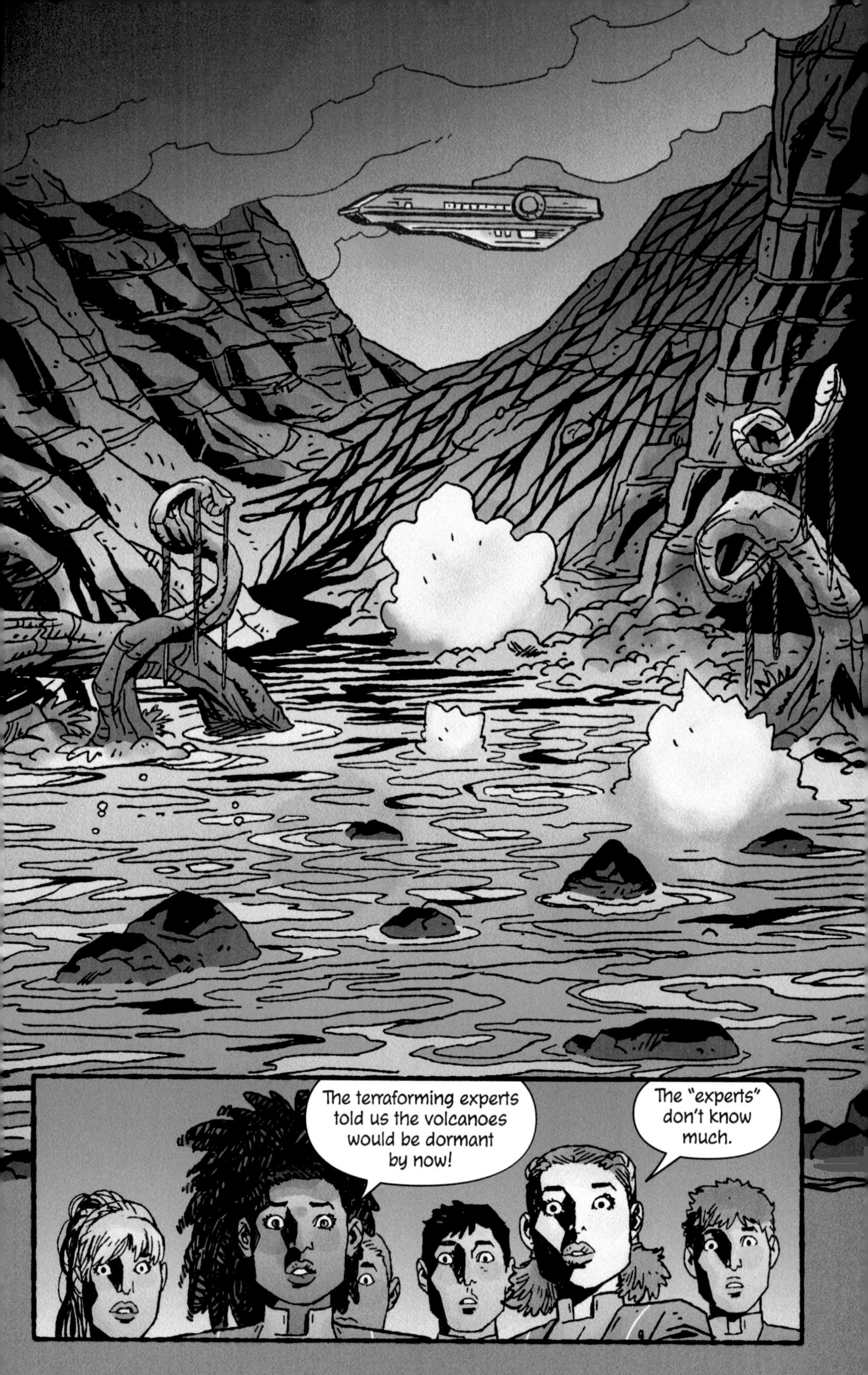
The terraforming experts told us the volcanoes would be dormant by now!
The "experts" don't know much.

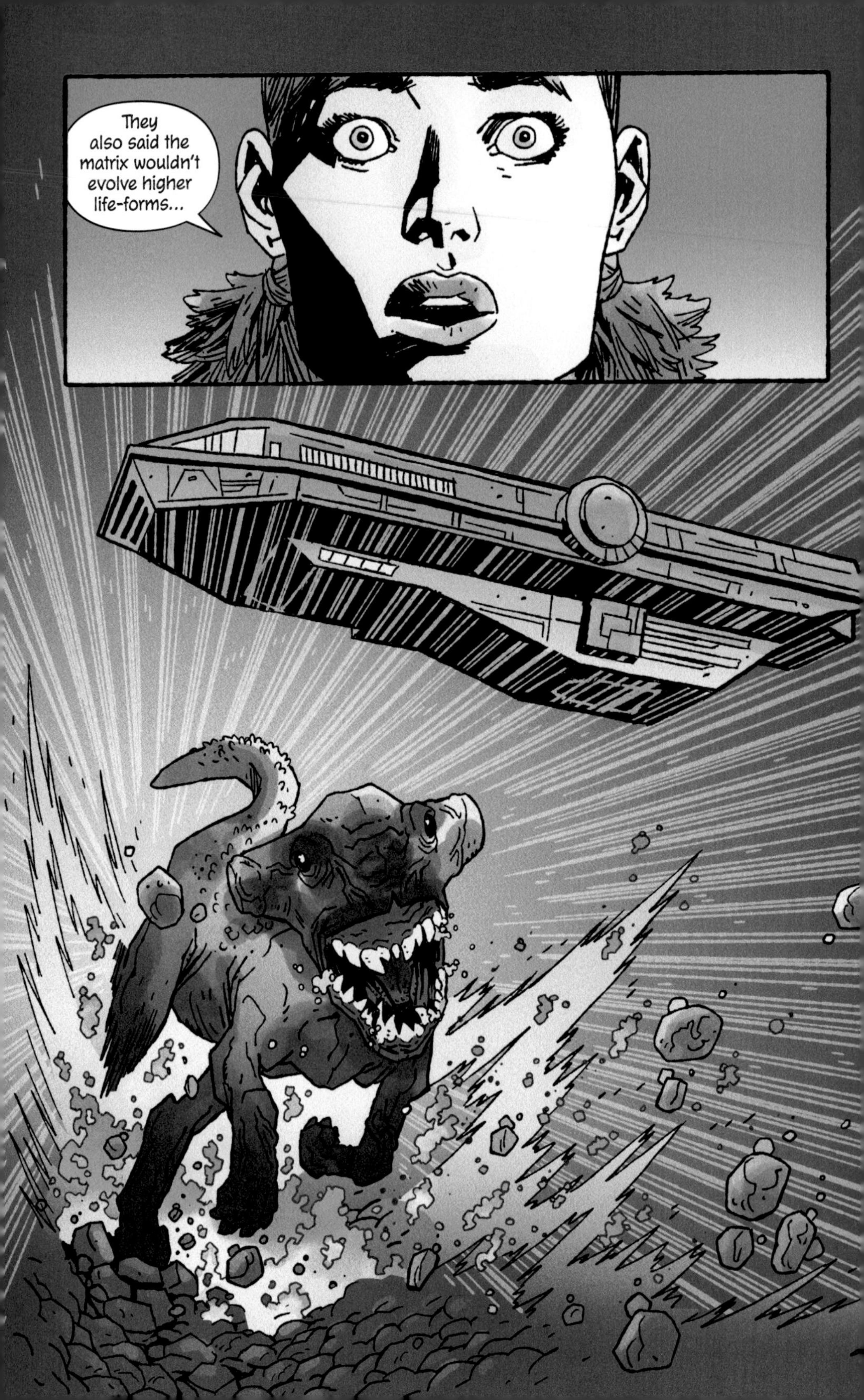
They also said the matrix wouldn't evolve higher life-forms...

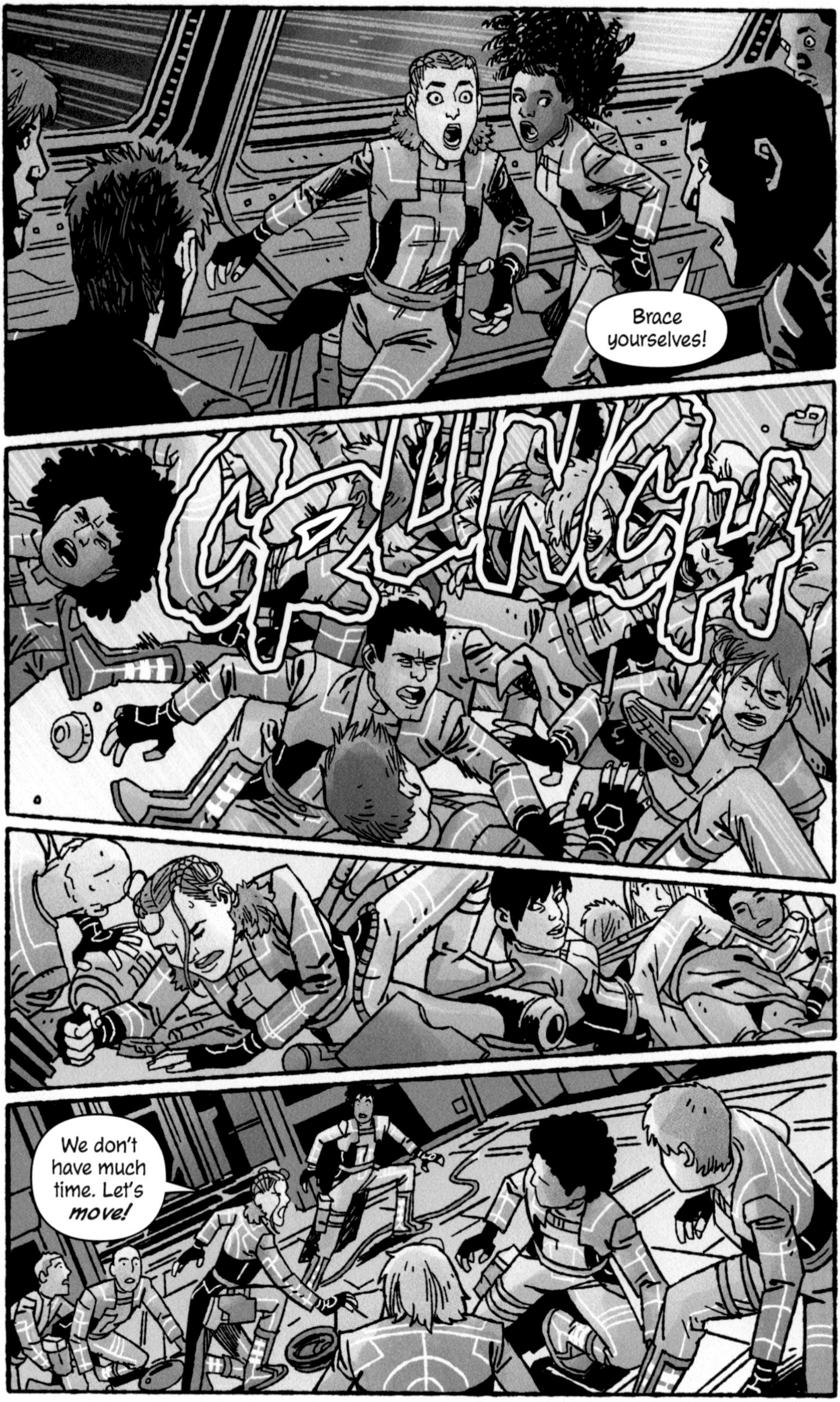
Brace yourselves!
We don't have much time. Let's *move!*

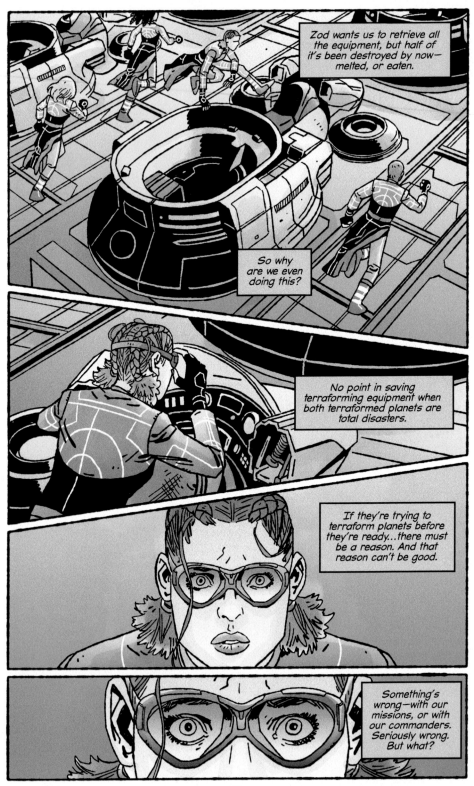

Zod wants us to retrieve all the equipment, but half of it's been destroyed by now— melted, or eaten.

So why are we even doing this?

No point in saving terraforming equipment when both terraformed planets are total disasters.

If they're trying to terraform planets before they're ready...there must be a reason. And that reason can't be good.

Something's wrong—with our missions, or with our commanders. Seriously wrong. But what?

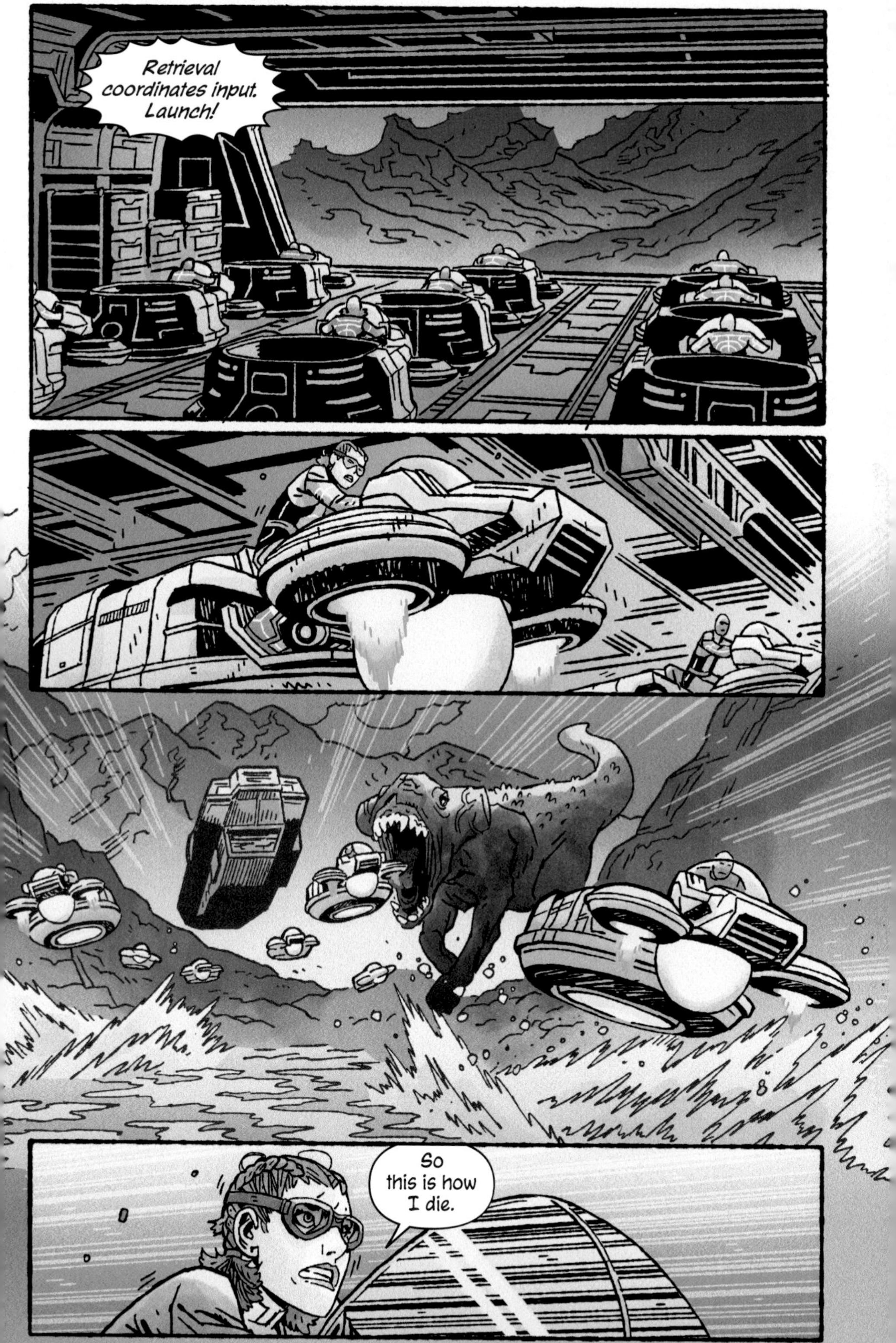
Retrieval coordinates input. Launch!
So this is how I die.

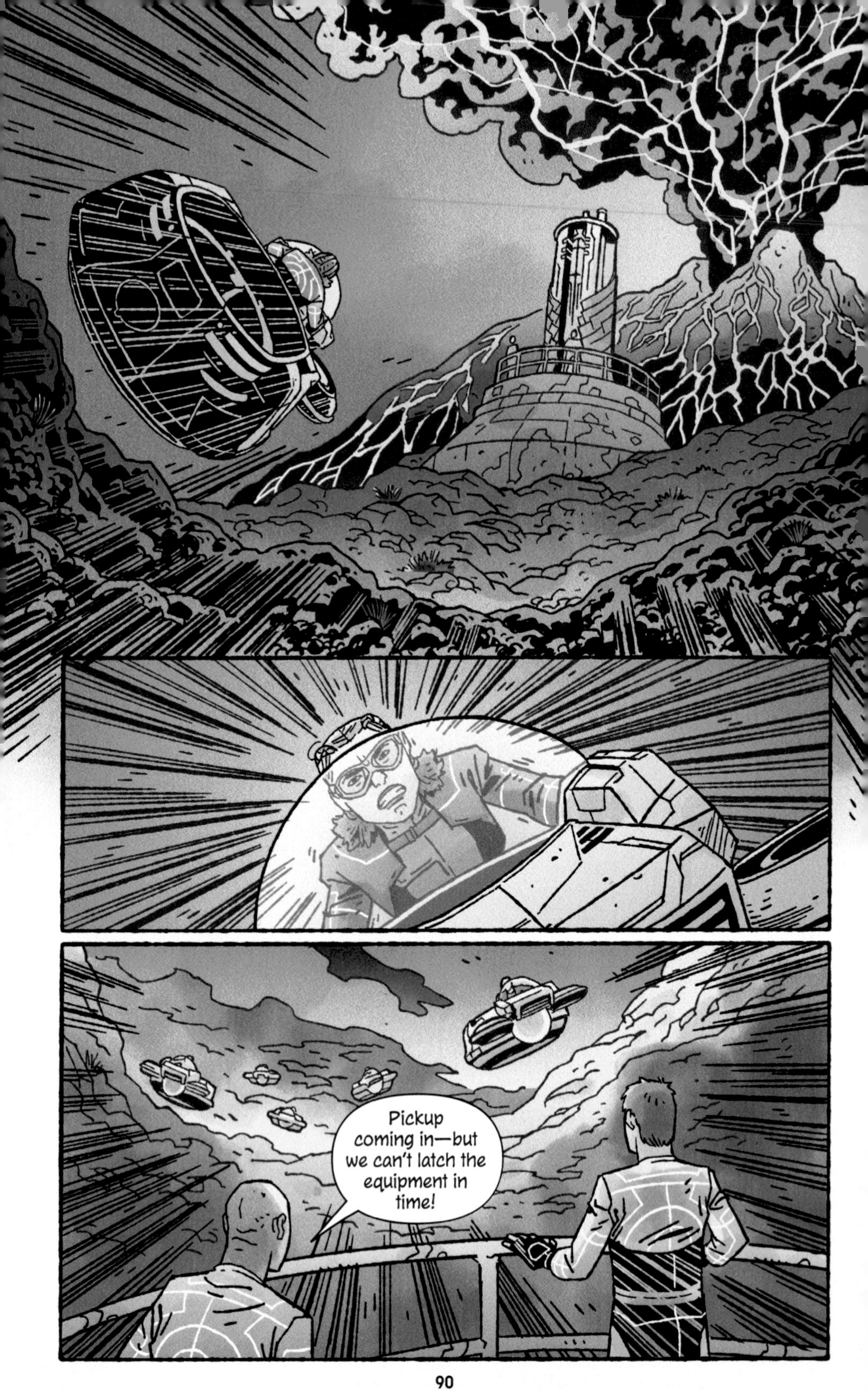
Pickup coming in—but we can't latch the equipment in time!

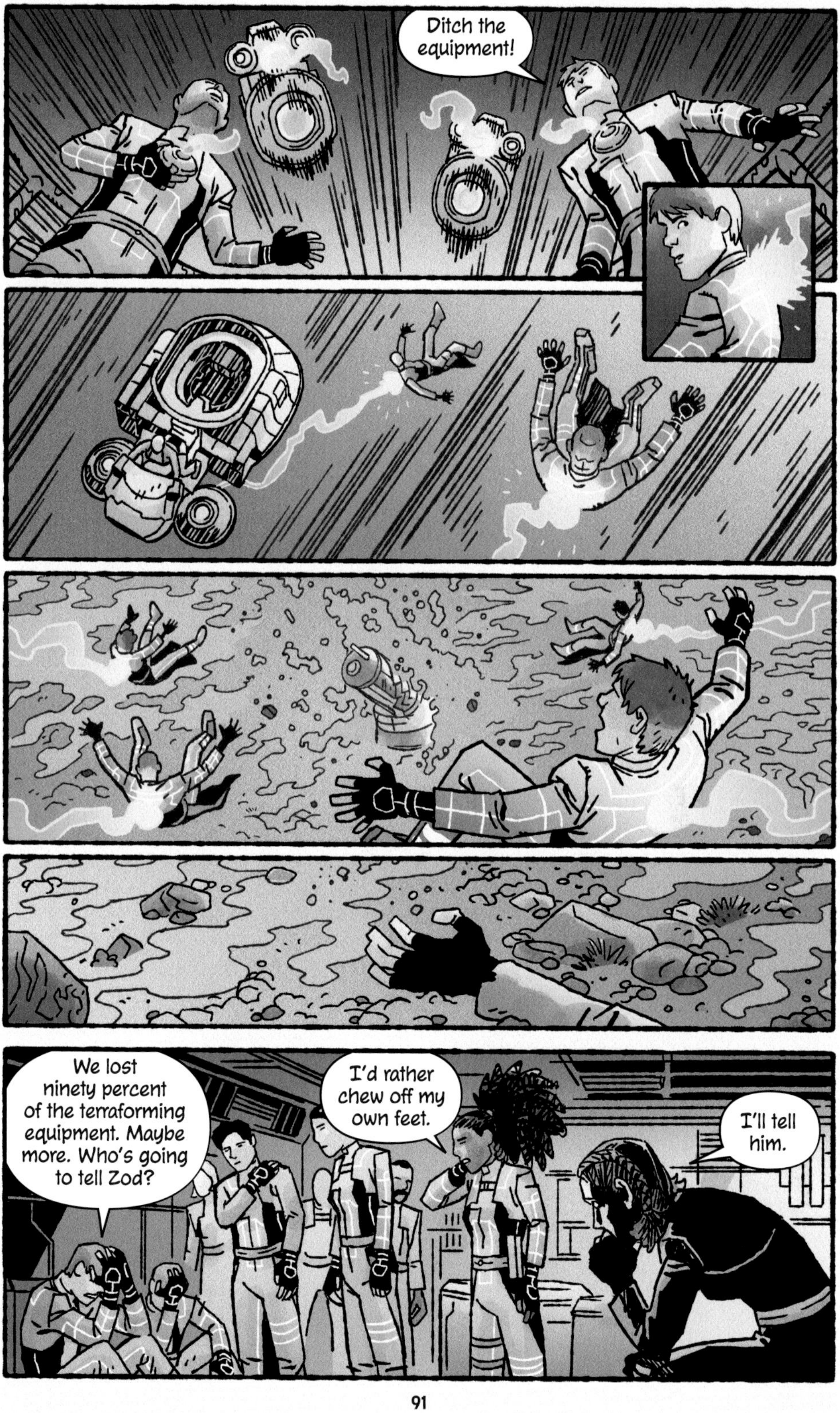
Ditch the equipment!
We lost ninety percent of the terraforming equipment. Maybe more. Who's going to tell Zod?
I'd rather chew off my own feet.
I'll tell him.

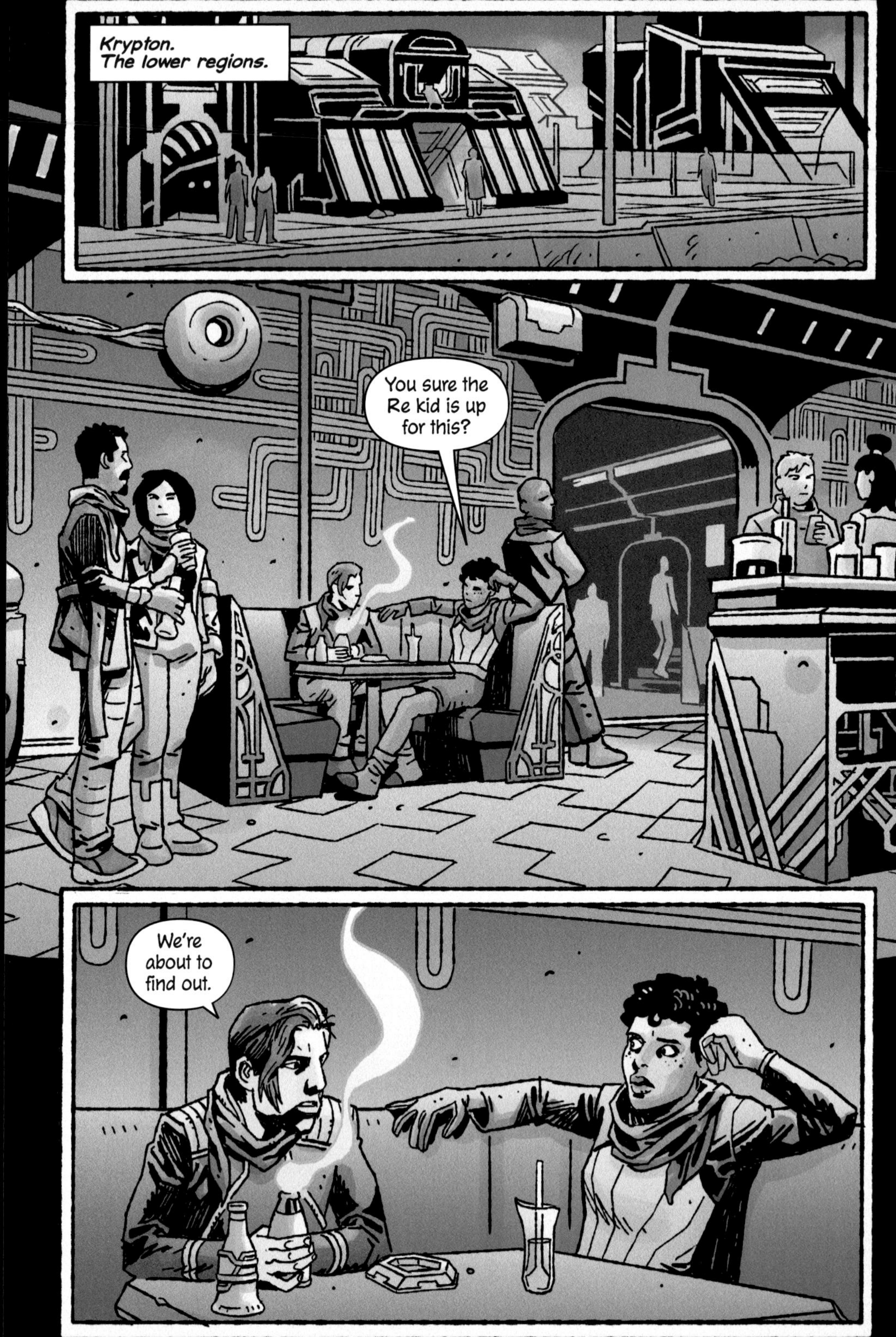
Krypton.
The lower regions.
You sure the Re kid is up for this?
We're about to find out.

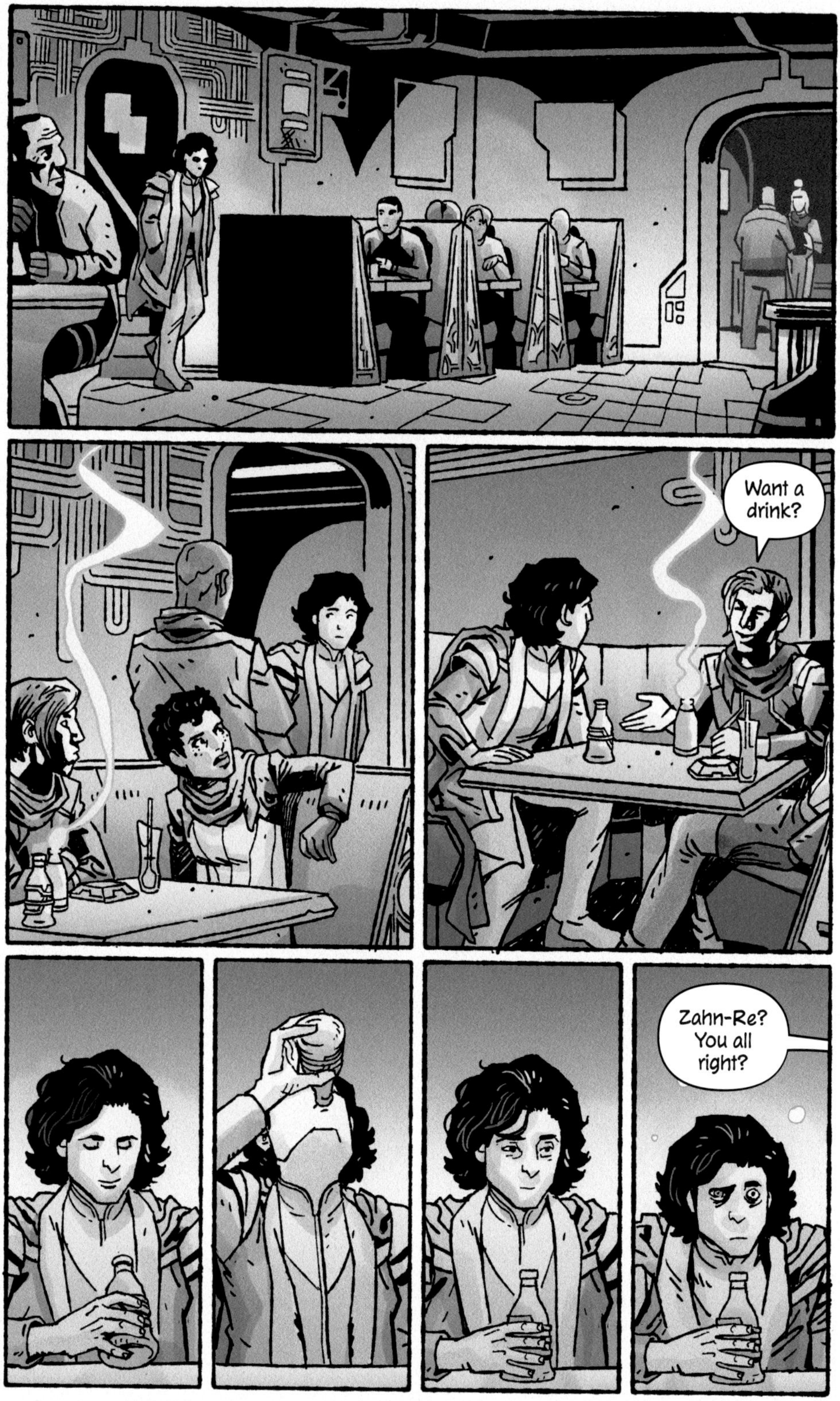
Want a drink?
Zahn-Re? You all right?

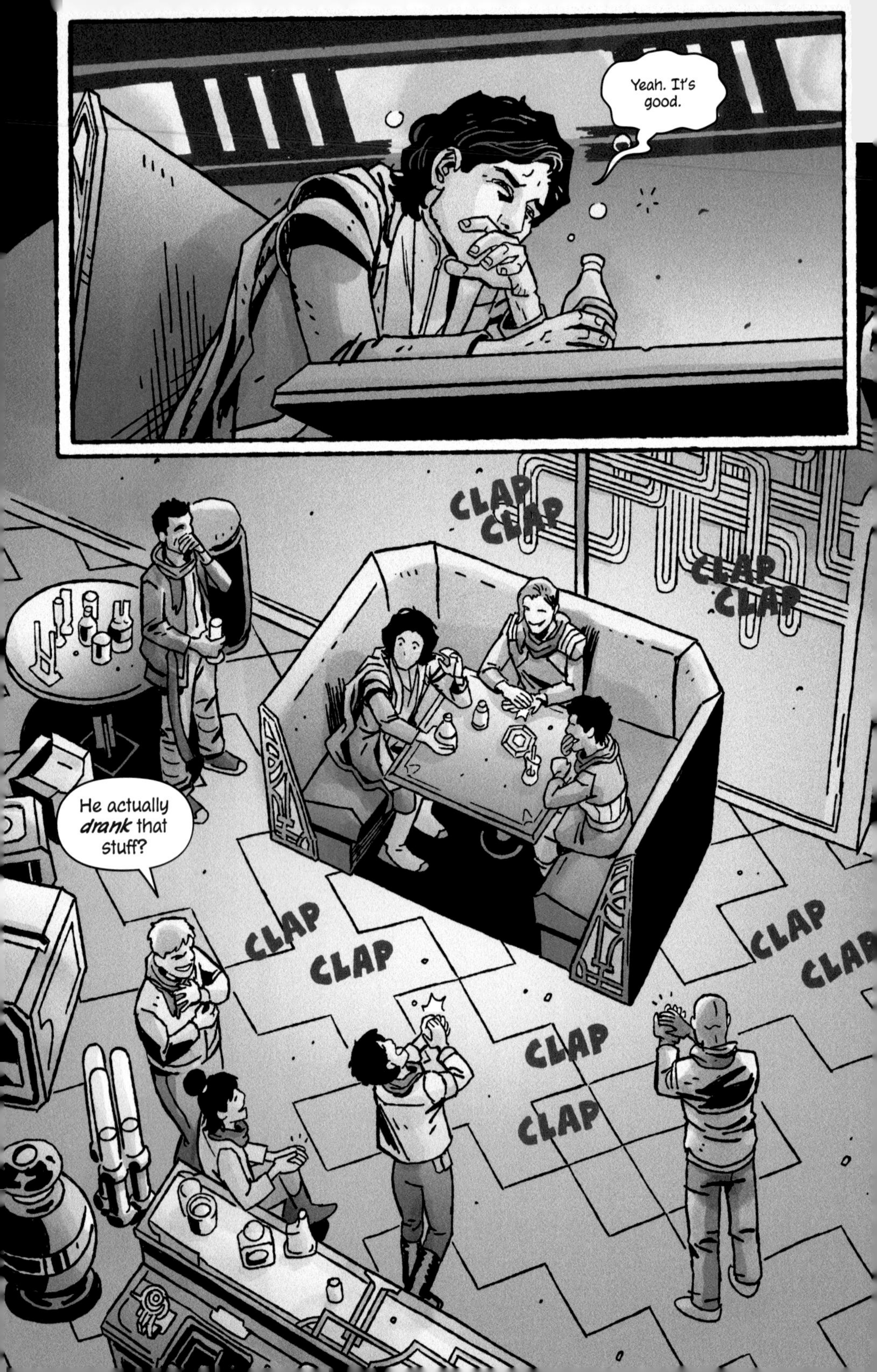
Yeah. It's good.
CLAP
CLAP
CLAP
CLAP
He actually *drank* that stuff?
CLAP
CLAP
CLAP
CLAP
CLAP
CLAP

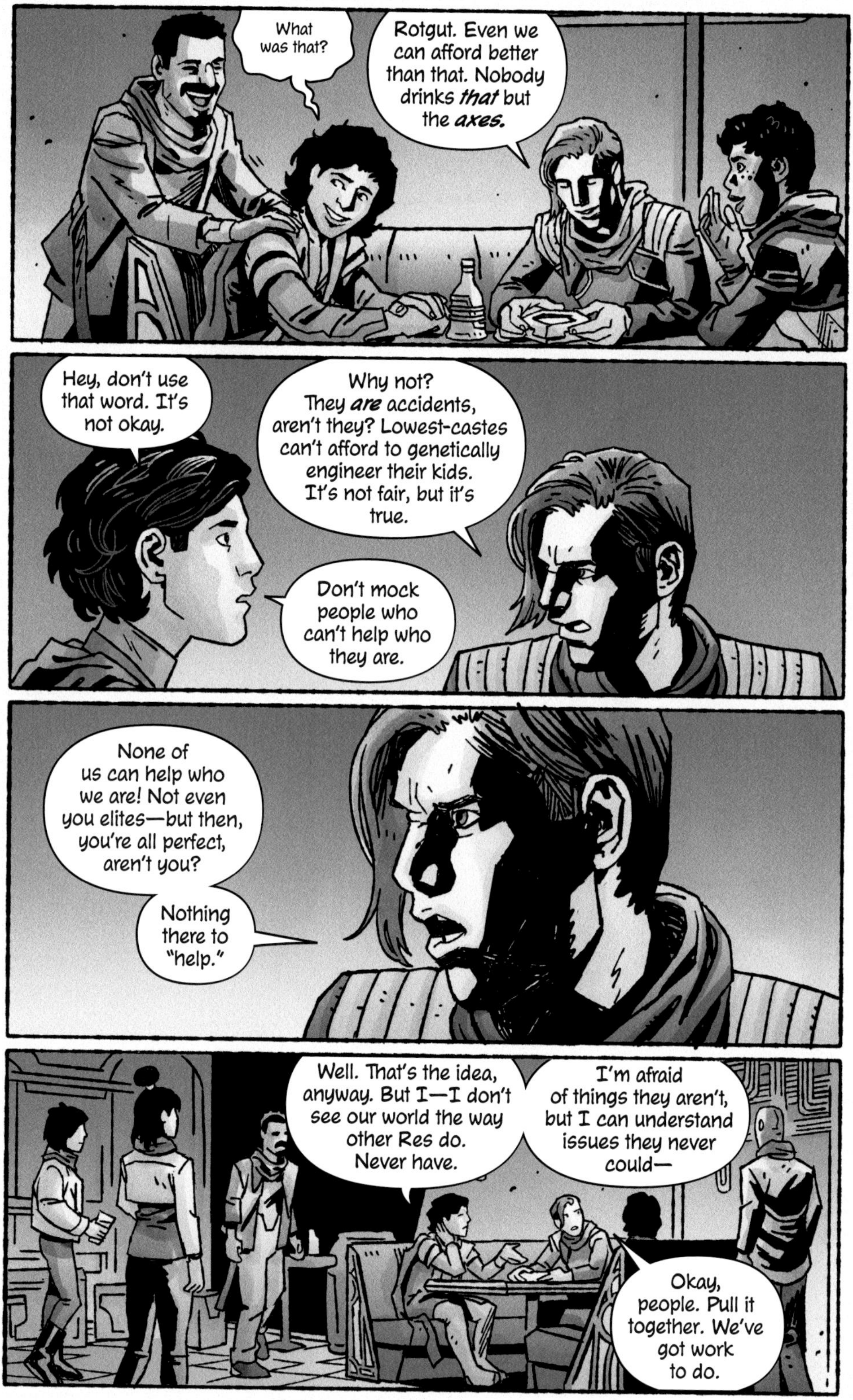
What was that?
Rotgut. Even we can afford better than that. Nobody drinks *that* but the *axes.*
Hey, don't use that word. It's not okay.
Why not? They *are* accidents, aren't they? Lowest-castes can't afford to genetically engineer their kids. It's not fair, but it's true.
Don't mock people who can't help who they are.
None of us can help who we are! Not even you elites—but then, you're all perfect, aren't you?
Nothing there to "help."
Well. That's the idea, anyway. But I—I don't see our world the way other Res do. Never have.
I'm afraid of things they aren't, but I can understand issues they never could—
Okay, people. Pull it together. We've got work to do.

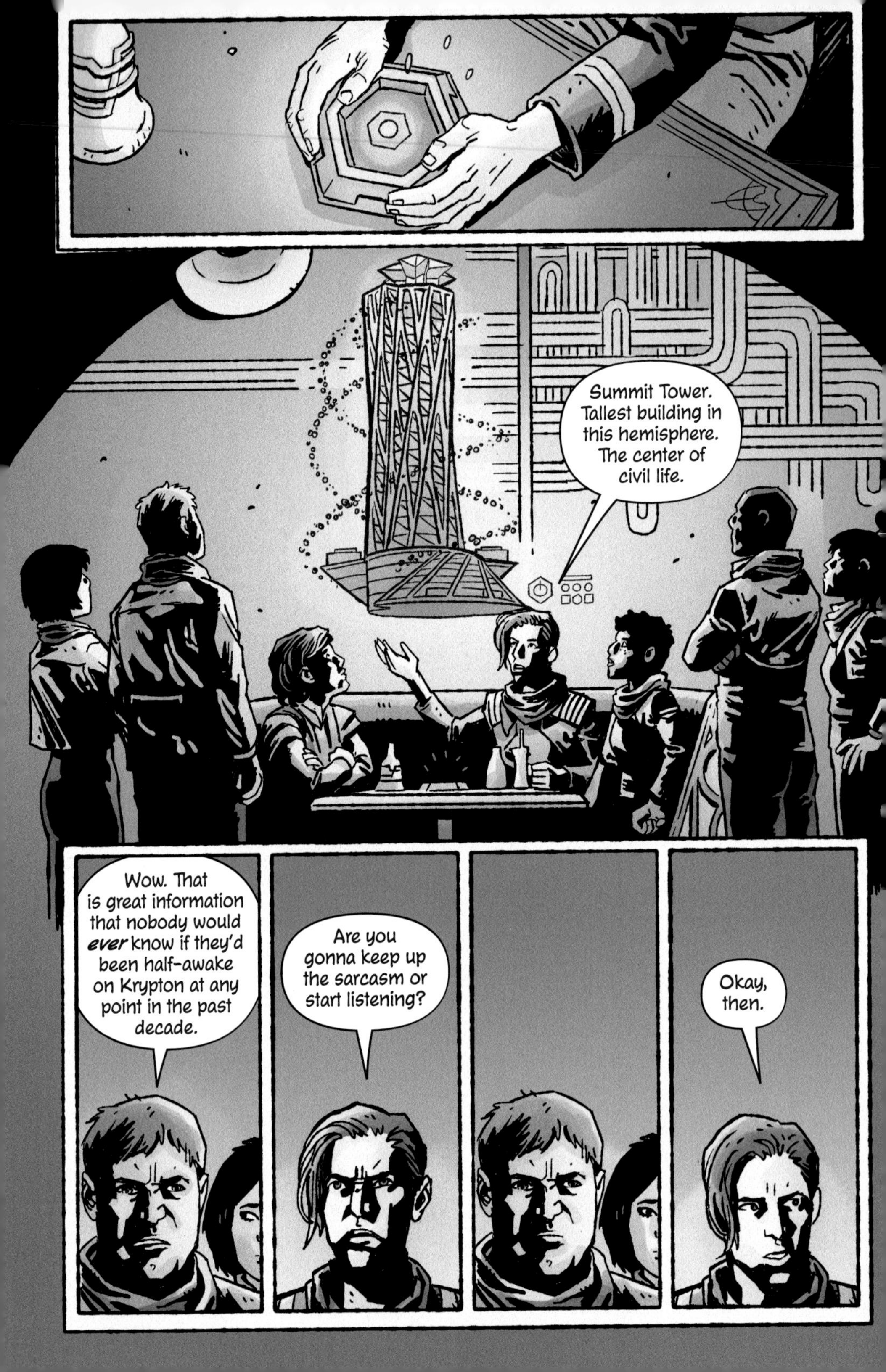

Summit Tower. Tallest building in this hemisphere. The center of civil life.
Wow. That is great information that nobody would *ever* know if they'd been half-awake on Krypton at any point in the past decade.
Are you gonna keep up the sarcasm or start listening?
Okay, then.

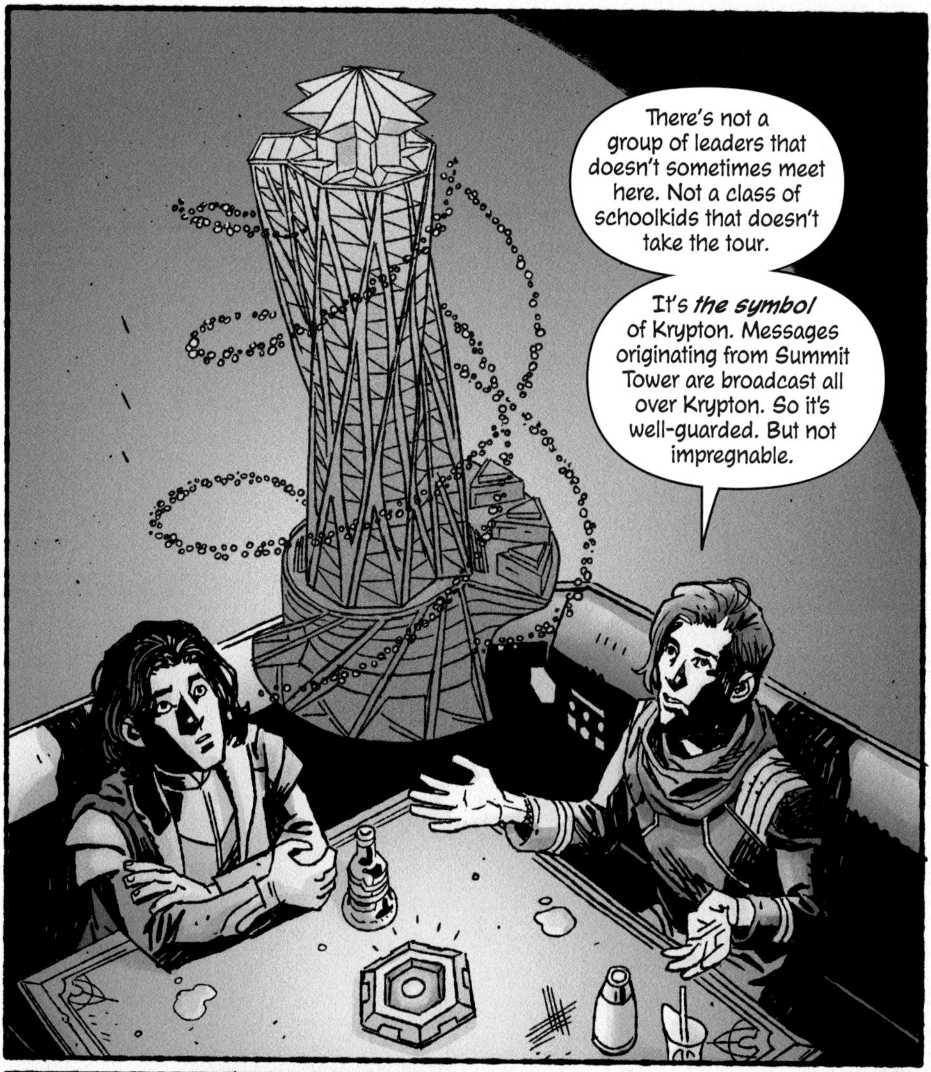
There's not a group of leaders that doesn't sometimes meet here. Not a class of schoolkids that doesn't take the tour.
It's *the symbol* of Krypton. Messages originating from Summit Tower are broadcast all over Krypton. So it's well-guarded. But not impregnable.

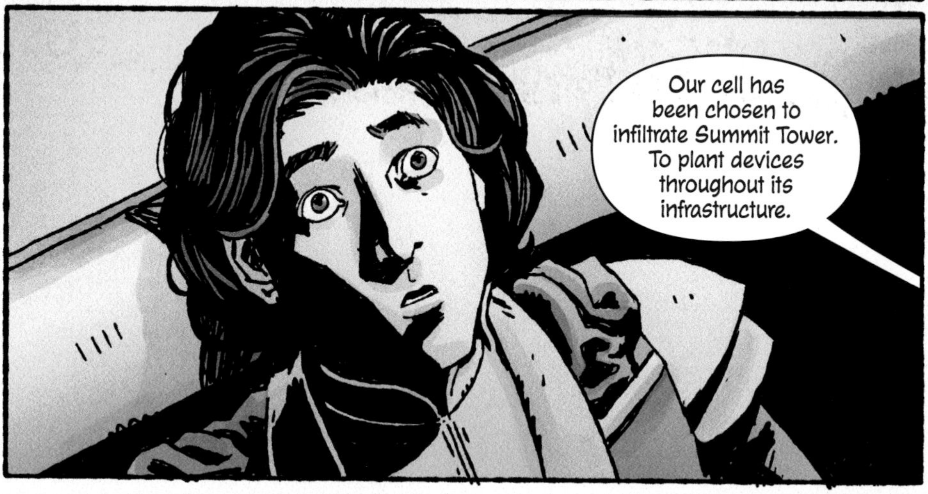
Our cell has been chosen to infiltrate Summit Tower. To plant devices throughout its infrastructure.

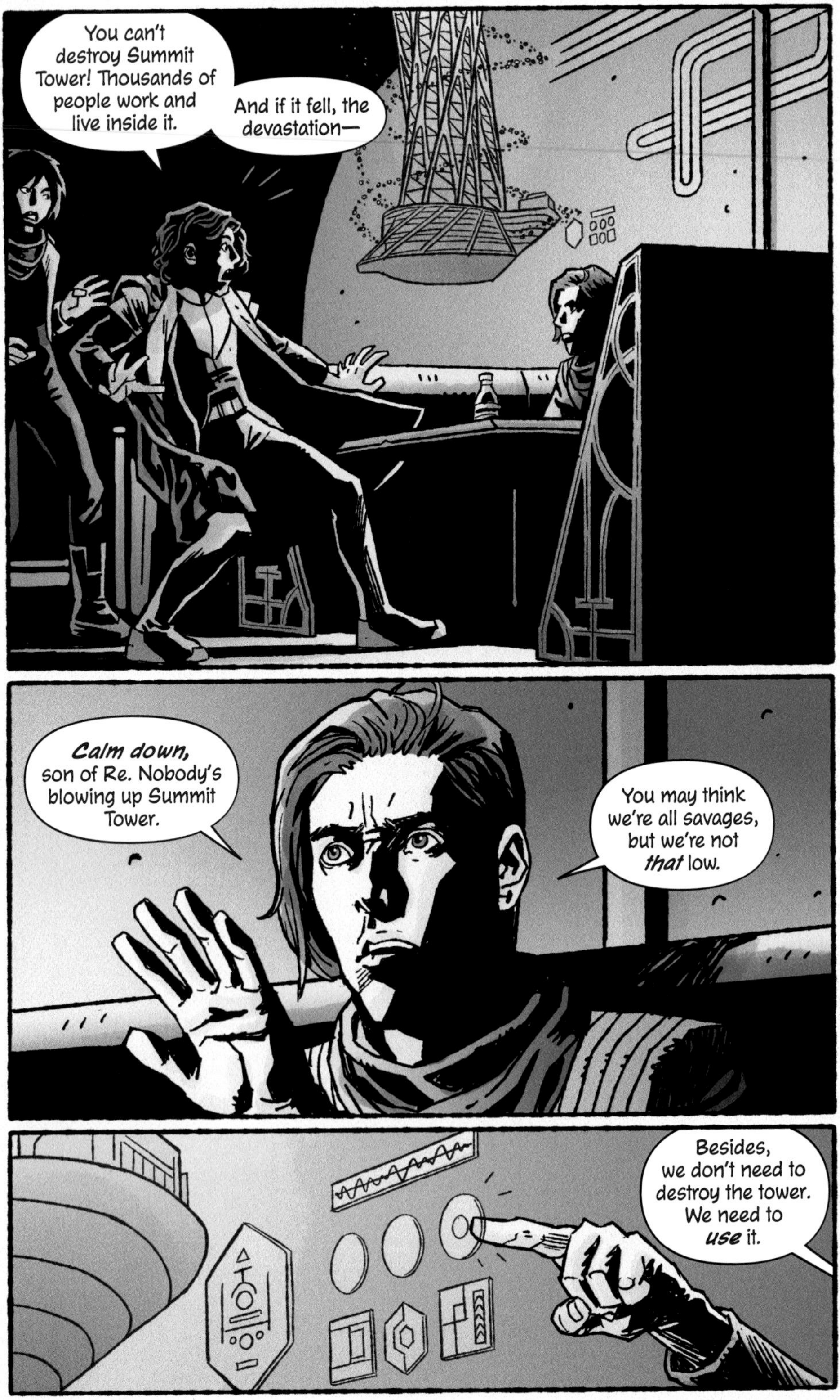
You can't destroy Summit Tower! Thousands of people work and live inside it.
And if it fell, the devastation—
Calm down, son of Re. Nobody's blowing up Summit Tower.
You may think we're all savages, but we're not *that* low.
Besides, we don't need to destroy the tower. We need to *use* it.

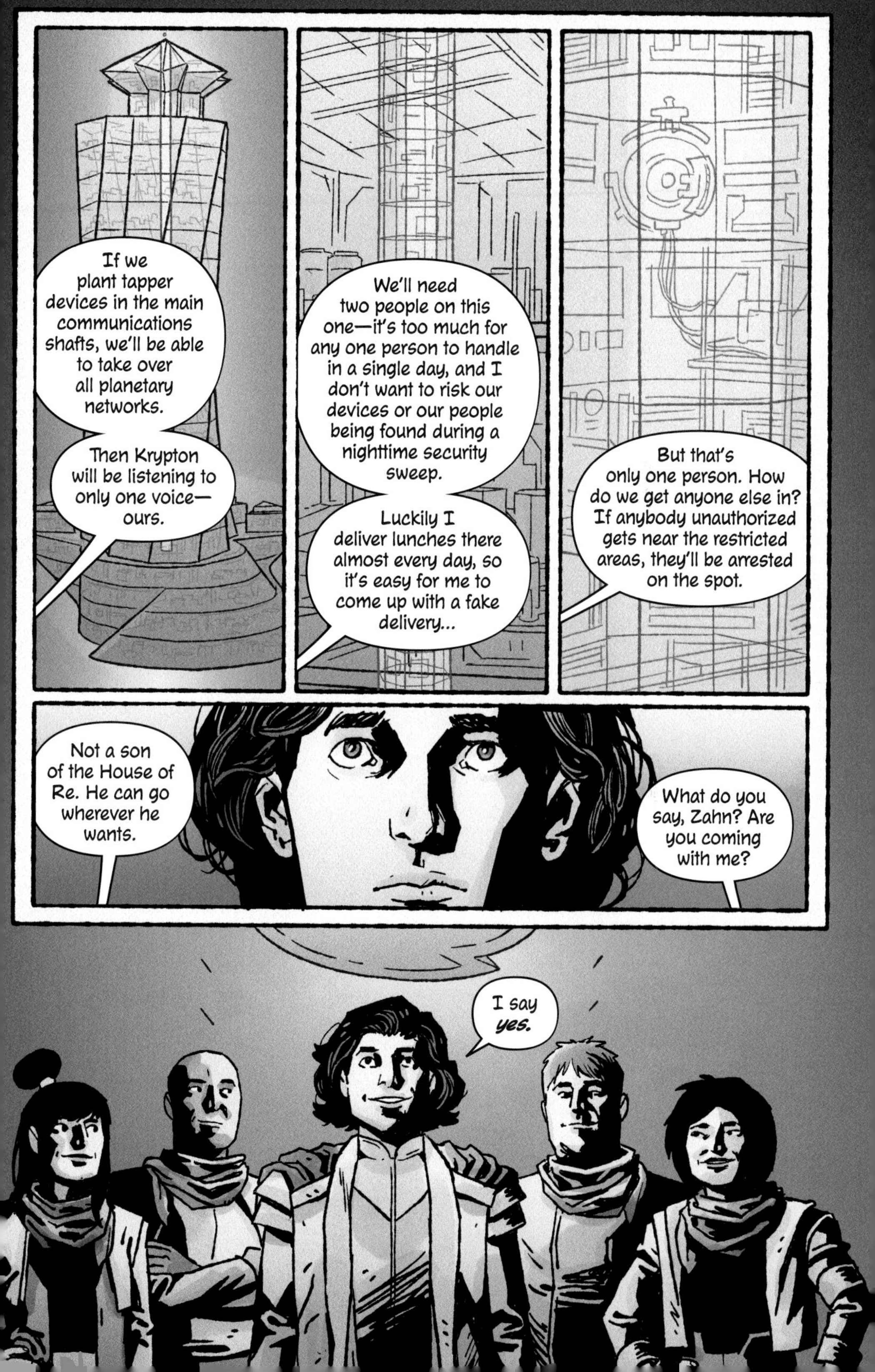
If we plant tapper devices in the main communications shafts, we'll be able to take over all planetary networks.
Then Krypton will be listening to only one voice—ours.
We'll need two people on this one—it's too much for any one person to handle in a single day, and I don't want to risk our devices or our people being found during a nighttime security sweep.
Luckily I deliver lunches there almost every day, so it's easy for me to come up with a fake delivery...
But that's only one person. How do we get anyone else in? If anybody unauthorized gets near the restricted areas, they'll be arrested on the spot.
Not a son of the House of Re. He can go wherever he wants.
What do you say, Zahn? Are you coming with me?
I say *yes.*

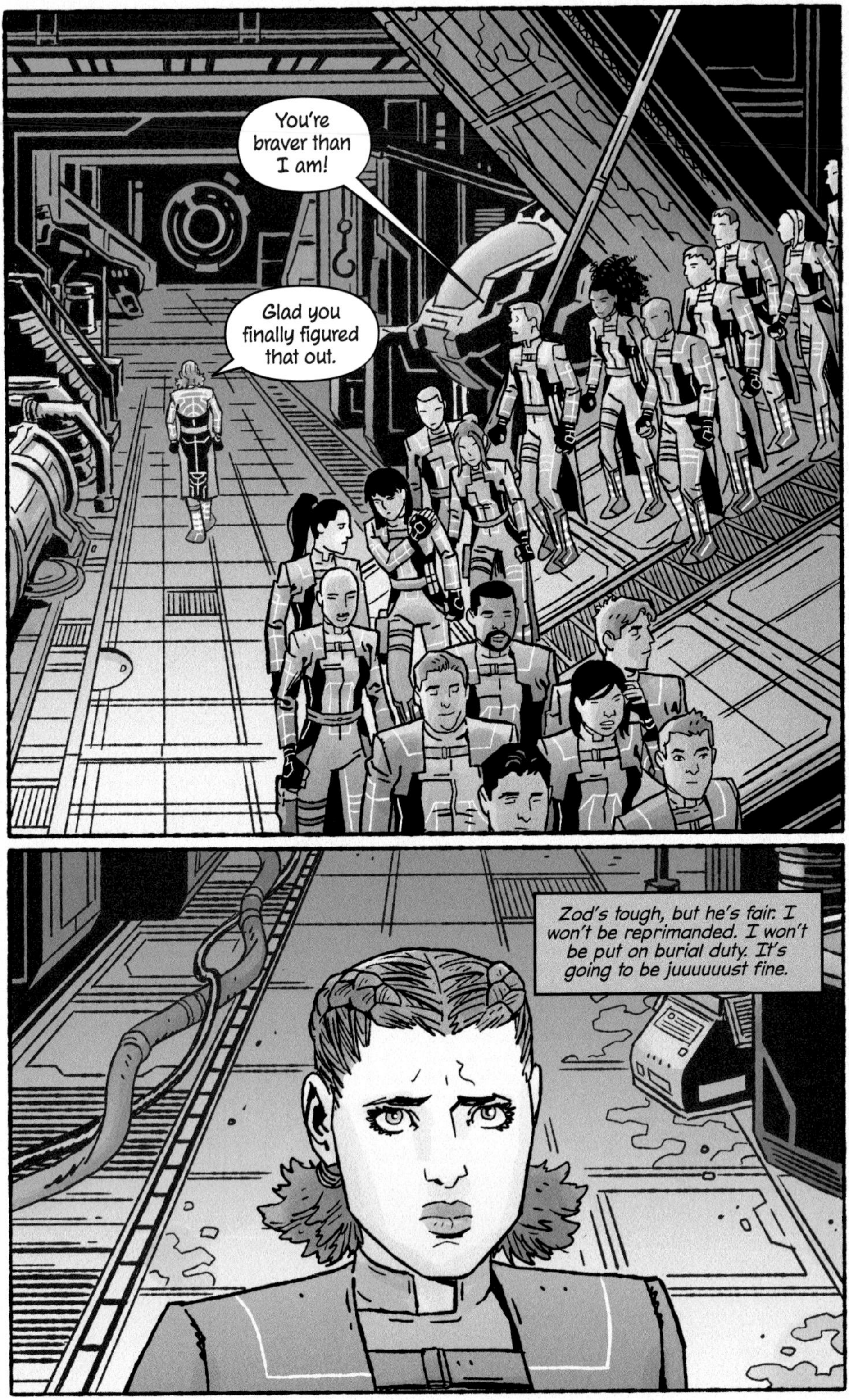
You're braver than I am!
Glad you finally figured that out.
Zod's tough, but he's fair. I won't be reprimanded. I won't be put on burial duty. It's going to be juuuuuust fine.

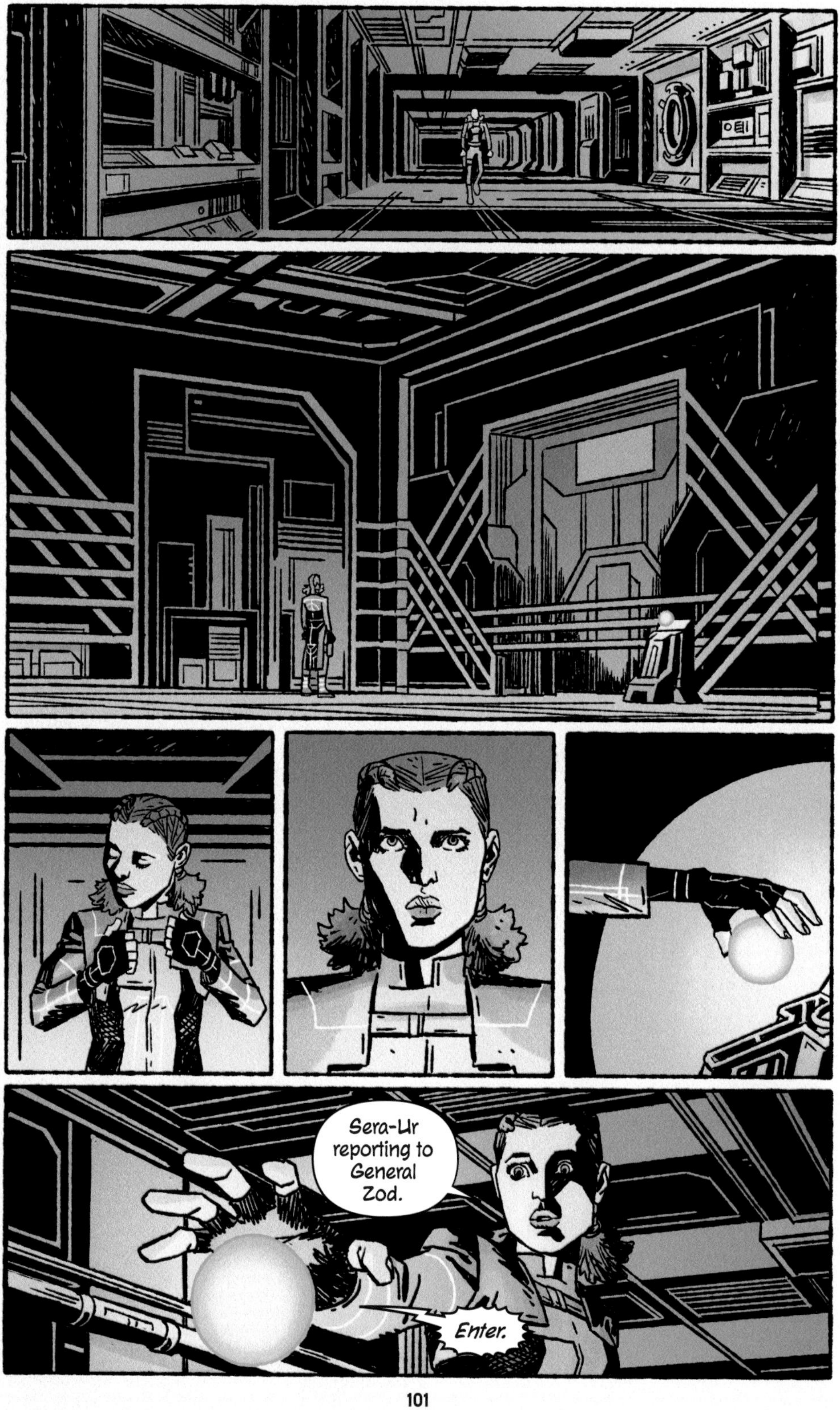
Sera-Ur reporting to General Zod.
Enter.

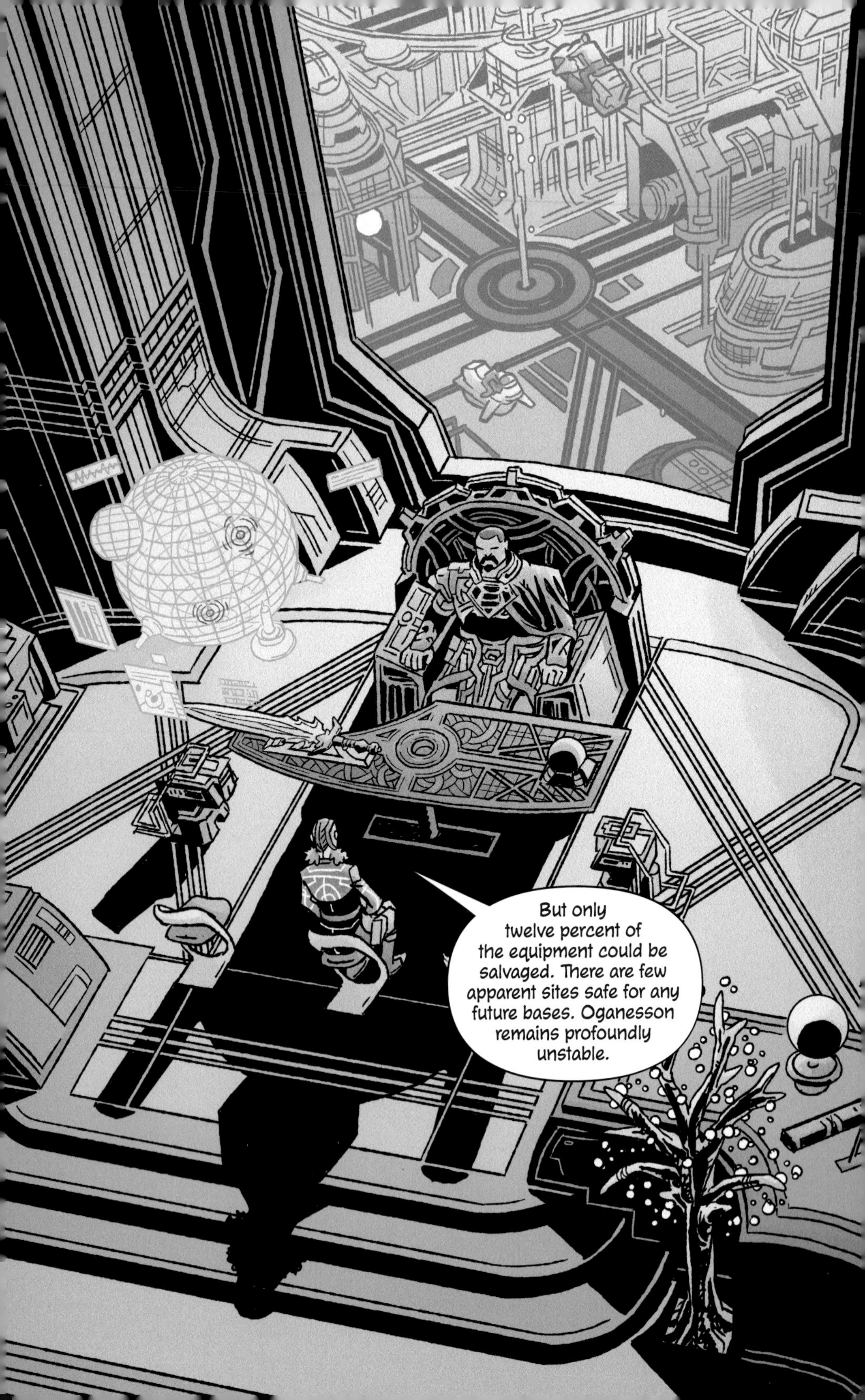
But only twelve percent of the equipment could be salvaged. There are few apparent sites safe for any future bases. Oganesson remains profoundly unstable.

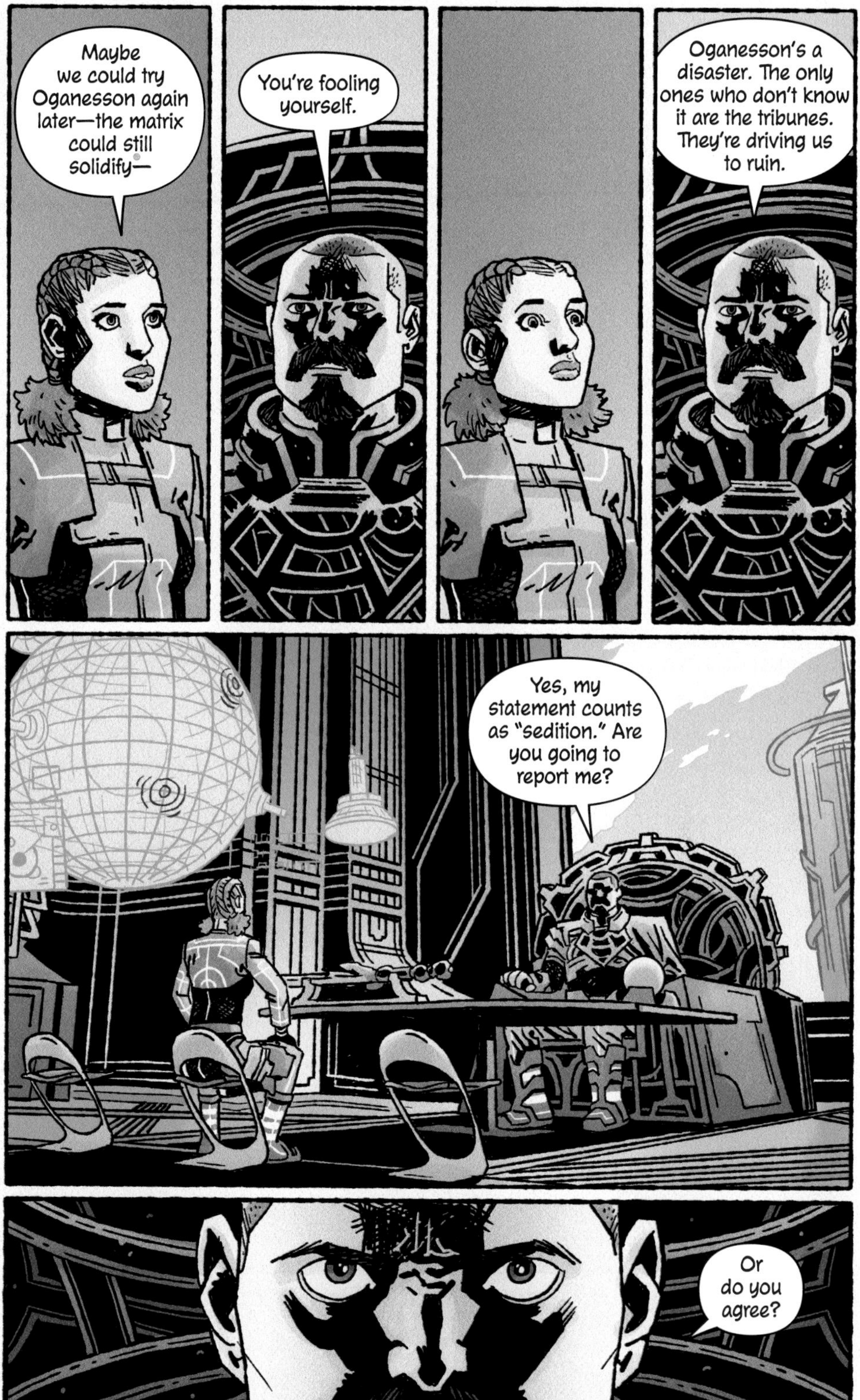
Maybe we could try Oganesson again later—the matrix could still solidify—
You're fooling yourself.
Oganesson's a disaster. The only ones who don't know it are the tribunes. They're driving us to ruin.
Yes, my statement counts as "sedition." Are you going to report me?
Or do you agree?

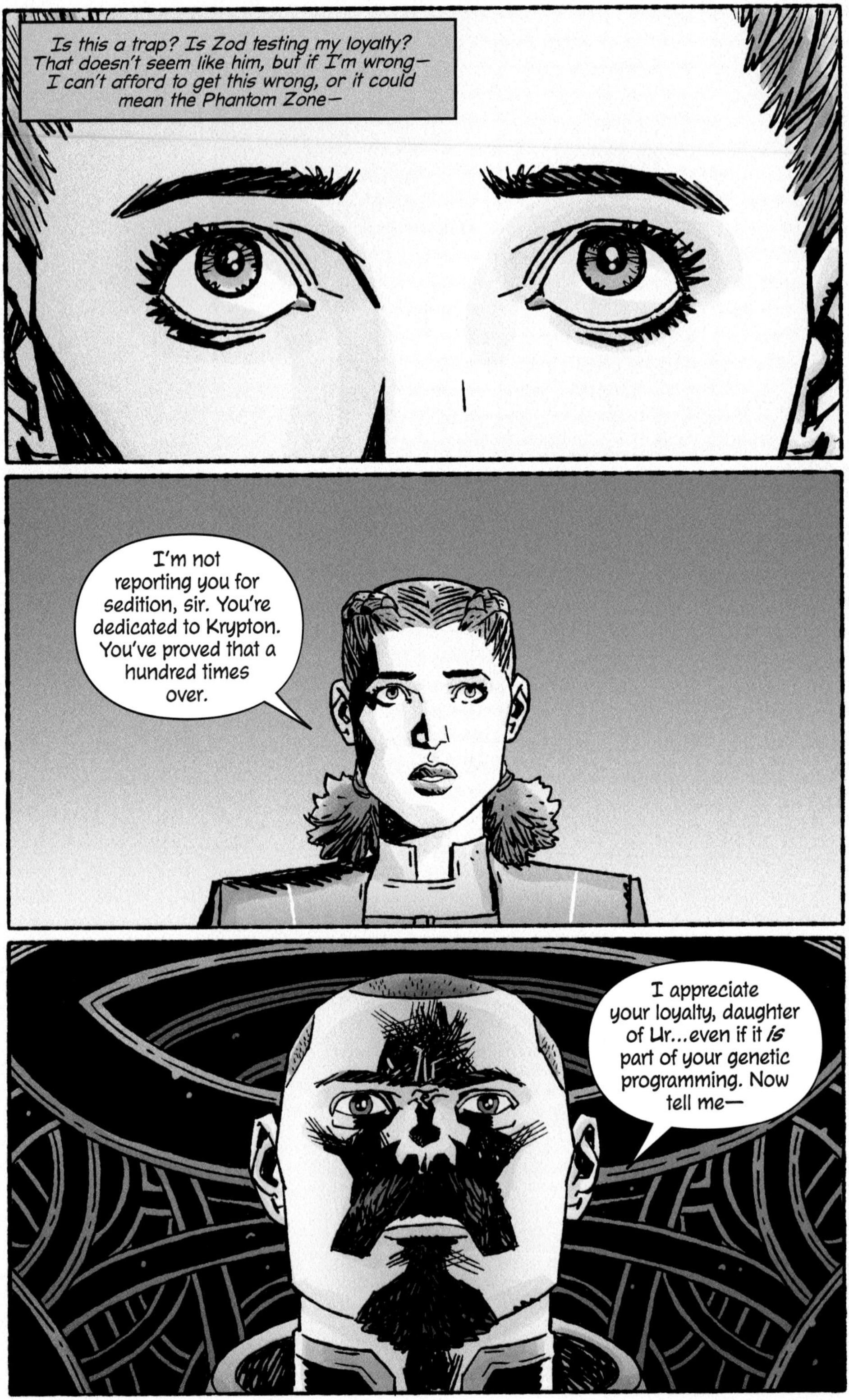
Is this a trap? Is Zod testing my loyalty? That doesn't seem like him, but if I'm wrong— I can't afford to get this wrong, or it could mean the Phantom Zone—
I'm not reporting you for sedition, sir. You're dedicated to Krypton. You've proved that a hundred times over.
I appreciate your loyalty, daughter of Ur...even if it *is* part of your genetic programming. Now tell me—

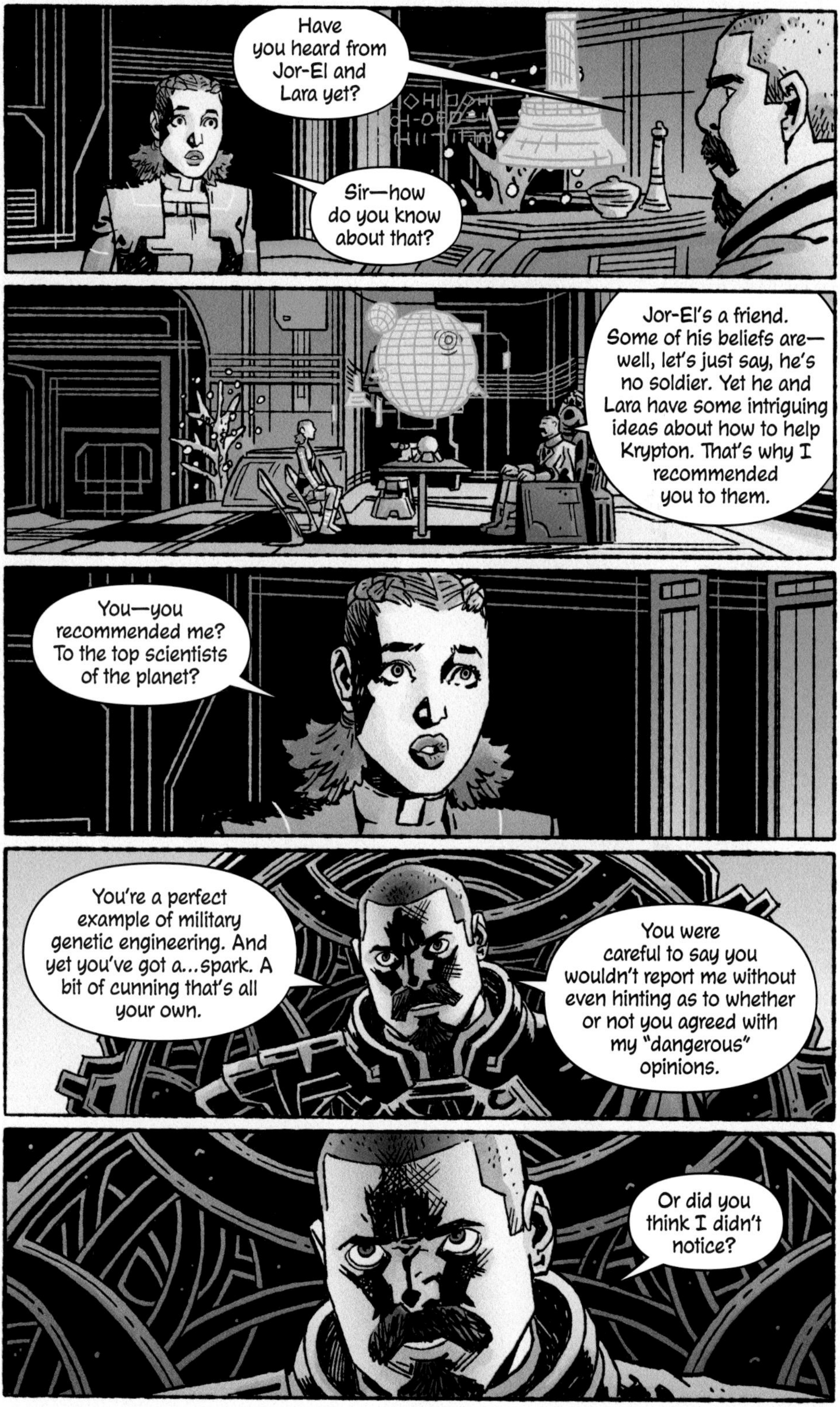
Have you heard from Jor-El and Lara yet?
Sir—how do you know about that?
Jor-El's a friend. Some of his beliefs are—well, let's just say, he's no soldier. Yet he and Lara have some intriguing ideas about how to help Krypton. That's why I recommended you to them.
You—you recommended me? To the top scientists of the planet?
You're a perfect example of military genetic engineering. And yet you've got a...spark. A bit of cunning that's all your own.
You were careful to say you wouldn't report me without even hinting as to whether or not you agreed with my "dangerous" opinions.
Or did you think I didn't notice?

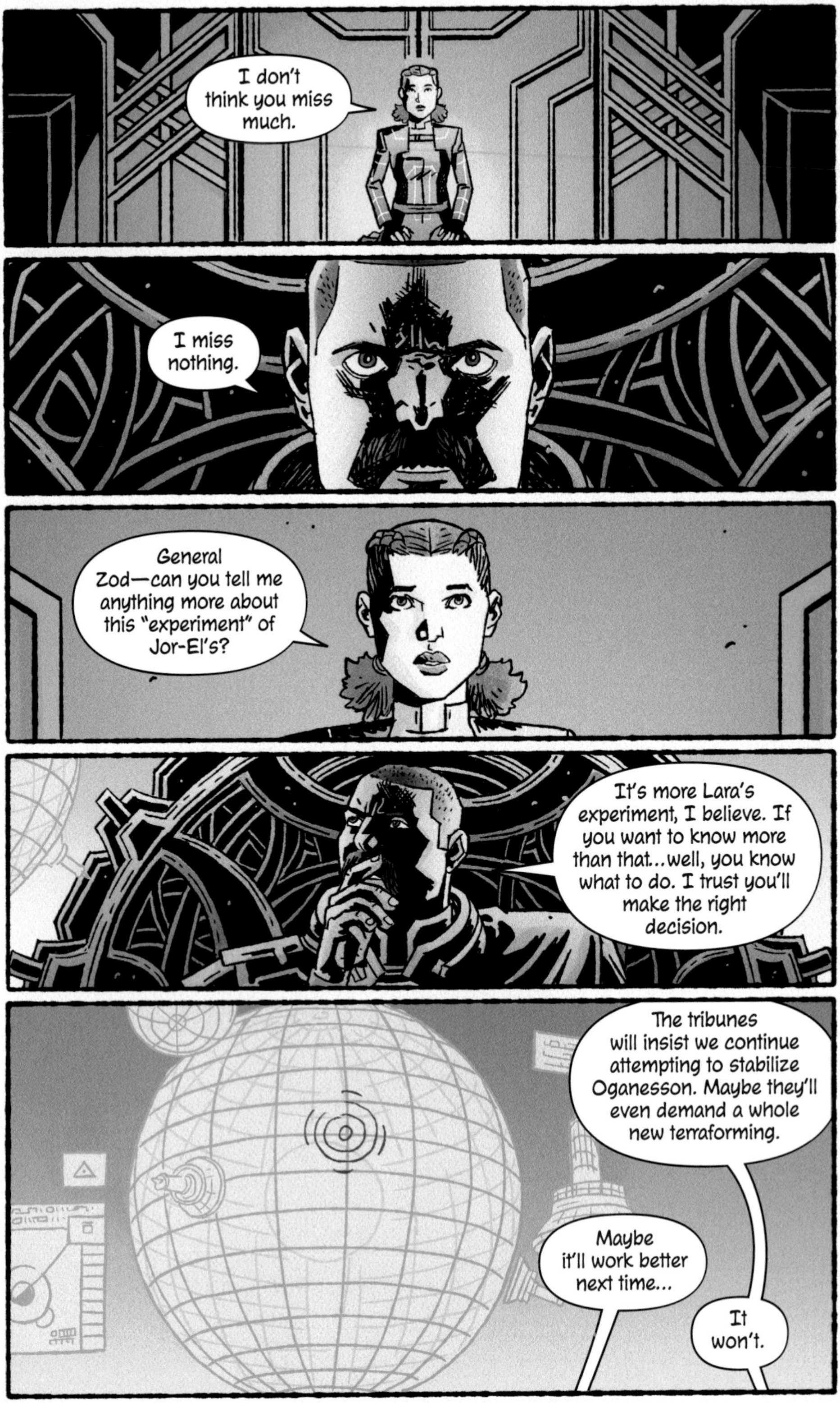
I don't think you miss much.
I miss nothing.
General Zod—can you tell me anything more about this "experiment" of Jor-El's?
It's more Lara's experiment, I believe. If you want to know more than that...well, you know what to do. I trust you'll make the right decision.
The tribunes will insist we continue attempting to stabilize Oganesson. Maybe they'll even demand a whole new terraforming.
Maybe it'll work better next time...
It won't.

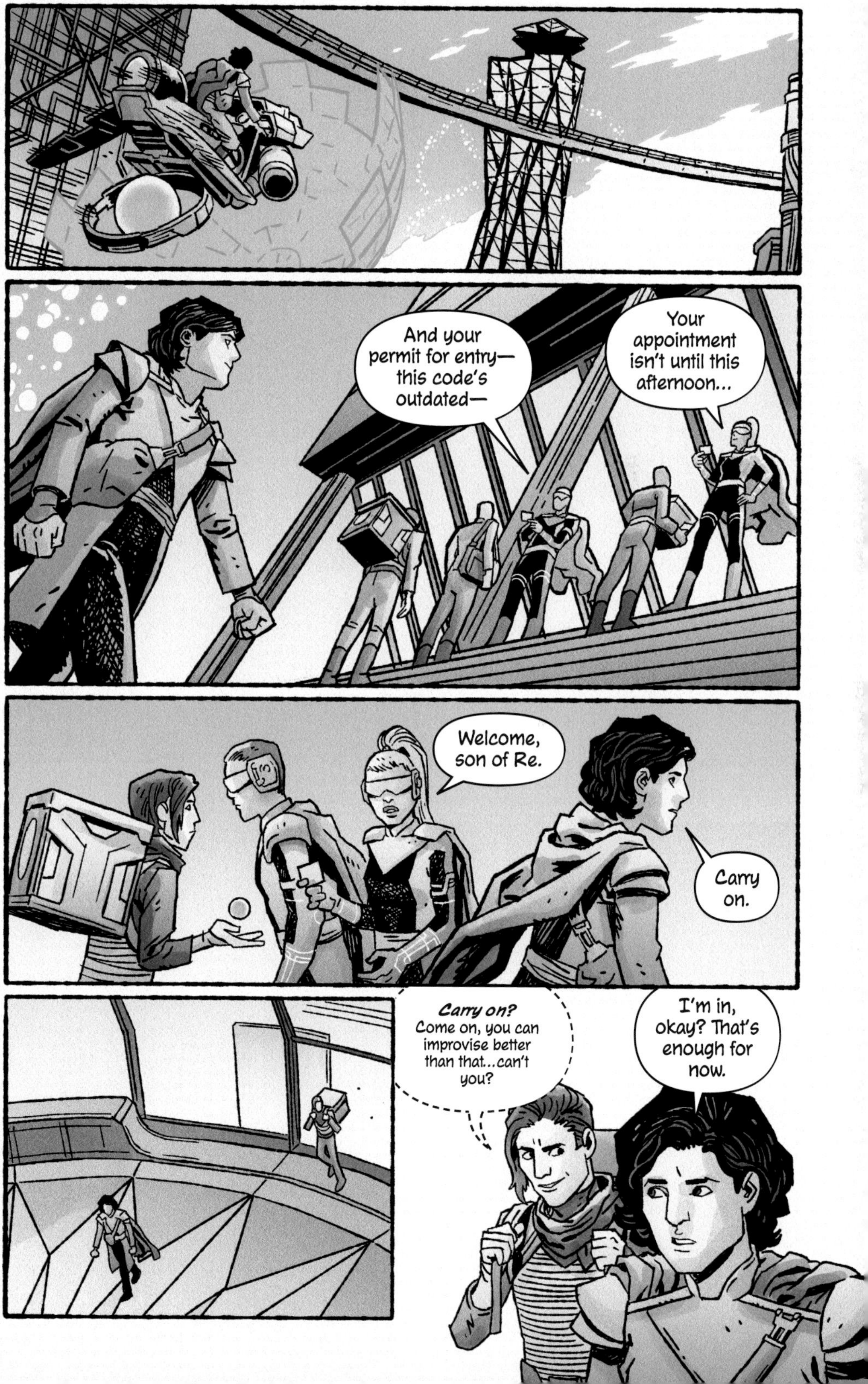
And your permit for entry—this code's outdated—
Your appointment isn't until this afternoon...
Welcome, son of Re.
Carry on.
Carry on? Come on, you can improvise better than that...can't you?
I'm in, okay? That's enough for now.

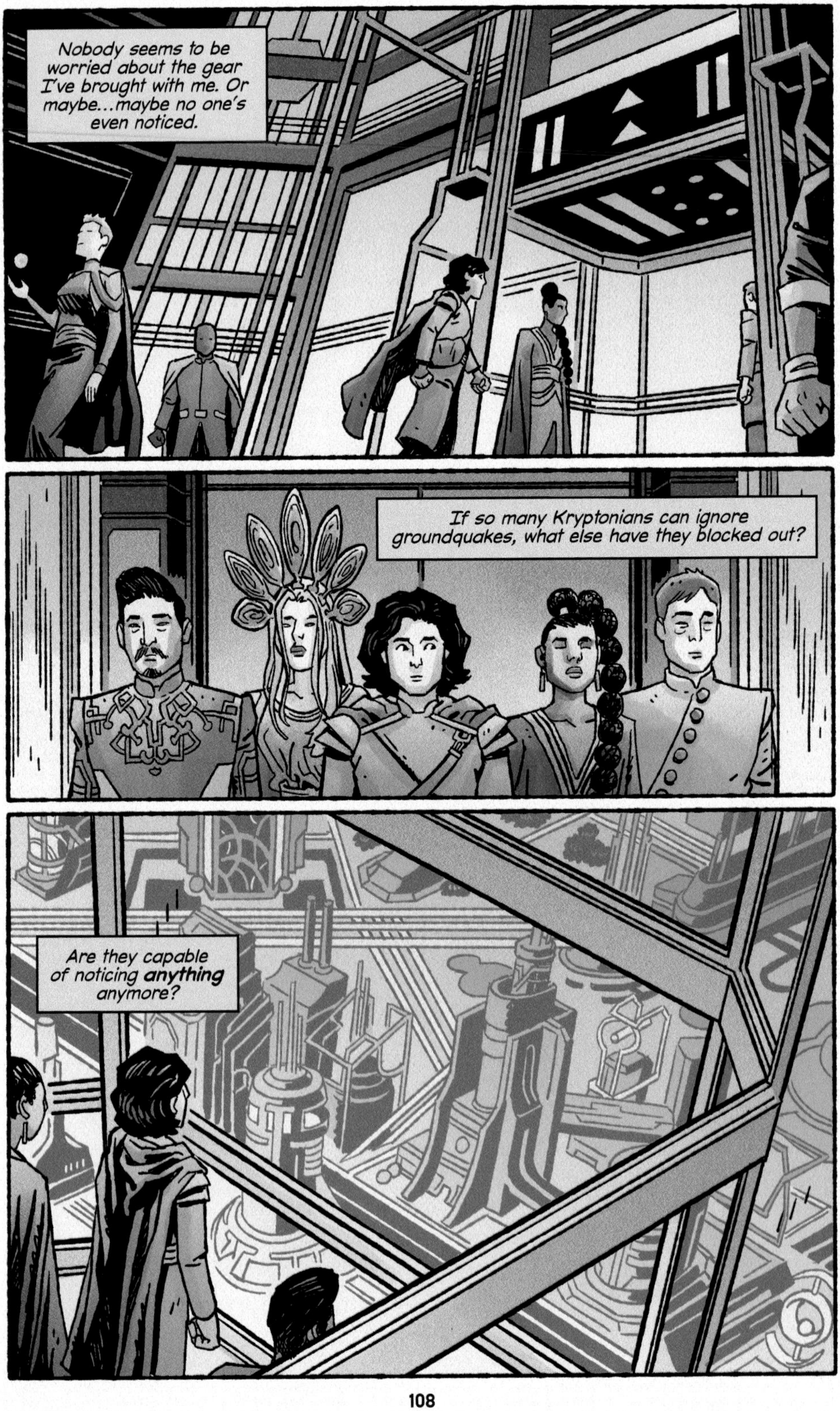
Nobody seems to be worried about the gear I've brought with me. Or maybe...maybe no one's even noticed.
If so many Kryptonians can ignore groundquakes, what else have they blocked out?
Are they capable of noticing **anything** anymore?

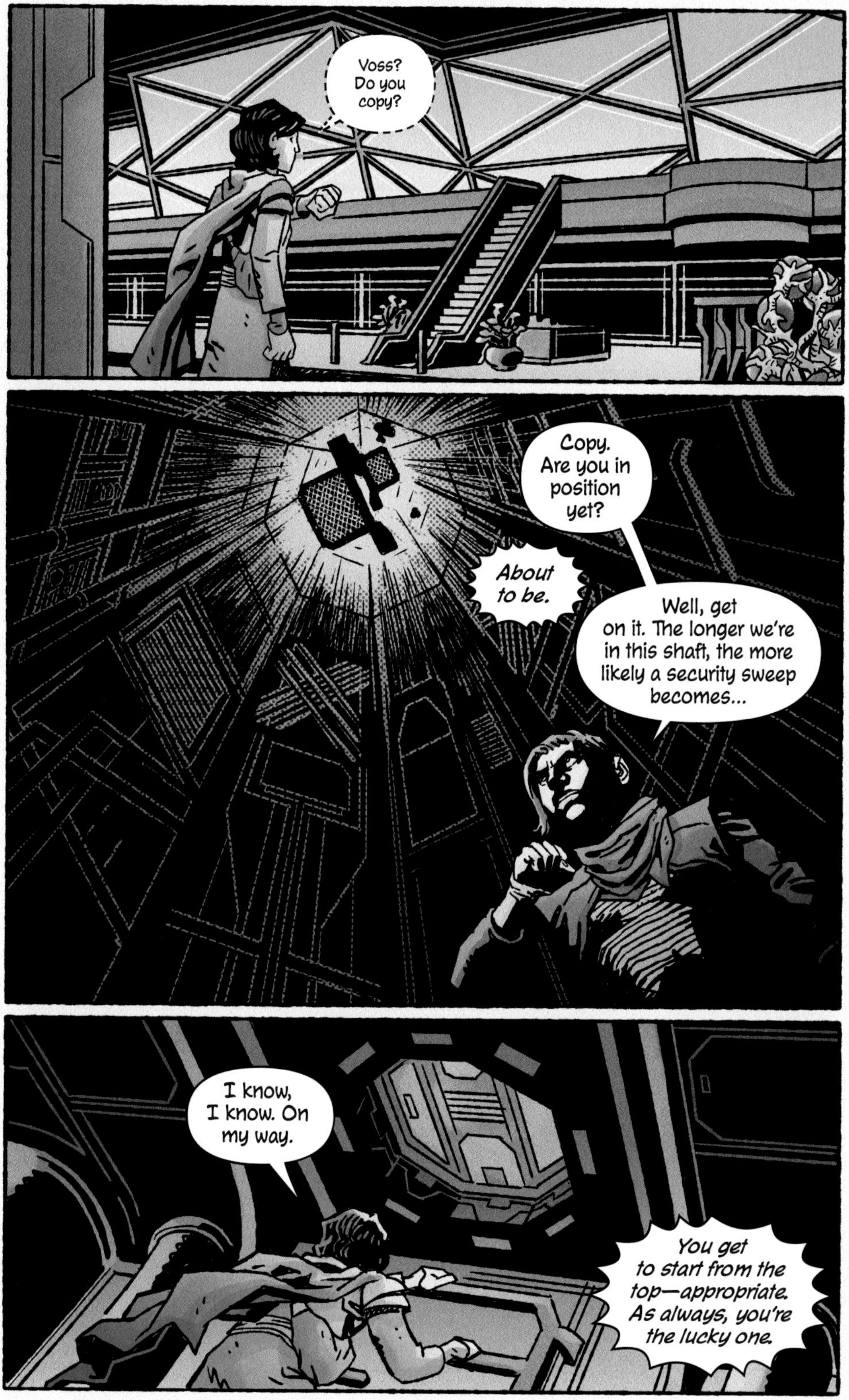
Voss? Do you copy?
Copy. Are you in position yet?
About to be.
Well, get on it. The longer we're in this shaft, the more likely a security sweep becomes...
I know, I know. On my way.
You get to start from the top—appropriate. As always, you're the lucky one.

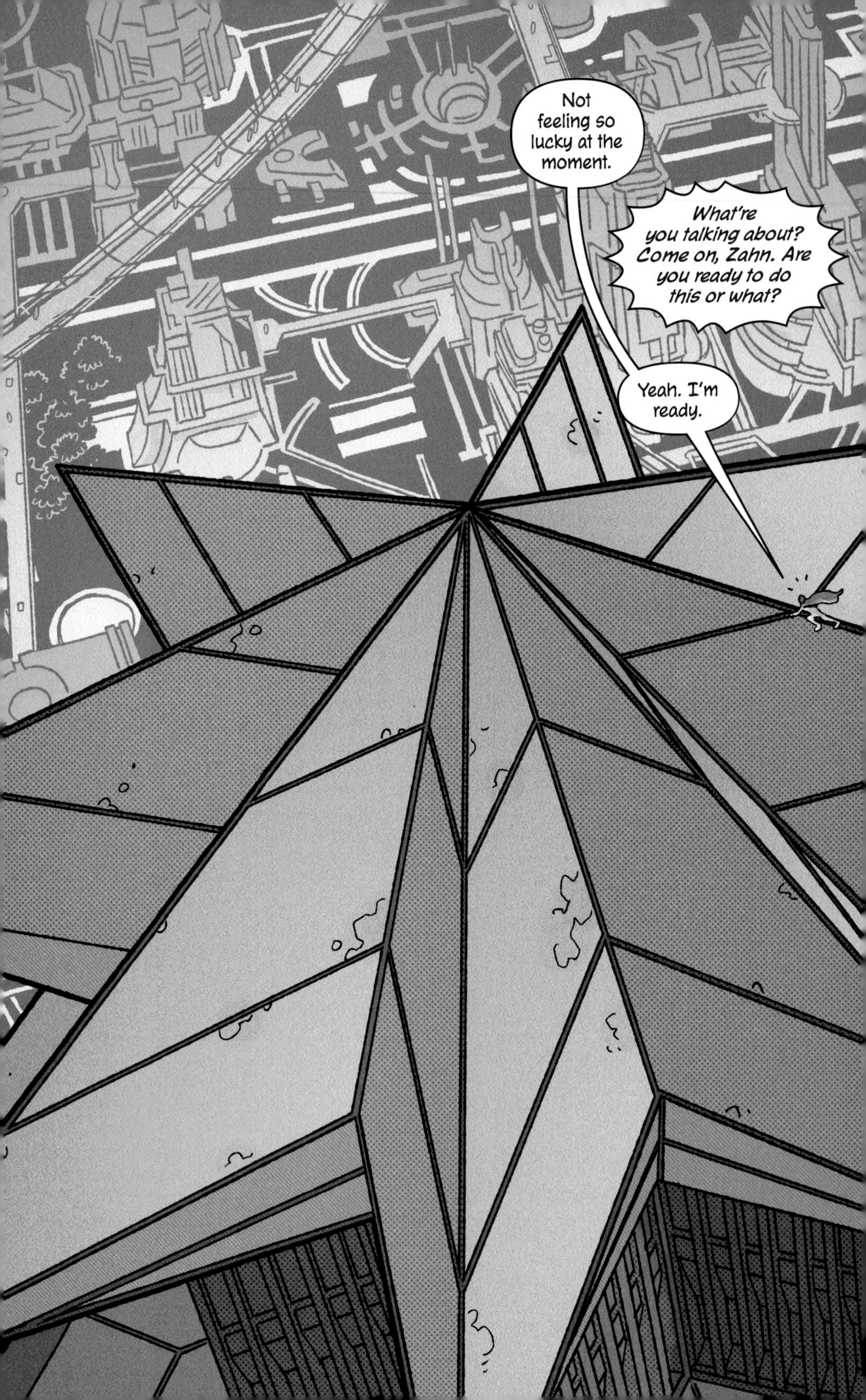
Not feeling so lucky at the moment.
What're you talking about? Come on, Zahn. Are you ready to do this or what?
Yeah. I'm ready.

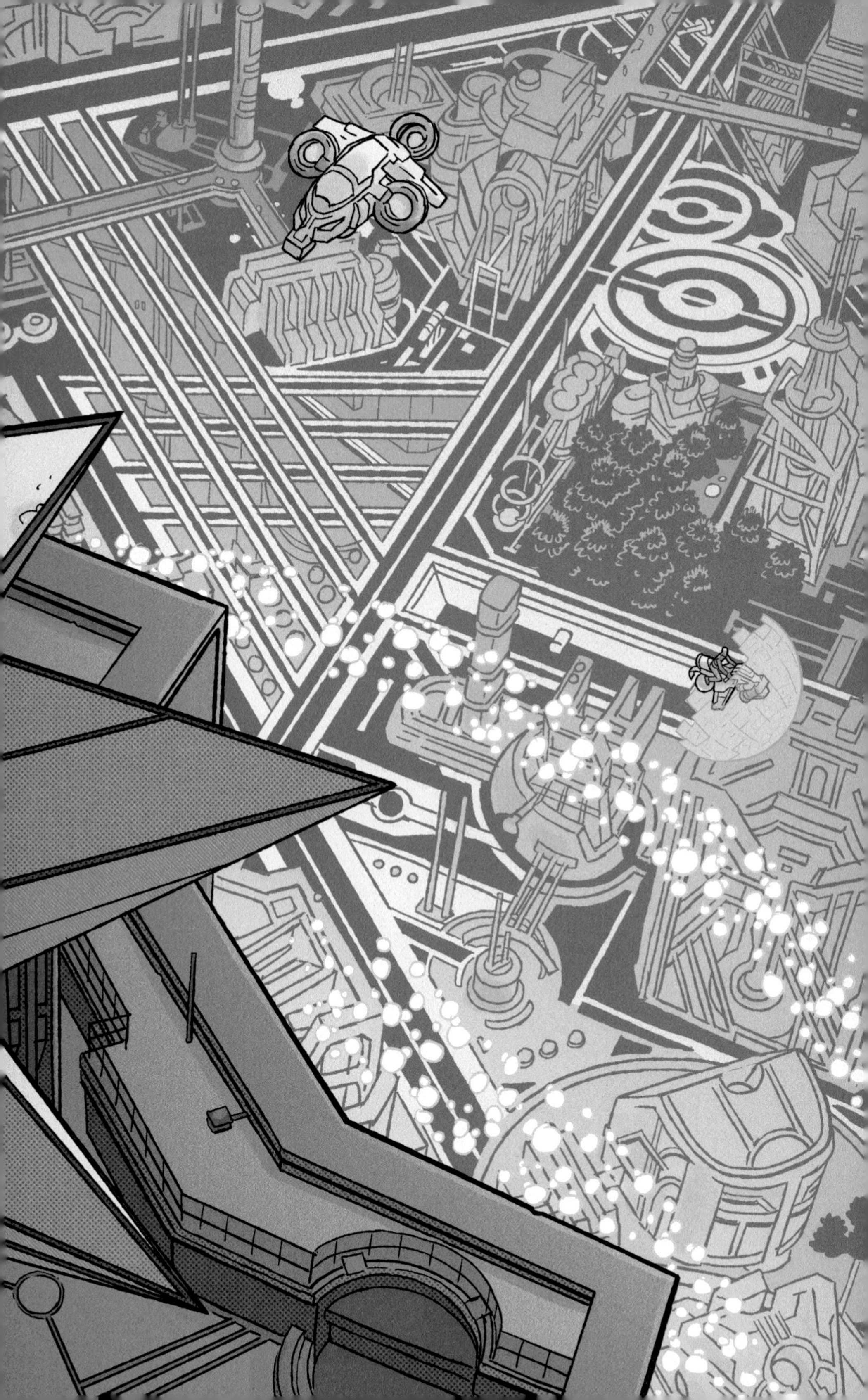

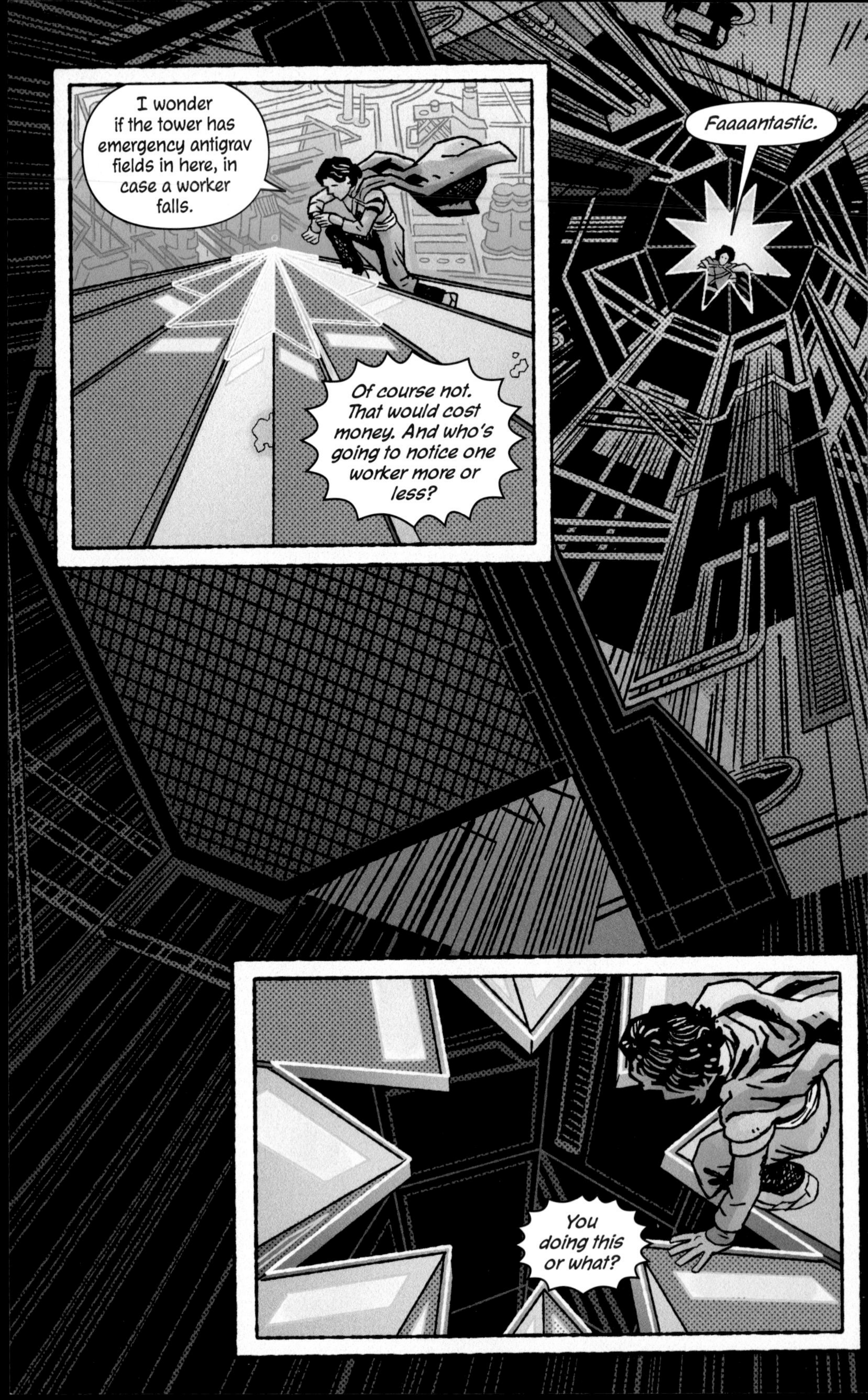
I wonder if the tower has emergency antigrav fields in here, in case a worker falls.
Of course not. That would cost money. And who's going to notice one worker more or less?
Faaaantastic.
You doing this or what?

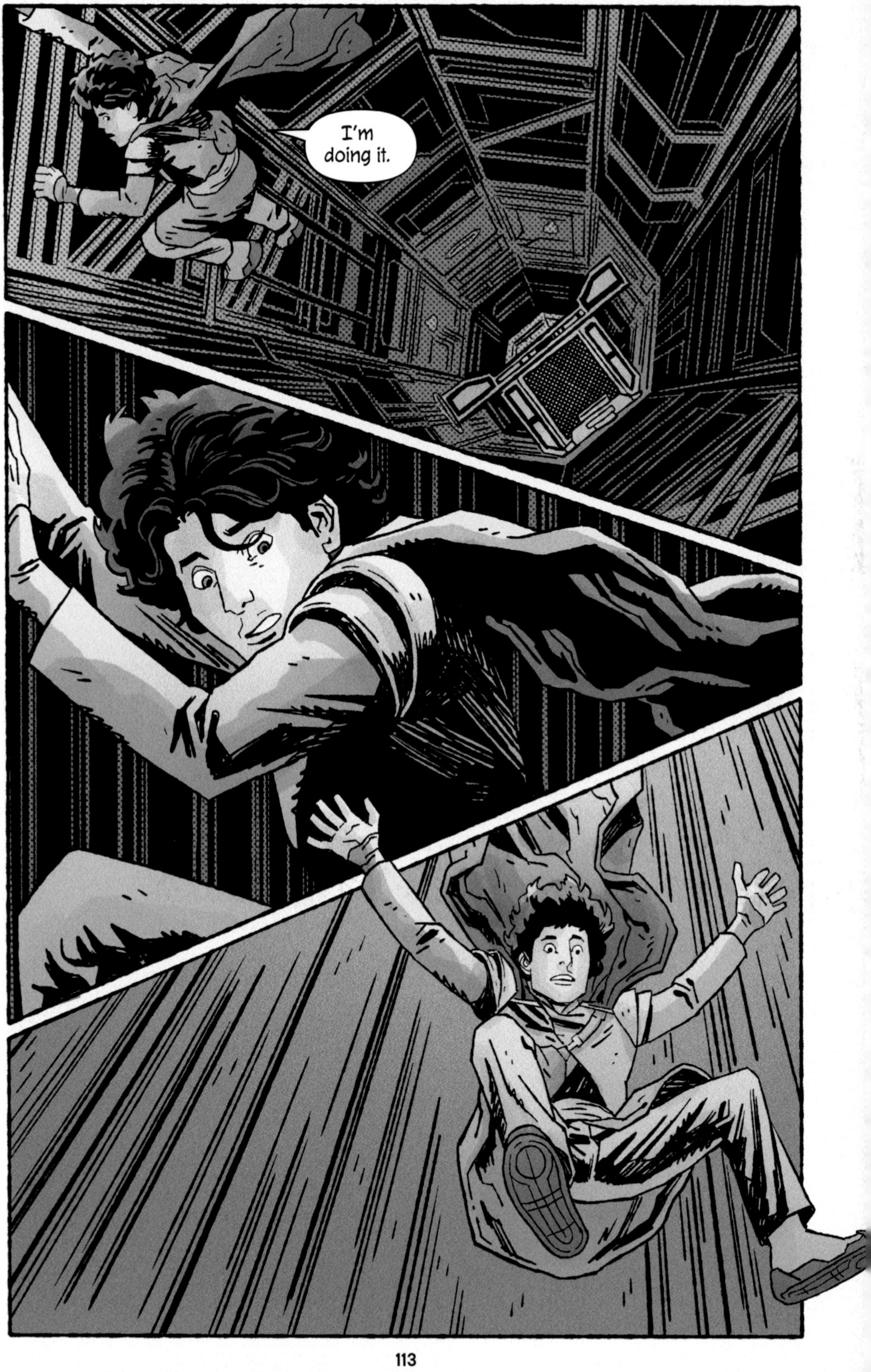
I'm doing it.

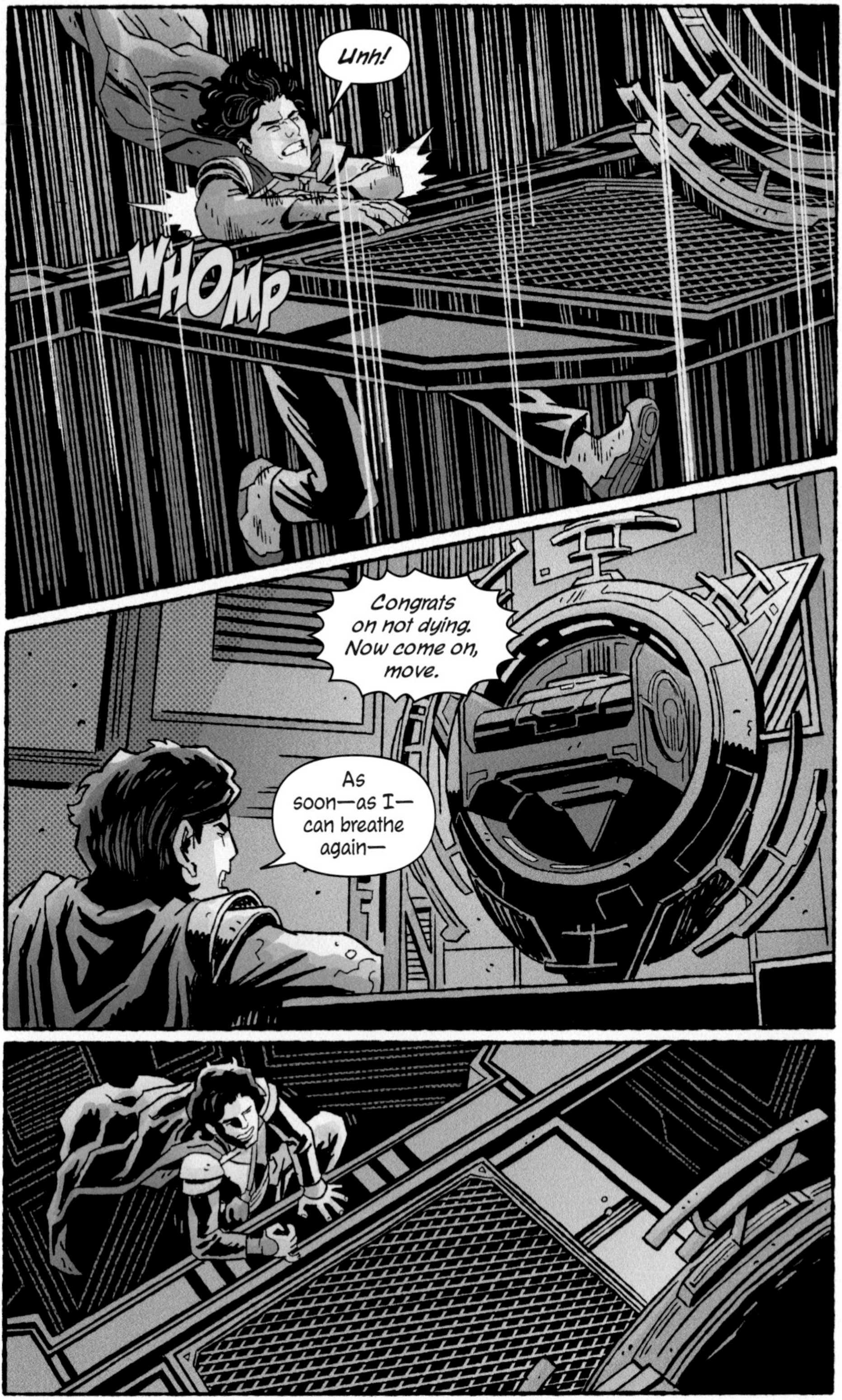
Unh!
WHOMP
Congrats on not dying. Now come on, move.
As soon—as I—can breathe again—

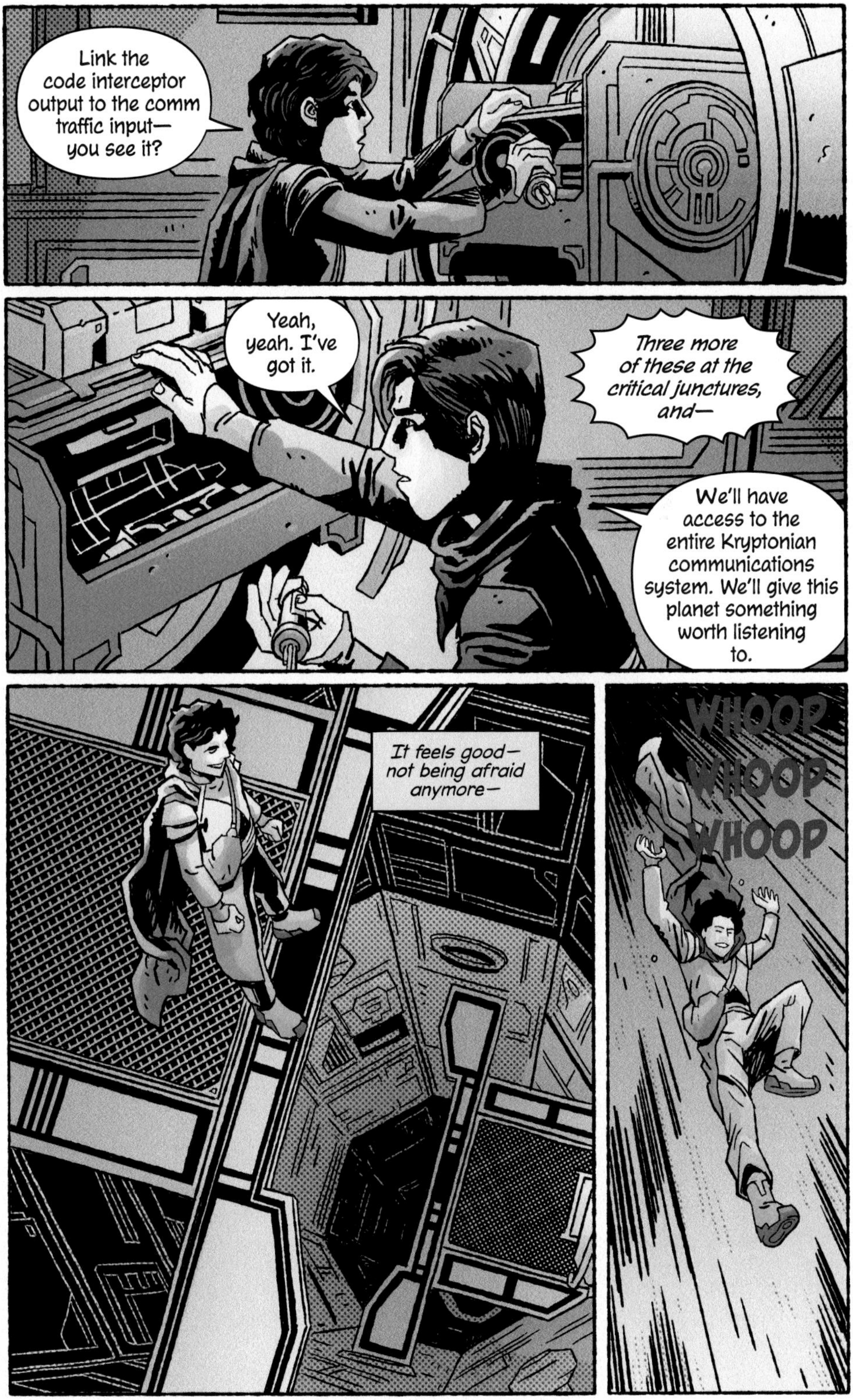
Link the code interceptor output to the comm traffic input— you see it?
Yeah, yeah. I've got it.
Three more of these at the critical junctures, and—
We'll have access to the entire Kryptonian communications system. We'll give this planet something worth listening to.
It feels good— not being afraid anymore—
WHOOP
WHOOP
WHOOP

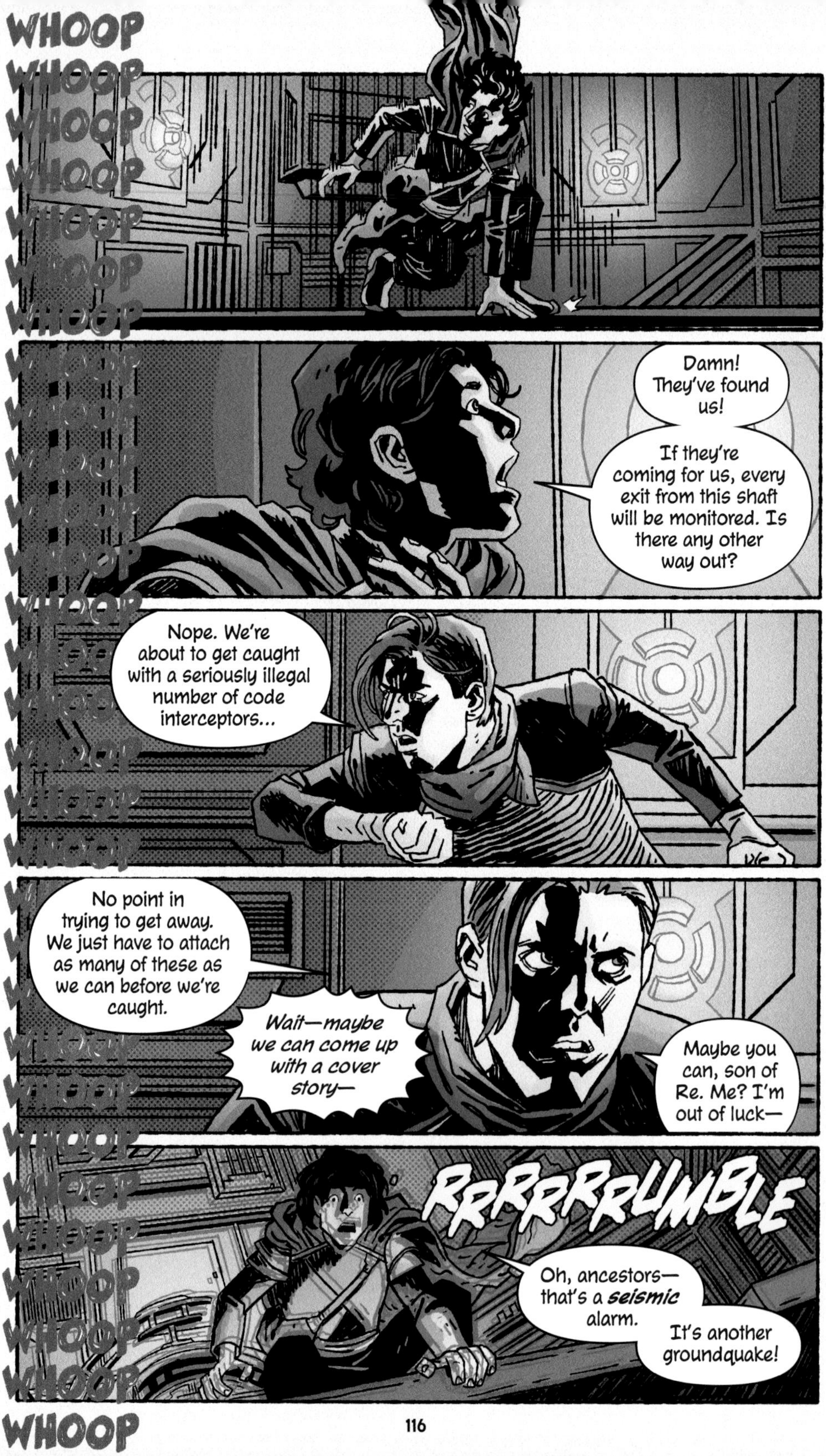
WHOOP
Damn! They've found us!
If they're coming for us, every exit from this shaft will be monitored. Is there any other way out?
Nope. We're about to get caught with a seriously illegal number of code interceptors...
No point in trying to get away. We just have to attach as many of these as we can before we're caught.
Wait—maybe we can come up with a cover story—
Maybe you can, son of Re. Me? I'm out of luck—
RRRRRRUMBLE
Oh, ancestors—that's a *seismic* alarm.
It's another groundquake!
WHOOP

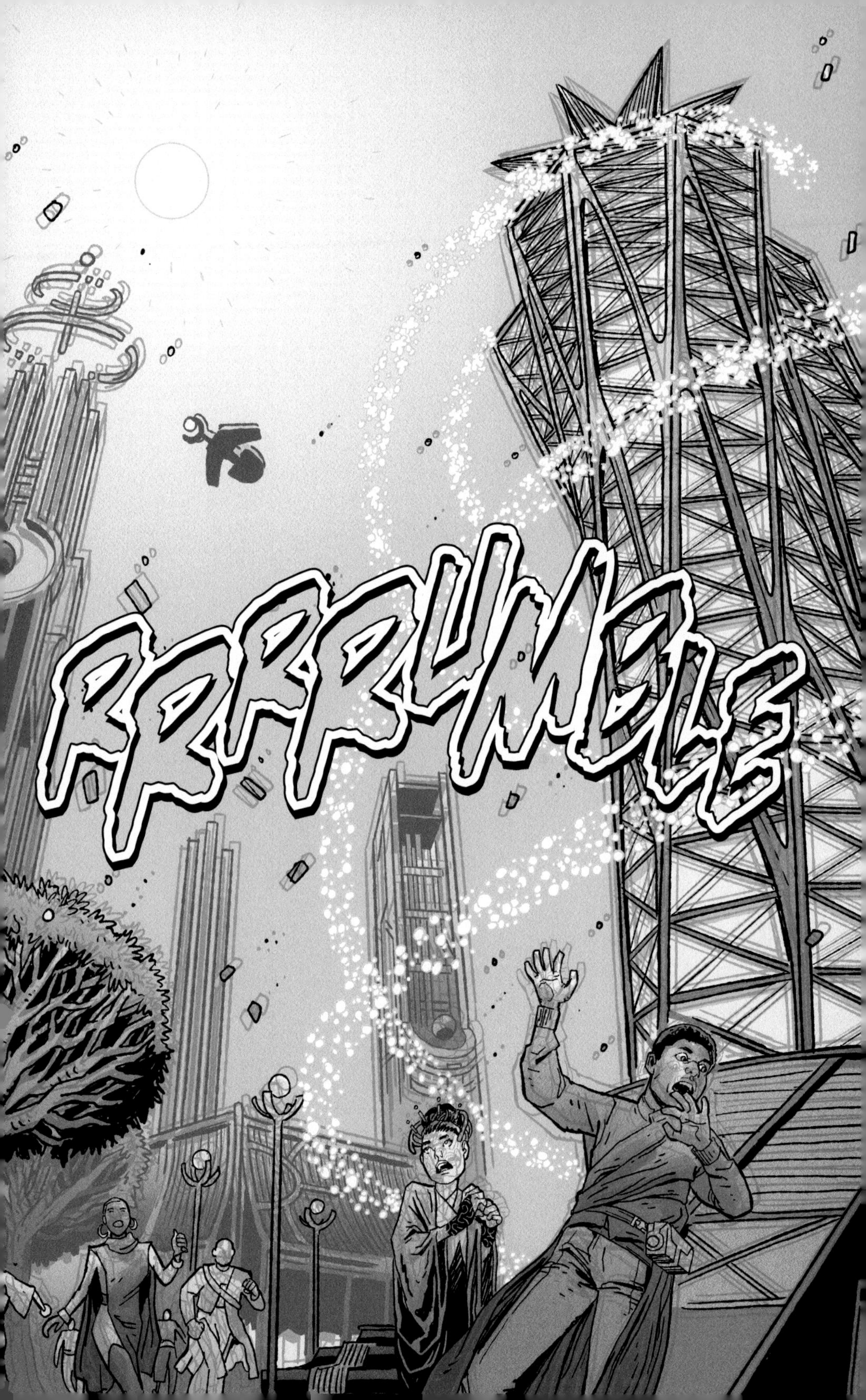
RRRRUMBLE

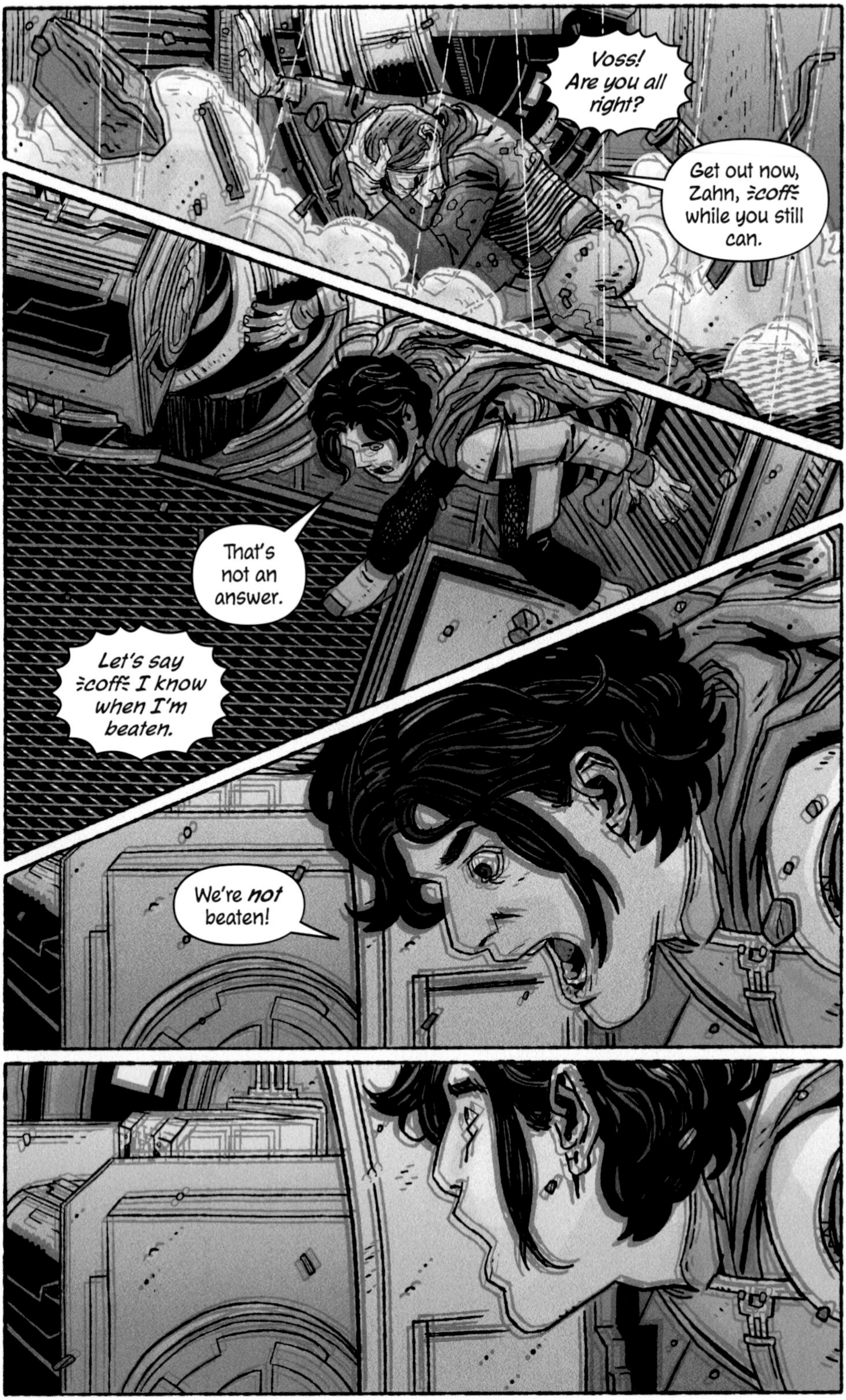
Voss! Are you all right?
Get out now, Zahn, ≈coff≈ while you still can.
That's not an answer.
Let's say ≈coff≈ I know when I'm beaten.
We're *not* beaten!

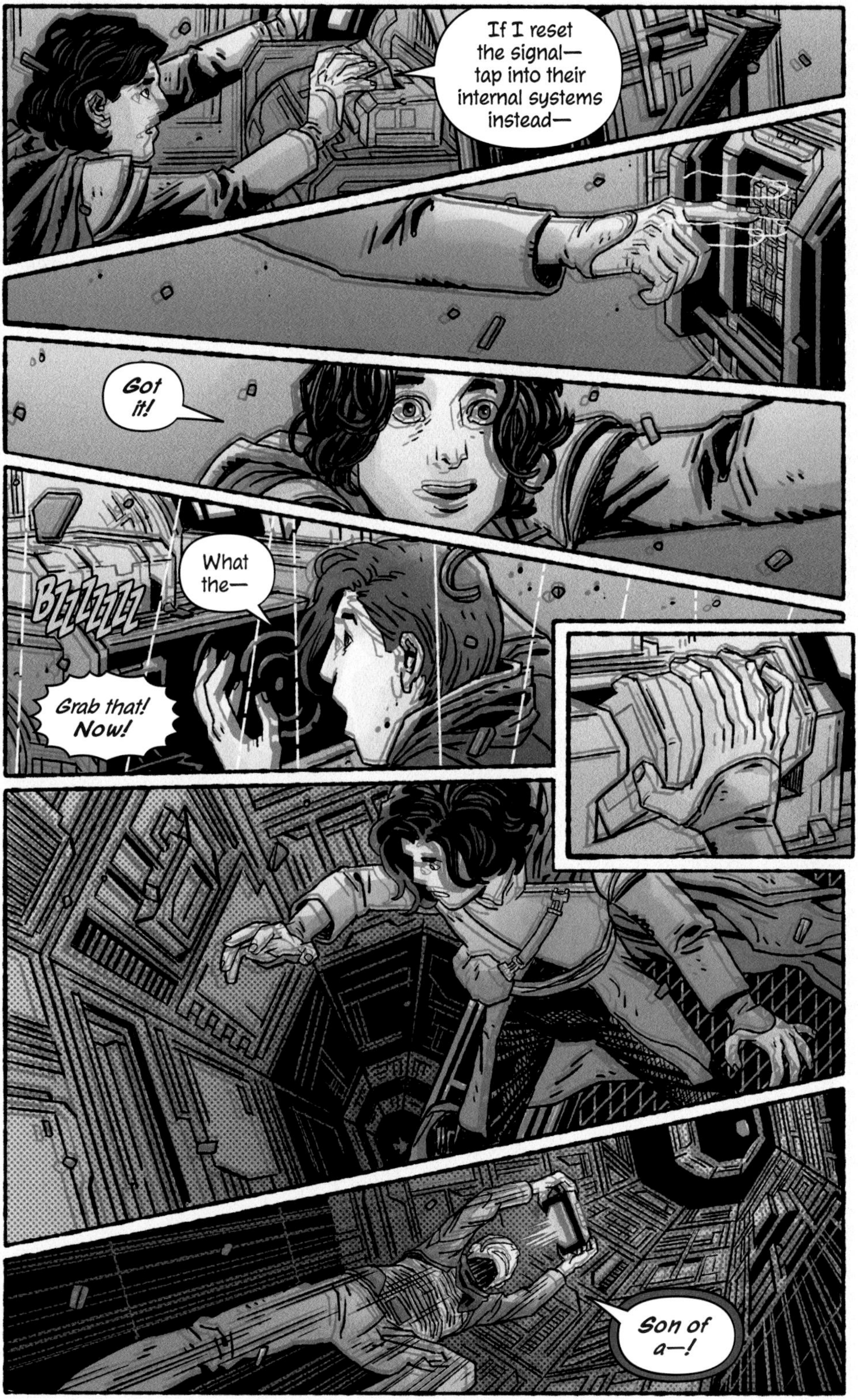
If I reset the signal— tap into their internal systems instead—
Got it!
BZZZZZZ
What the—
Grab that! Now!
Son of a—!

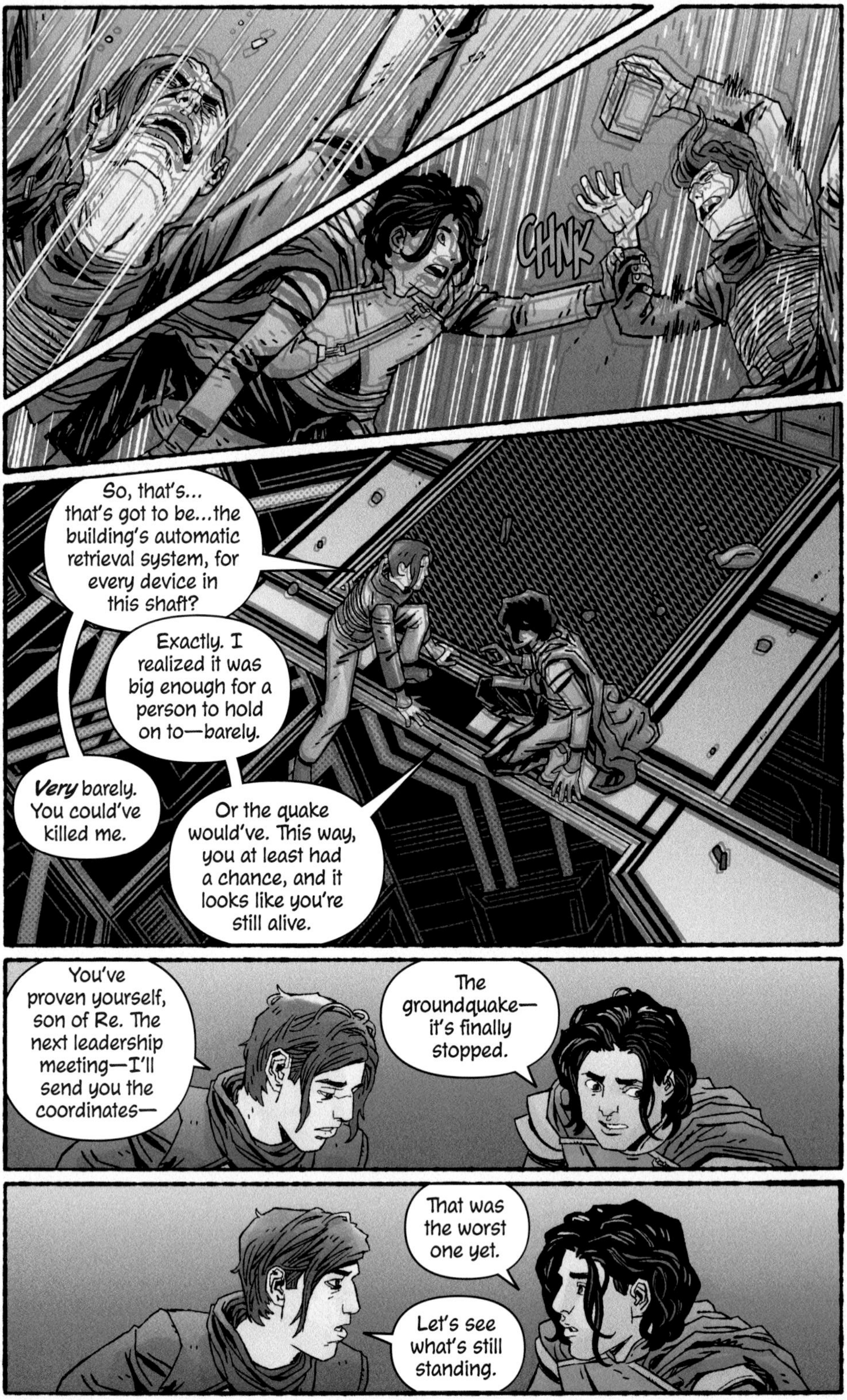
CHNK
So, that's... that's got to be...the building's automatic retrieval system, for every device in this shaft?
Exactly. I realized it was big enough for a person to hold on to—barely.
Very barely. You could've killed me.
Or the quake would've. This way, you at least had a chance, and it looks like you're still alive.
You've proven yourself, son of Re. The next leadership meeting—I'll send you the coordinates—
The groundquake—it's finally stopped.
That was the worst one yet.
Let's see what's still standing.

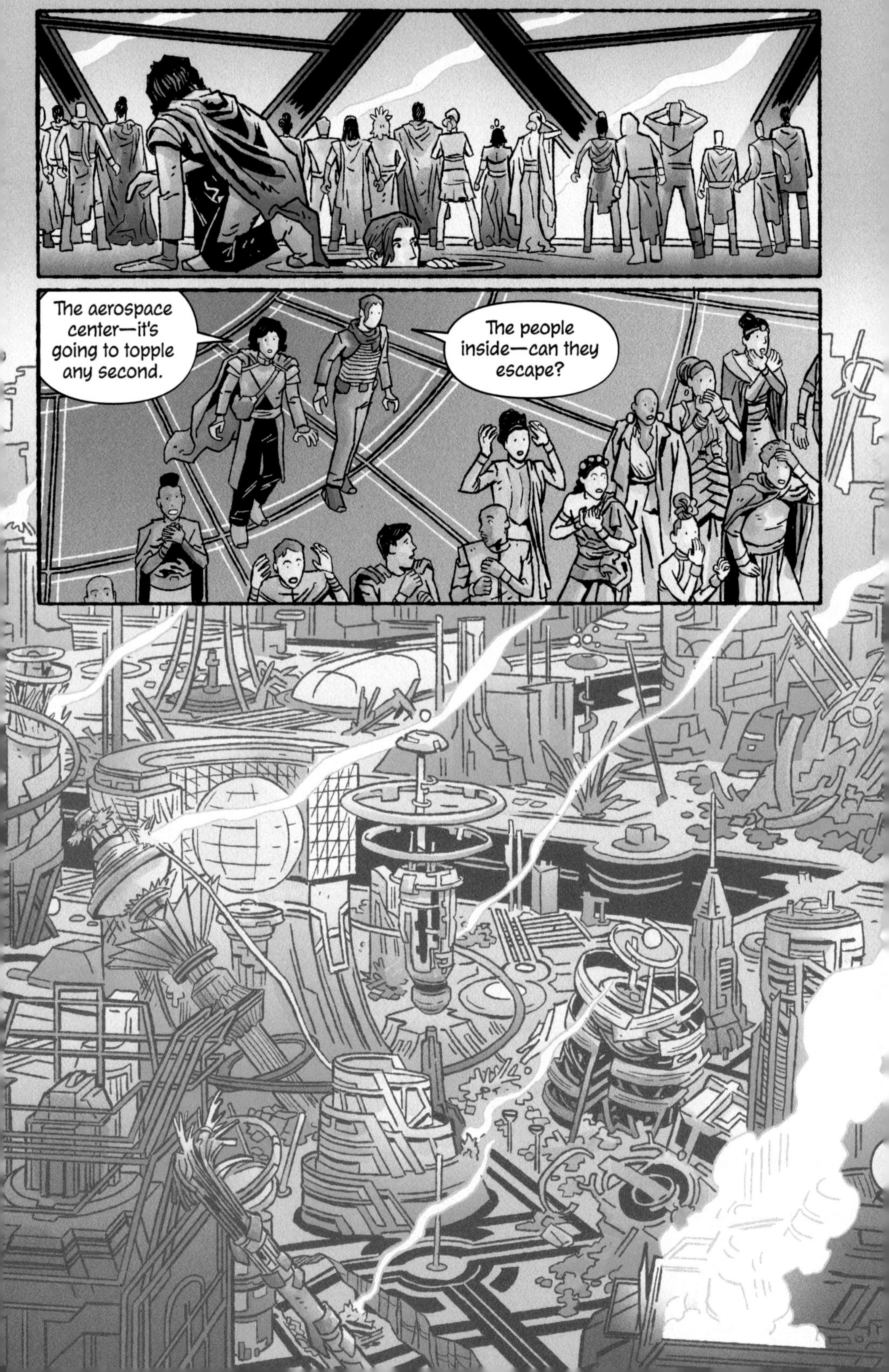
The aerospace center—it's going to topple any second.
The people inside—can they escape?

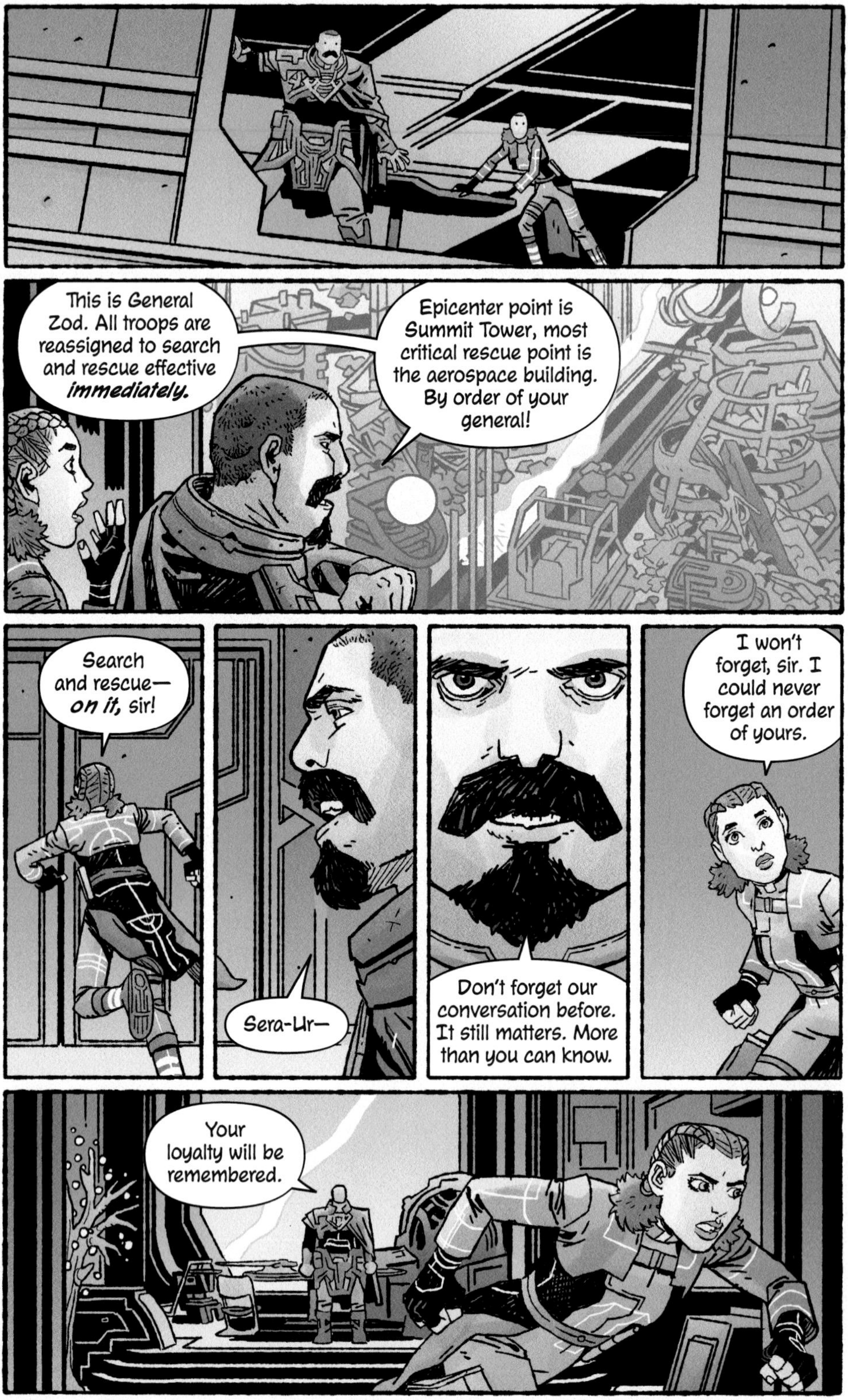
This is General Zod. All troops are reassigned to search and rescue effective *immediately.*
Epicenter point is Summit Tower, most critical rescue point is the aerospace building. By order of your general!
Search and rescue— *on it,* sir!
Sera-Ur—
Don't forget our conversation before. It still matters. More than you can know.
I won't forget, sir. I could never forget an order of yours.
Your loyalty will be remembered.

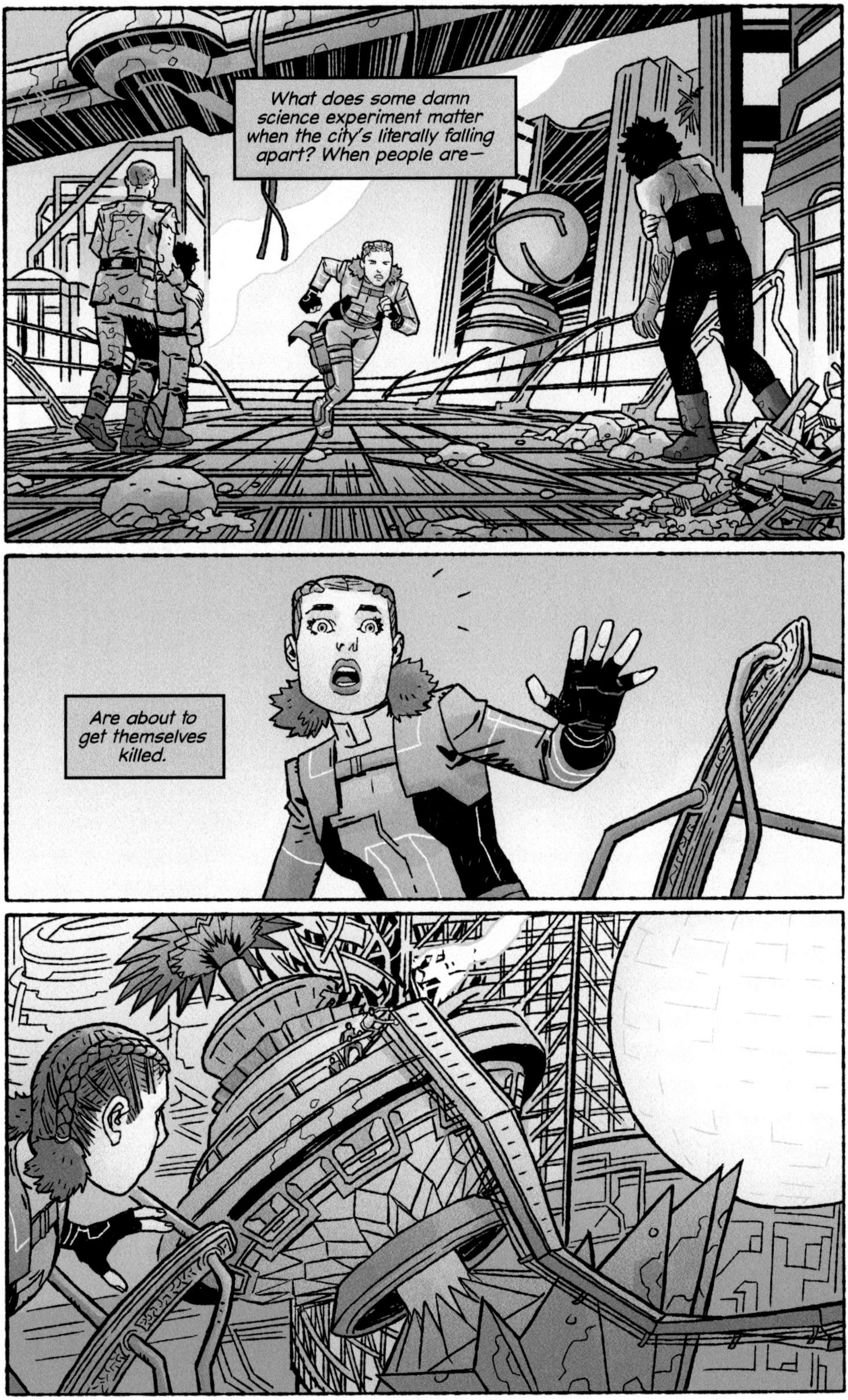
What does some damn science experiment matter when the city's literally falling apart? When people are—
Are about to get themselves killed.

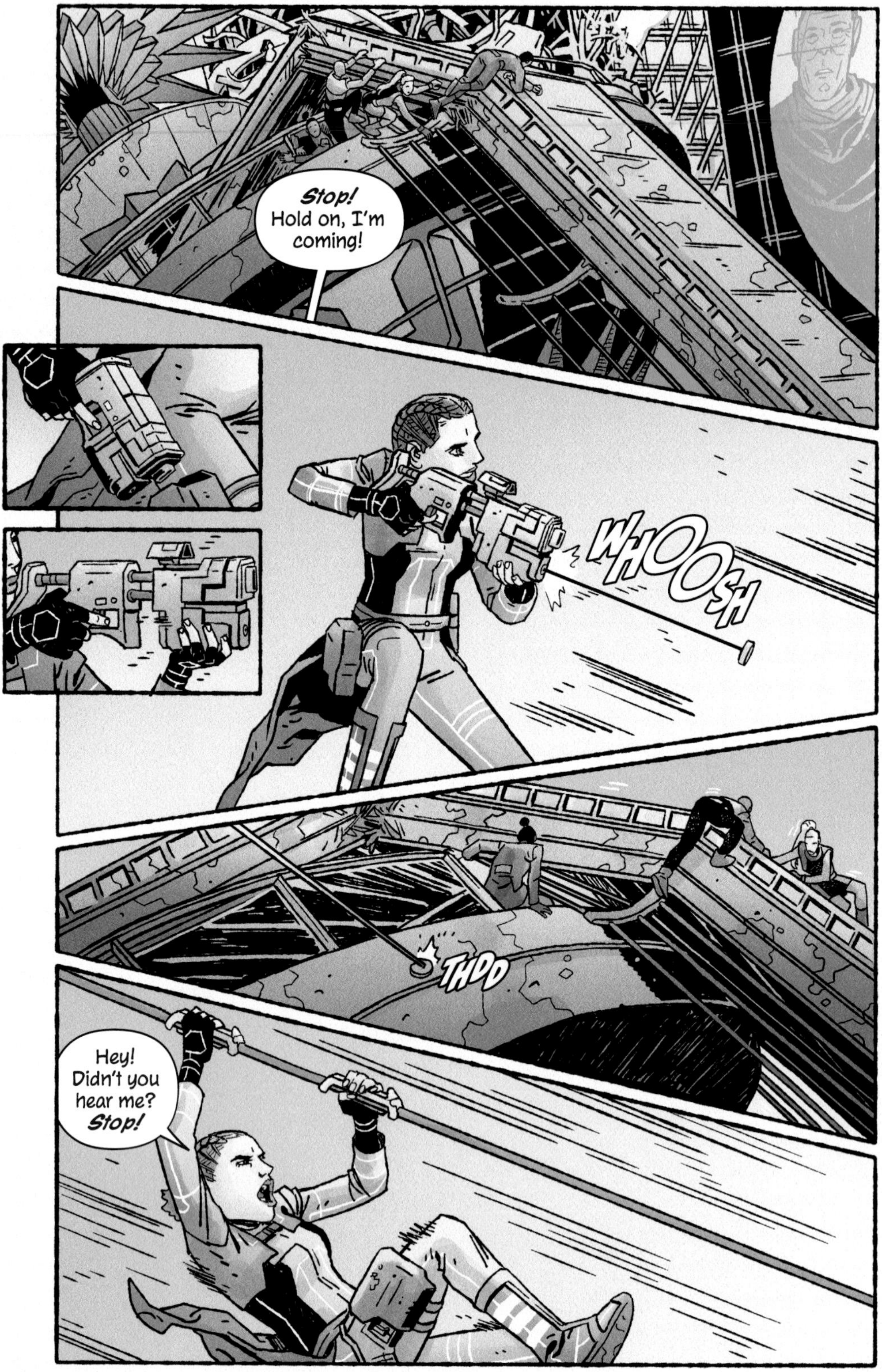
Stop!
Hold on, I'm coming!
WHOOSH
THDD
Hey! Didn't you hear me? Stop!

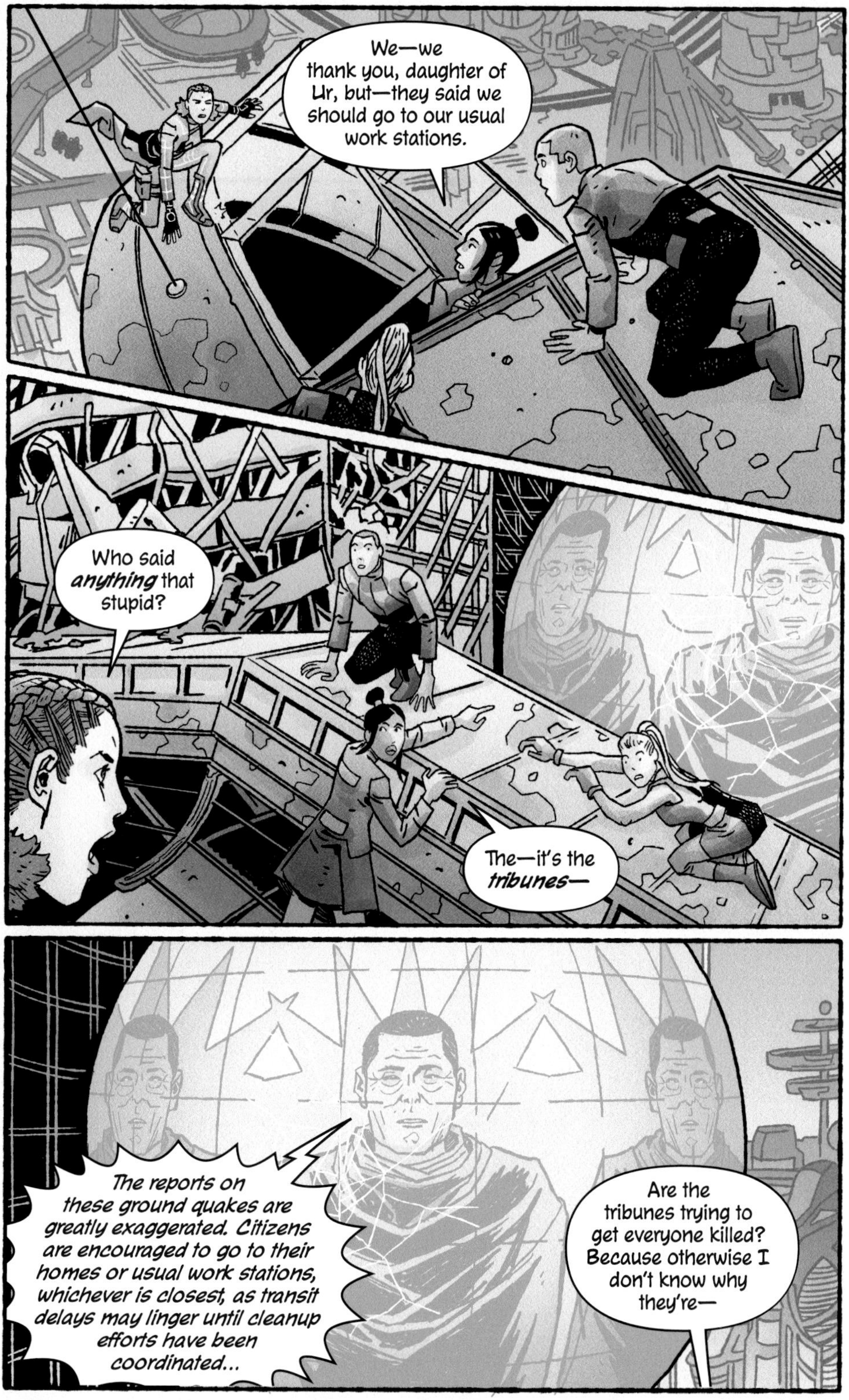
We—we thank you, daughter of Ur, but—they said we should go to our usual work stations.
Who said *anything* that stupid?
The—it's the *tribunes*—
The reports on these ground quakes are greatly exaggerated. Citizens are encouraged to go to their homes or usual work stations, whichever is closest, as transit delays may linger until cleanup efforts have been coordinated...
Are the tribunes trying to get everyone killed? Because otherwise I don't know why they're—

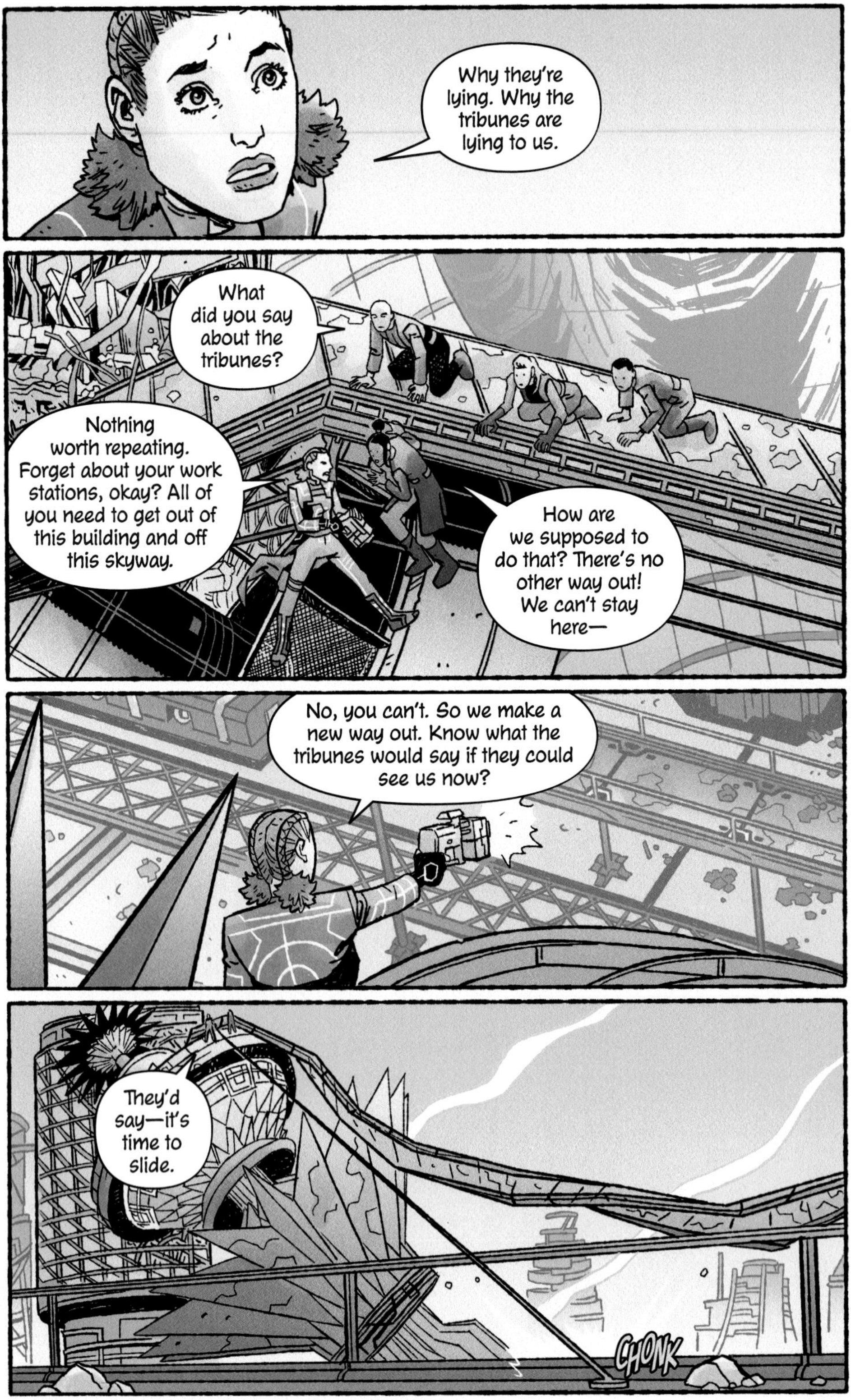
Why they're lying. Why the tribunes are lying to us.
What did you say about the tribunes?
Nothing worth repeating. Forget about your work stations, okay? All of you need to get out of this building and off this skyway.
How are we supposed to do that? There's no other way out! We can't stay here—
No, you can't. So we make a new way out. Know what the tribunes would say if they could see us now?
They'd say—it's time to slide.
CHONK

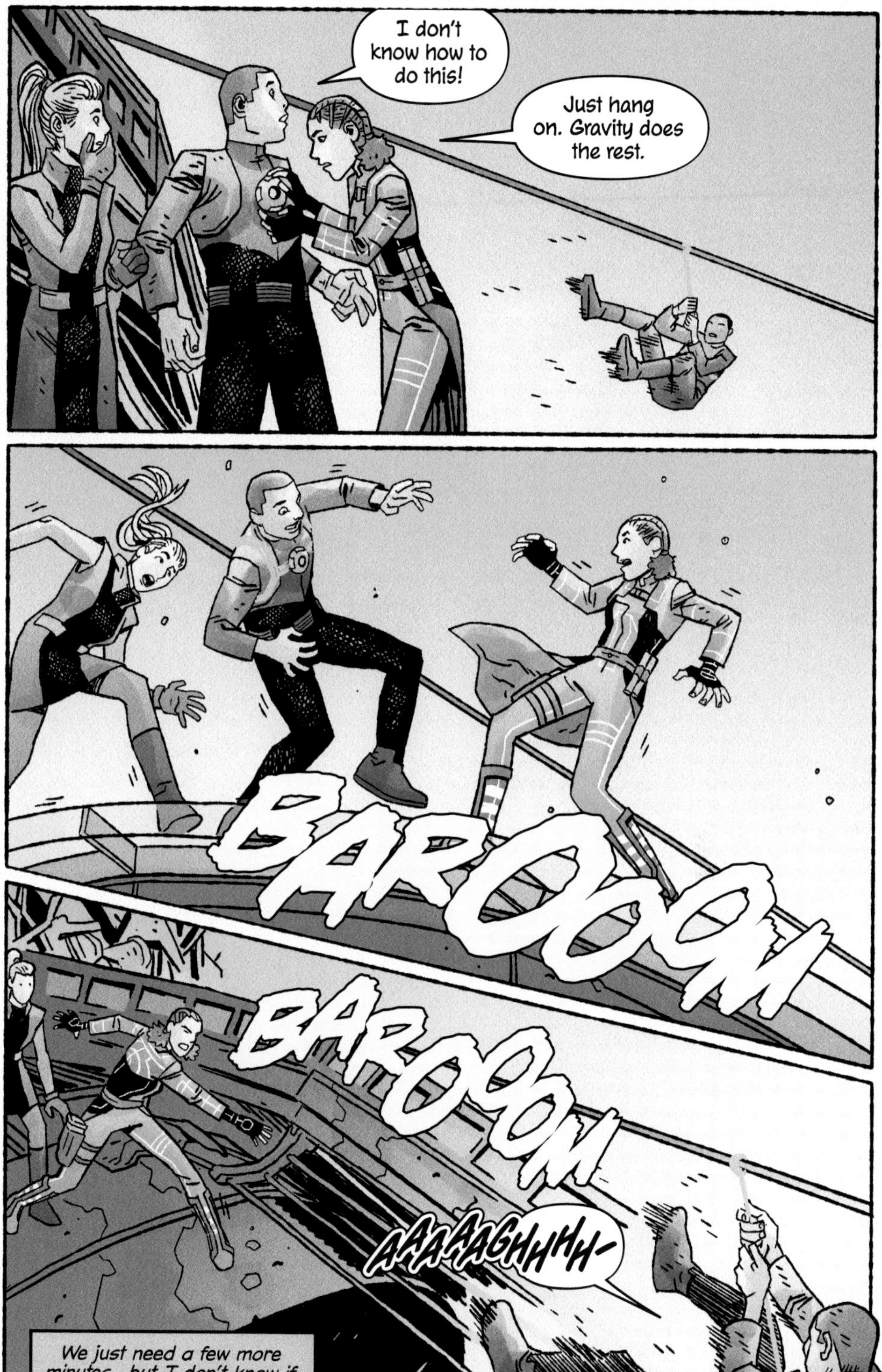
I don't know how to do this!
Just hang on. Gravity does the rest.
BAROOOM
BAROOOM
AAAAAAGHHHHH-
We just need a few more minutes...but I don't know if we're going to get them...

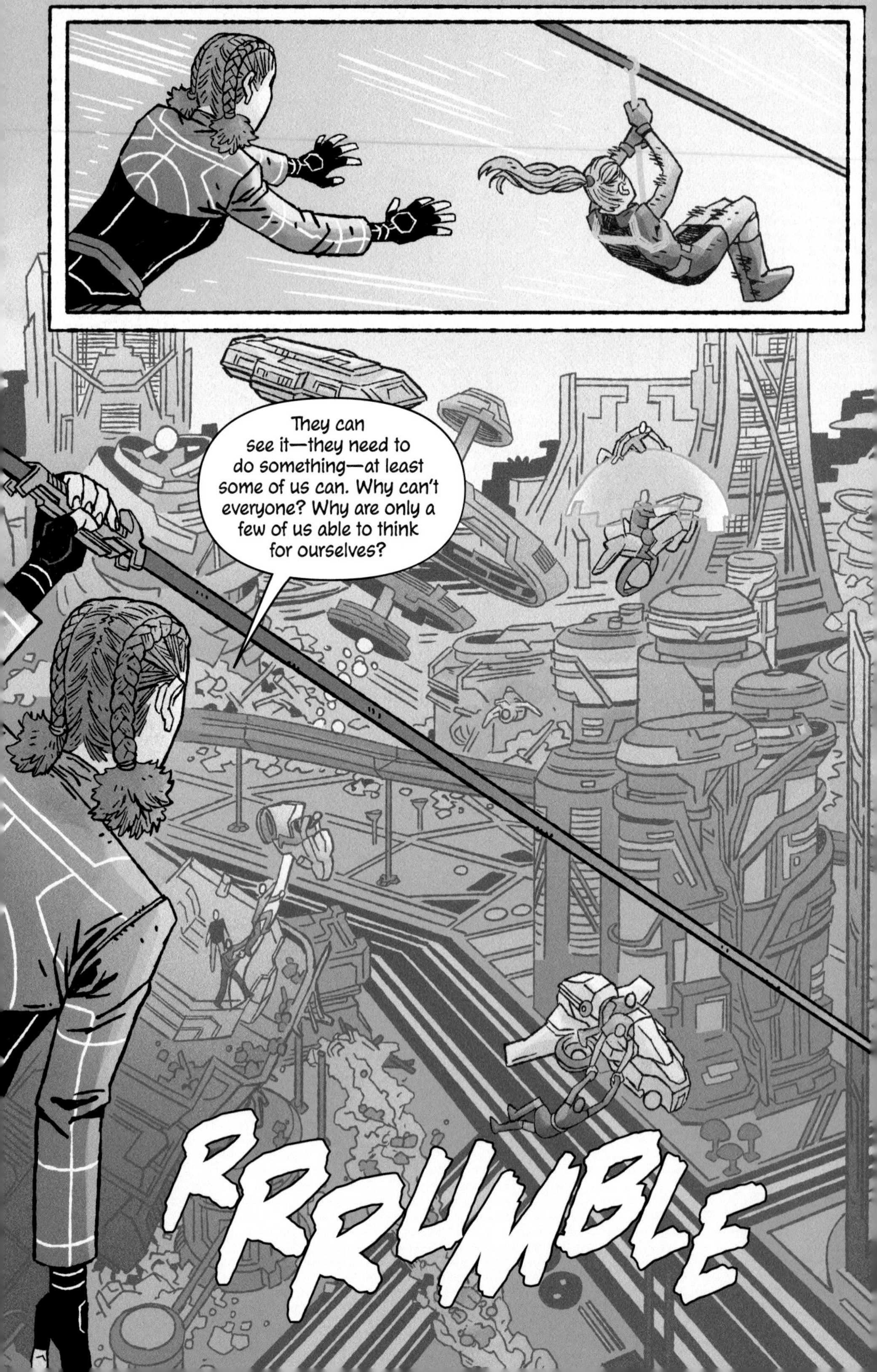
They can see it—they need to do something—at least some of us can. Why can't everyone? Why are only a few of us able to think for ourselves?
PRRRUMBLE

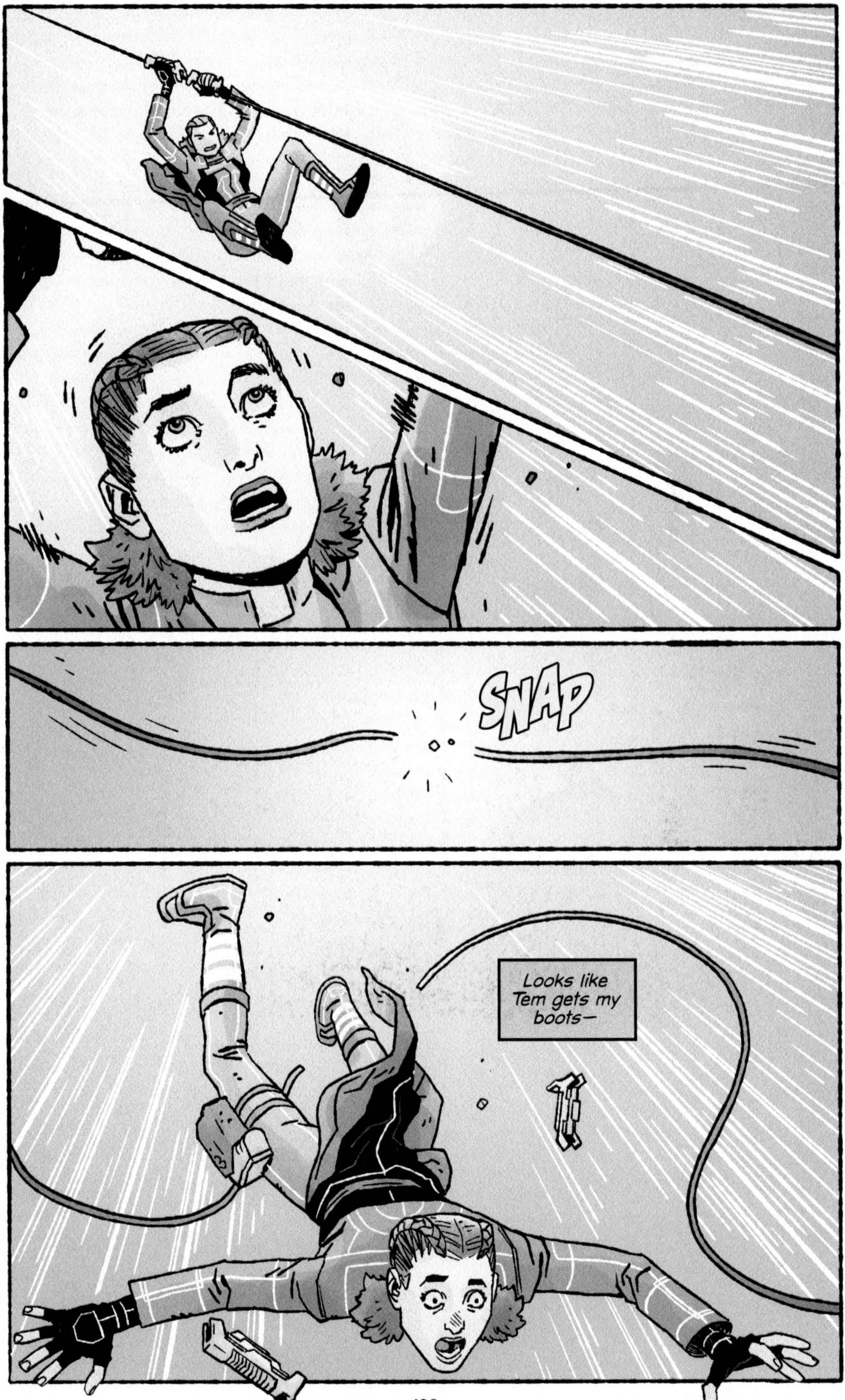
SNAP
Looks like Tem gets my boots—

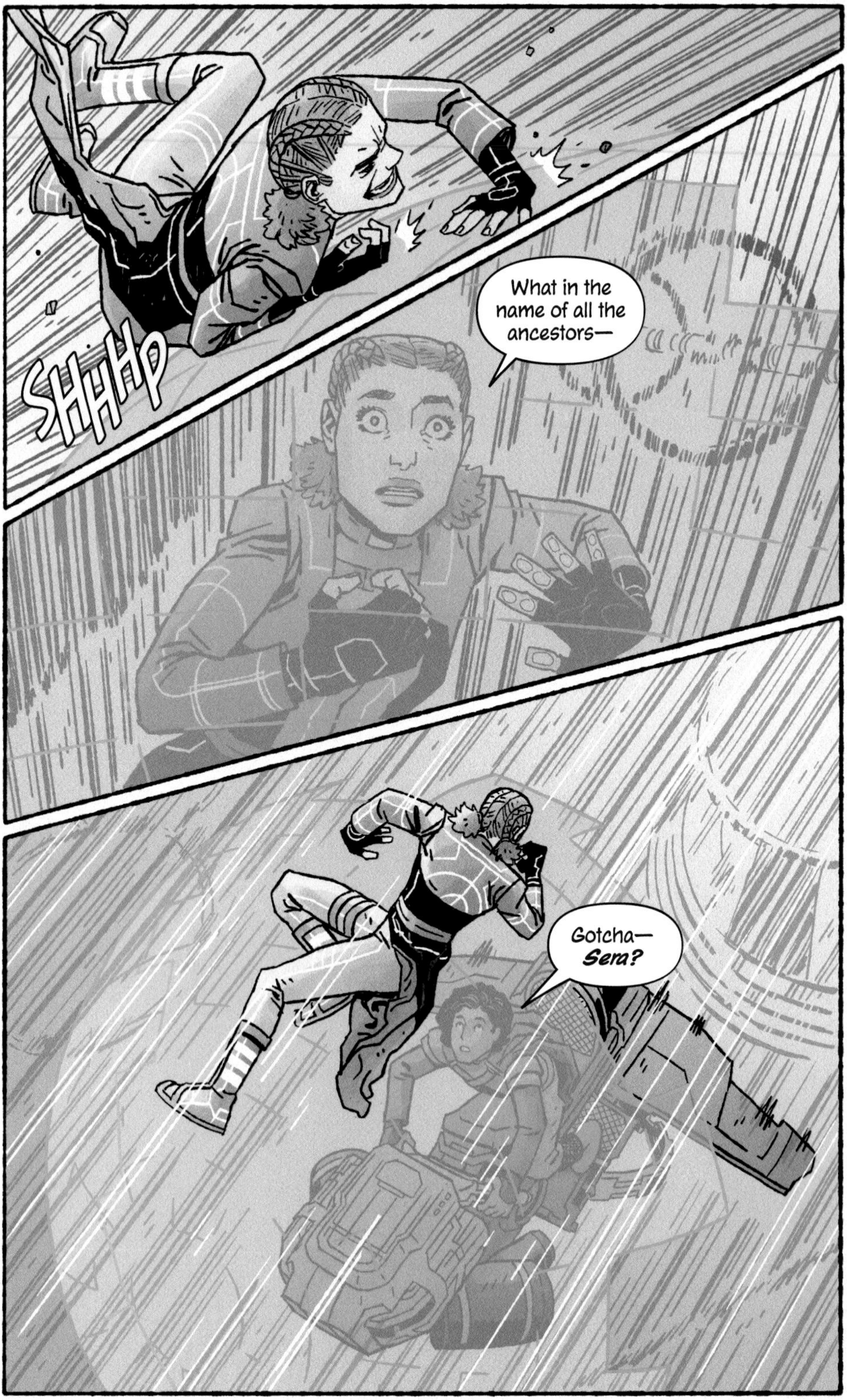
SHHHP
What in the name of all the ancestors—
Gotcha—
Sera?

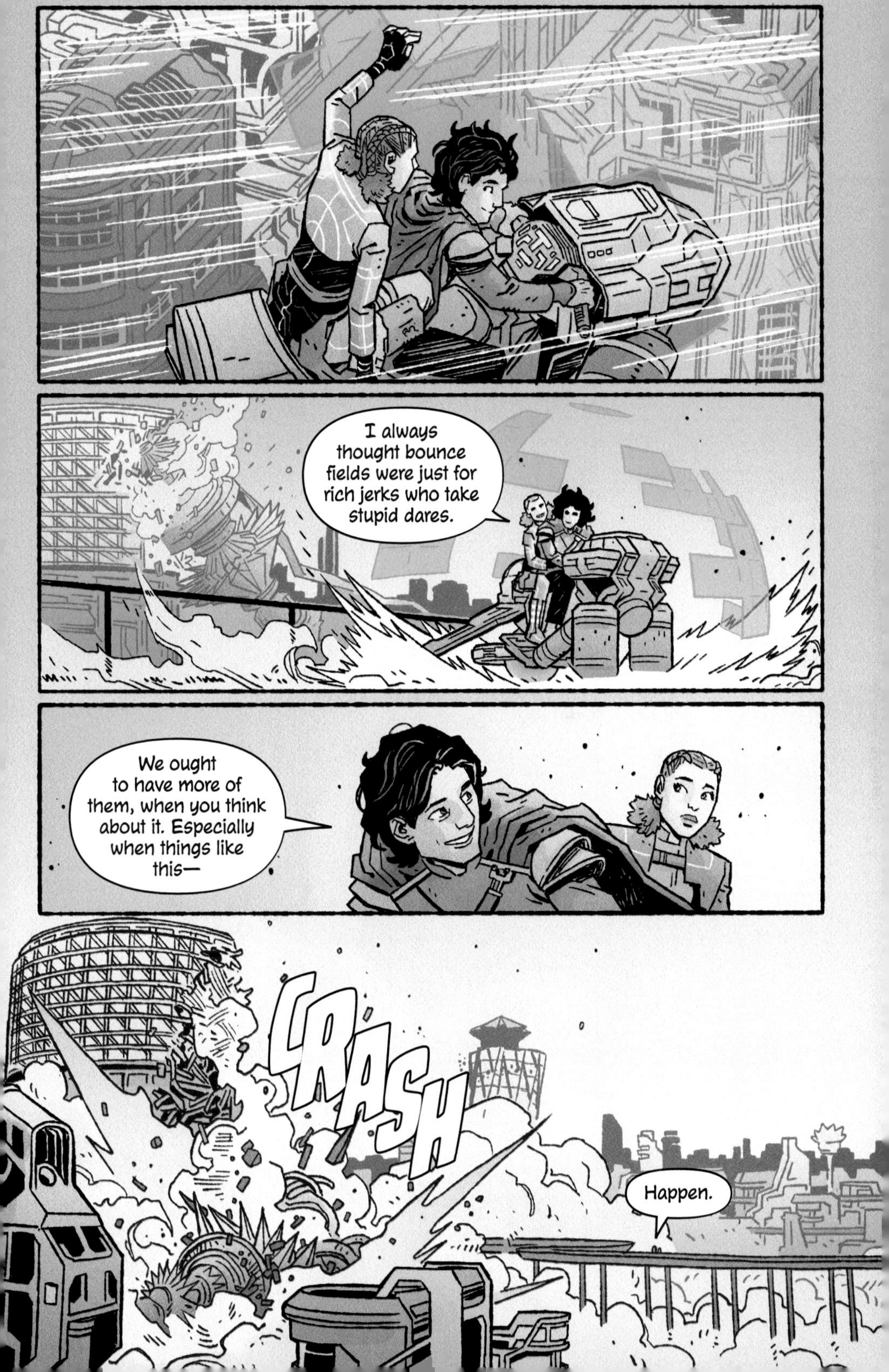
I always thought bounce fields were just for rich jerks who take stupid dares.
We ought to have more of them, when you think about it. Especially when things like this—
CRASH
Happen.

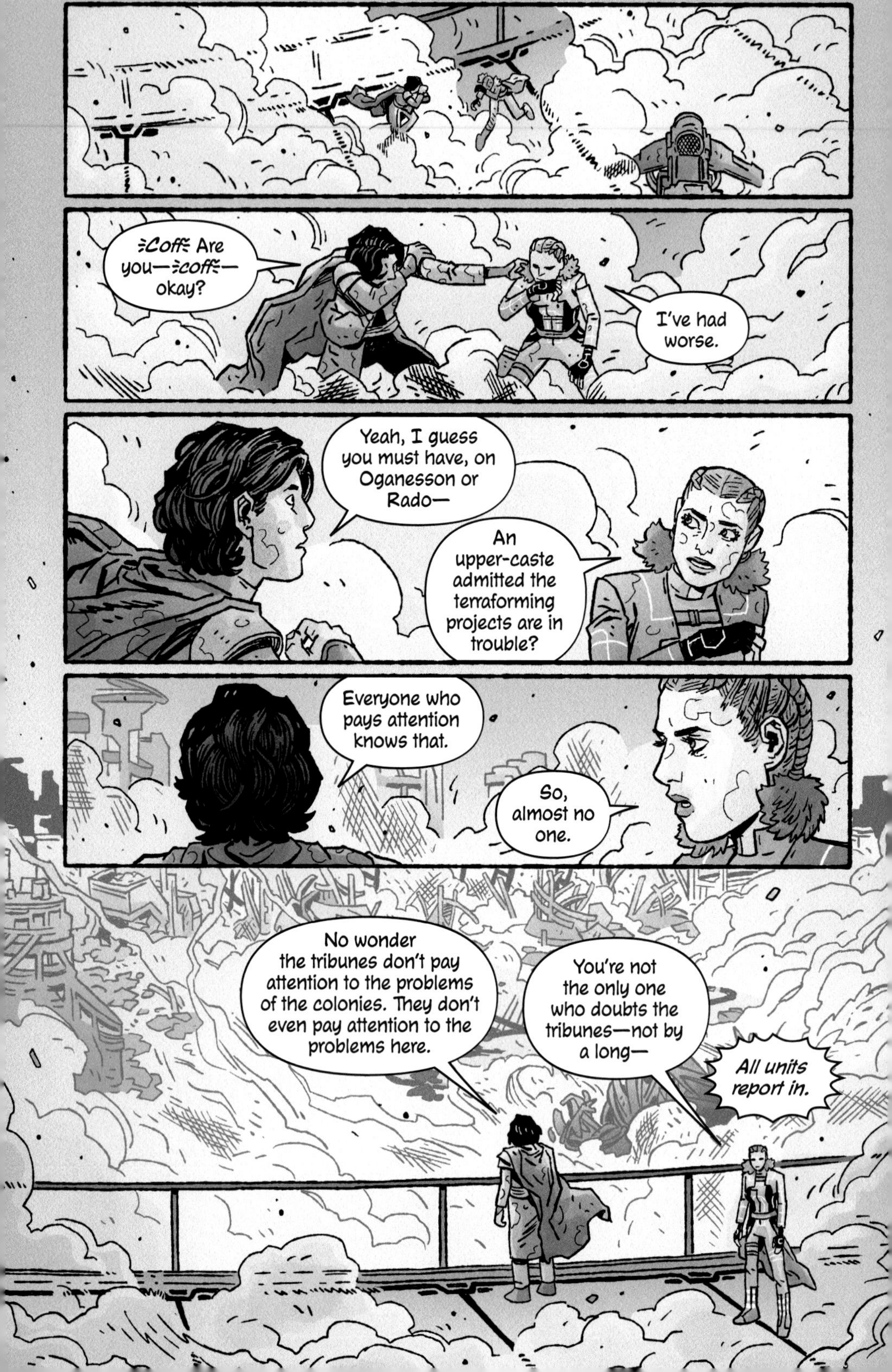

Coff Are you—*coff*—okay?
I've had worse.
Yeah, I guess you must have, on Oganesson or Rado—
An upper-caste admitted the terraforming projects are in trouble?
Everyone who pays attention knows that.
So, almost no one.
No wonder the tribunes don't pay attention to the problems of the colonies. They don't even pay attention to the problems here.
You're not the only one who doubts the tribunes—not by a long—
All units report in.

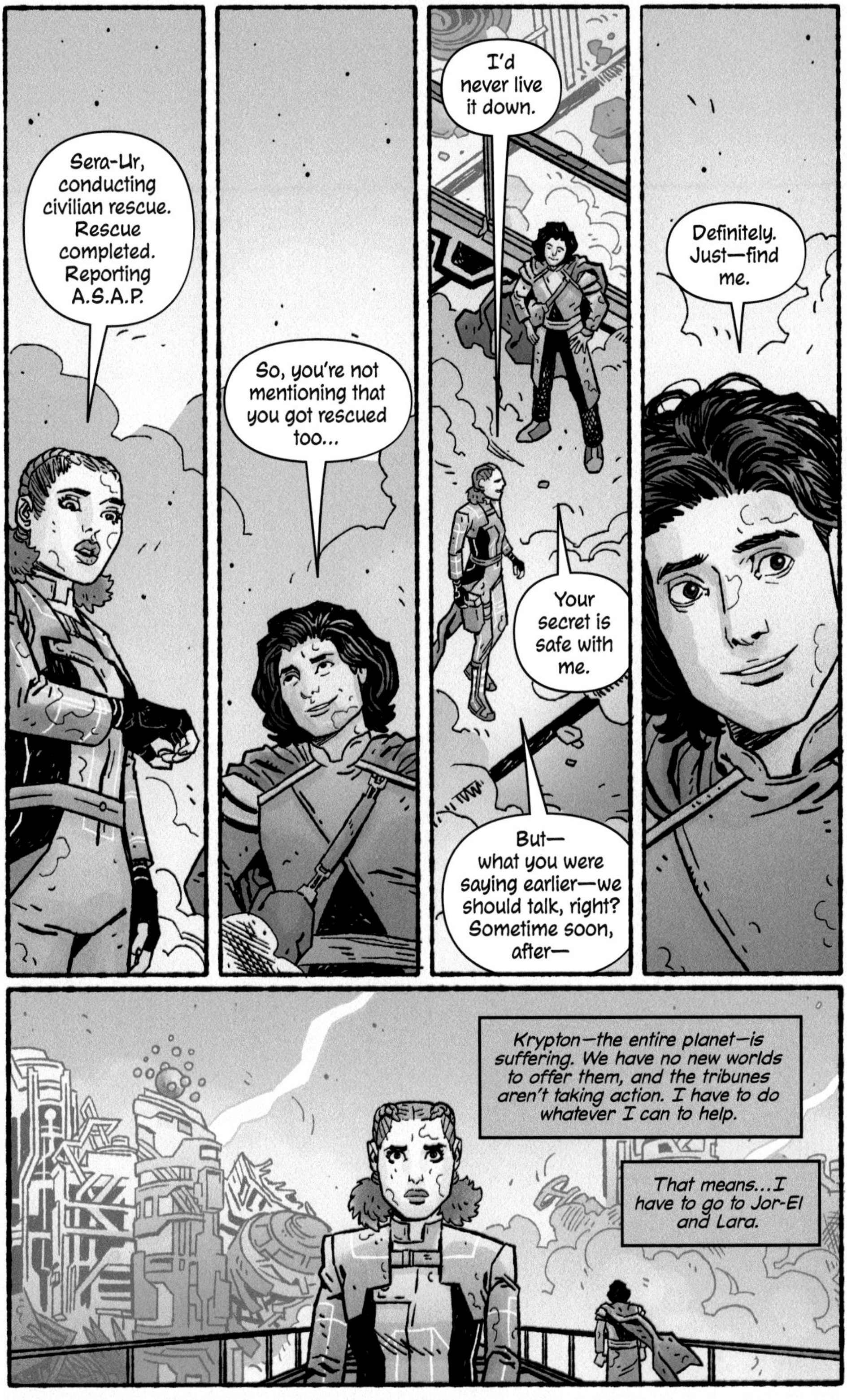

Sera-Ur, conducting civilian rescue. Rescue completed. Reporting A.S.A.P.
So, you're not mentioning that you got rescued too...
I'd never live it down.
Your secret is safe with me.
But—what you were saying earlier—we should talk, right? Sometime soon, after—
Definitely. Just—find me.
Krypton—the entire planet—is suffering. We have no new worlds to offer them, and the tribunes aren't taking action. I have to do whatever I can to help.
That means...I have to go to Jor-El and Lara.

CHAPTER THREE

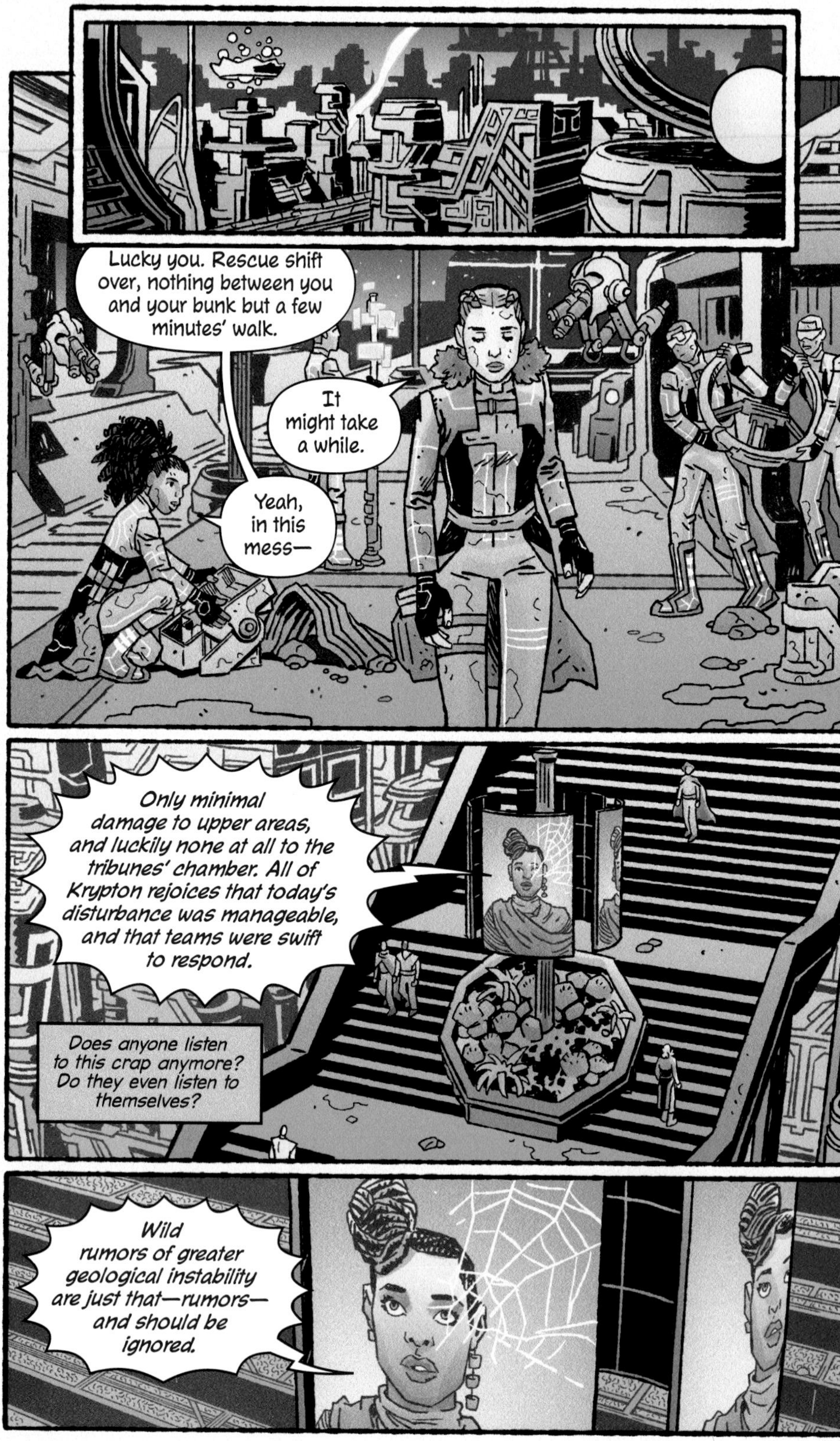

Lucky you. Rescue shift over, nothing between you and your bunk but a few minutes' walk.
It might take a while.
Yeah, in this mess—
Only minimal damage to upper areas, and luckily none at all to the tribunes' chamber. All of Krypton rejoices that today's disturbance was manageable, and that teams were swift to respond.
Does anyone listen to this crap anymore? Do they even listen to themselves?
Wild rumors of greater geological instability are just that—rumors—and should be ignored.

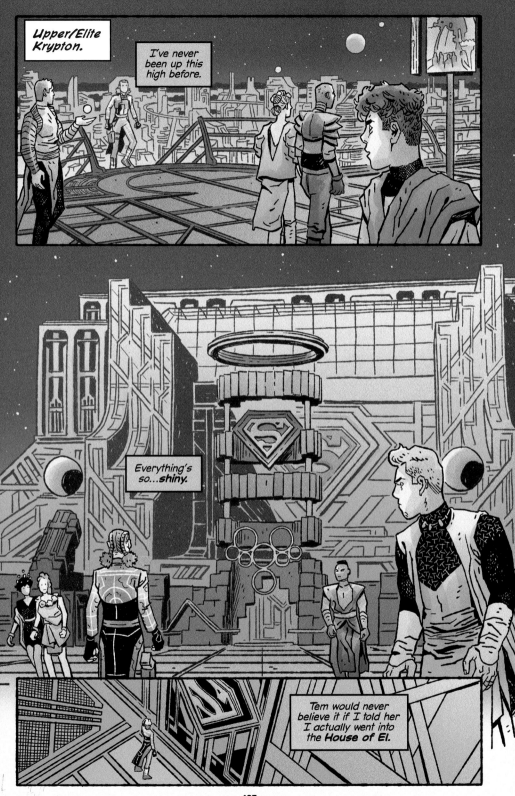

Upper/Elite Krypton.

I've never been up this high before.

Everything's so...*shiny.*

Tem would never believe it if I told her I actually went into the *House of El.*

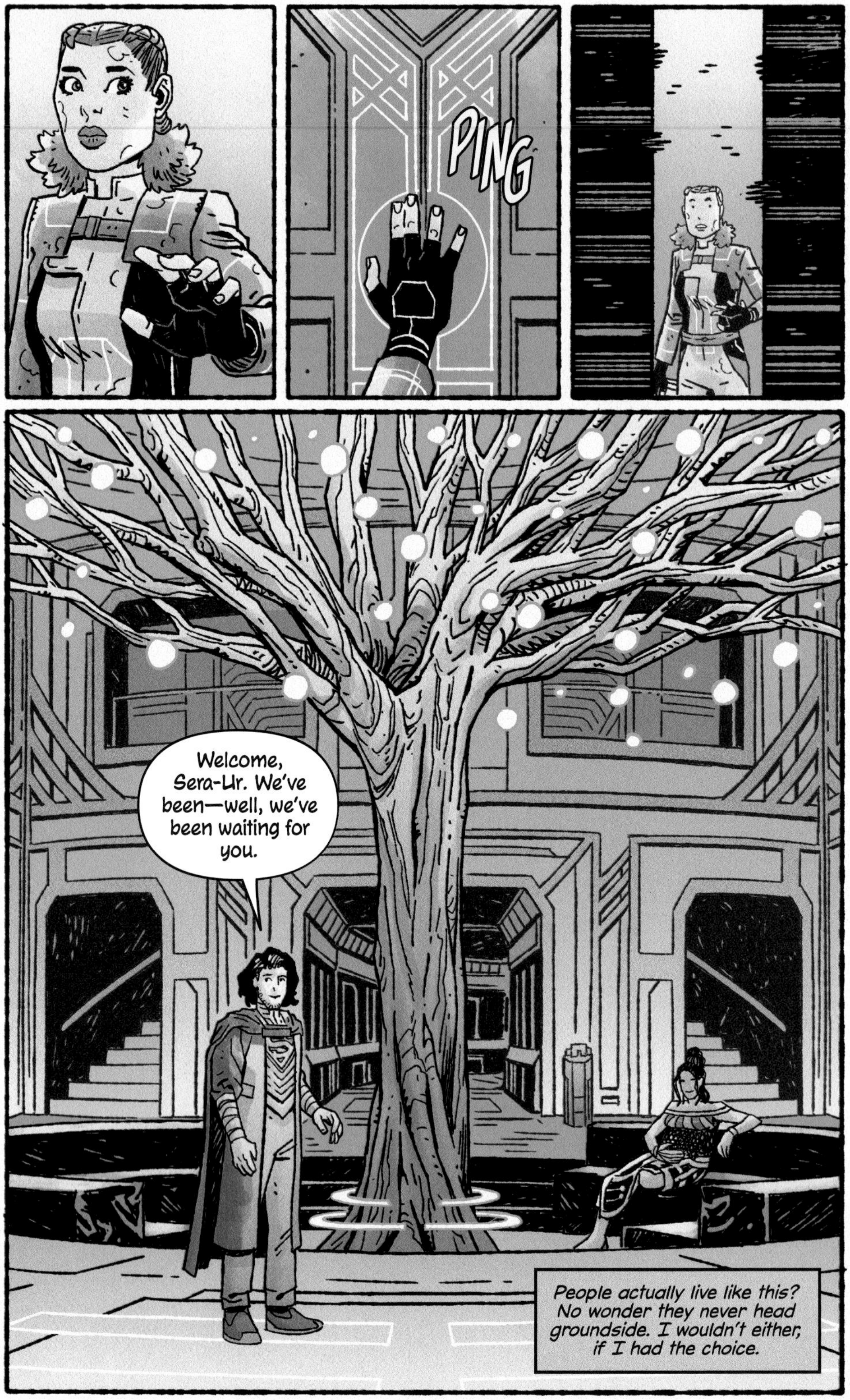
PING
Welcome, Sera-Ur. We've been—well, we've been waiting for you.
People actually live like this? No wonder they never head groundside. I wouldn't either, if I had the choice.

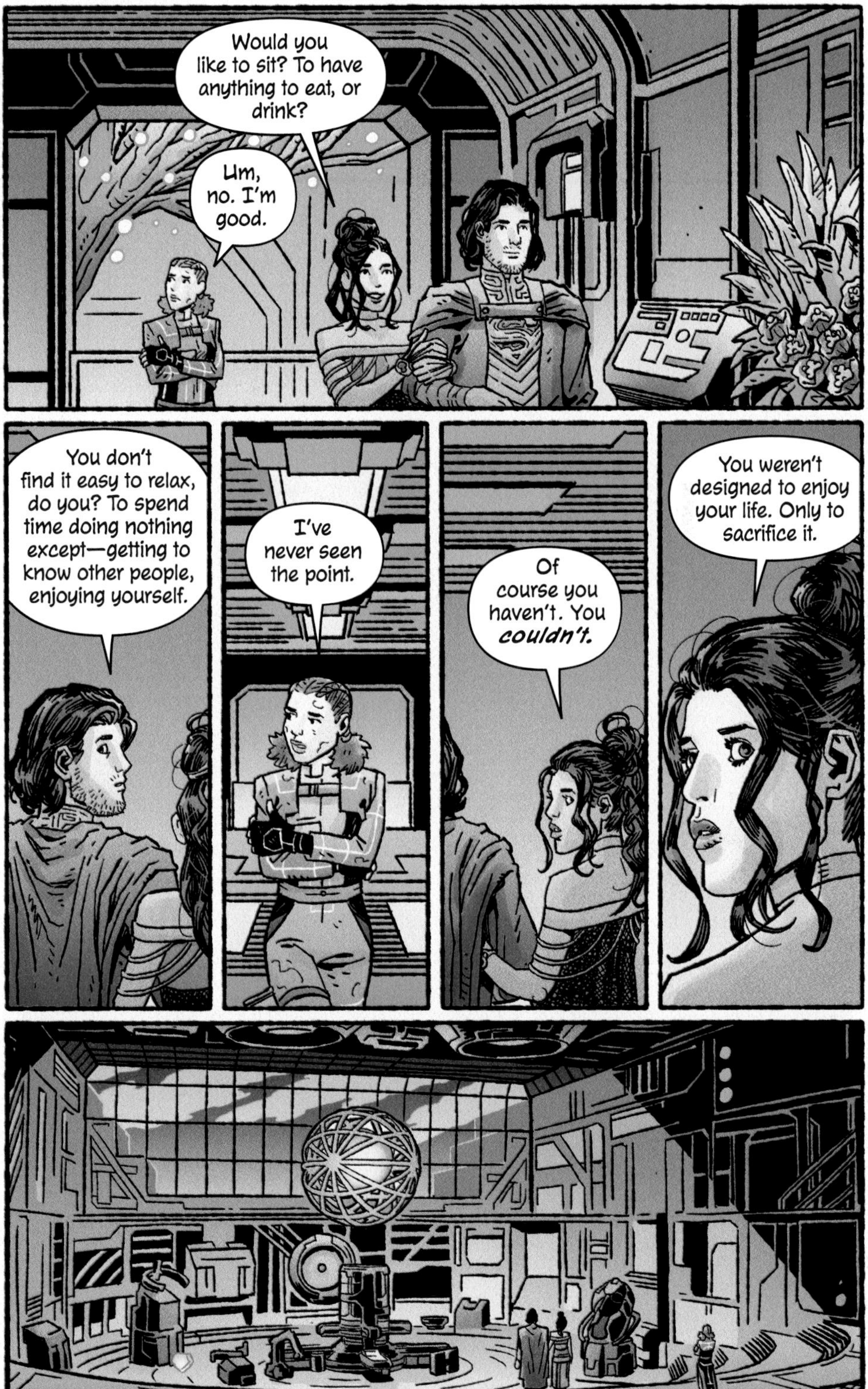
Would you like to sit? To have anything to eat, or drink?
Um, no. I'm good.
You don't find it easy to relax, do you? To spend time doing nothing except—getting to know other people, enjoying yourself.
I've never seen the point.
Of course you haven't. You *couldn't.*
You weren't designed to enjoy your life. Only to sacrifice it.

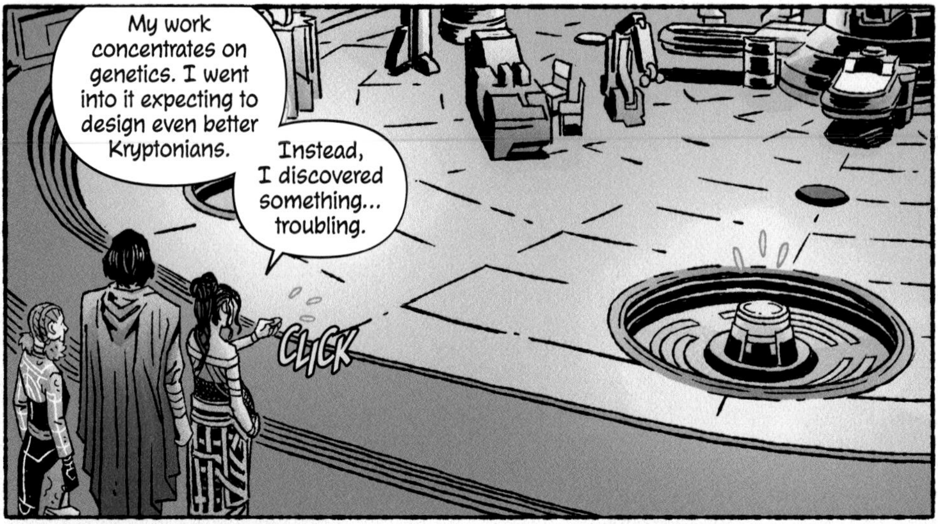
My work concentrates on genetics. I went into it expecting to design even better Kryptonians.
Instead, I discovered something... troubling.
CLICK

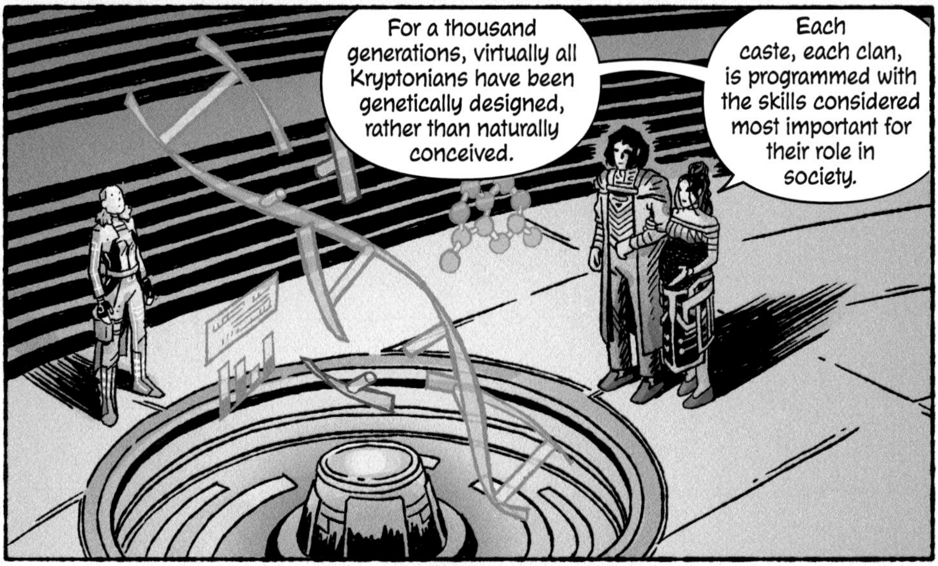
For a thousand generations, virtually all Kryptonians have been genetically designed, rather than naturally conceived.
Each caste, each clan, is programmed with the skills considered most important for their role in society.

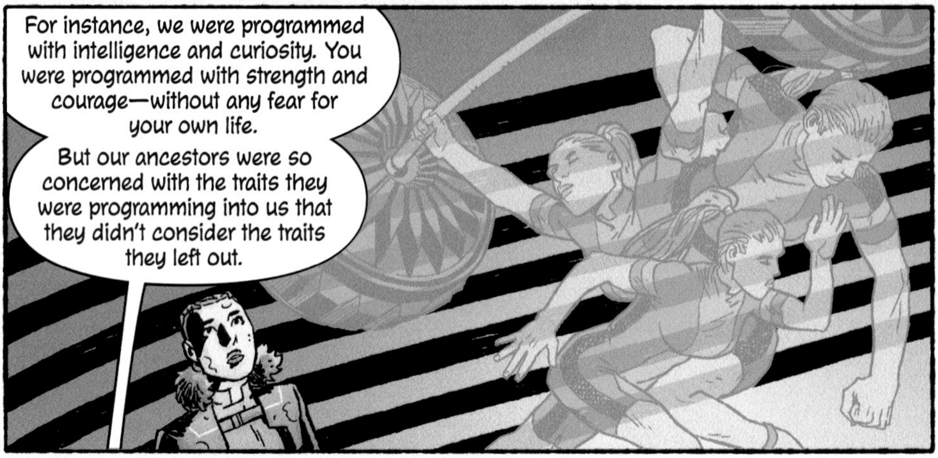
For instance, we were programmed with intelligence and curiosity. You were programmed with strength and courage—without any fear for your own life.
But our ancestors were so concerned with the traits they were programming into us that they didn't consider the traits they left out.

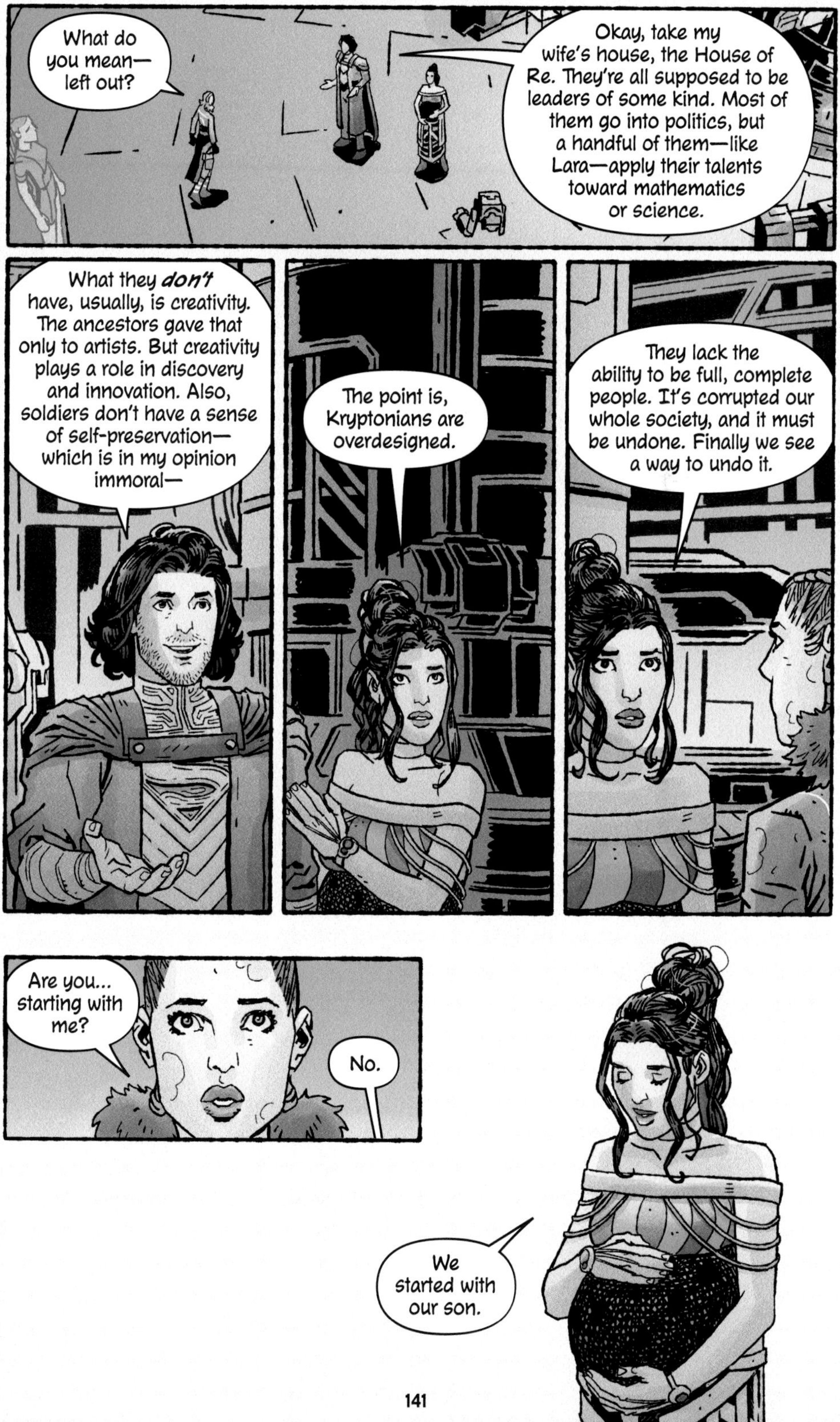
What do you mean—left out?
Okay, take my wife's house, the House of Re. They're all supposed to be leaders of some kind. Most of them go into politics, but a handful of them—like Lara—apply their talents toward mathematics or science.
What they *don't* have, usually, is creativity. The ancestors gave that only to artists. But creativity plays a role in discovery and innovation. Also, soldiers don't have a sense of self-preservation—which is in my opinion immoral—
The point is, Kryptonians are overdesigned.
They lack the ability to be full, complete people. It's corrupted our whole society, and it must be undone. Finally we see a way to undo it.
Are you... starting with me?
No.
We started with our son.

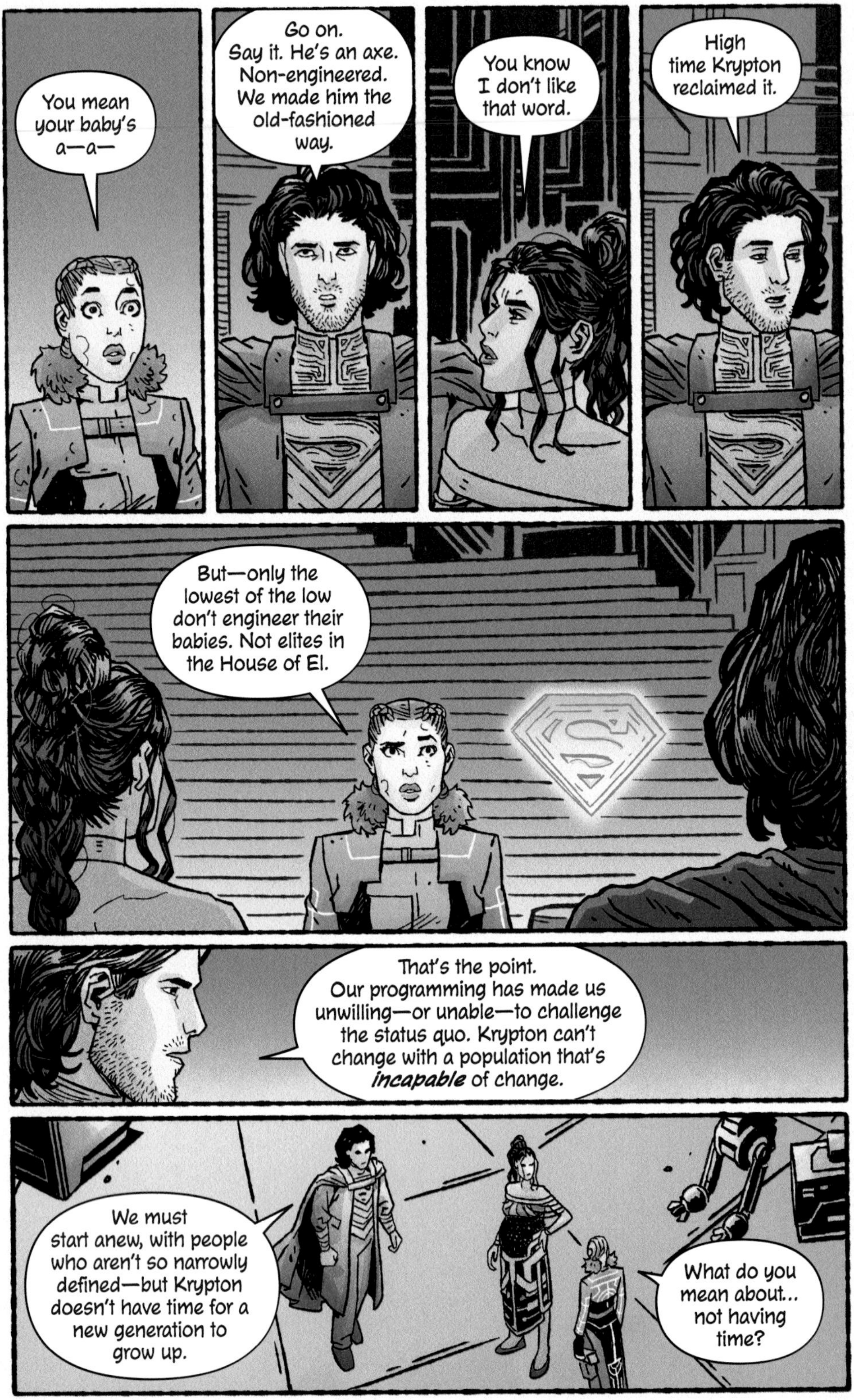

You mean your baby's a—a—
Go on. Say it. He's an axe. Non-engineered. We made him the old-fashioned way.
You know I don't like that word.
High time Krypton reclaimed it.
But—only the lowest of the low don't engineer their babies. Not elites in the House of El.
That's the point. Our programming has made us unwilling—or unable—to challenge the status quo. Krypton can't change with a population that's *incapable* of change.
We must start anew, with people who aren't so narrowly defined—but Krypton doesn't have time for a new generation to grow up.
What do you mean about... not having time?

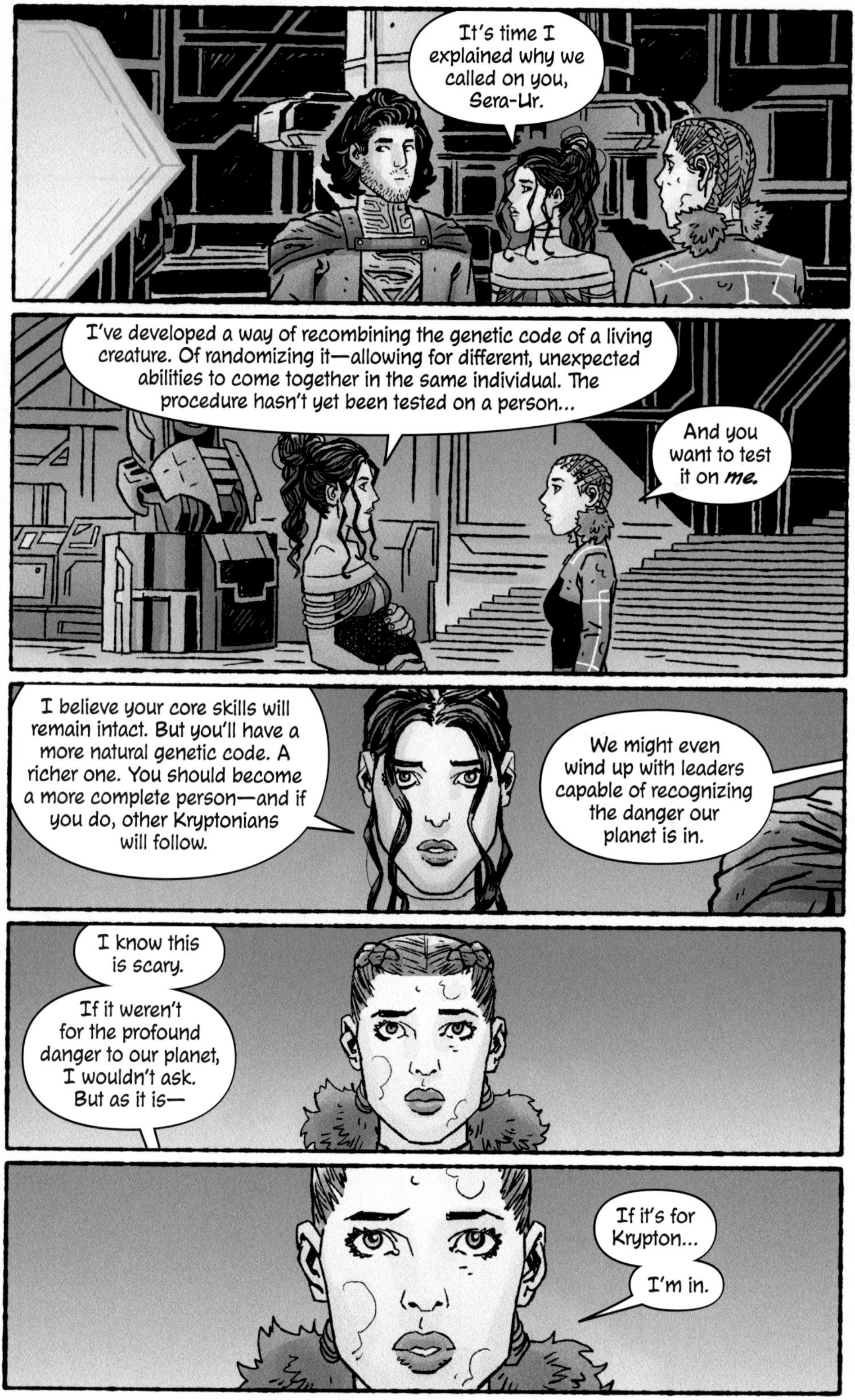
It's time I explained why we called on you, Sera-Ur.
I've developed a way of recombining the genetic code of a living creature. Of randomizing it—allowing for different, unexpected abilities to come together in the same individual. The procedure hasn't yet been tested on a person...
And you want to test it on *me.*
I believe your core skills will remain intact. But you'll have a more natural genetic code. A richer one. You should become a more complete person—and if you do, other Kryptonians will follow.
We might even wind up with leaders capable of recognizing the danger our planet is in.
I know this is scary.
If it weren't for the profound danger to our planet, I wouldn't ask. But as it is—
If it's for Krypton...
I'm in.

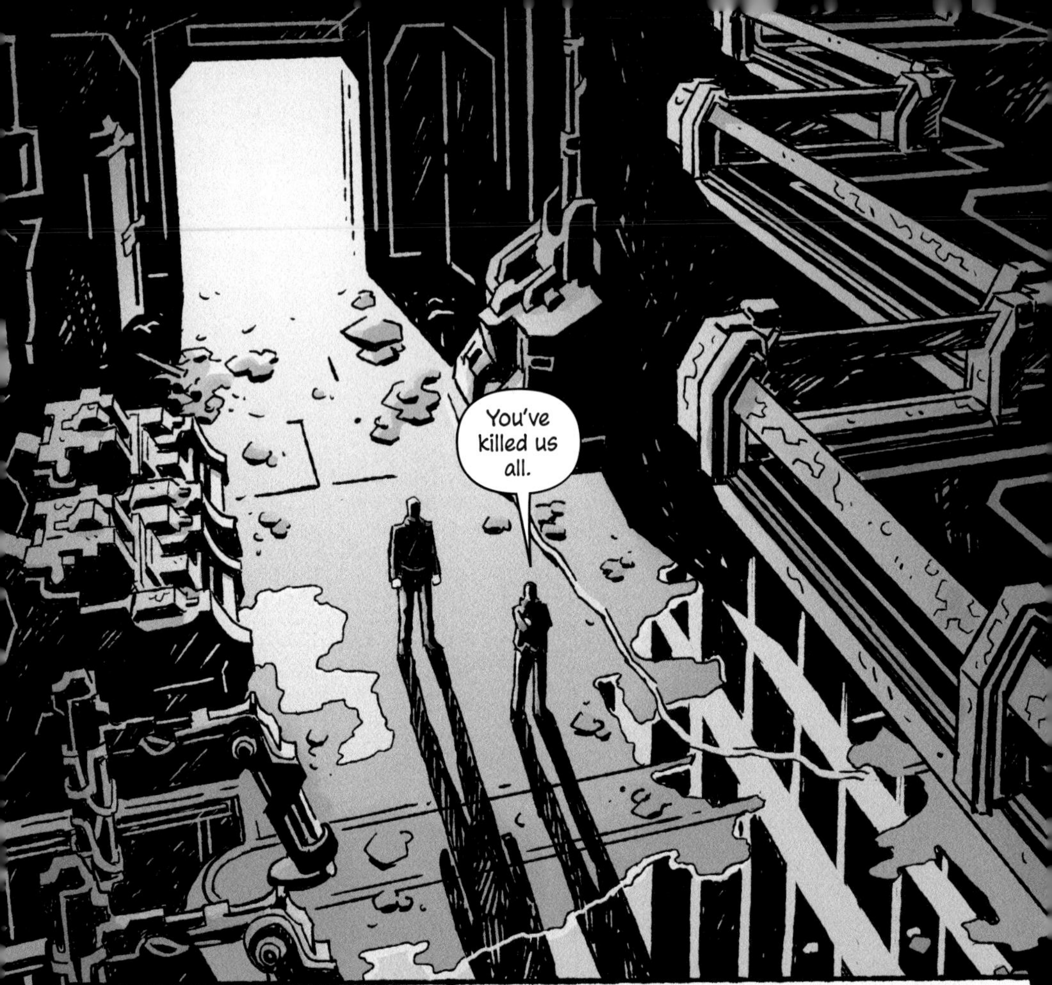
You've killed us all.

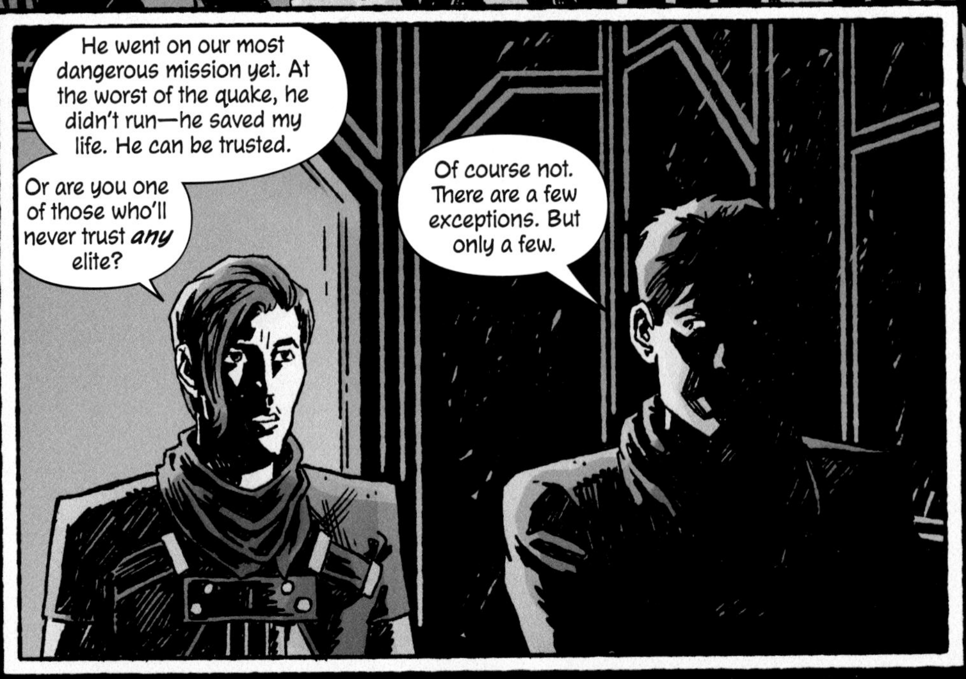
He went on our most dangerous mission yet. At the worst of the quake, he didn't run—he saved my life. He can be trusted.
Or are you one of those who'll never trust *any* elite?
Of course not. There are a few exceptions. But only a few.

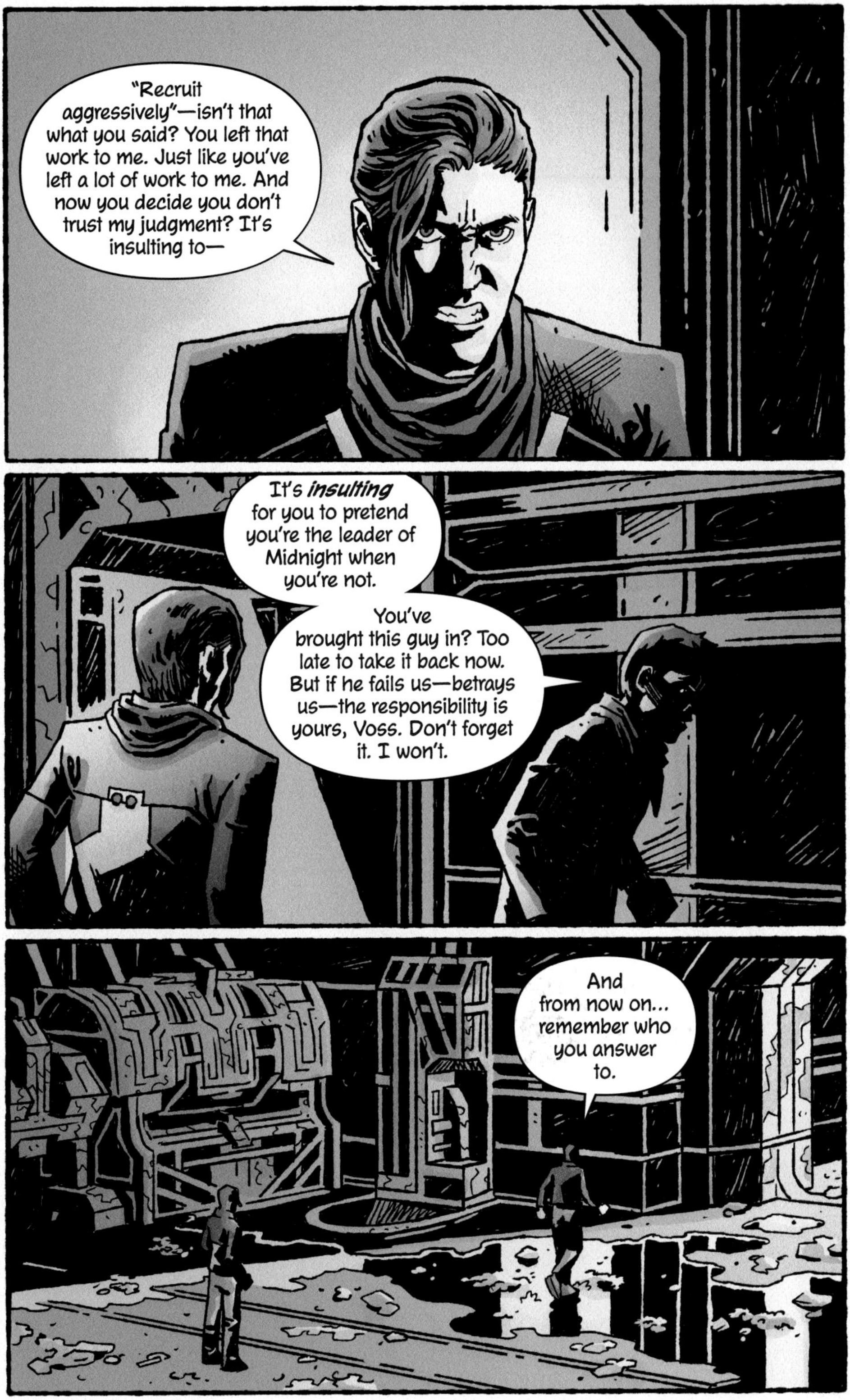
"Recruit aggressively"—isn't that what you said? You left that work to me. Just like you've left a lot of work to me. And now you decide you don't trust my judgment? It's insulting to—
It's *insulting* for you to pretend you're the leader of Midnight when you're not.
You've brought this guy in? Too late to take it back now. But if he fails us—betrays us—the responsibility is yours, Voss. Don't forget it. I won't.
And from now on... remember who you answer to.

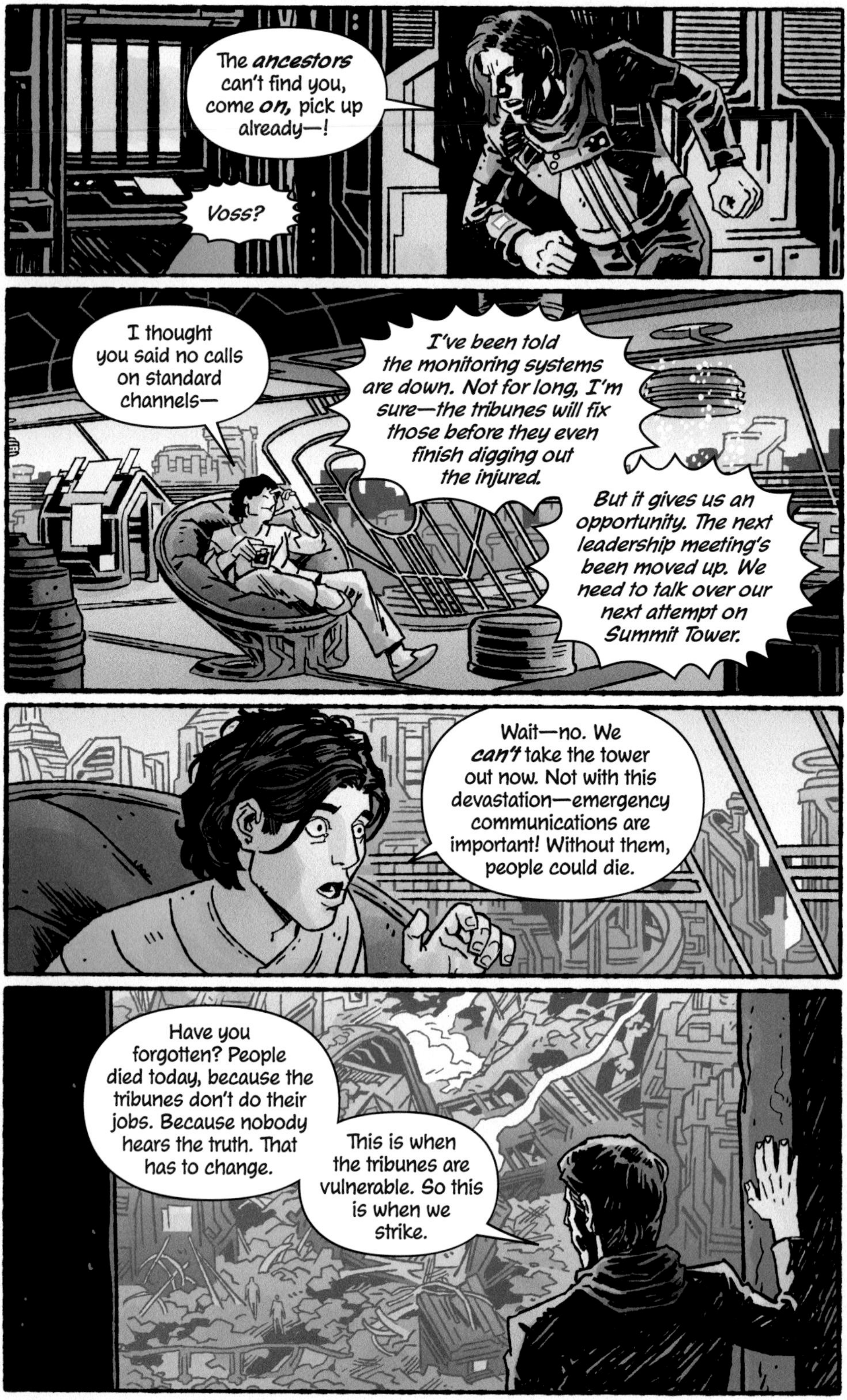
The *ancestors* can't find you, come *on,* pick up already—!
Voss?
I thought you said no calls on standard channels—
I've been told the monitoring systems are down. Not for long, I'm sure—the tribunes will fix those before they even finish digging out the injured.
But it gives us an opportunity. The next leadership meeting's been moved up. We need to talk over our next attempt on Summit Tower.
Wait—no. We ***can't*** take the tower out now. Not with this devastation—emergency communications are important! Without them, people could die.
Have you forgotten? People died today, because the tribunes don't do their jobs. Because nobody hears the truth. That has to change.
This is when the tribunes are vulnerable. So this is when we strike.

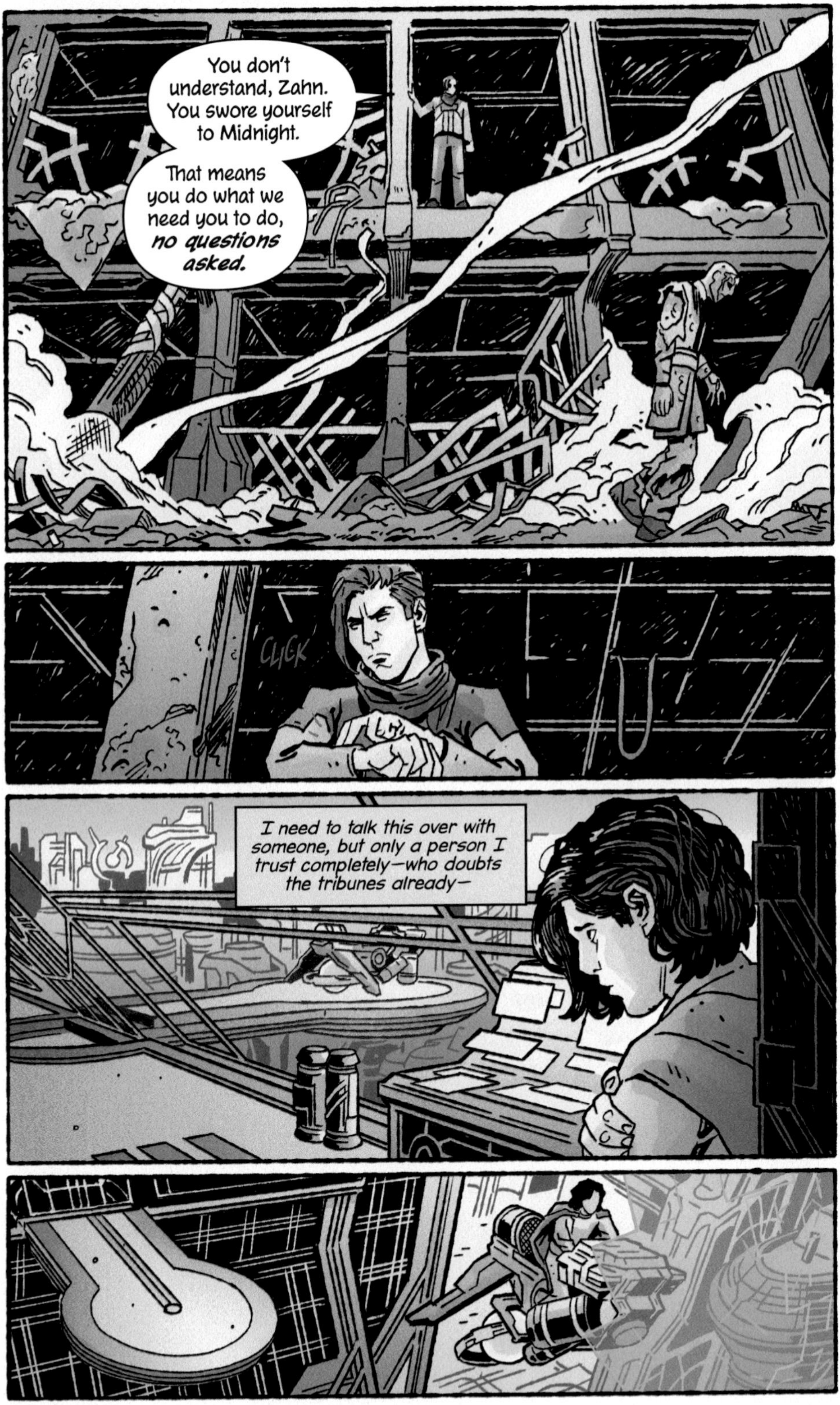
You don't understand, Zahn. You swore yourself to Midnight.
That means you do what we need you to do, ***no questions asked.***
CLICK
I need to talk this over with someone, but only a person I trust completely—who doubts the tribunes already—

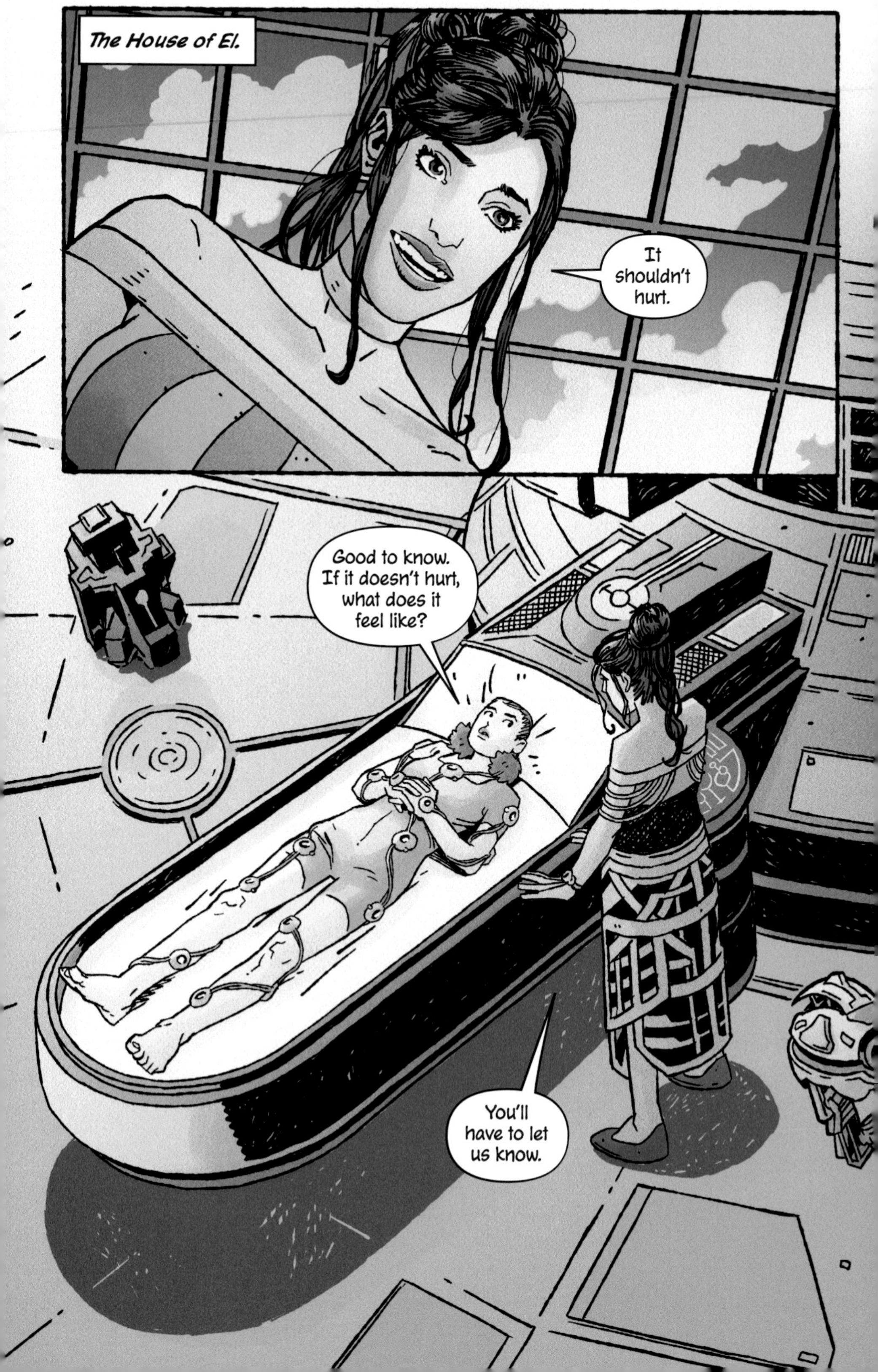
The House of El.
It shouldn't hurt.
Good to know. If it doesn't hurt, what does it feel like?
You'll have to let us know.

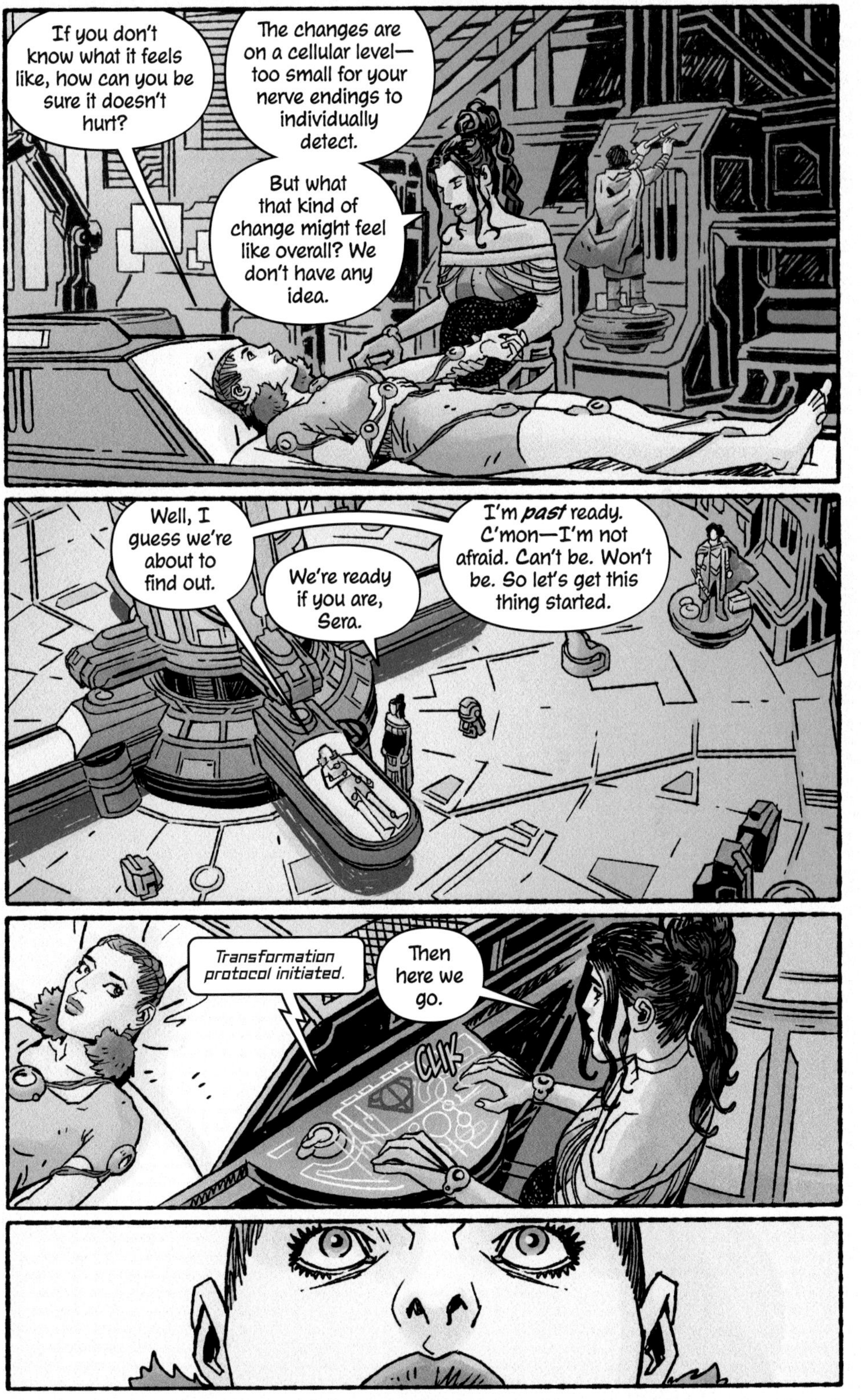
If you don't know what it feels like, how can you be sure it doesn't hurt?
The changes are on a cellular level—too small for your nerve endings to individually detect.
But what that kind of change might feel like overall? We don't have any idea.
Well, I guess we're about to find out.
I'm *past* ready. C'mon—I'm not afraid. Can't be. Won't be. So let's get this thing started.
We're ready if you are, Sera.
Transformation protocol initiated.
Then here we go.
CLIK

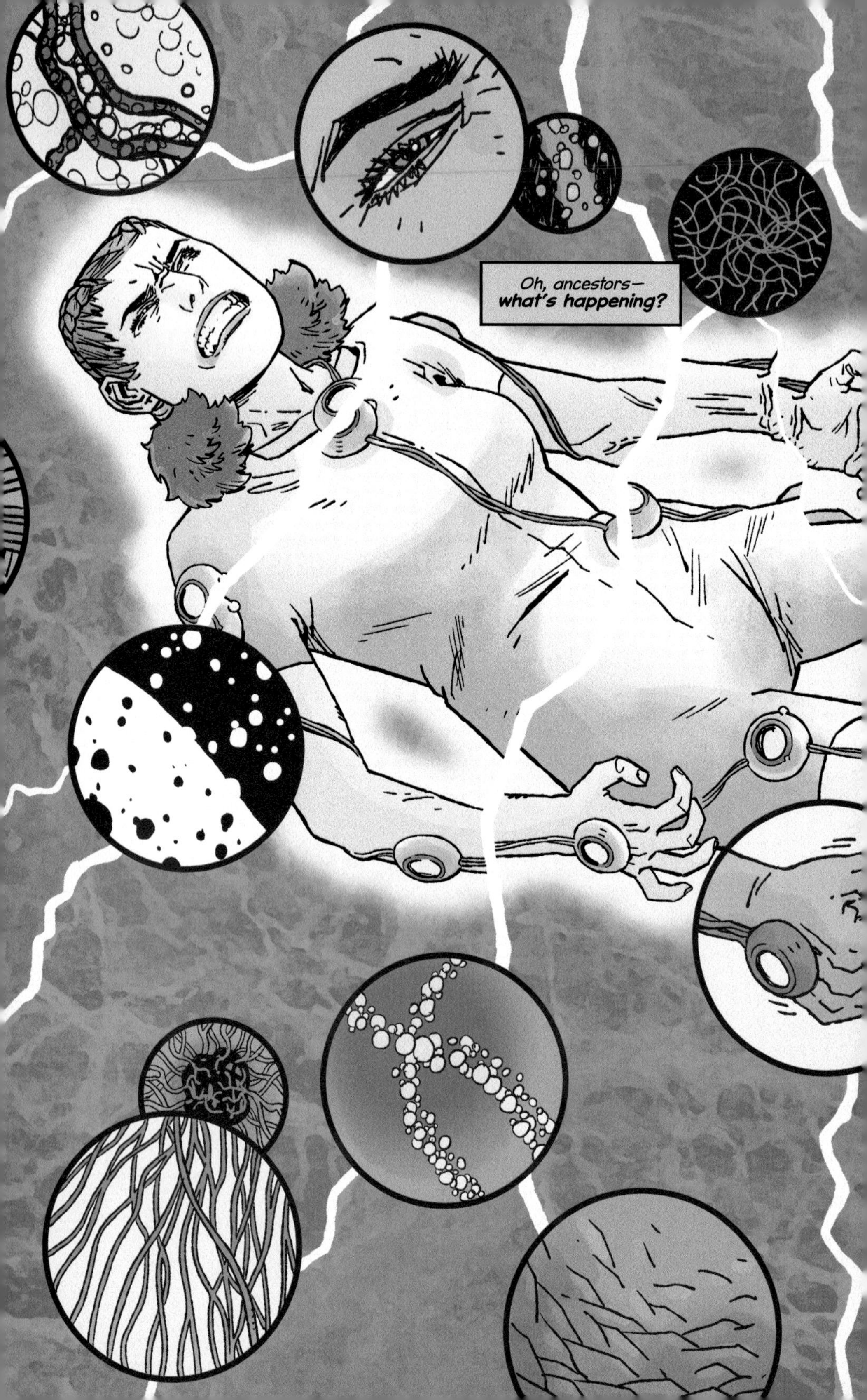
Oh, ancestors—
what's happening?

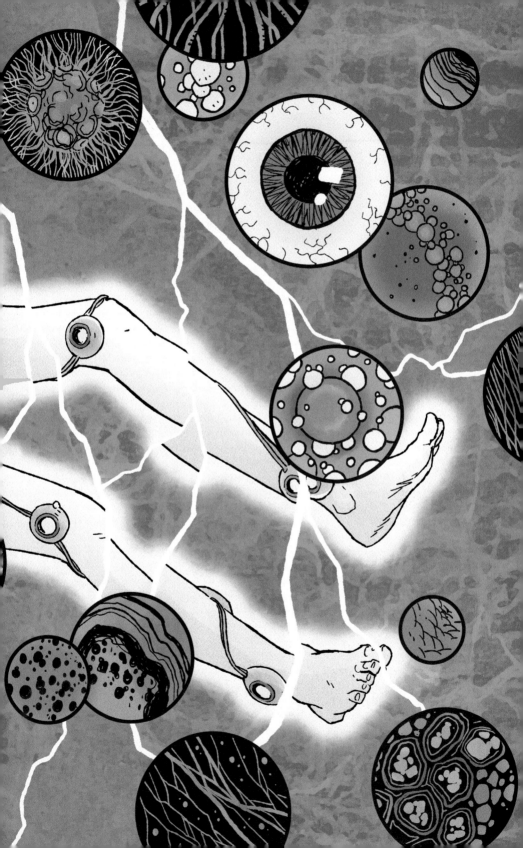

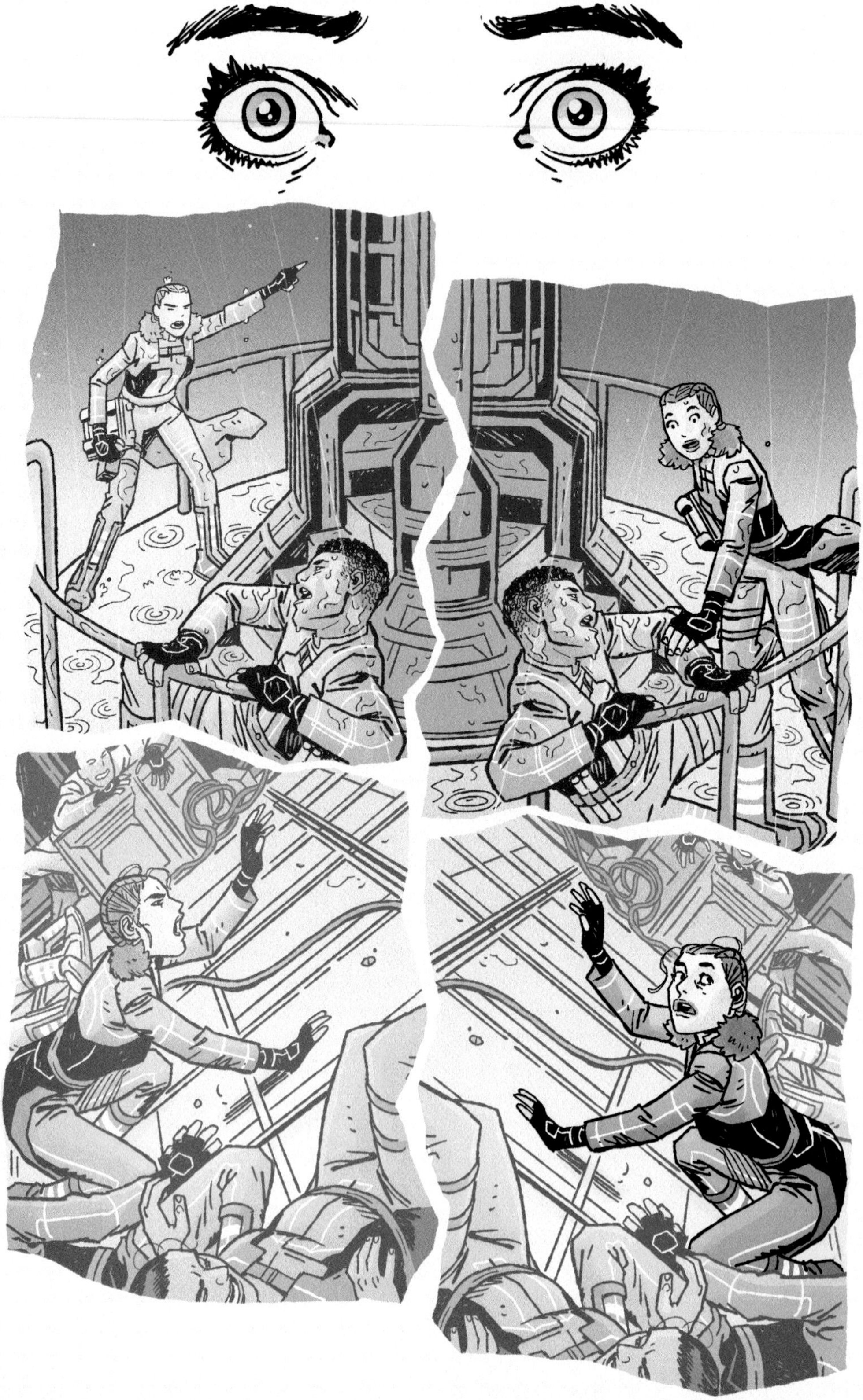

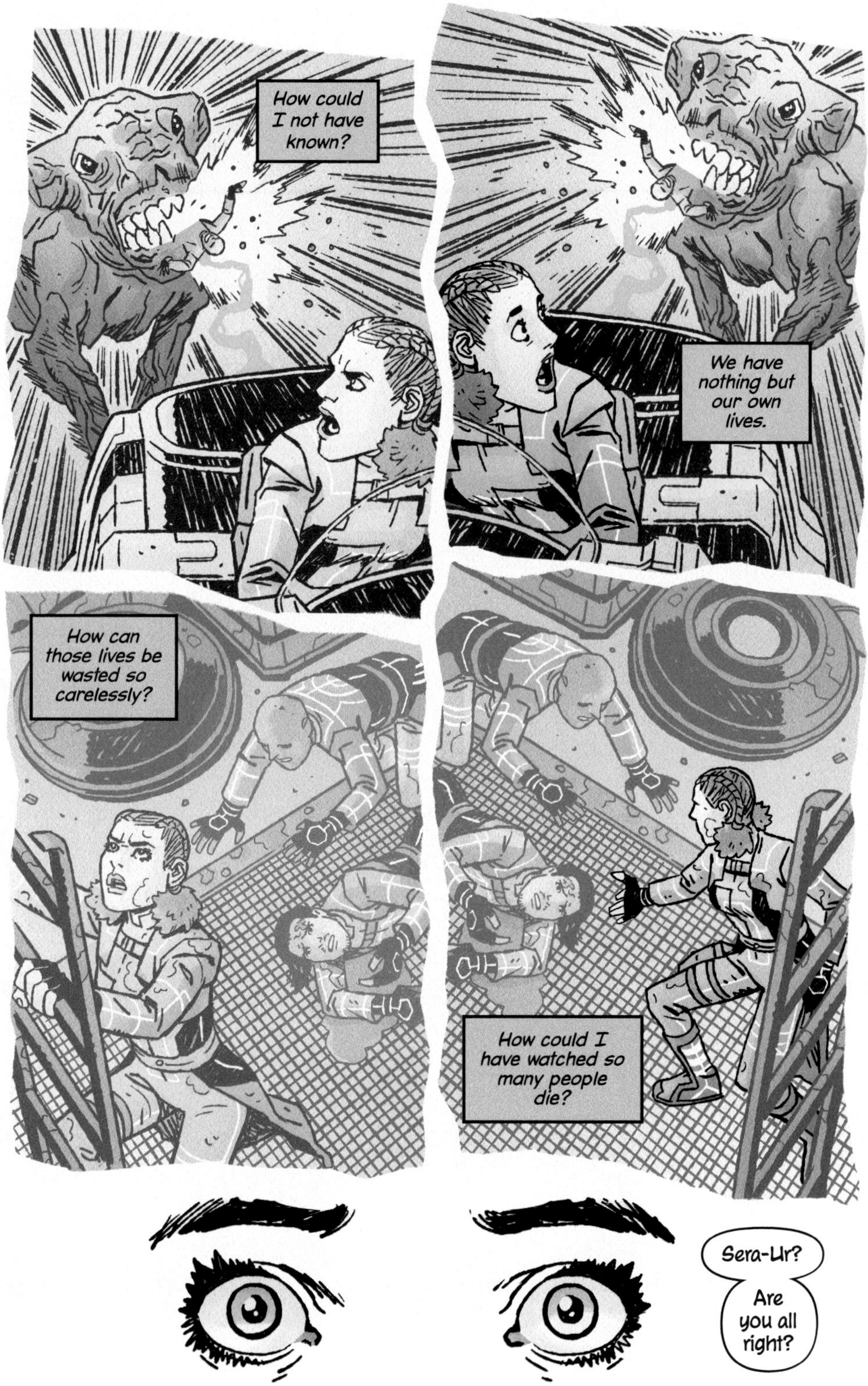
How could I not have known?
We have nothing but our own lives.
How can those lives be wasted so carelessly?
How could I have watched so many people die?
Sera-Ur?
Are you all right?

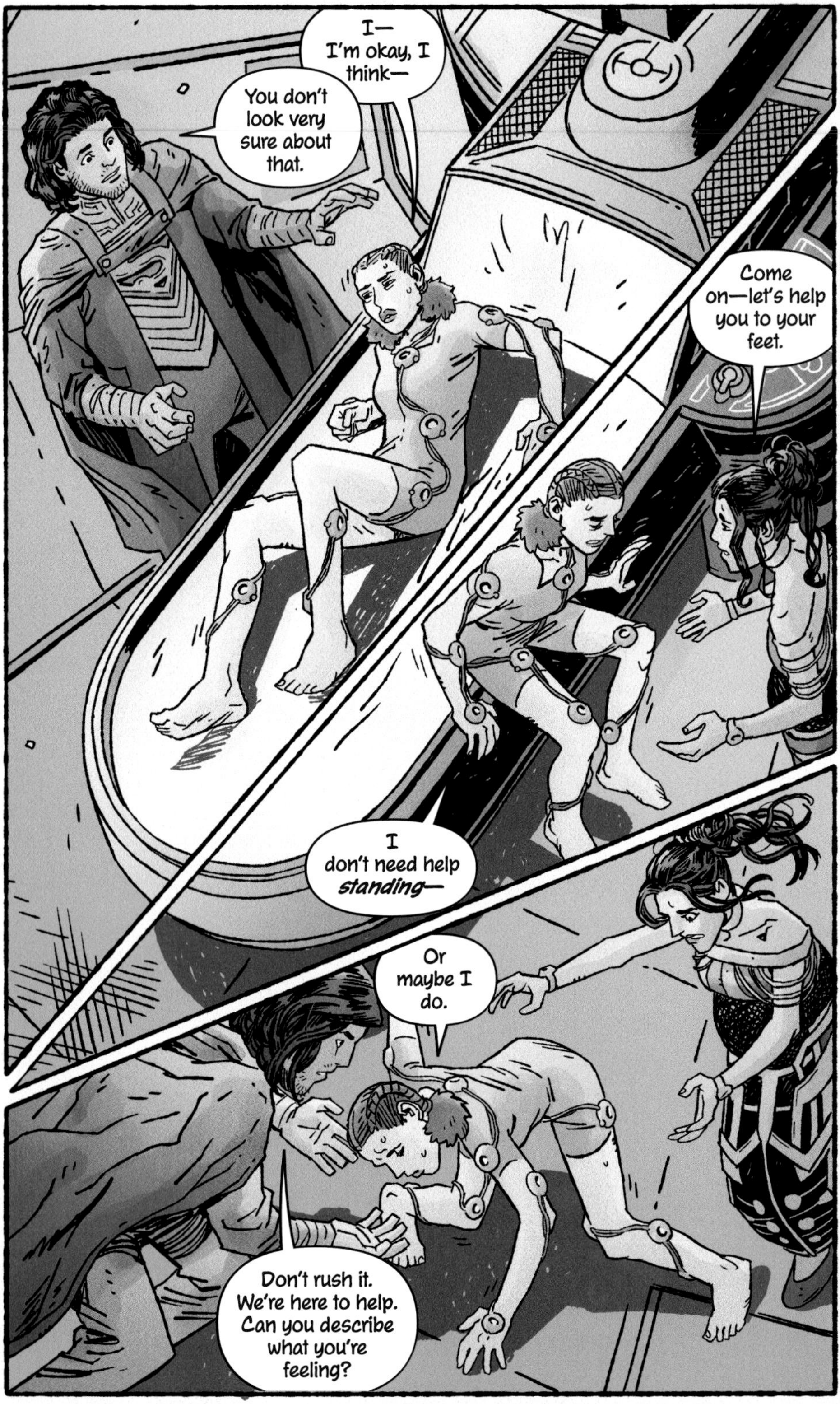
I—
I'm okay, I think—
You don't look very sure about that.
Come on—let's help you to your feet.
I don't need help *standing*—
Or maybe I do.
Don't rush it. We're here to help. Can you describe what you're feeling?

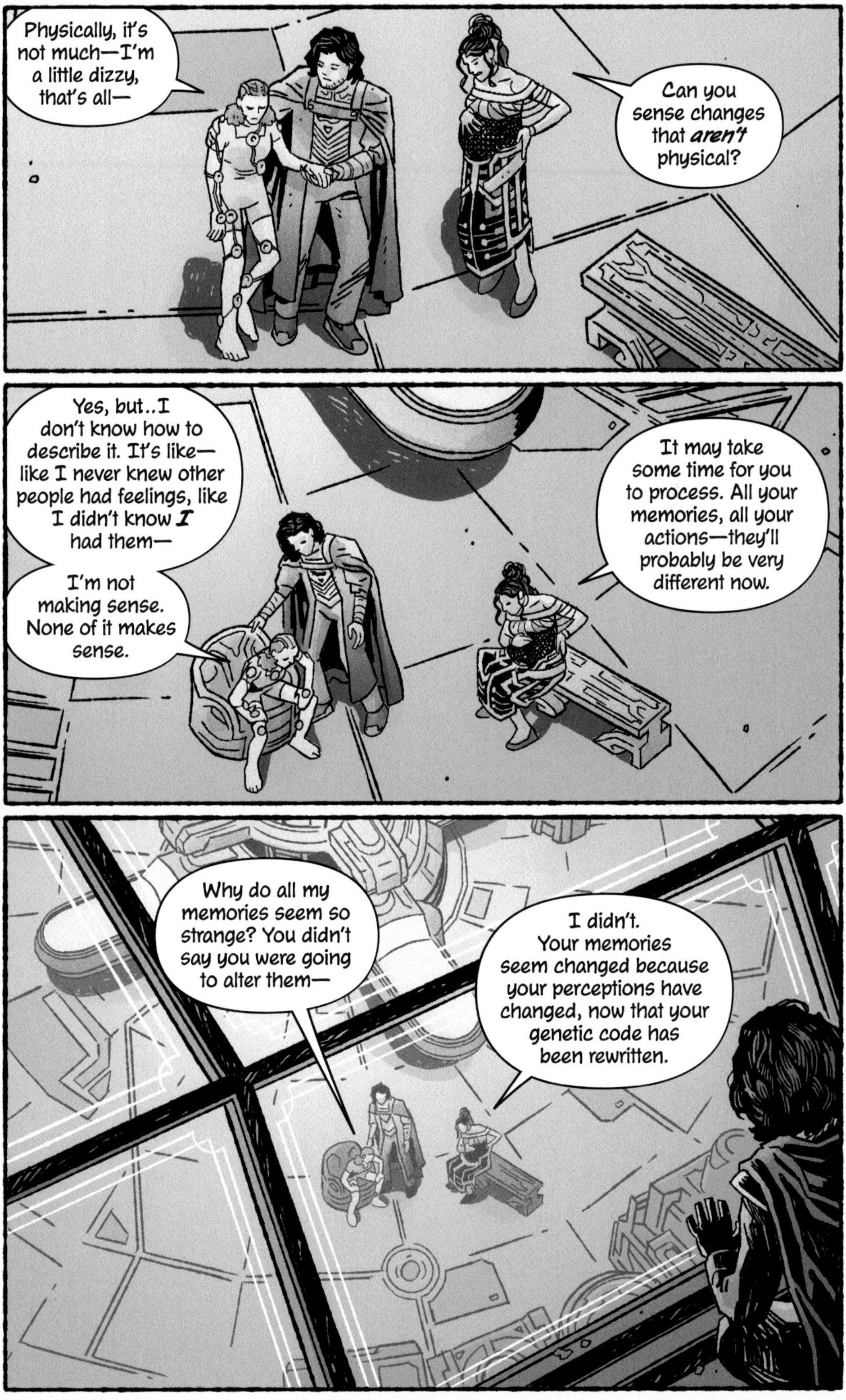

Physically, it's not much—I'm a little dizzy, that's all—
Can you sense changes that *aren't* physical?
Yes, but..I don't know how to describe it. It's like—like I never knew other people had feelings, like I didn't know *I* had them—
I'm not making sense. None of it makes sense.
It may take some time for you to process. All your memories, all your actions—they'll probably be very different now.
Why do all my memories seem so strange? You didn't say you were going to alter them—
I didn't. Your memories seem changed because your perceptions have changed, now that your genetic code has been rewritten.

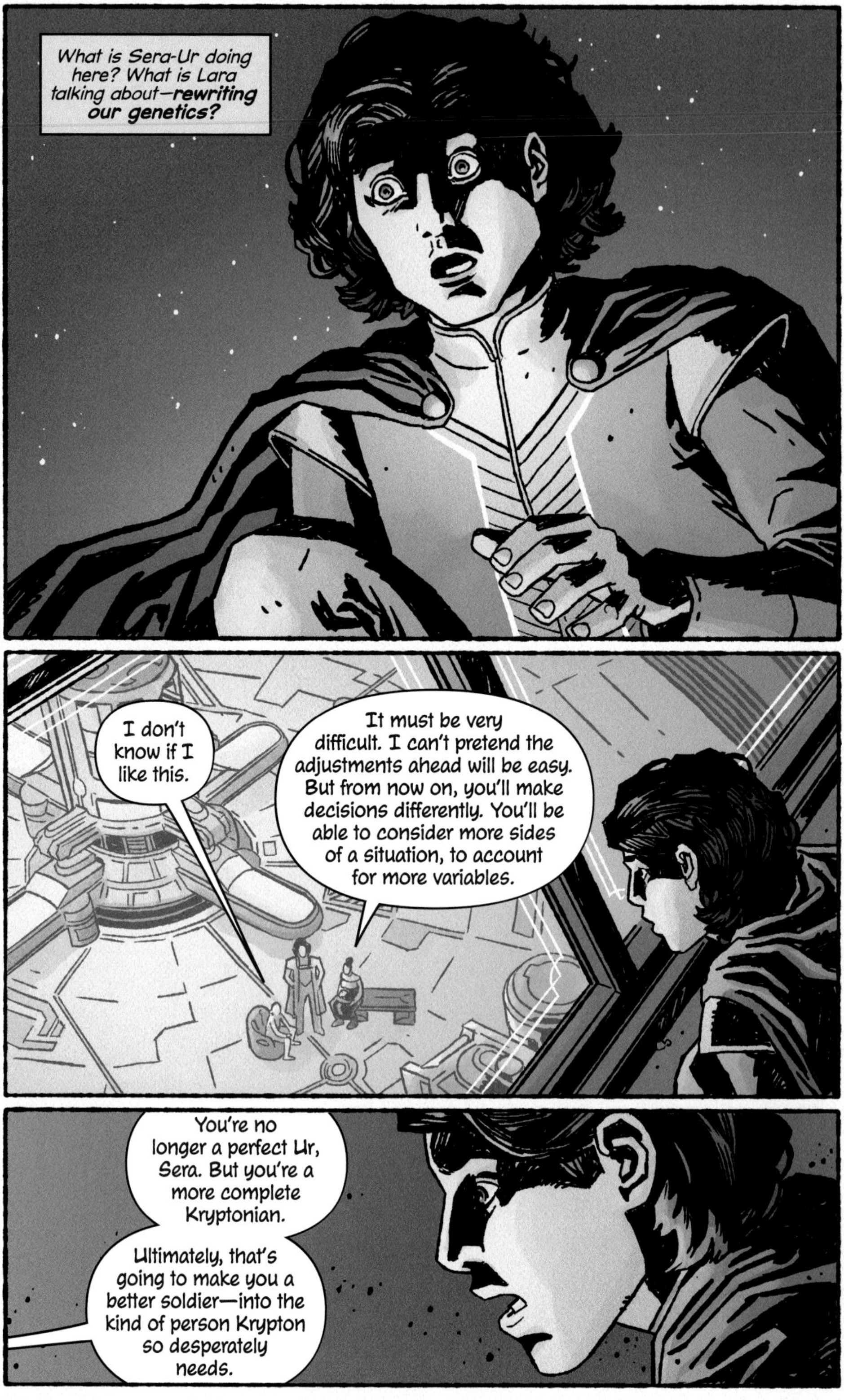
What is Sera-Ur doing here? What is Lara talking about—**rewriting our genetics?**
I don't know if I like this.
It must be very difficult. I can't pretend the adjustments ahead will be easy. But from now on, you'll make decisions differently. You'll be able to consider more sides of a situation, to account for more variables.
You're no longer a perfect Ur, Sera. But you're a more complete Kryptonian.
Ultimately, that's going to make you a better soldier—into the kind of person Krypton so desperately needs.

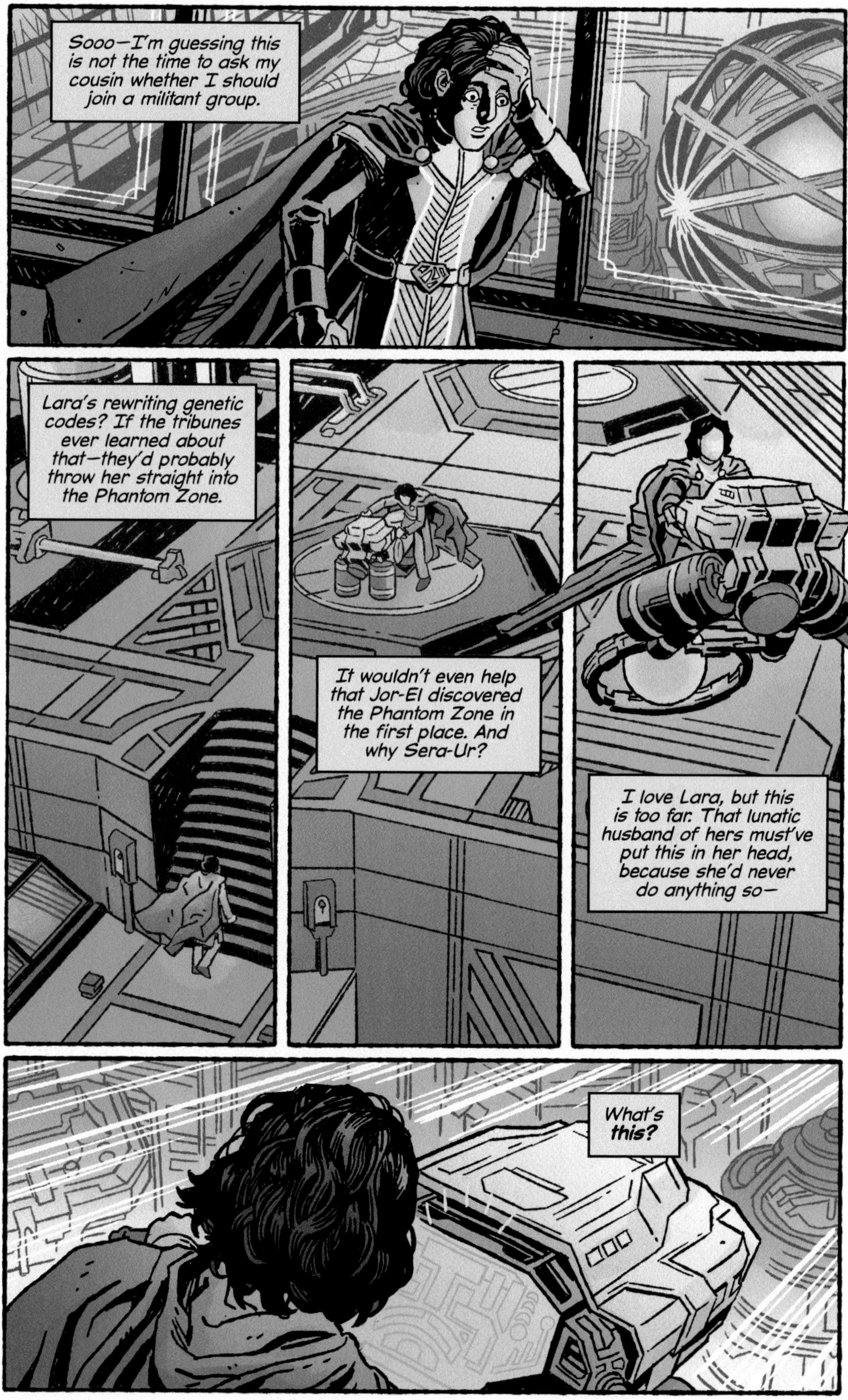
Sooo—I'm guessing this is not the time to ask my cousin whether I should join a militant group.
Lara's rewriting genetic codes? If the tribunes ever learned about that—they'd probably throw her straight into the Phantom Zone.
It wouldn't even help that Jor-El discovered the Phantom Zone in the first place. And why Sera-Ur?
I love Lara, but this is too far. That lunatic husband of hers must've put this in her head, because she'd never do anything so—
What's this?

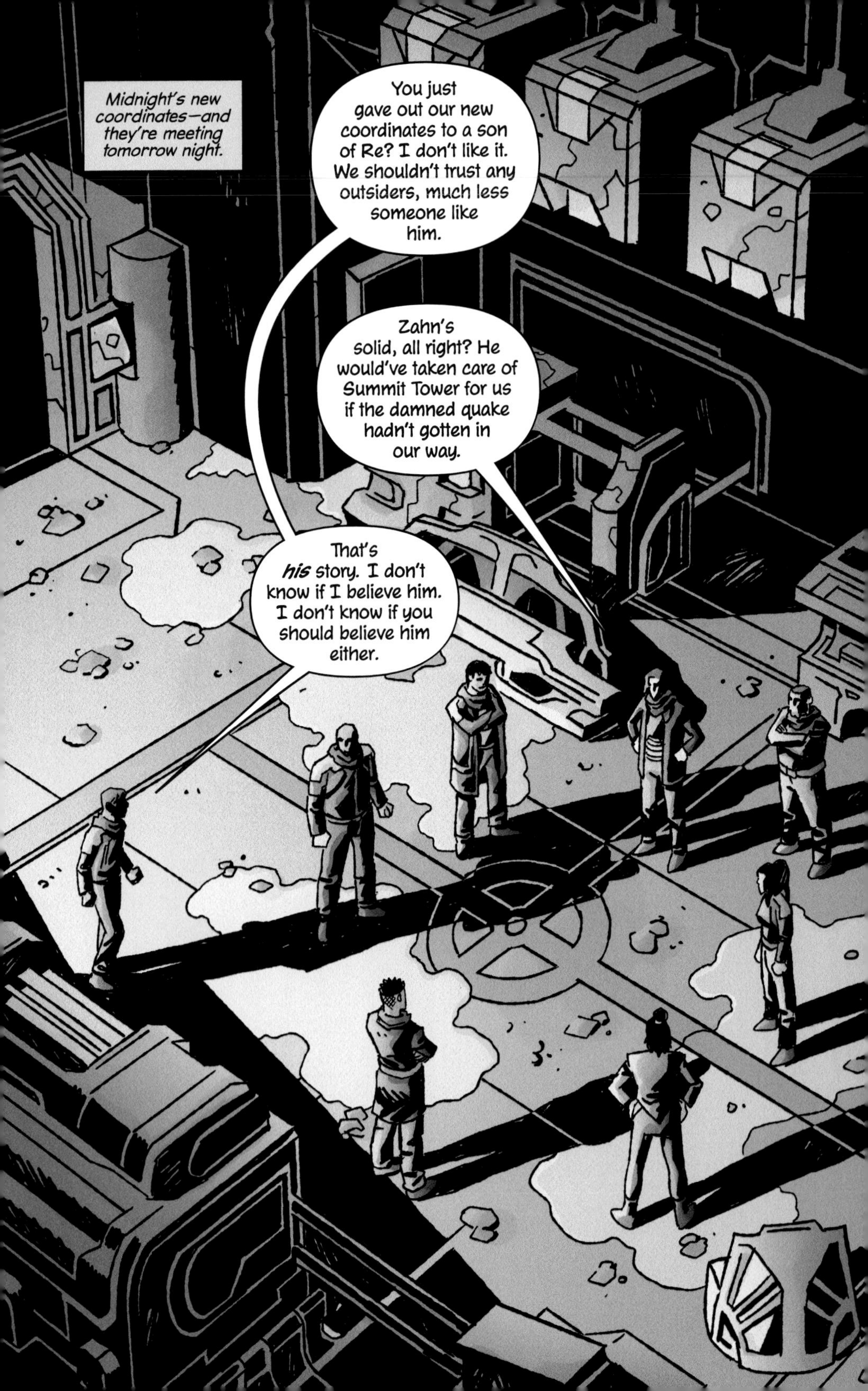
Midnight's new coordinates—and they're meeting tomorrow night.
You just gave out our new coordinates to a son of Re? I don't like it. We shouldn't trust any outsiders, much less someone like him.
Zahn's solid, all right? He would've taken care of Summit Tower for us if the damned quake hadn't gotten in our way.
That's *his* story. I don't know if I believe him. I don't know if you should believe him either.

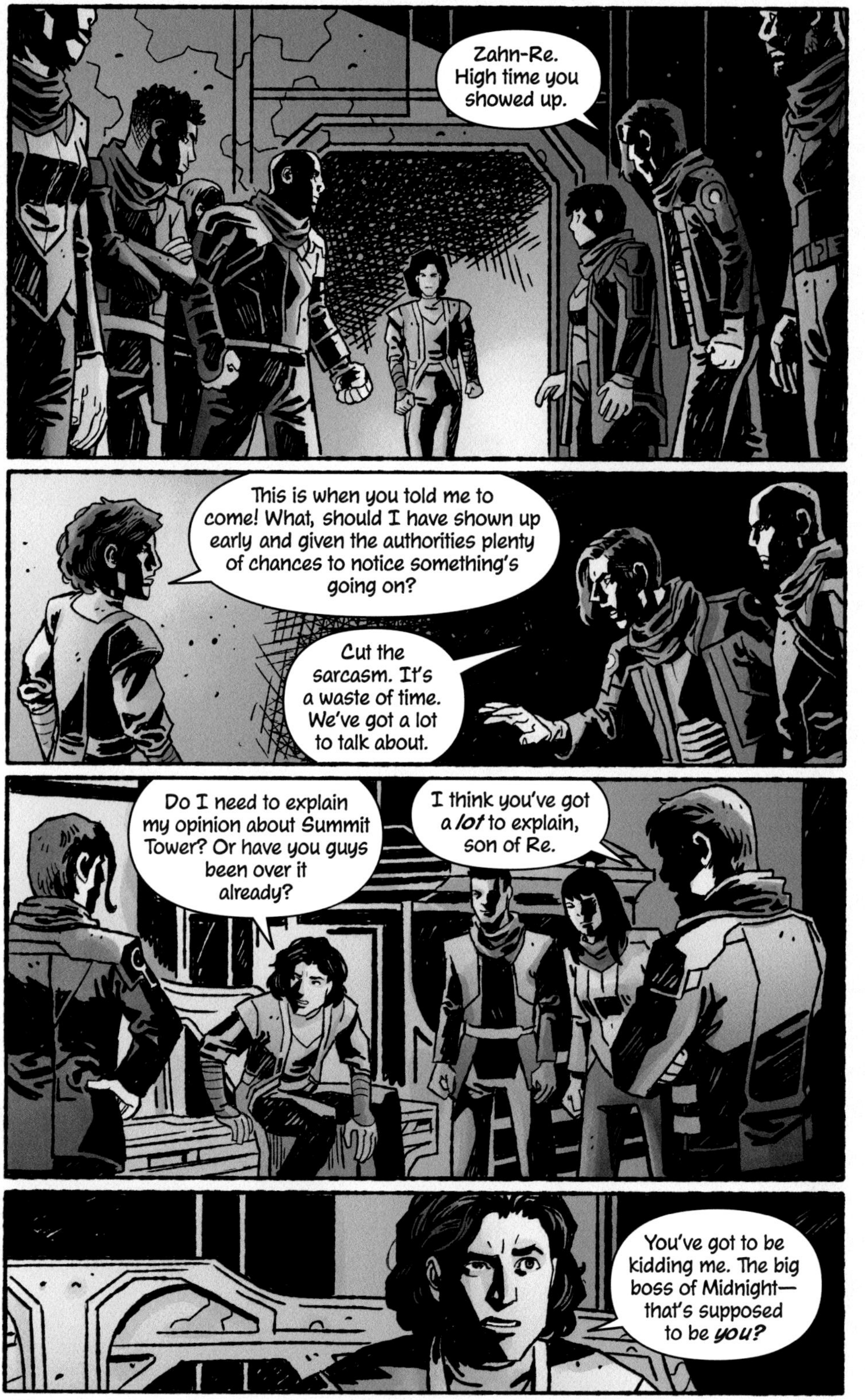
Zahn-Re. High time you showed up.
This is when you told me to come! What, should I have shown up early and given the authorities plenty of chances to notice something's going on?
Cut the sarcasm. It's a waste of time. We've got a lot to talk about.
Do I need to explain my opinion about Summit Tower? Or have you guys been over it already?
I think you've got a *lot* to explain, son of Re.
You've got to be kidding me. The big boss of Midnight— that's supposed to be ***you?***

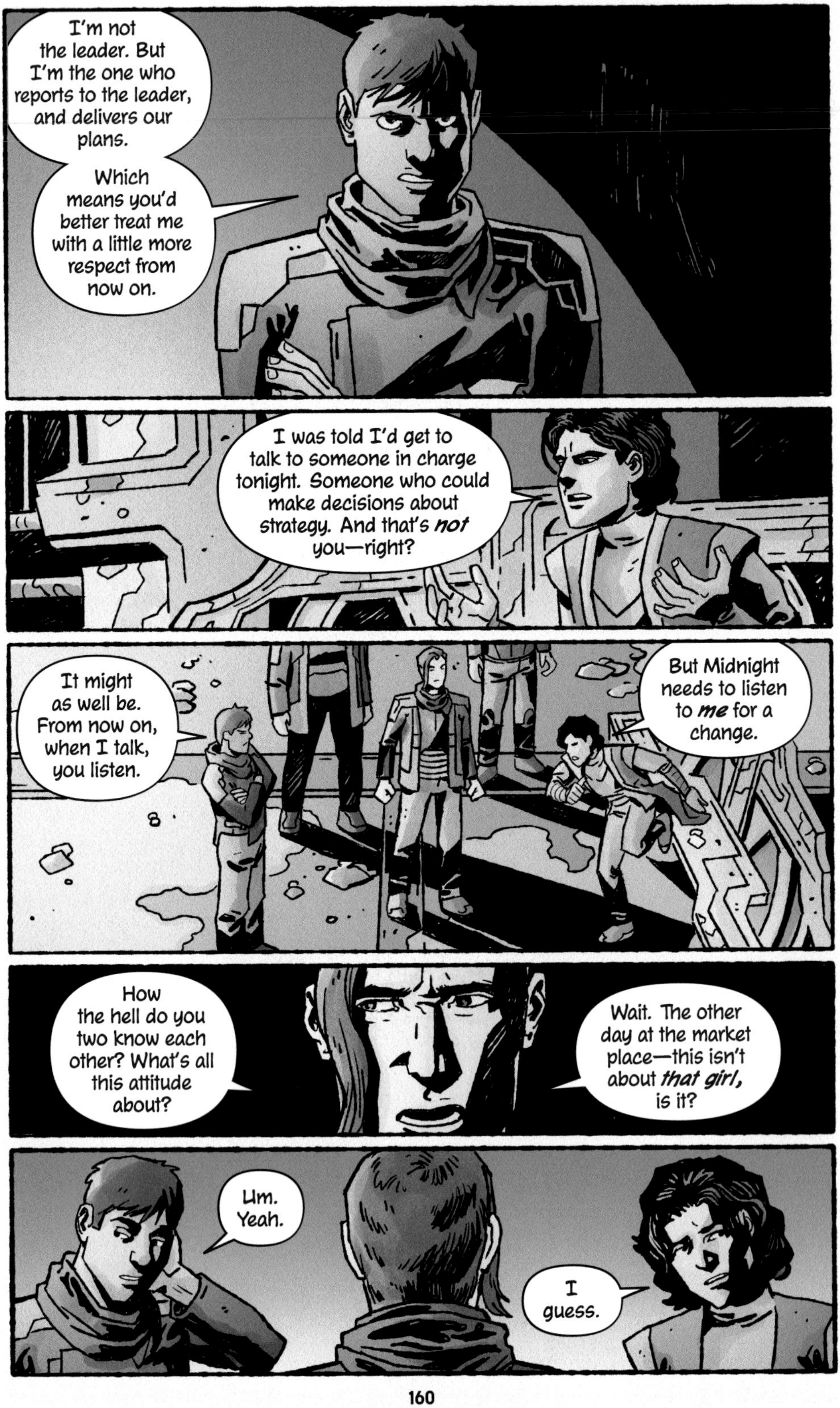
I'm not the leader. But I'm the one who reports to the leader, and delivers our plans.
Which means you'd better treat me with a little more respect from now on.
I was told I'd get to talk to someone in charge tonight. Someone who could make decisions about strategy. And that's *not* you—right?
It might as well be. From now on, when I talk, you listen.
But Midnight needs to listen to *me* for a change.
How the hell do you two know each other? What's all this attitude about?
Wait. The other day at the market place—this isn't about *that girl,* is it?
Um. Yeah.
I guess.

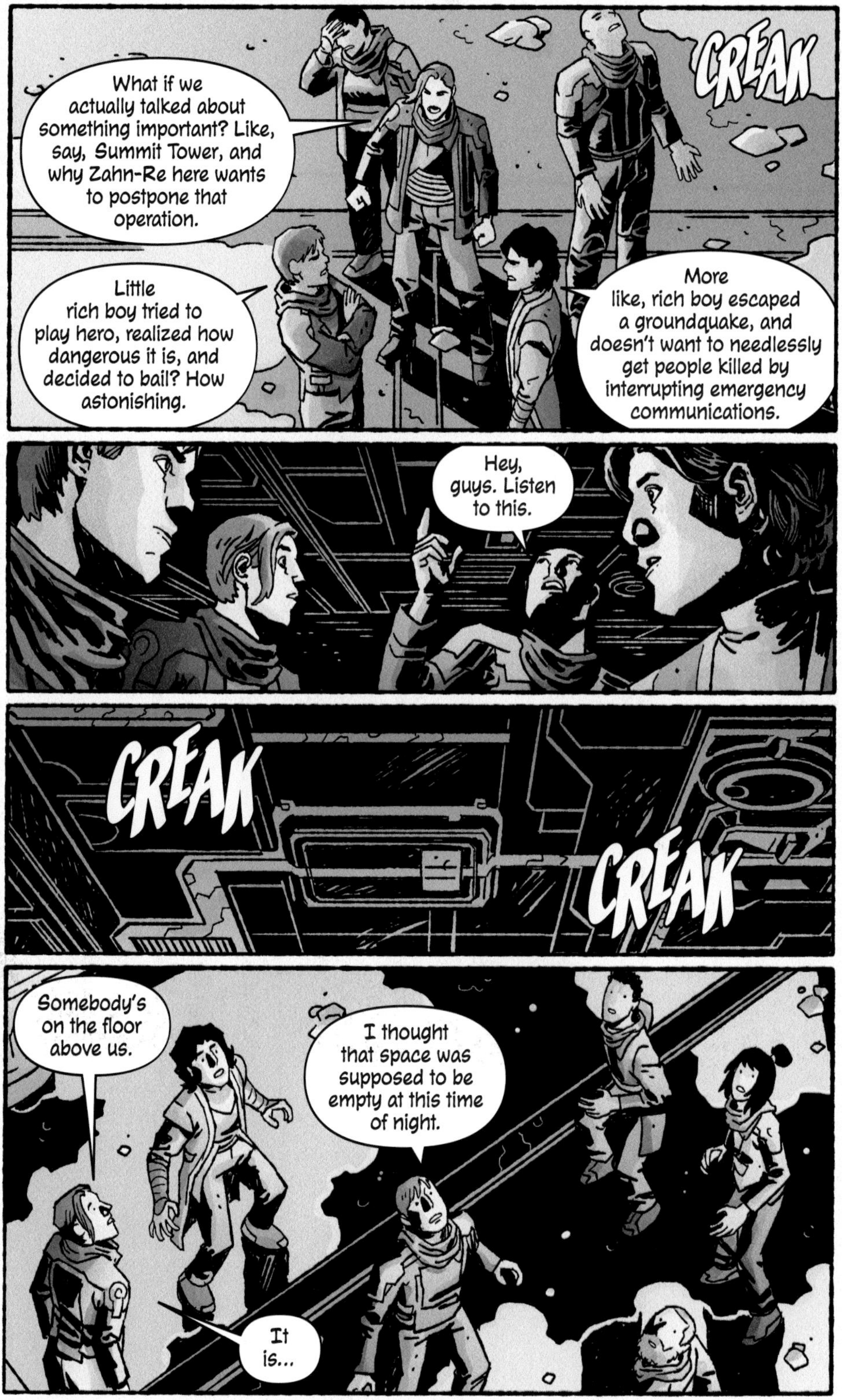
CREAK
What if we actually talked about something important? Like, say, Summit Tower, and why Zahn-Re here wants to postpone that operation.
Little rich boy tried to play hero, realized how dangerous it is, and decided to bail? How astonishing.
More like, rich boy escaped a groundquake, and doesn't want to needlessly get people killed by interrupting emergency communications.
Hey, guys. Listen to this.
CREAK
CREAK
Somebody's on the floor above us.
I thought that space was supposed to be empty at this time of night.
It is...

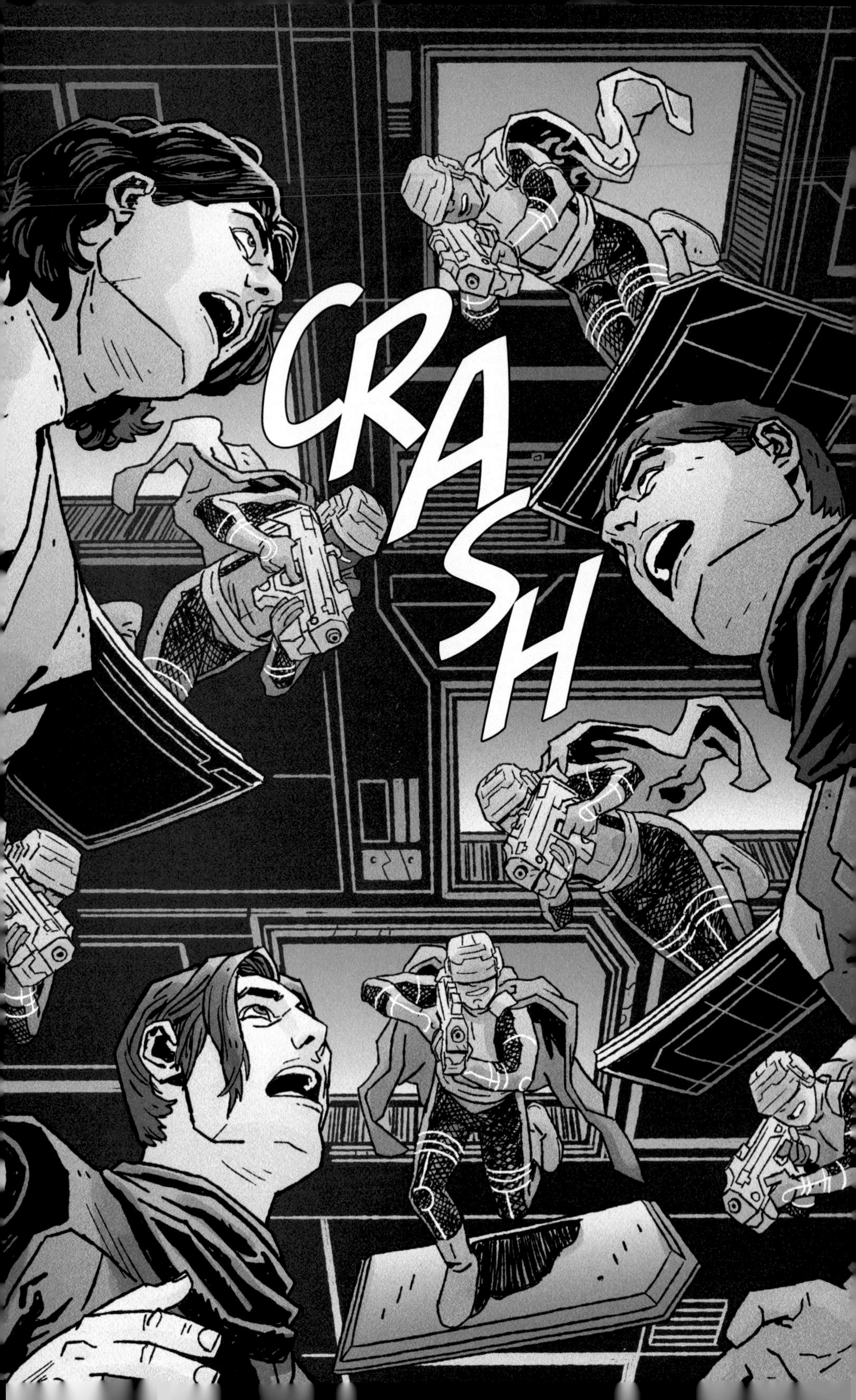
CRASH

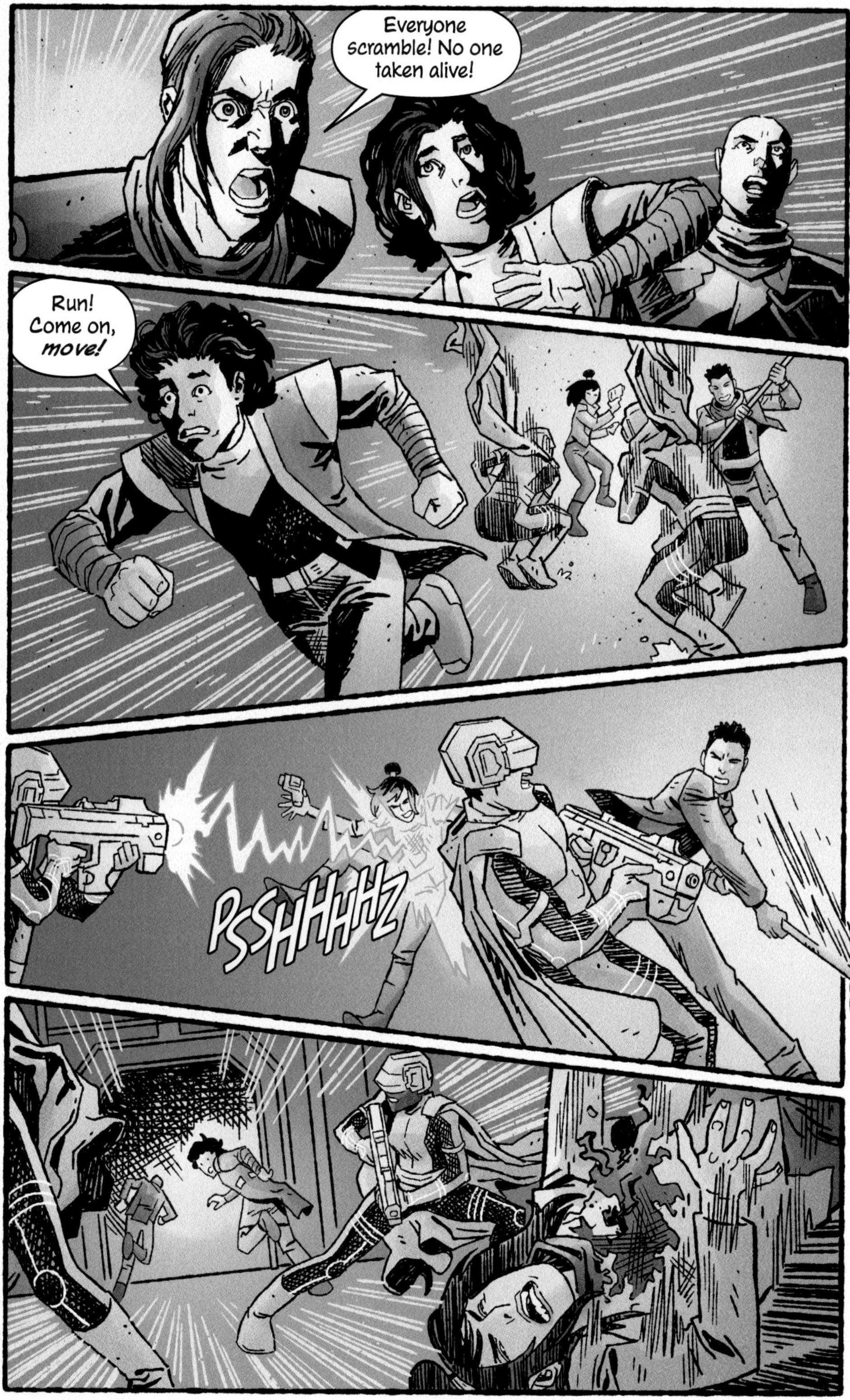
Everyone scramble! No one taken alive!
Run! Come on, *move!*
PSSHHHHZ

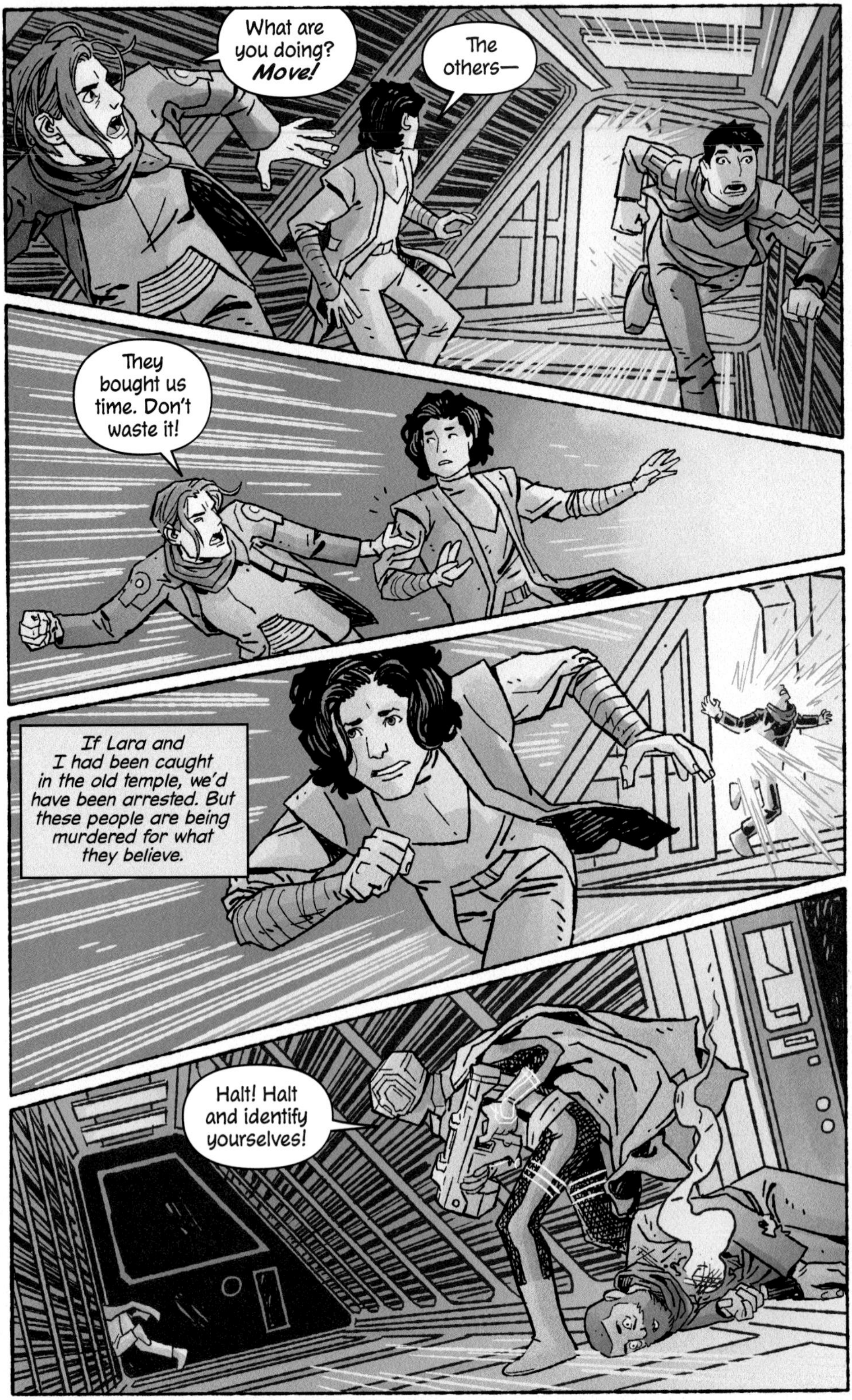
What are you doing? *Move!*
The others—
They bought us time. Don't waste it!
If Lara and I had been caught in the old temple, we'd have been arrested. But these people are being murdered for what they believe.
Halt! Halt and identify yourselves!

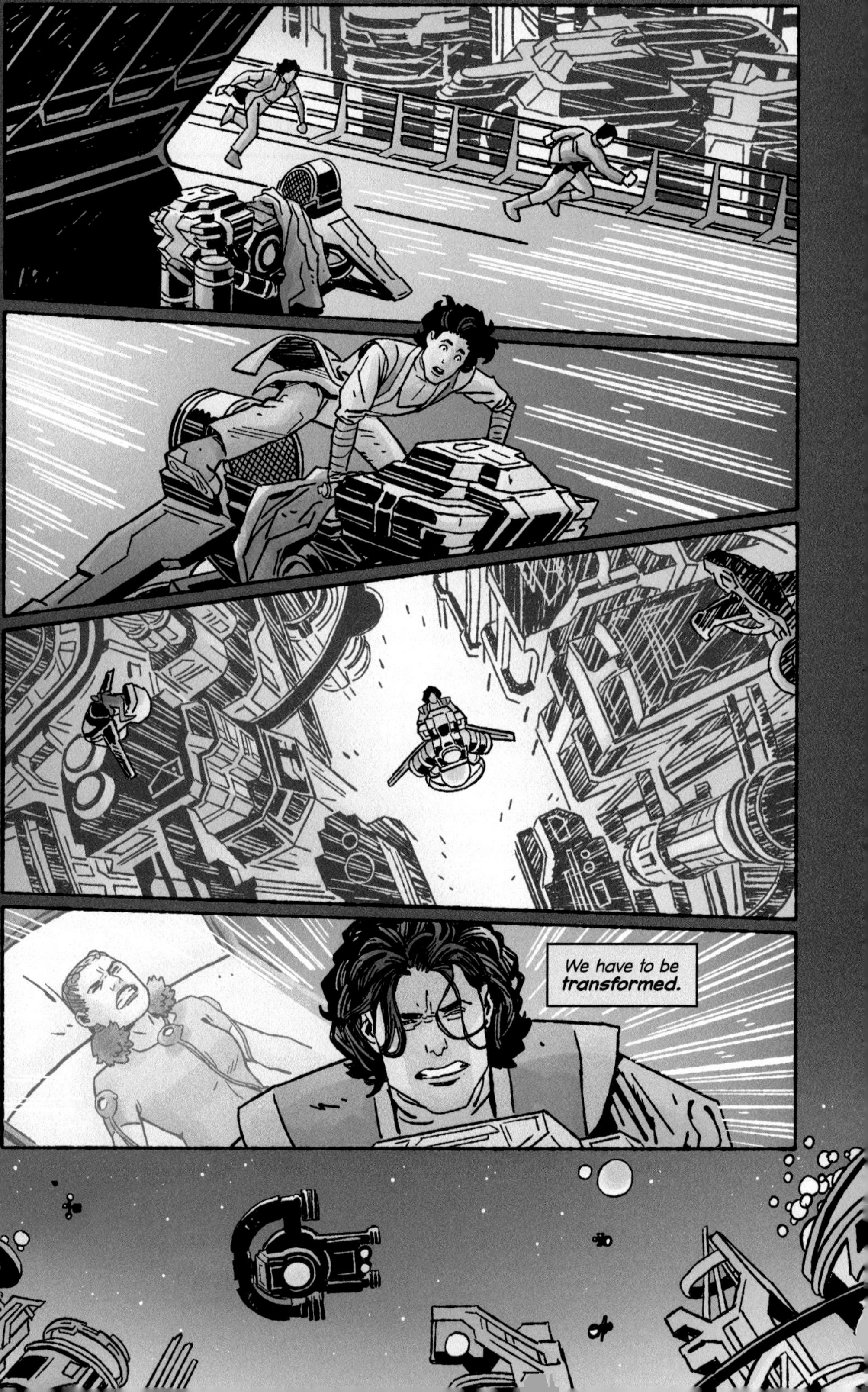
We have to be transformed.

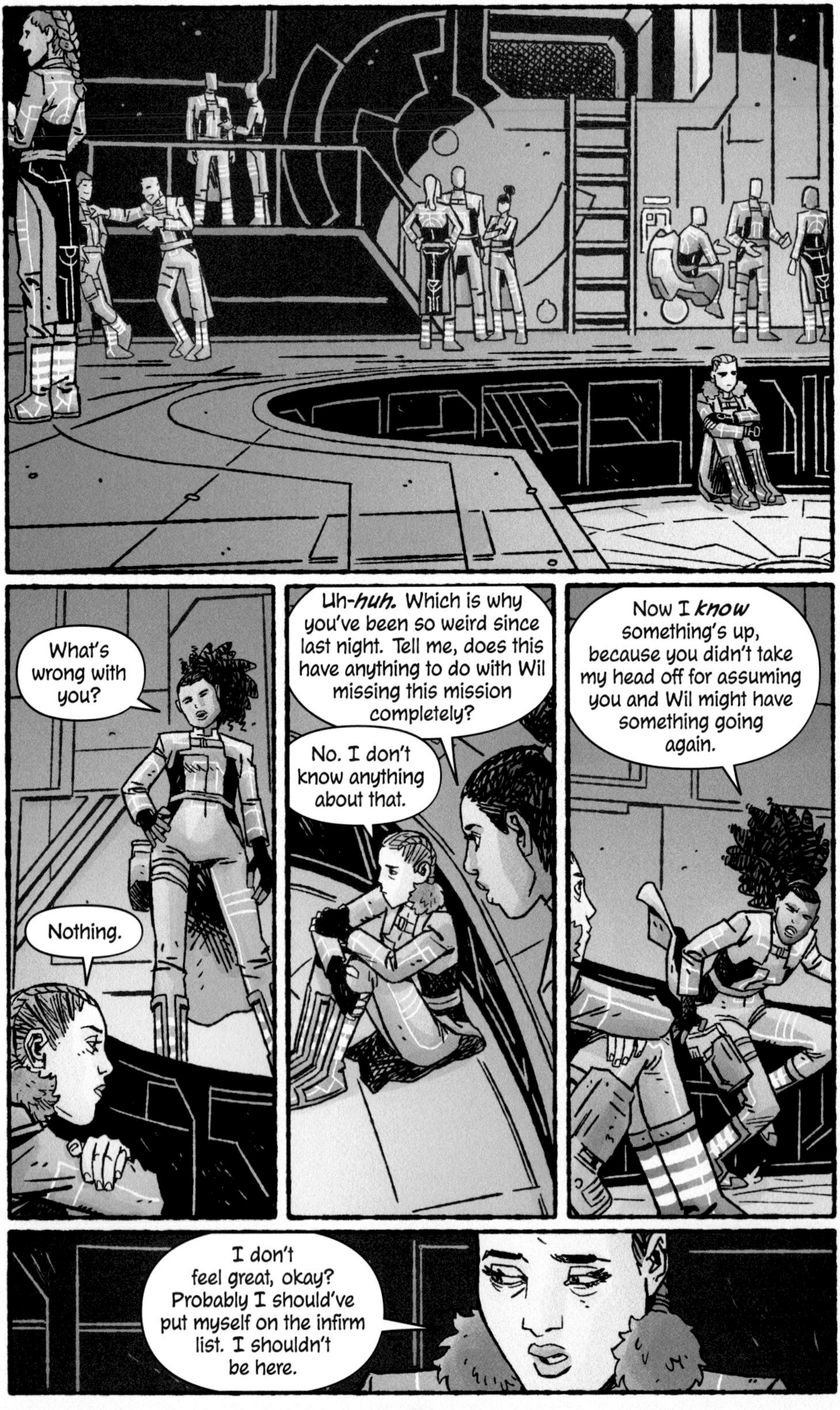
What's wrong with you?
Nothing.
Uh-huh. Which is why you've been so weird since last night. Tell me, does this have anything to do with Wil missing this mission completely?
No. I don't know anything about that.
Now I know something's up, because you didn't take my head off for assuming you and Wil might have something going again.
I don't feel great, okay? Probably I should've put myself on the infirm list. I shouldn't be here.

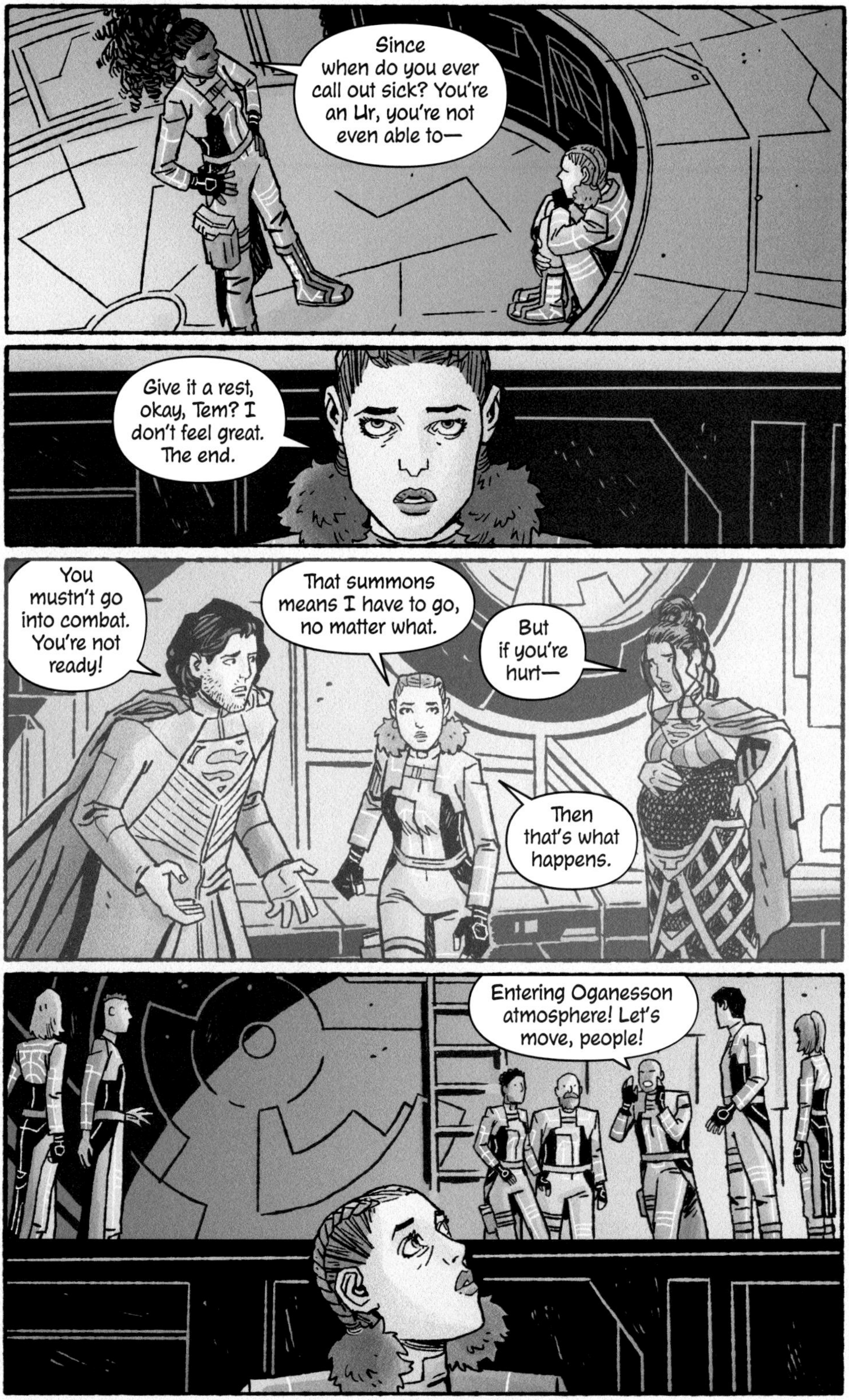
Since when do you ever call out sick? You're an Ur, you're not even able to—
Give it a rest, okay, Tem? I don't feel great. The end.
You mustn't go into combat. You're not ready!
That summons means I have to go, no matter what.
But if you're hurt—
Then that's what happens.
Entering Oganesson atmosphere! Let's move, people!

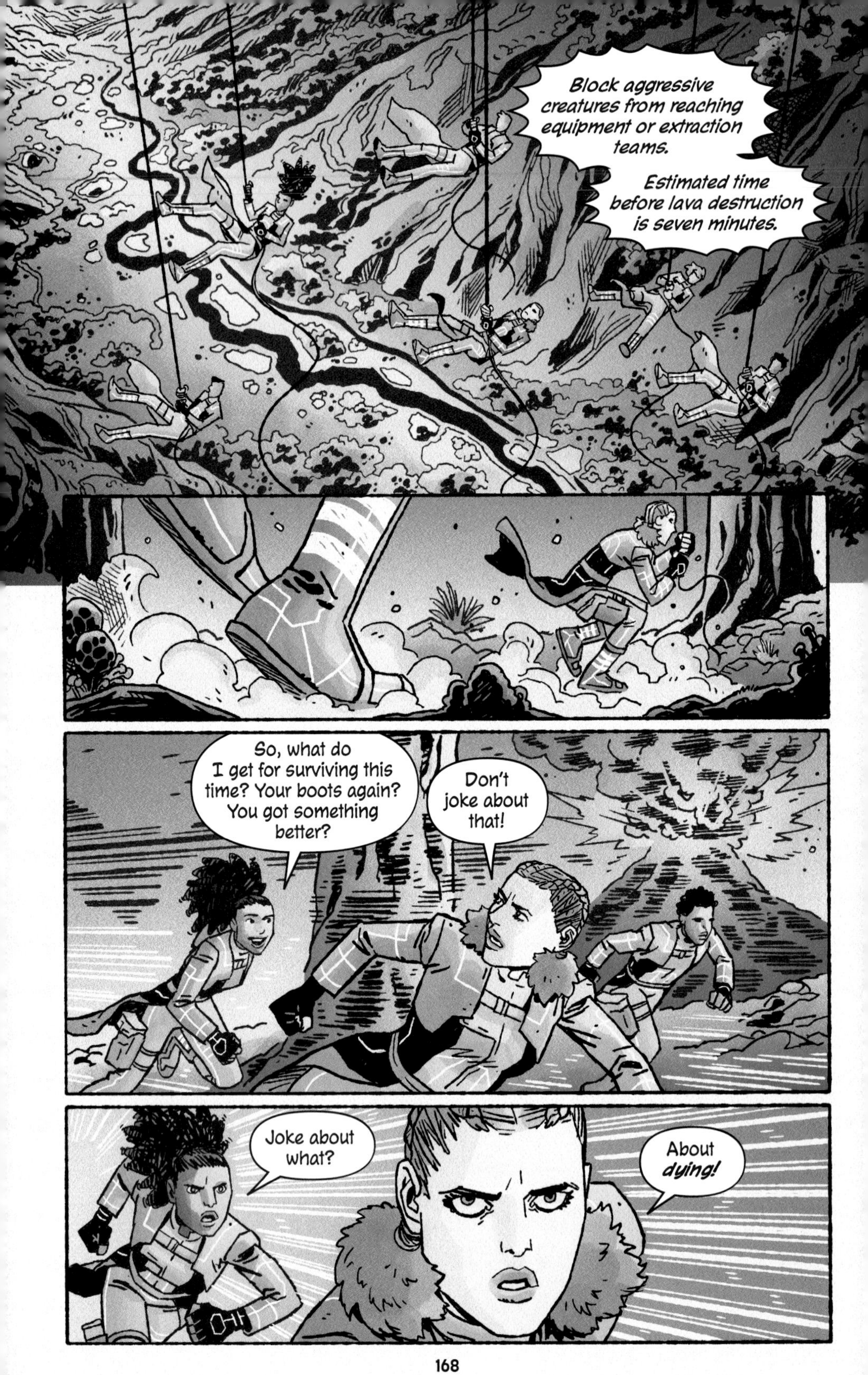
Block aggressive creatures from reaching equipment or extraction teams.
Estimated time before lava destruction is seven minutes.
So, what do I get for surviving this time? Your boots again? You got something better?
Don't joke about that!
Joke about what?
About *dying!*

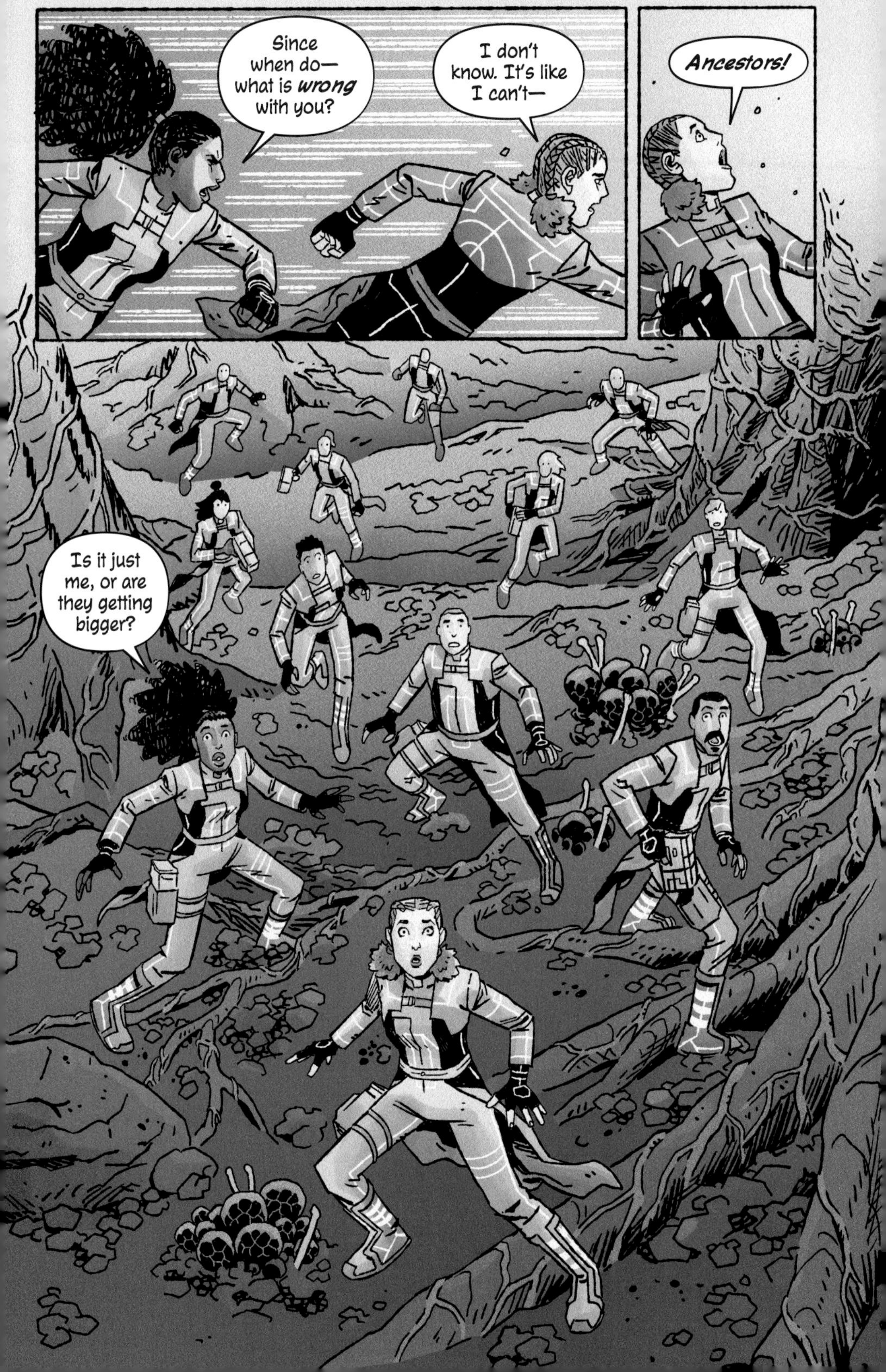
Since when do— what is *wrong* with you?
I don't know. It's like I can't—
Ancestors!
Is it just me, or are they getting bigger?

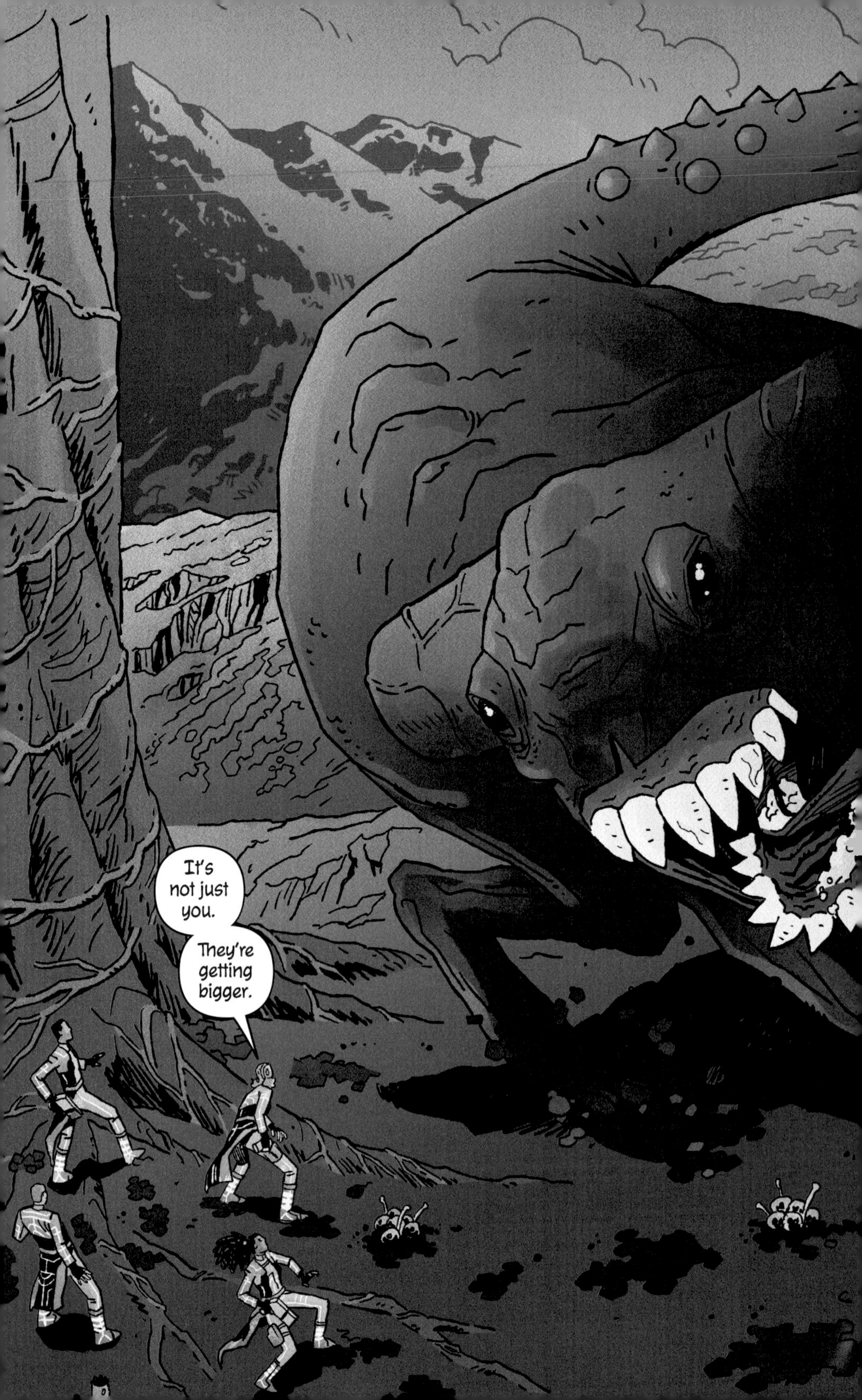
It's not just you.
They're getting bigger.

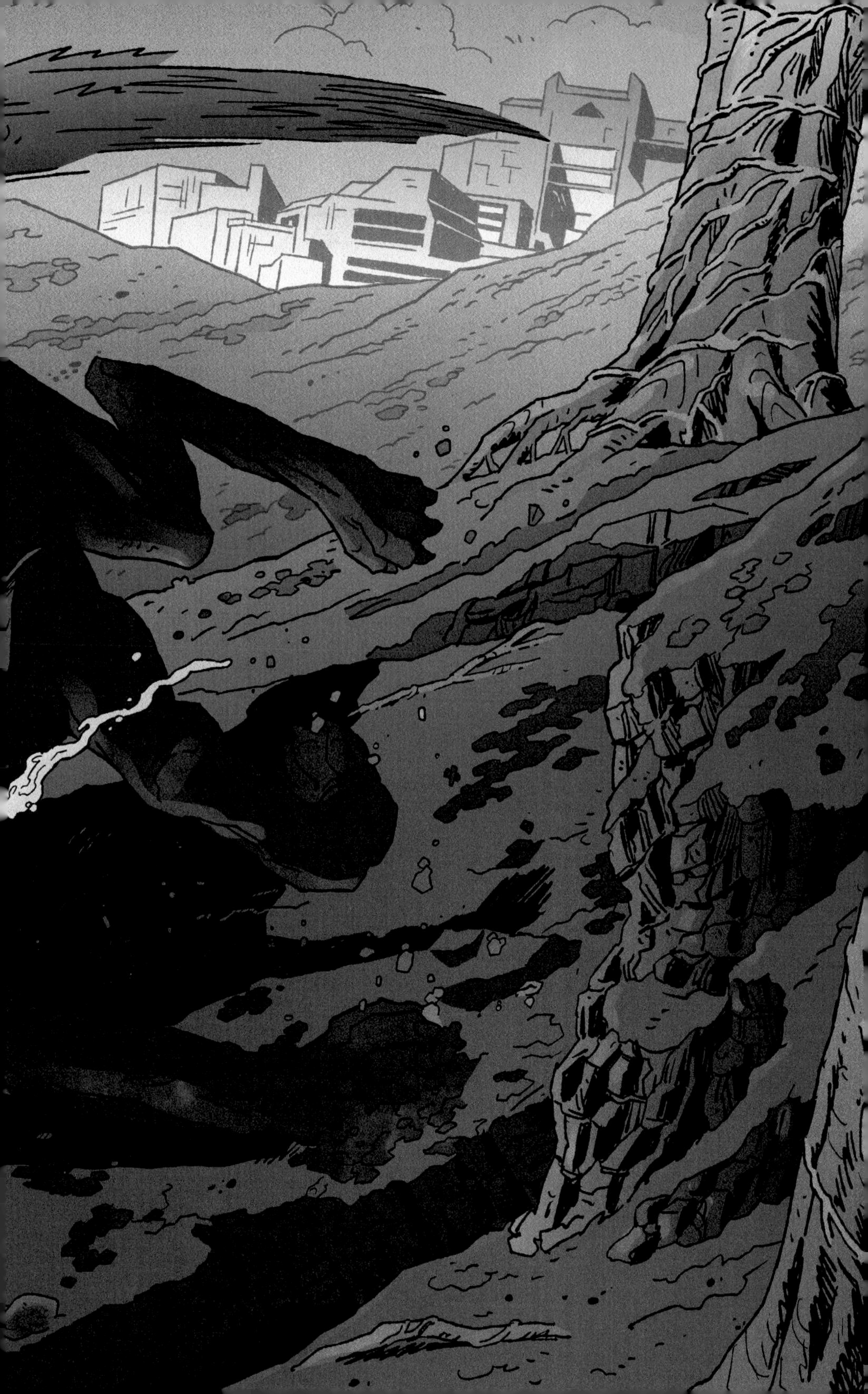

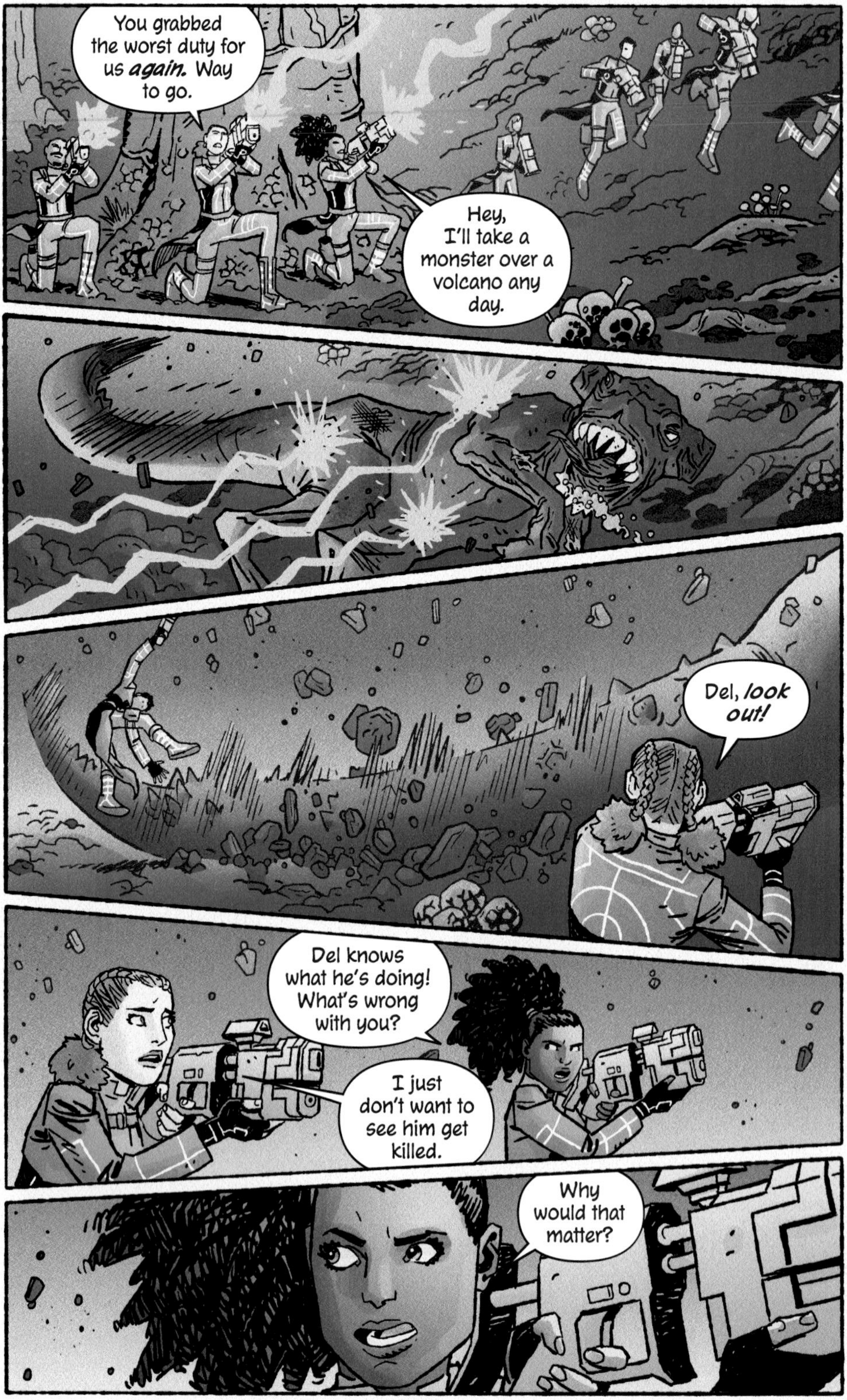
You grabbed the worst duty for us *again.* Way to go.
Hey, I'll take a monster over a volcano any day.
Del, *look out!*
Del knows what he's doing! What's wrong with you?
I just don't want to see him get killed.
Why would that matter?

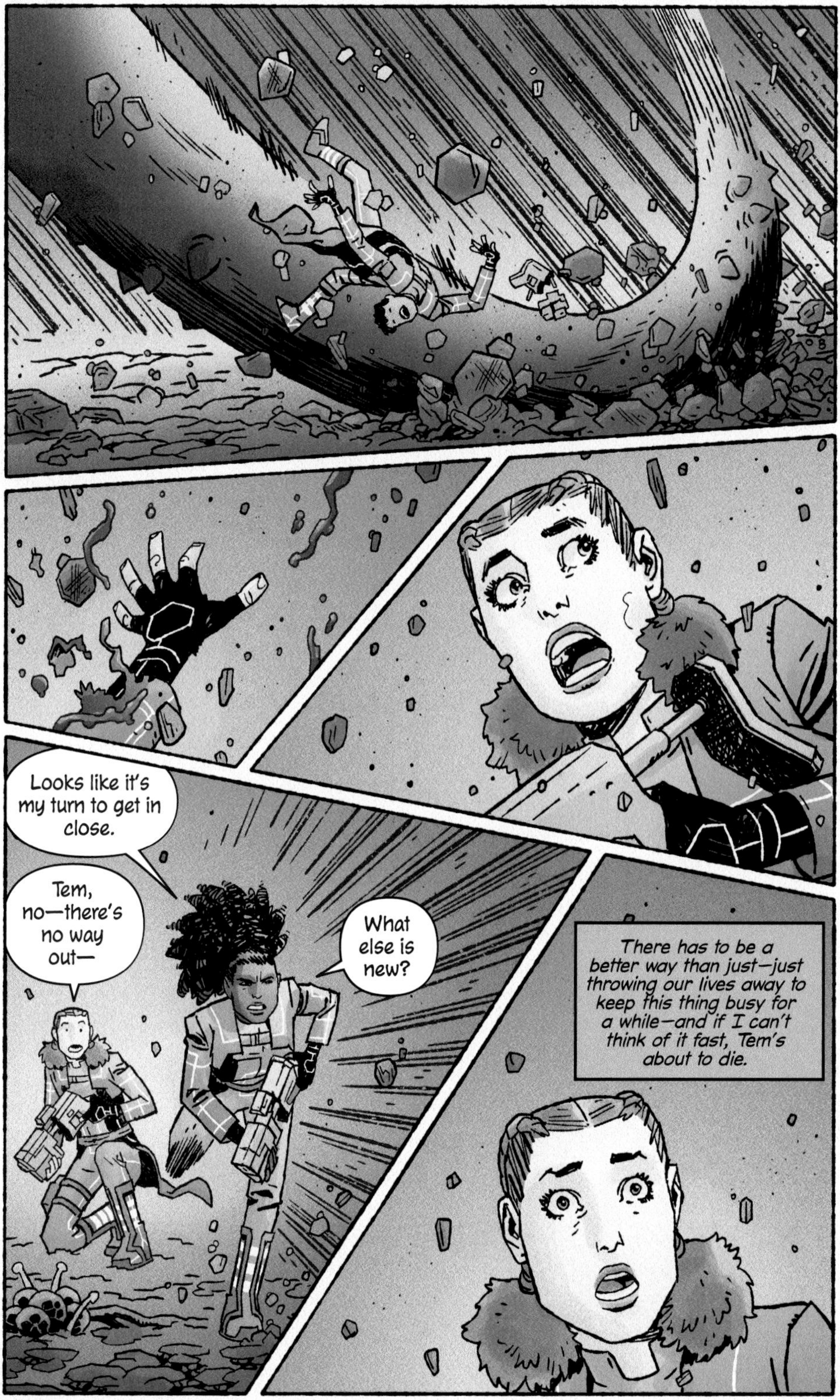
Looks like it's my turn to get in close.
Tem, no—there's no way out—
What else is new?
There has to be a better way than just—just throwing our lives away to keep this thing busy for a while—and if I can't think of it fast, Tem's about to die.

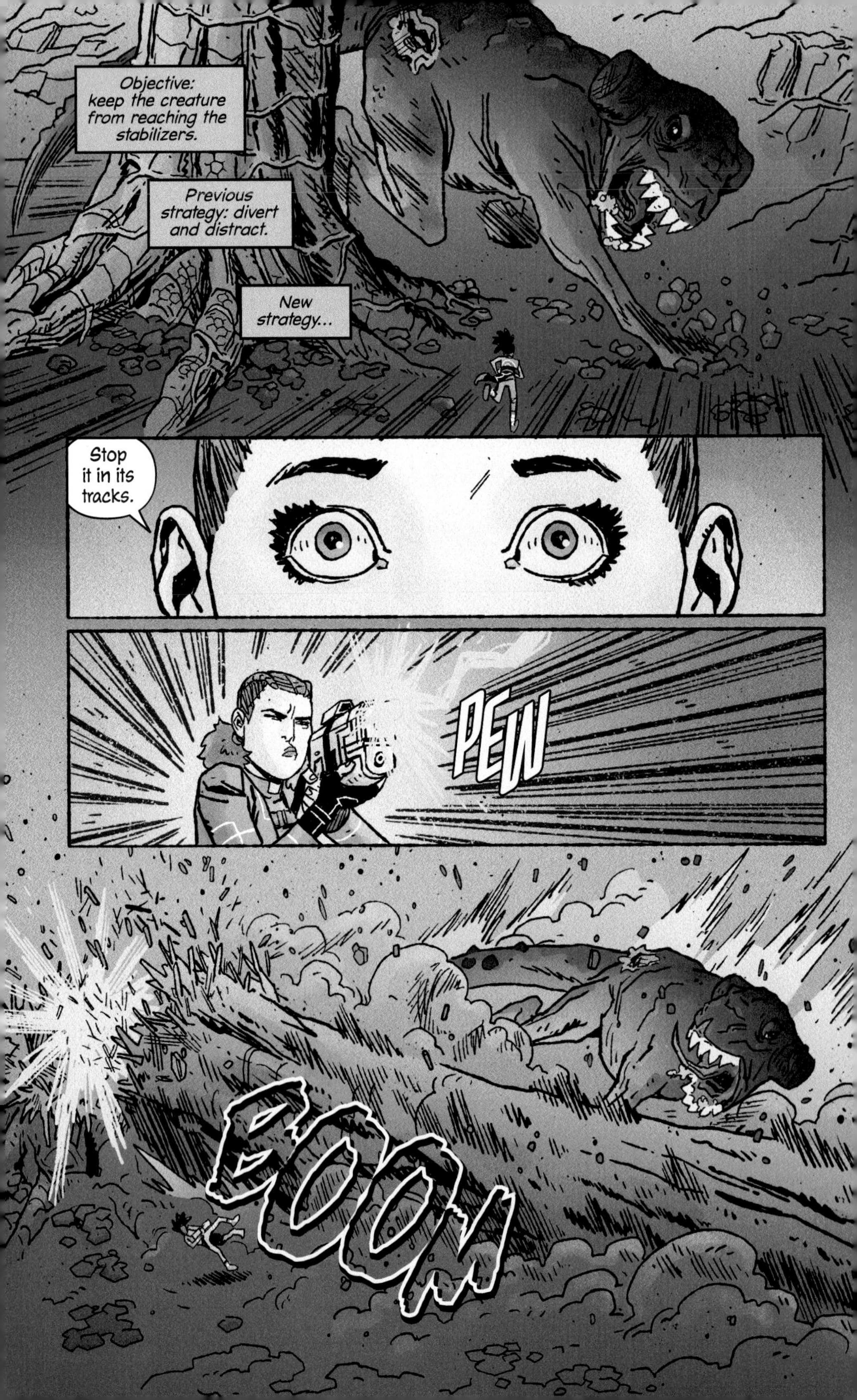
Objective: keep the creature from reaching the stabilizers.
Previous strategy: divert and distract.
New strategy...
Stop it in its tracks.
PEW
BOOM

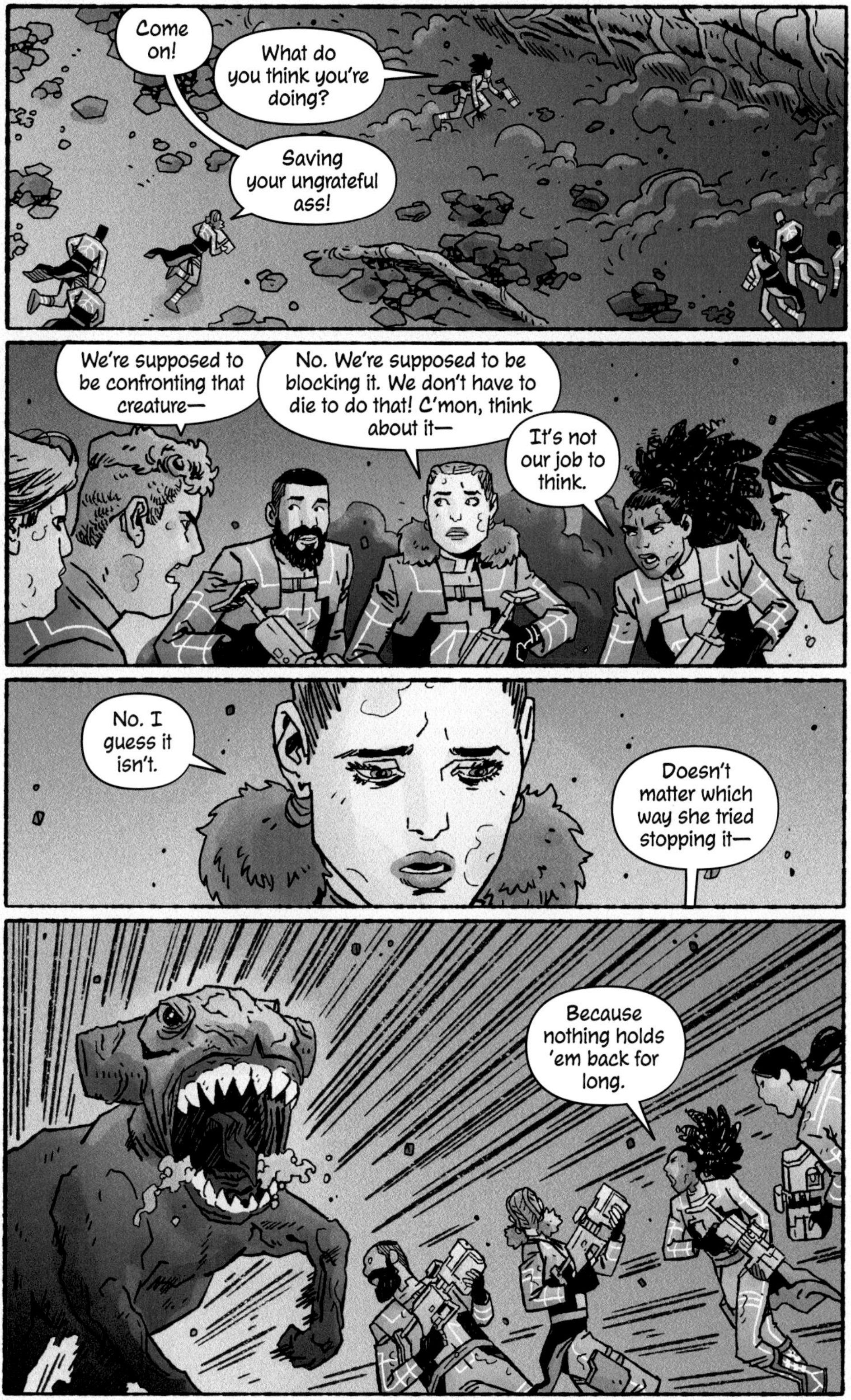
Come on!
What do you think you're doing?
Saving your ungrateful ass!
We're supposed to be confronting that creature—
No. We're supposed to be blocking it. We don't have to die to do that! C'mon, think about it—
It's not our job to think.
No. I guess it isn't.
Doesn't matter which way she tried stopping it—
Because nothing holds 'em back for long.

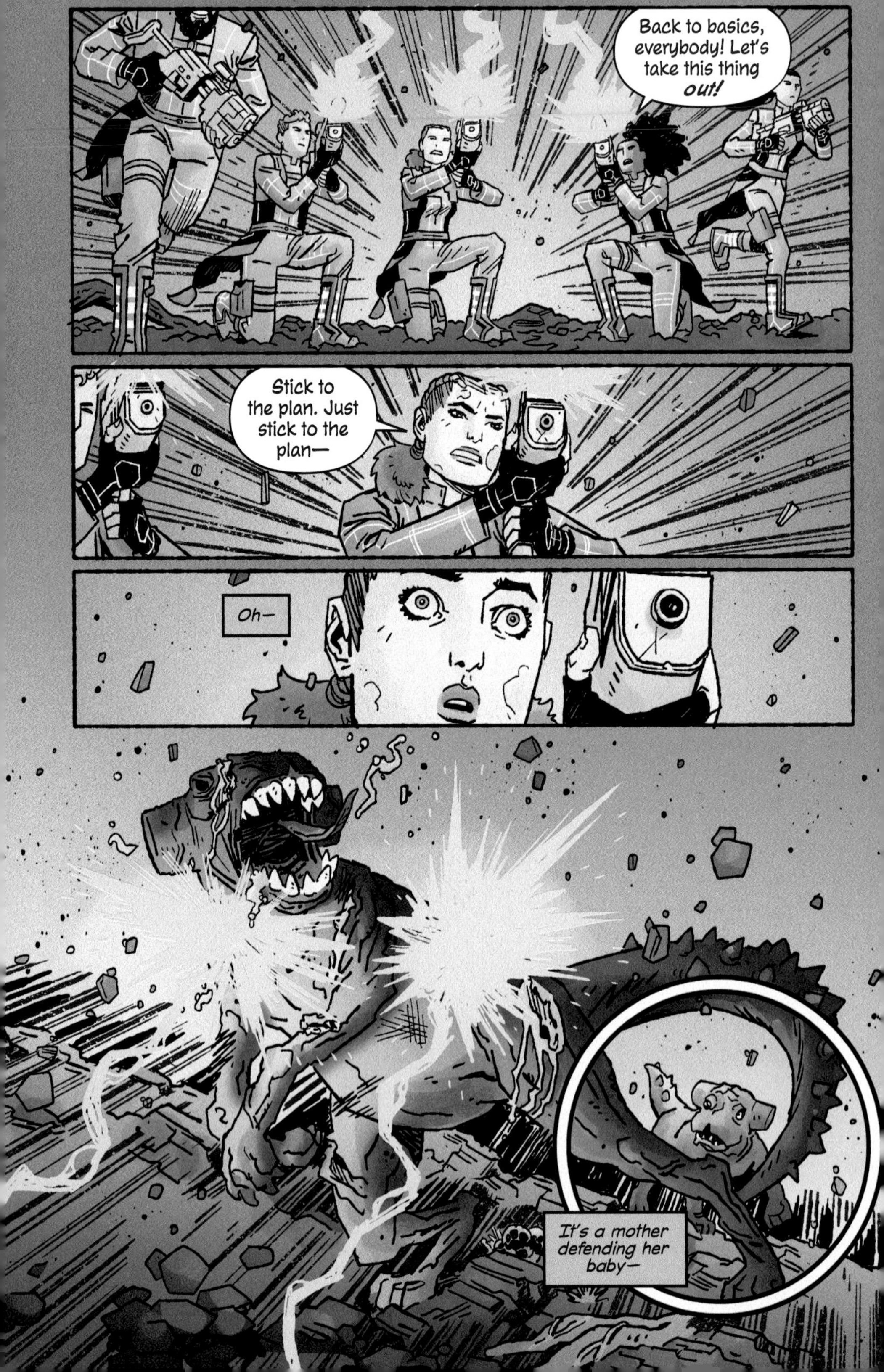
Back to basics, everybody! Let's take this thing *out!*
Stick to the plan. Just stick to the plan—
Oh—
It's a mother defending her baby—

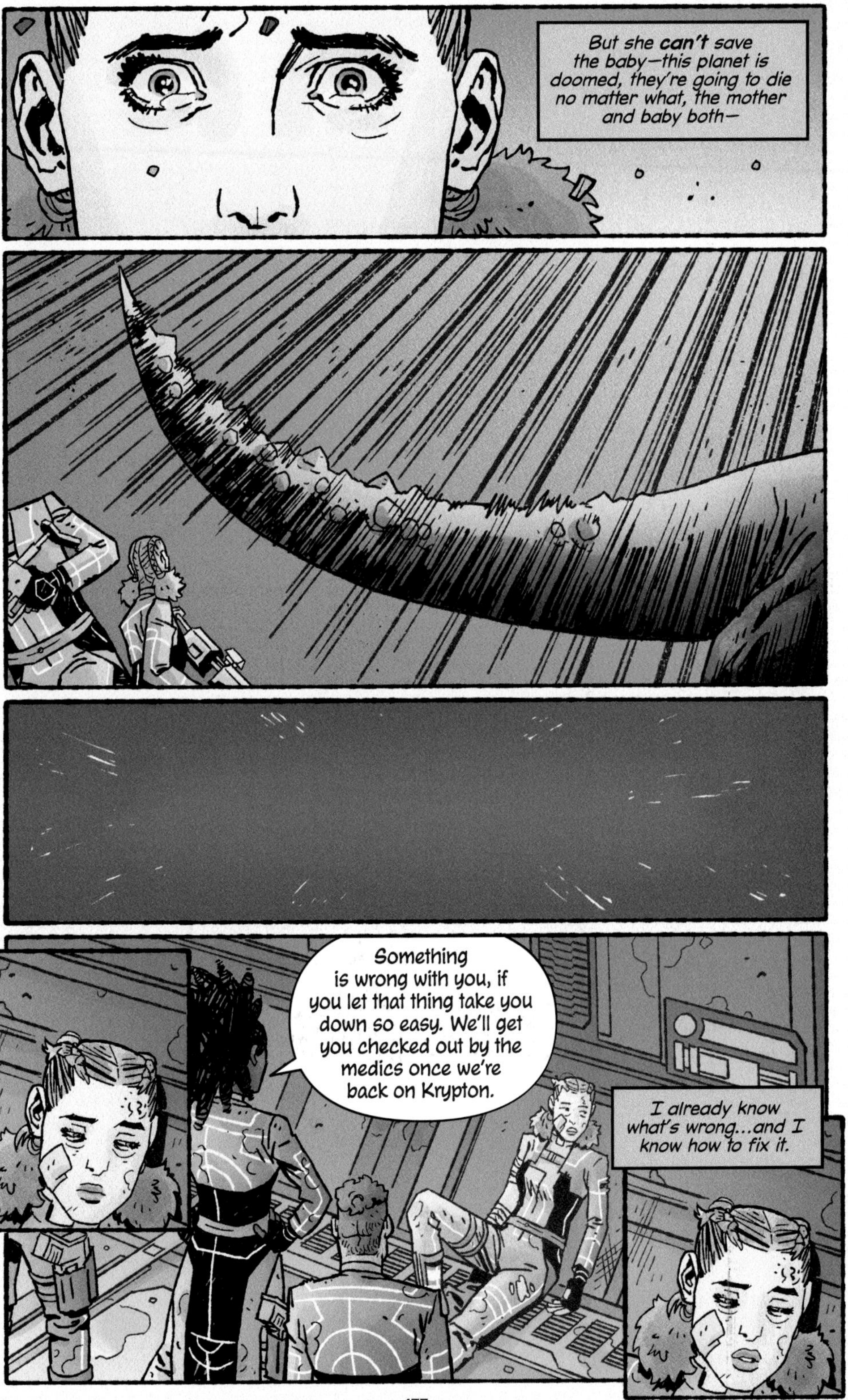

But she **can't** save the baby—this planet is doomed, they're going to die no matter what, the mother and baby both—
Something is wrong with you, if you let that thing take you down so easy. We'll get you checked out by the medics once we're back on Krypton.
I already know what's wrong...and I know how to fix it.

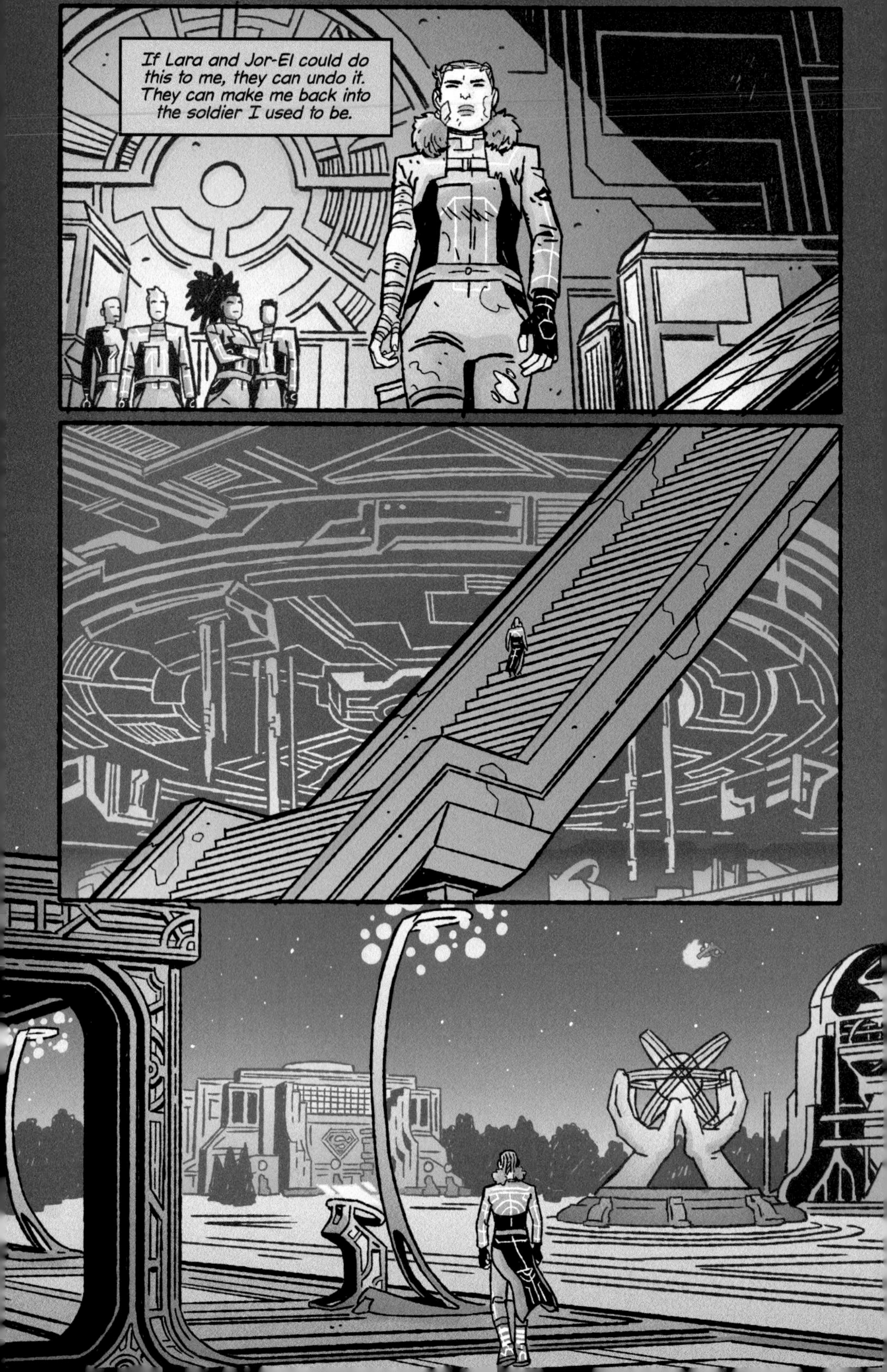
If Lara and Jor-El could do this to me, they can undo it. They can make me back into the soldier I used to be.

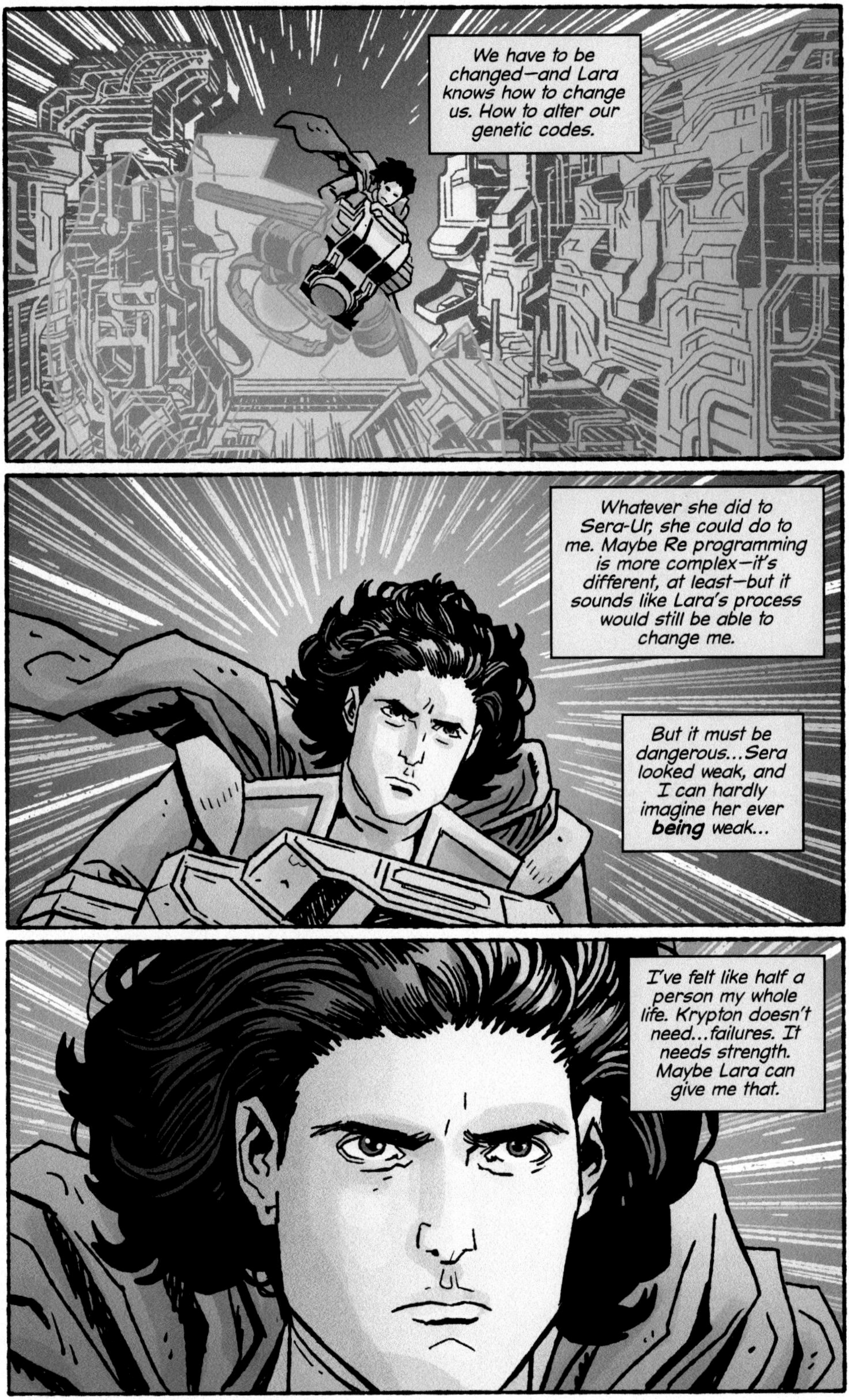
We have to be changed—and Lara knows how to change us. How to alter our genetic codes.
Whatever she did to Sera-Ur, she could do to me. Maybe Re programming is more complex—it's different, at least—but it sounds like Lara's process would still be able to change me.
But it must be dangerous...Sera looked weak, and I can hardly imagine her ever **being** weak...
I've felt like half a person my whole life. Krypton doesn't need...failures. It needs strength. Maybe Lara can give me that.

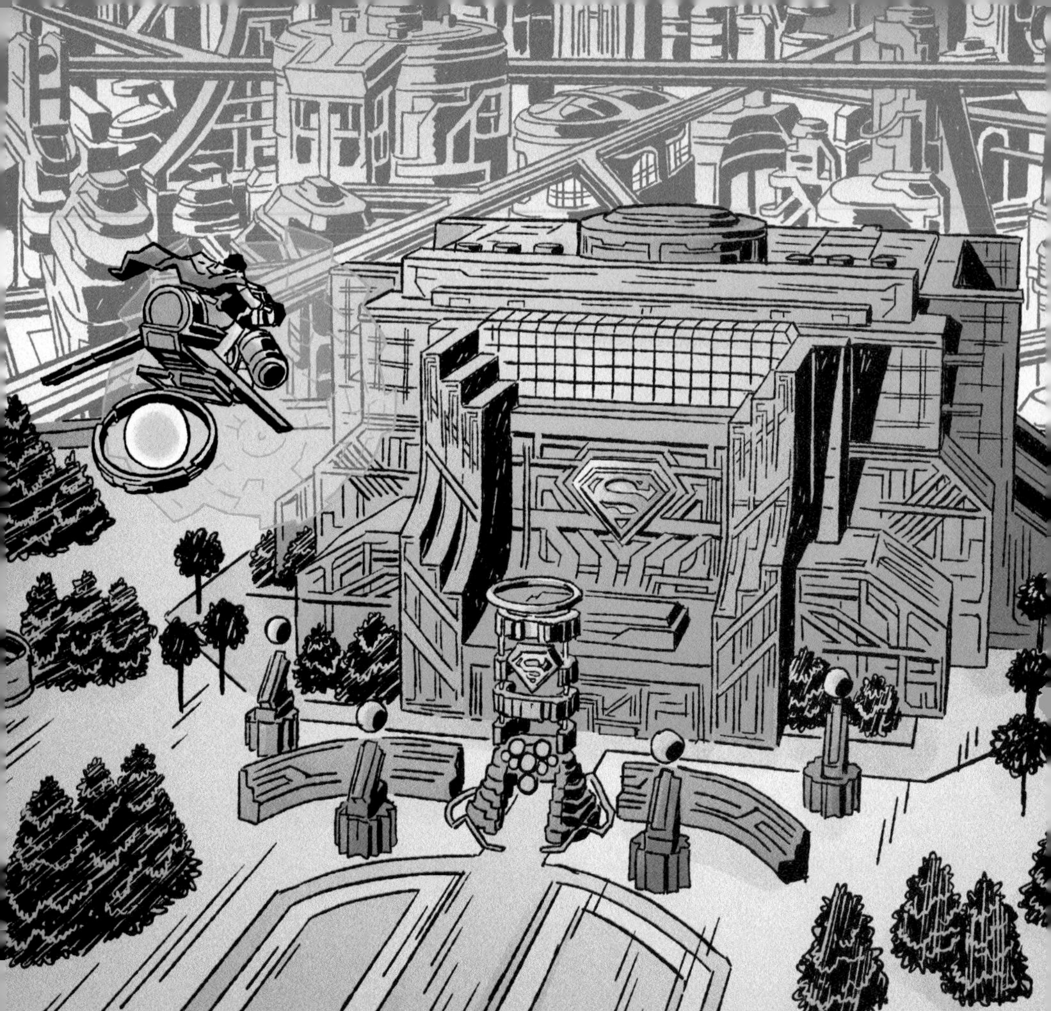

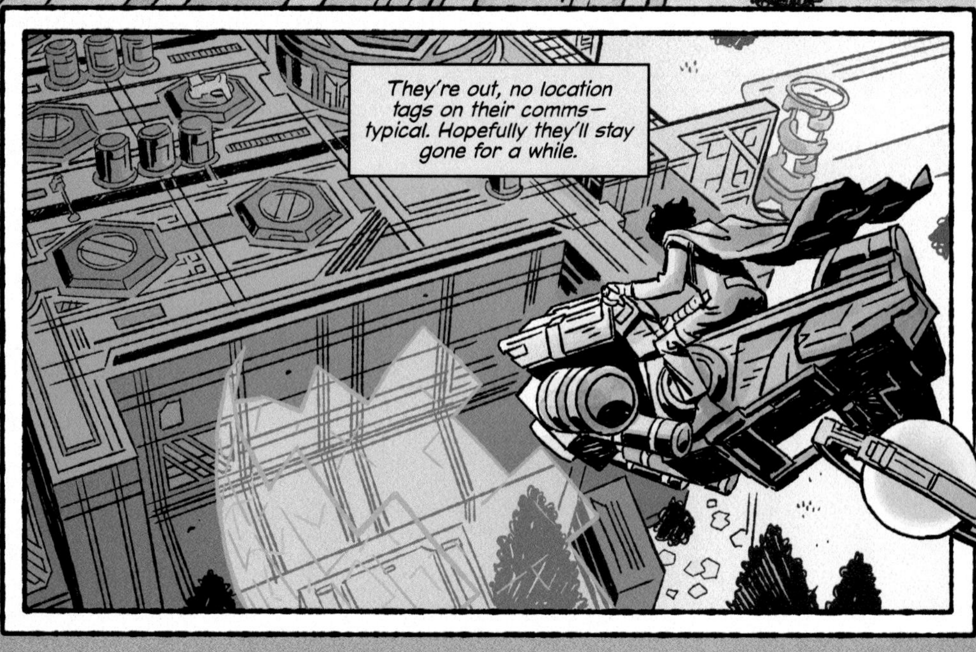
They're out, no location tags on their comms—typical. Hopefully they'll stay gone for a while.

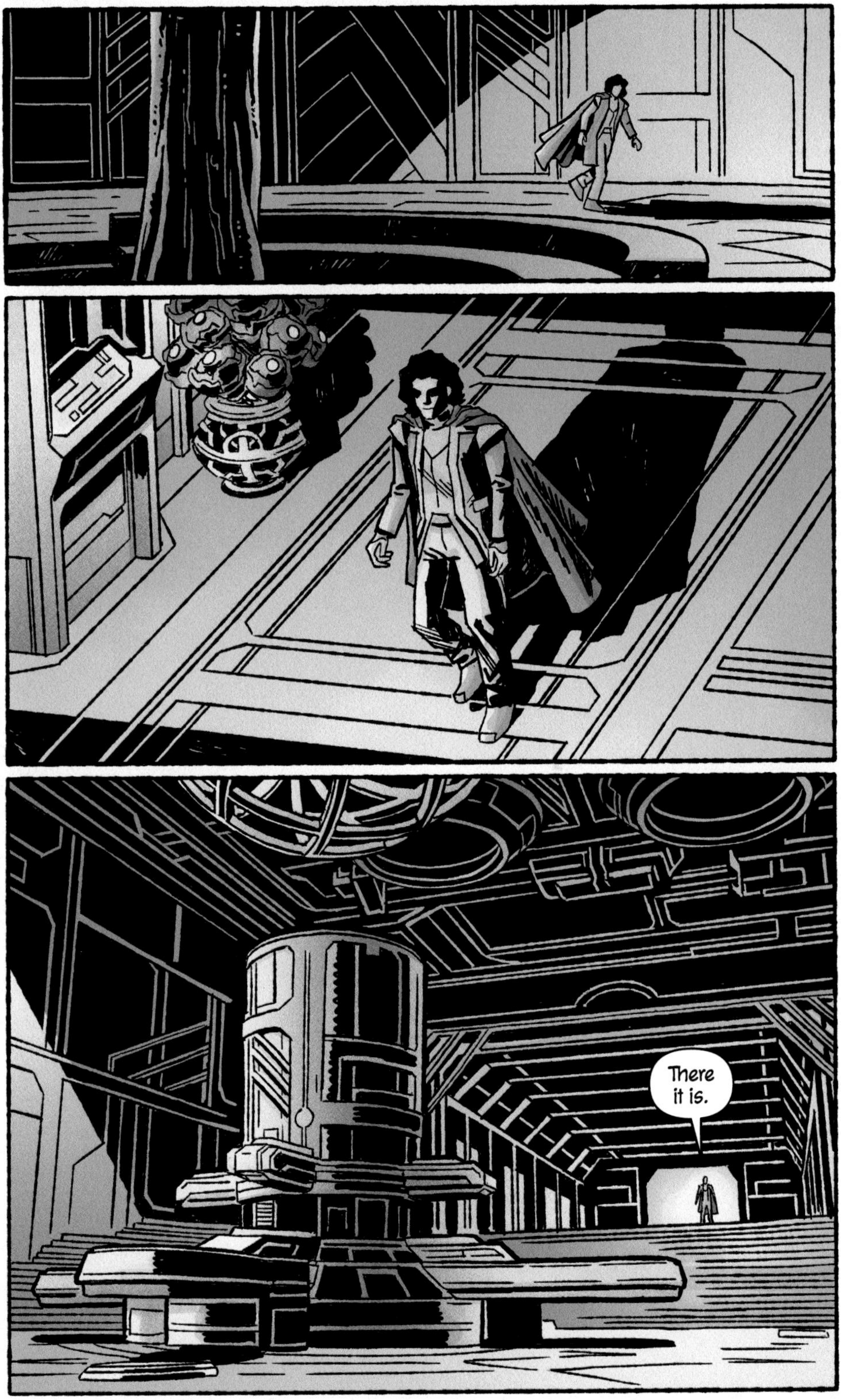
There it is.

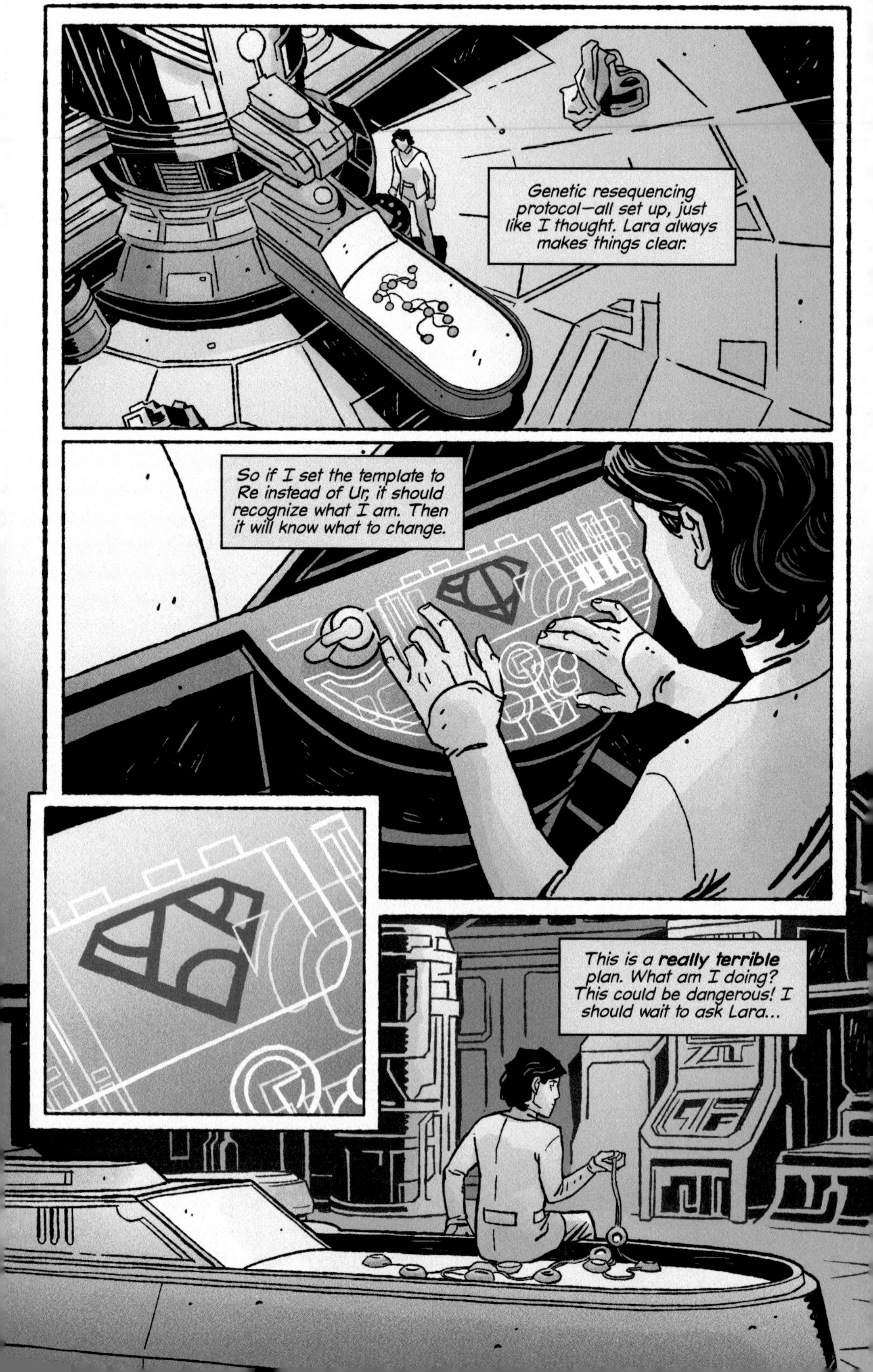
Genetic resequencing protocol—all set up, just like I thought. Lara always makes things clear.
So if I set the template to Re instead of Ur, it should recognize what I am. Then it will know what to change.
This is a **really terrible** plan. What am I doing? This could be dangerous! I should wait to ask Lara...

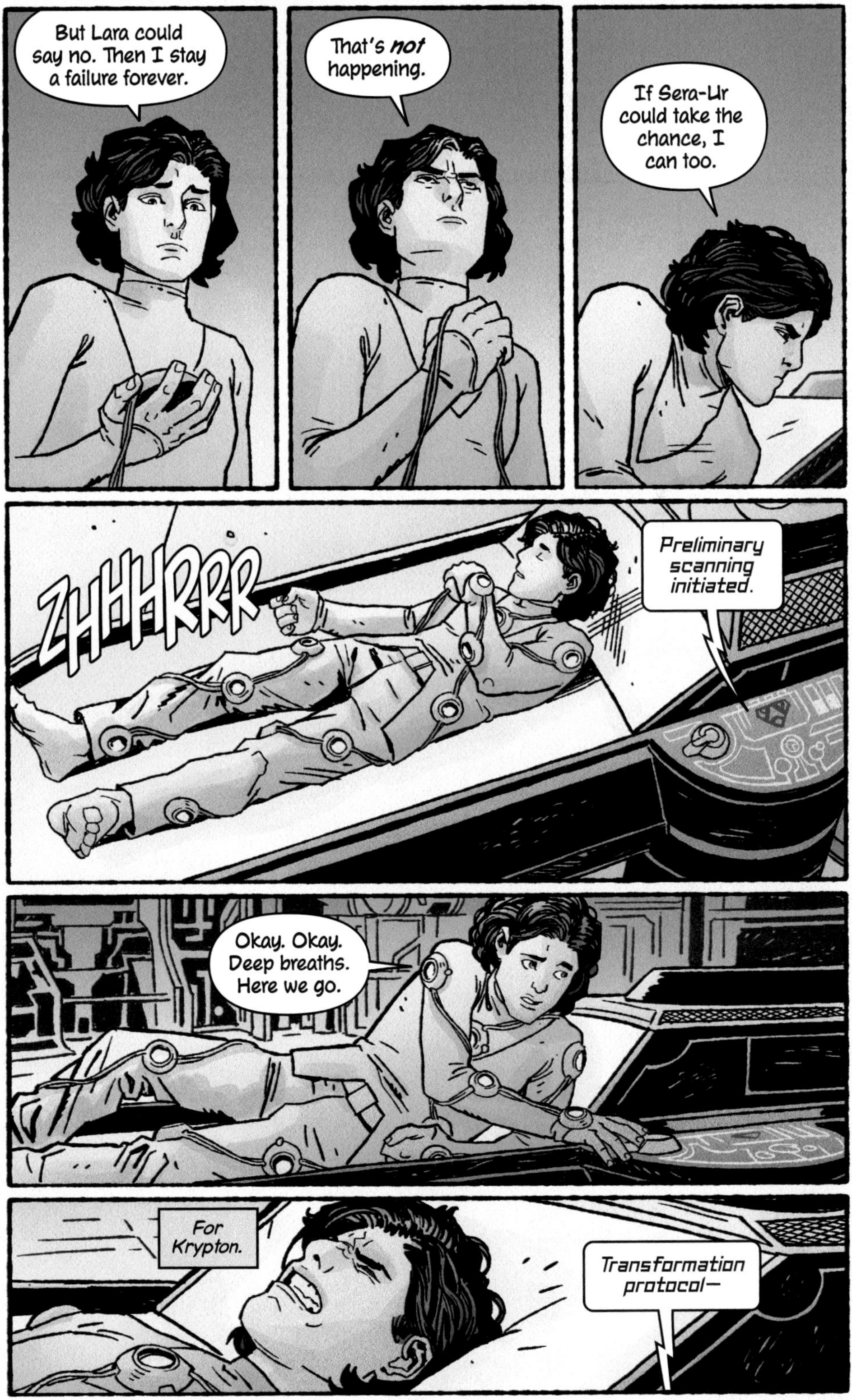
But Lara could say no. Then I stay a failure forever.
That's *not* happening.
If Sera-Ur could take the chance, I can too.
ZHHHRRR
Preliminary scanning initiated.
Okay. Okay. Deep breaths. Here we go.
For Krypton.
Transformation protocol—

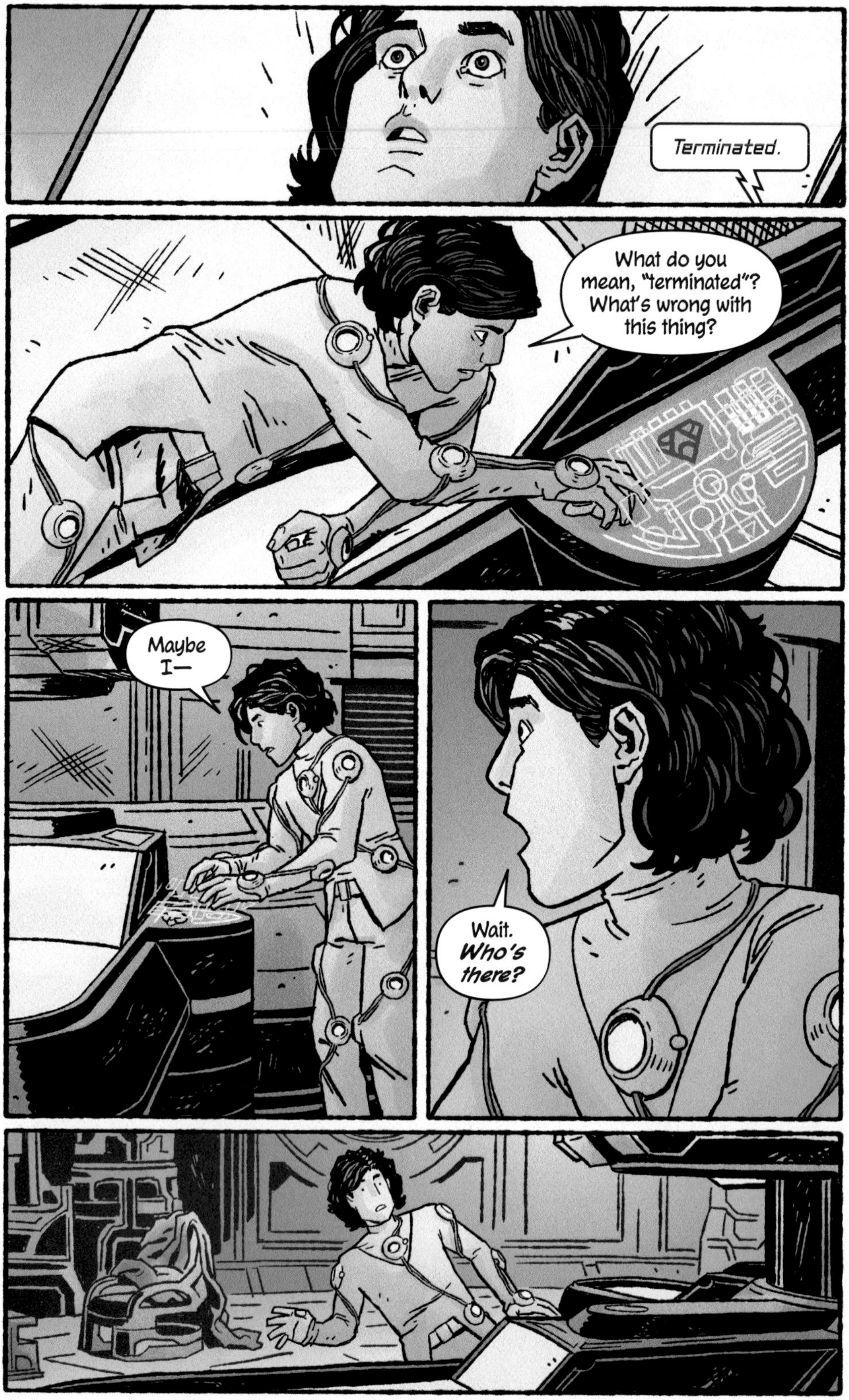
Terminated.
What do you mean, "terminated"? What's wrong with this thing?
Maybe I—
Wait. Who's there?

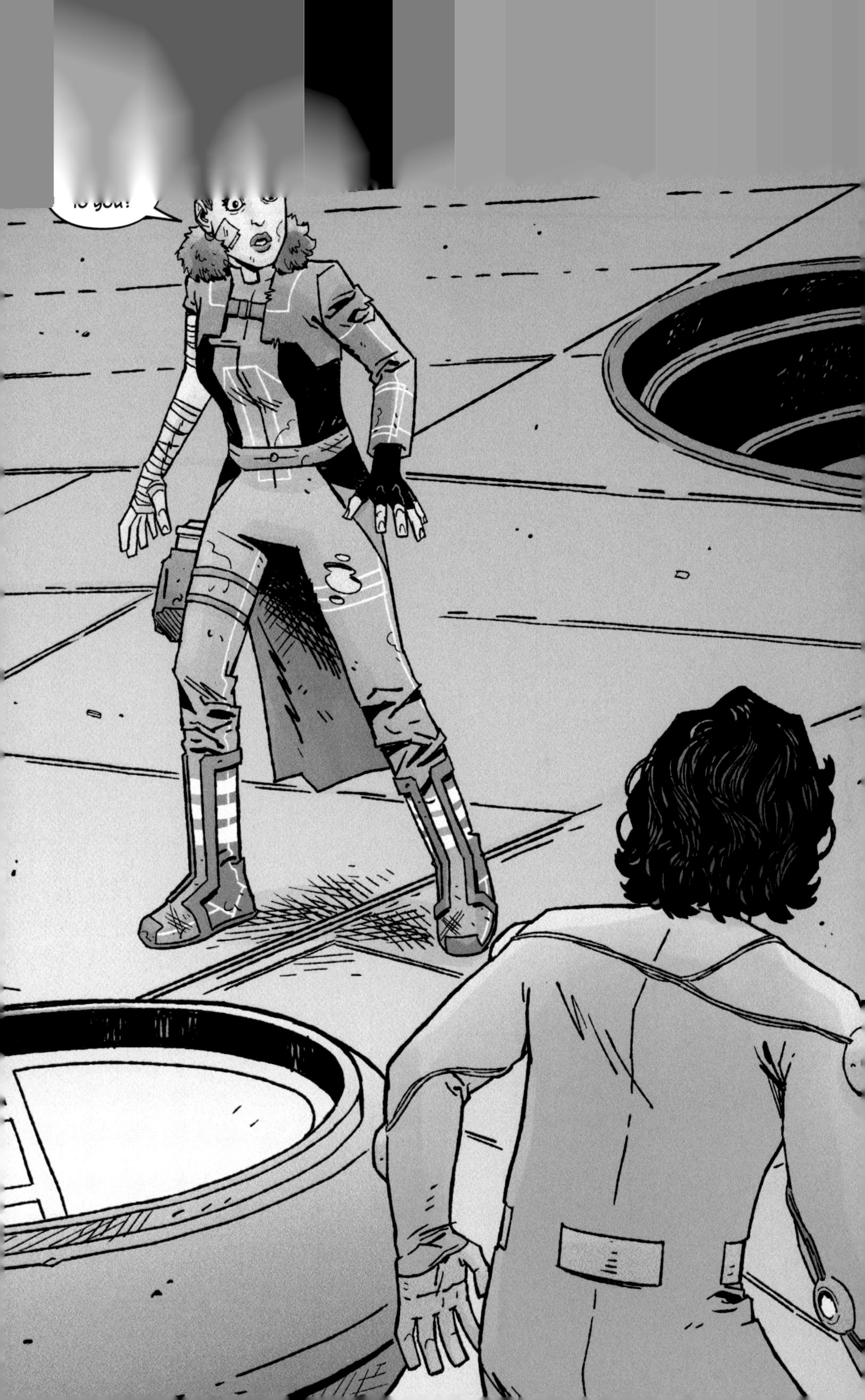

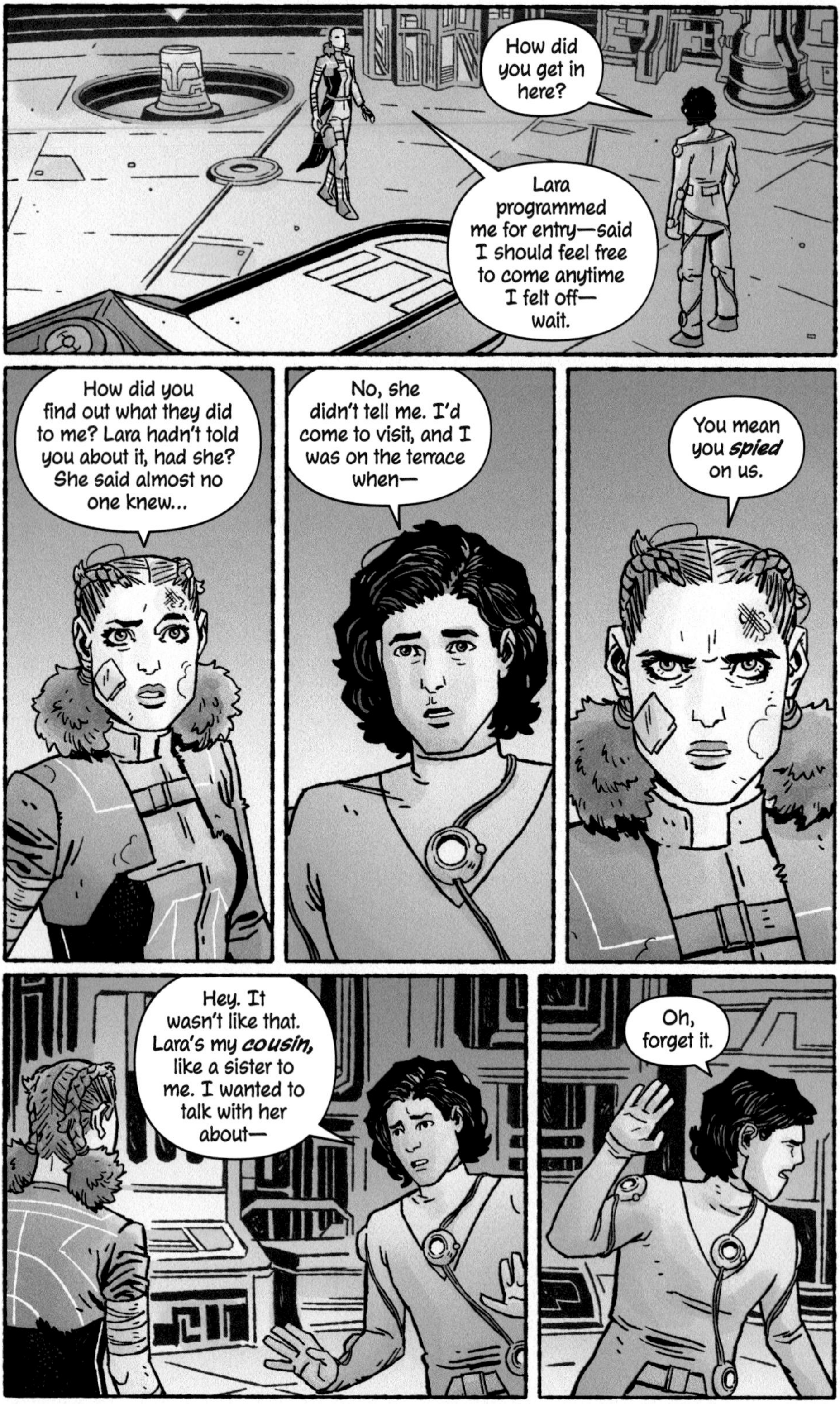
How did you get in here?
Lara programmed me for entry—said I should feel free to come anytime I felt off—wait.
How did you find out what they did to me? Lara hadn't told you about it, had she? She said almost no one knew...
No, she didn't tell me. I'd come to visit, and I was on the terrace when—
You mean you *spied* on us.
Hey. It wasn't like that. Lara's my *cousin,* like a sister to me. I wanted to talk with her about—
Oh, forget it.

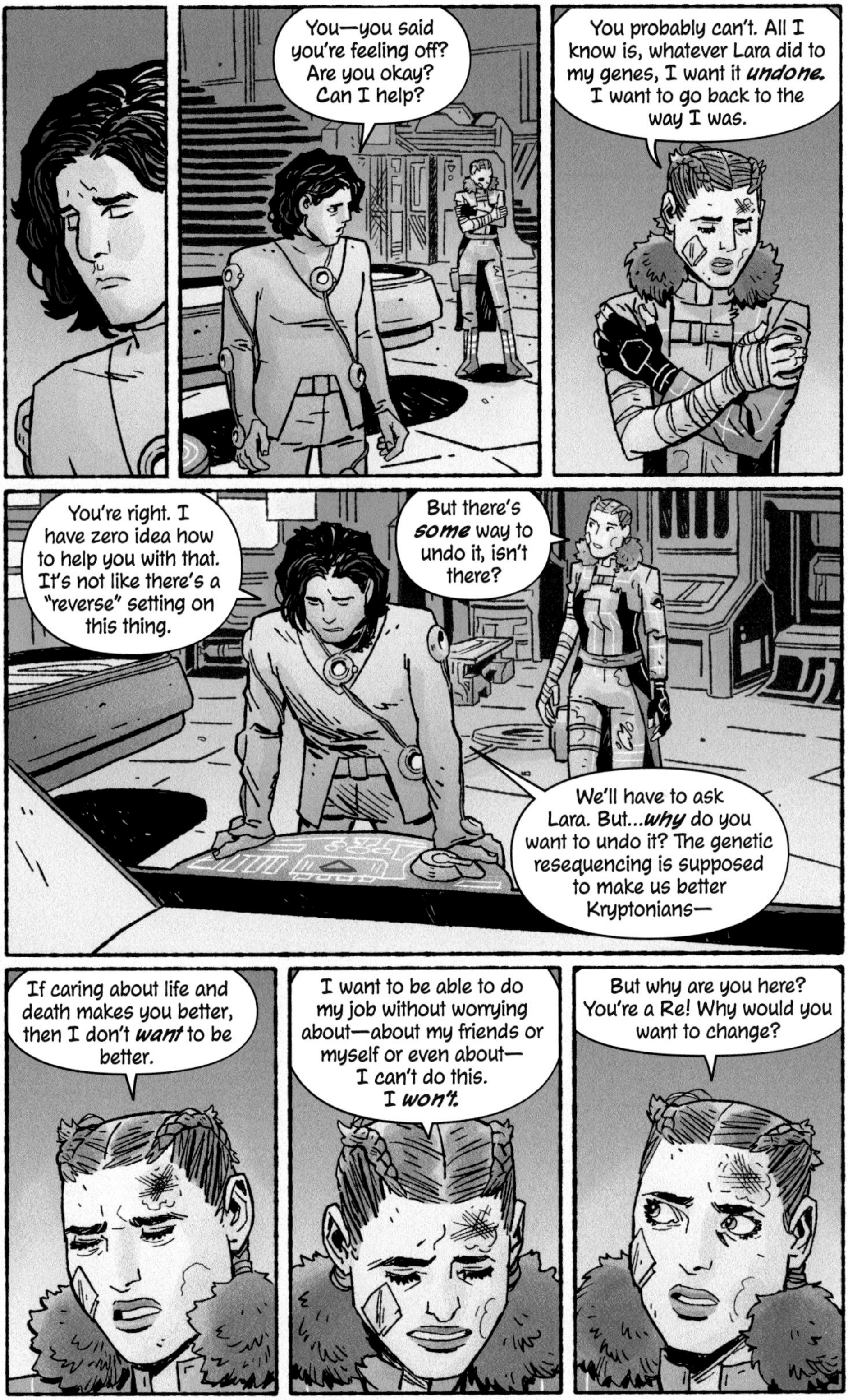
You—you said you're feeling off? Are you okay? Can I help?
You probably can't. All I know is, whatever Lara did to my genes, I want it *undone.* I want to go back to the way I was.
You're right. I have zero idea how to help you with that. It's not like there's a "reverse" setting on this thing.
But there's *some* way to undo it, isn't there?
We'll have to ask Lara. But...*why* do you want to undo it? The genetic resequencing is supposed to make us better Kryptonians—
If caring about life and death makes you better, then I don't *want* to be better.
I want to be able to do my job without worrying about—about my friends or myself or even about— I can't do this. I *won't.*
But why are you here? You're a Re! Why would you want to change?

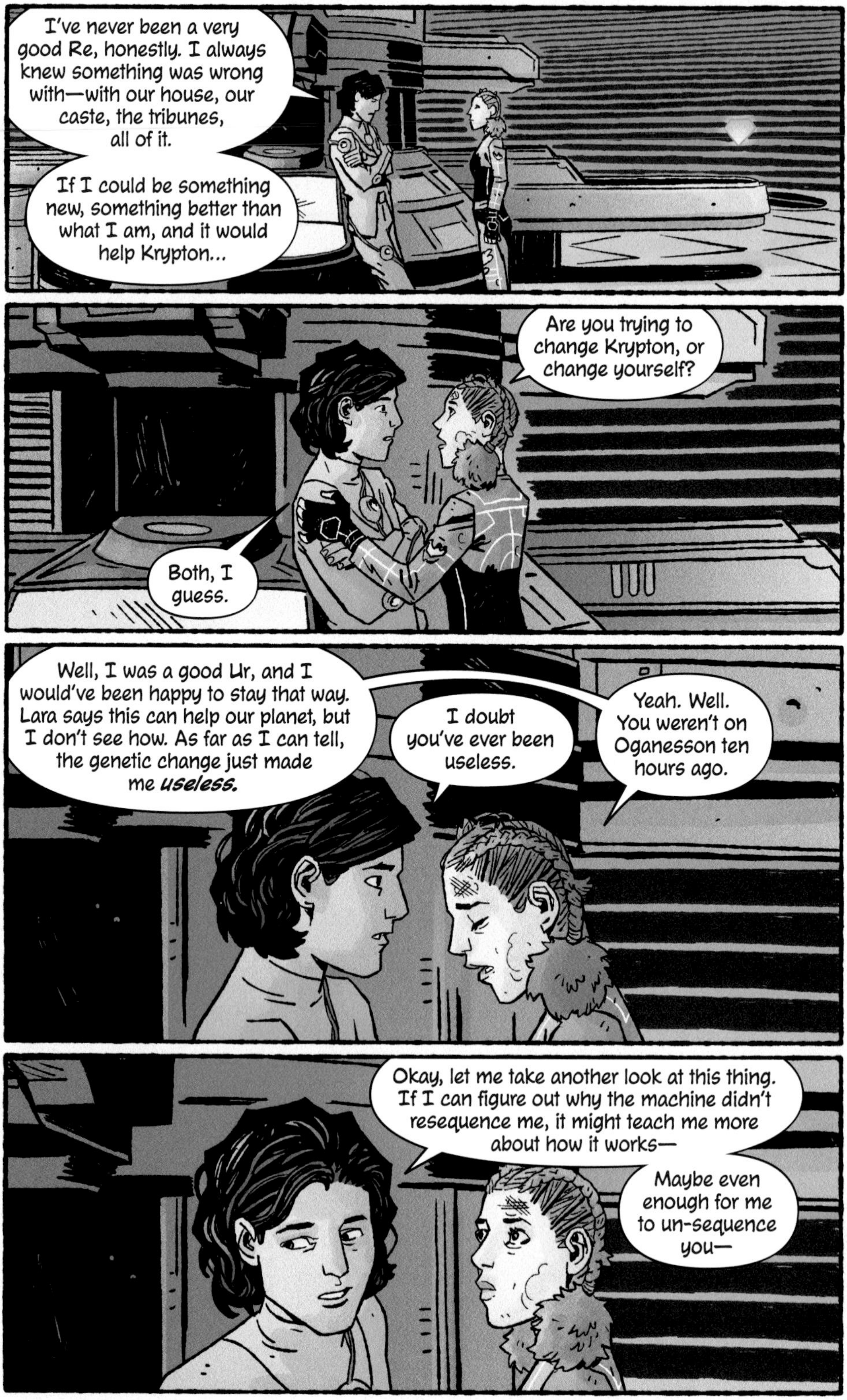
I've never been a very good Re, honestly. I always knew something was wrong with—with our house, our caste, the tribunes, all of it.
If I could be something new, something better than what I am, and it would help Krypton...
Are you trying to change Krypton, or change yourself?
Both, I guess.
Well, I was a good Ur, and I would've been happy to stay that way. Lara says this can help our planet, but I don't see how. As far as I can tell, the genetic change just made me *useless.*
I doubt you've ever been useless.
Yeah. Well. You weren't on Oganesson ten hours ago.
Okay, let me take another look at this thing. If I can figure out why the machine didn't resequence me, it might teach me more about how it works—
Maybe even enough for me to un-sequence you—

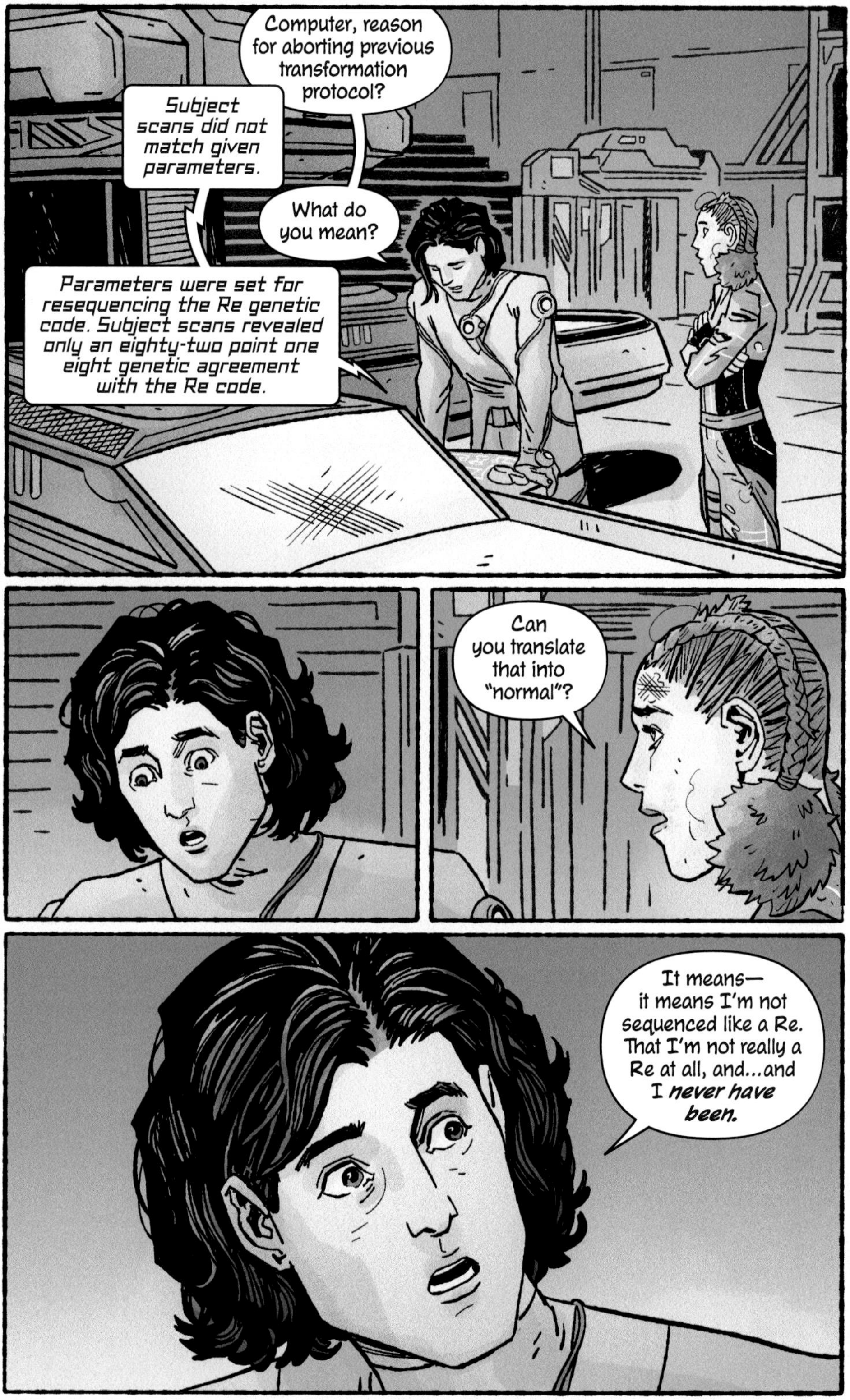
Computer, reason for aborting previous transformation protocol?
Subject scans did not match given parameters.
What do you mean?
Parameters were set for resequencing the Re genetic code. Subject scans revealed only an eighty-two point one eight genetic agreement with the Re code.
Can you translate that into "normal"?
It means— it means I'm not sequenced like a Re. That I'm not really a Re at all, and...and I ***never have been.***

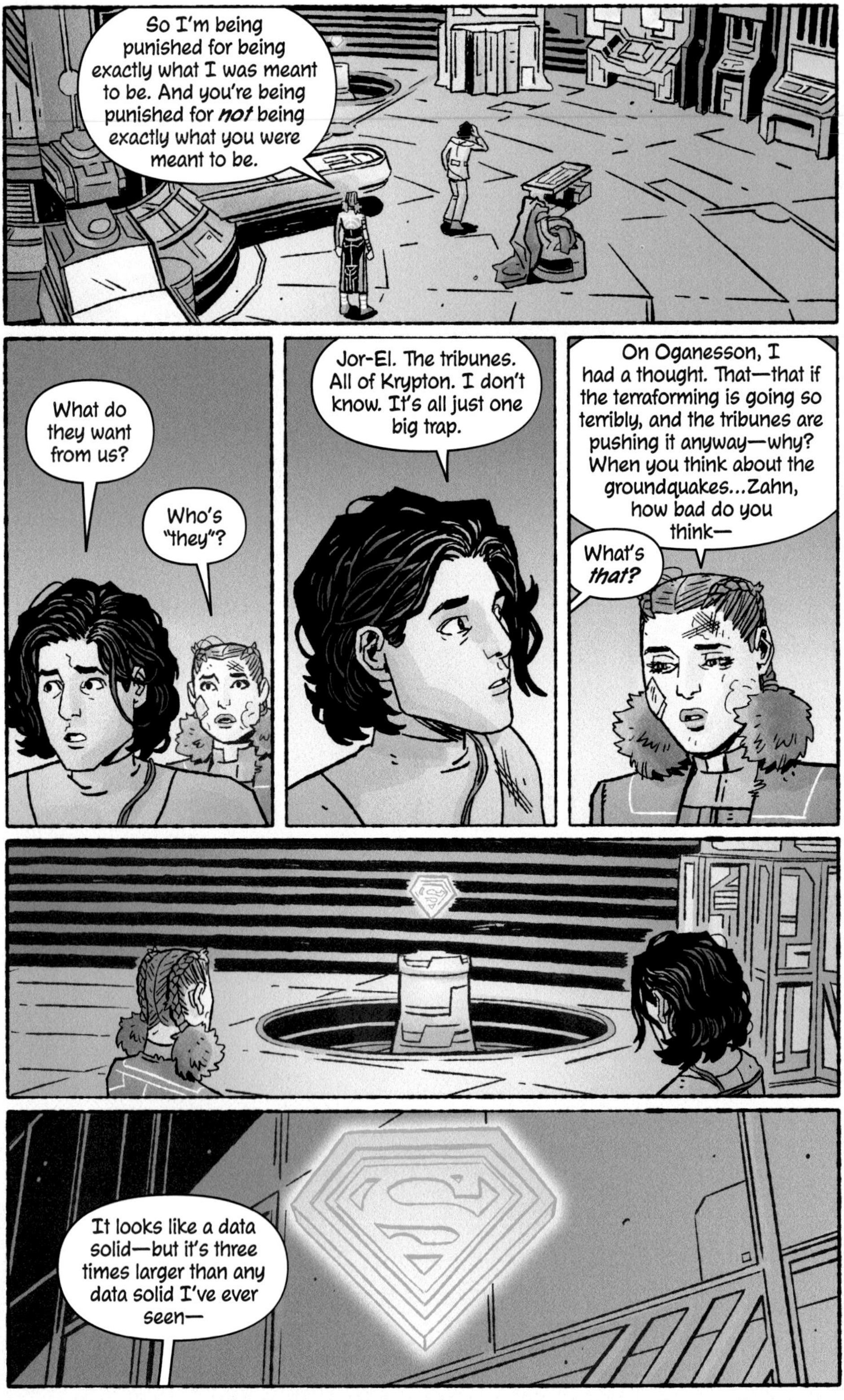
So I'm being punished for being exactly what I was meant to be. And you're being punished for *not* being exactly what you were meant to be.
What do they want from us?
Who's "they"?
Jor-El. The tribunes. All of Krypton. I don't know. It's all just one big trap.
On Oganesson, I had a thought. That—that if the terraforming is going so terribly, and the tribunes are pushing it anyway—why? When you think about the groundquakes...Zahn, how bad do you think—
What's *that?*
It looks like a data solid—but it's three times larger than any data solid I've ever seen—

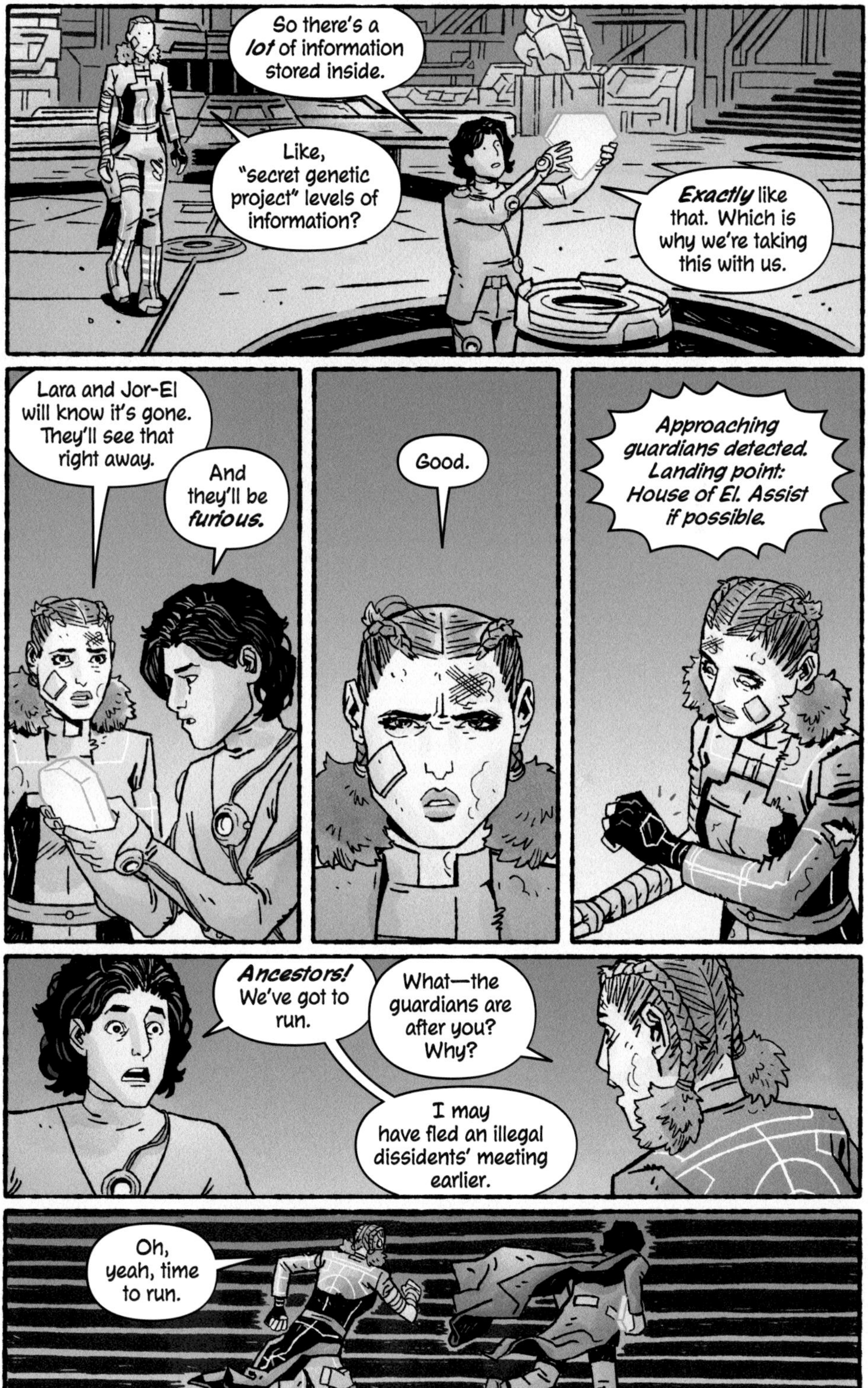
So there's a *lot* of information stored inside.
Like, "secret genetic project" levels of information?
Exactly like that. Which is why we're taking this with us.
Lara and Jor-El will know it's gone. They'll see that right away.
And they'll be *furious.*
Good.
Approaching guardians detected. Landing point: House of El. Assist if possible.
Ancestors! We've got to run.
What—the guardians are after you? Why?
I may have fled an illegal dissidents' meeting earlier.
Oh, yeah, time to run.

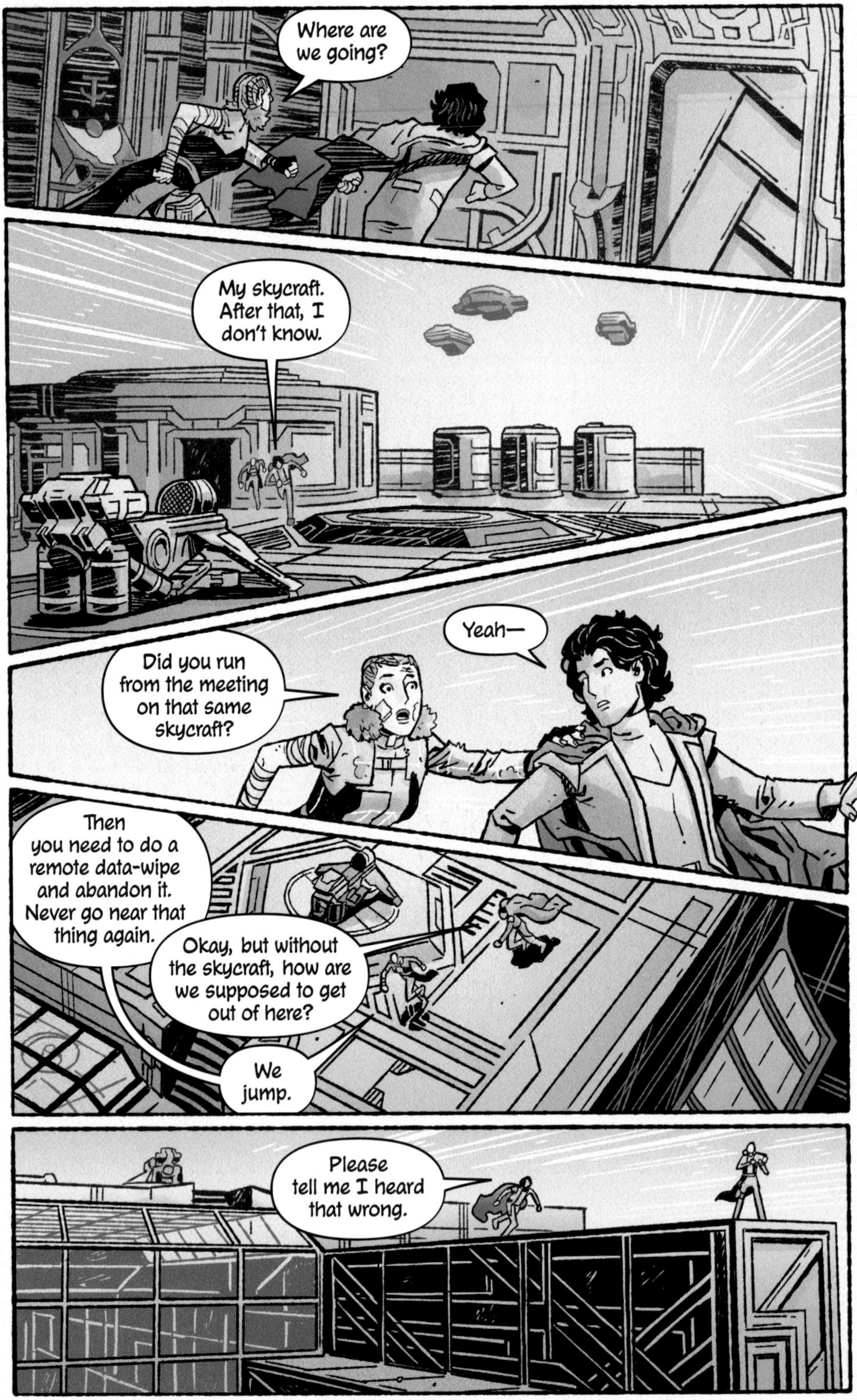
Where are we going?
My skycraft. After that, I don't know.
Did you run from the meeting on that same skycraft?
Yeah—
Then you need to do a remote data-wipe and abandon it. Never go near that thing again.
Okay, but without the skycraft, how are we supposed to get out of here?
We jump.
Please tell me I heard that wrong.

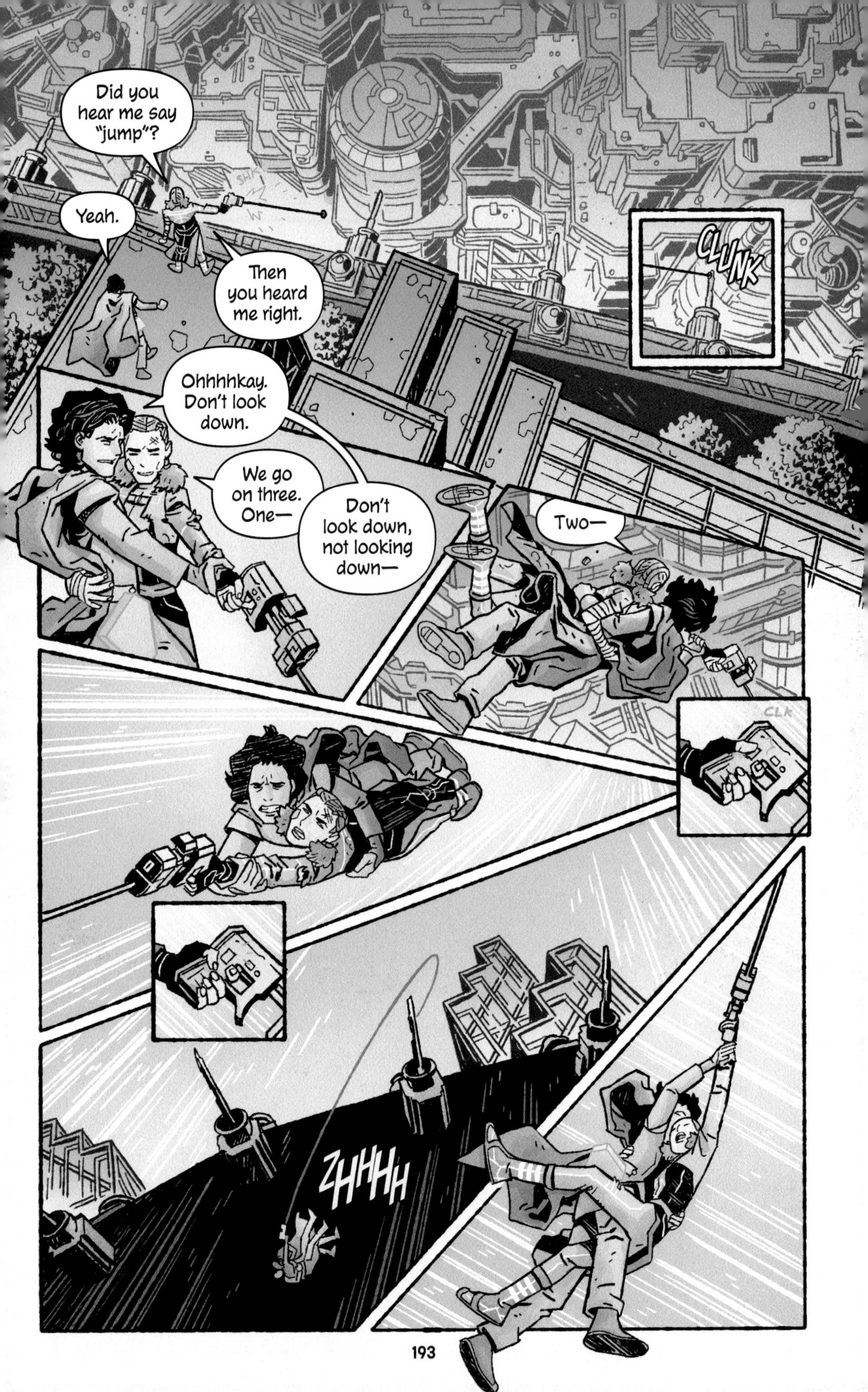

Did you hear me say "jump"?
Yeah.
Then you heard me right.
CLUNK
Ohhhhkay. Don't look down.
We go on three. One—
Don't look down, not looking down—
Two—
CLK
ZHHHH

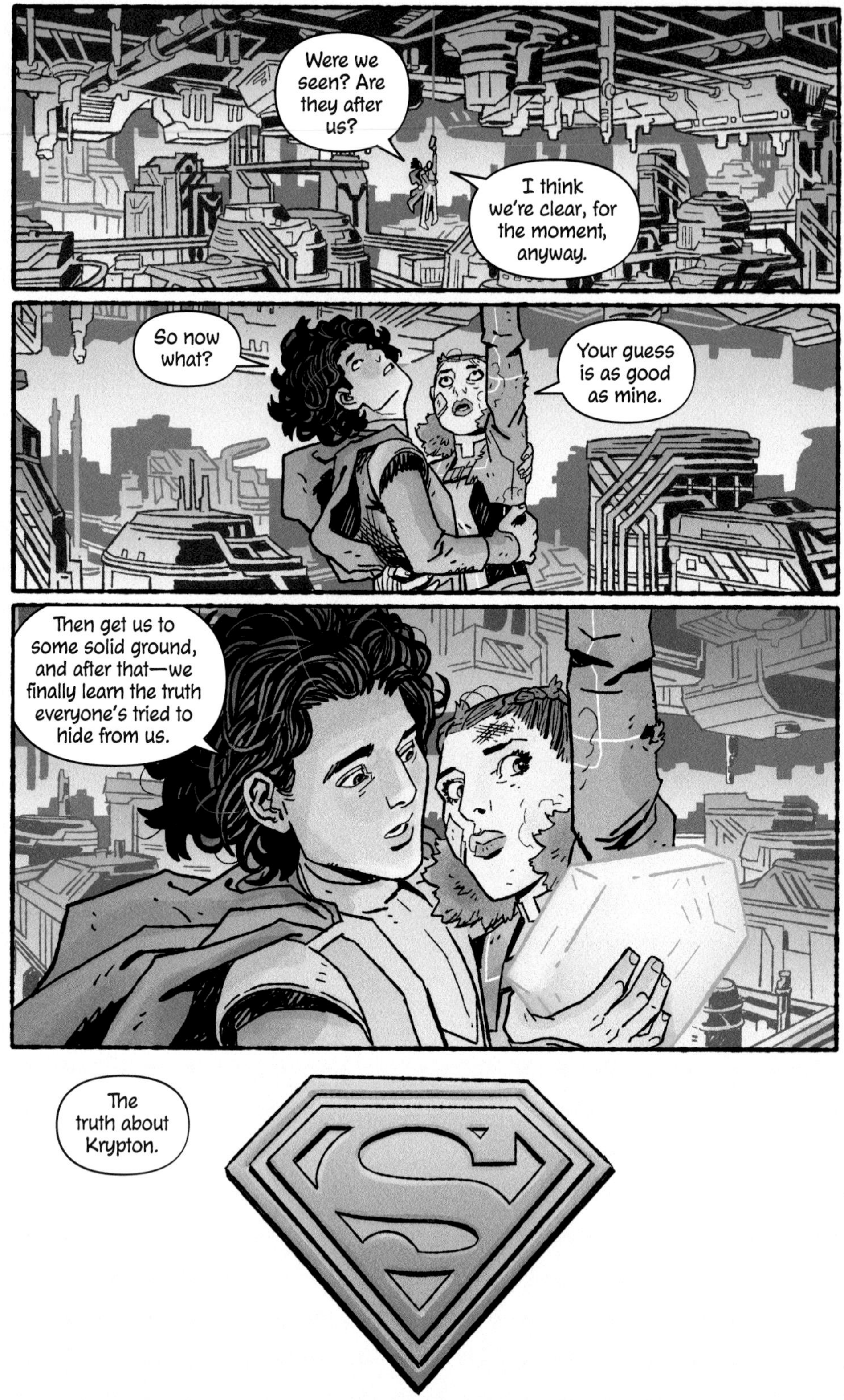
Were we seen? Are they after us?
I think we're clear, for the moment, anyway.
So now what?
Your guess is as good as mine.
Then get us to some solid ground, and after that—we finally learn the truth everyone's tried to hide from us.
The truth about Krypton.

TO BE
CONTINUED
IN

HOUSE of EL

BOOK TWO

THE
ENEMY
DELUSION

FALL 2021

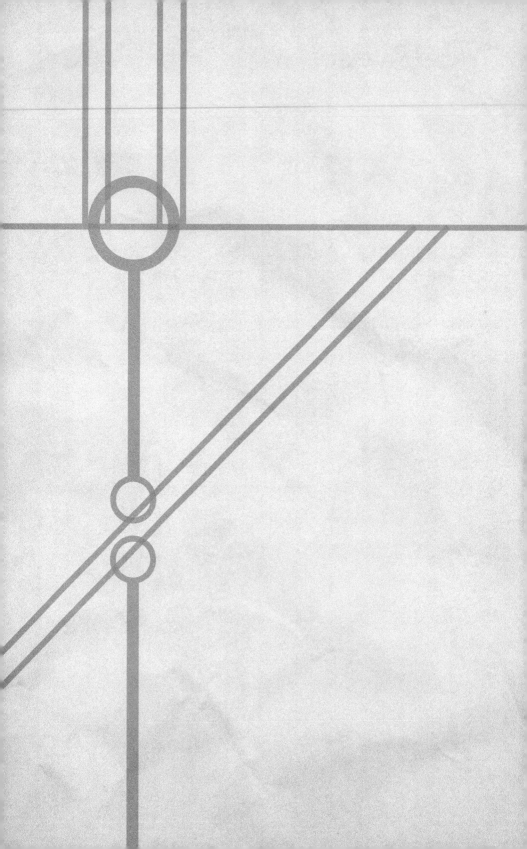

CLAUDIA GRAY

is the pseudonym of Amy Vincent. She is the writer of multiple young adult novels, including the Evernight series, the Firebird trilogy, and the Constellation trilogy. In addition, she's written several *Star Wars* novels, such as *Lost Stars* and *Bloodline*. She makes her home in New Orleans with her partner, Paul, and assorted small dogs.

ERIC ZAWADZKI

is a Canadian comic book artist who most recently worked on *Heart Attack* for Skybound/Image Comics. He's most well-known for his work on the critically acclaimed *The Dregs* and *Eternal* from Black Mask Studios. Eric is a recent transplant to Calgary, Alberta. He and his two hairless cats aren't handling the winters very well.

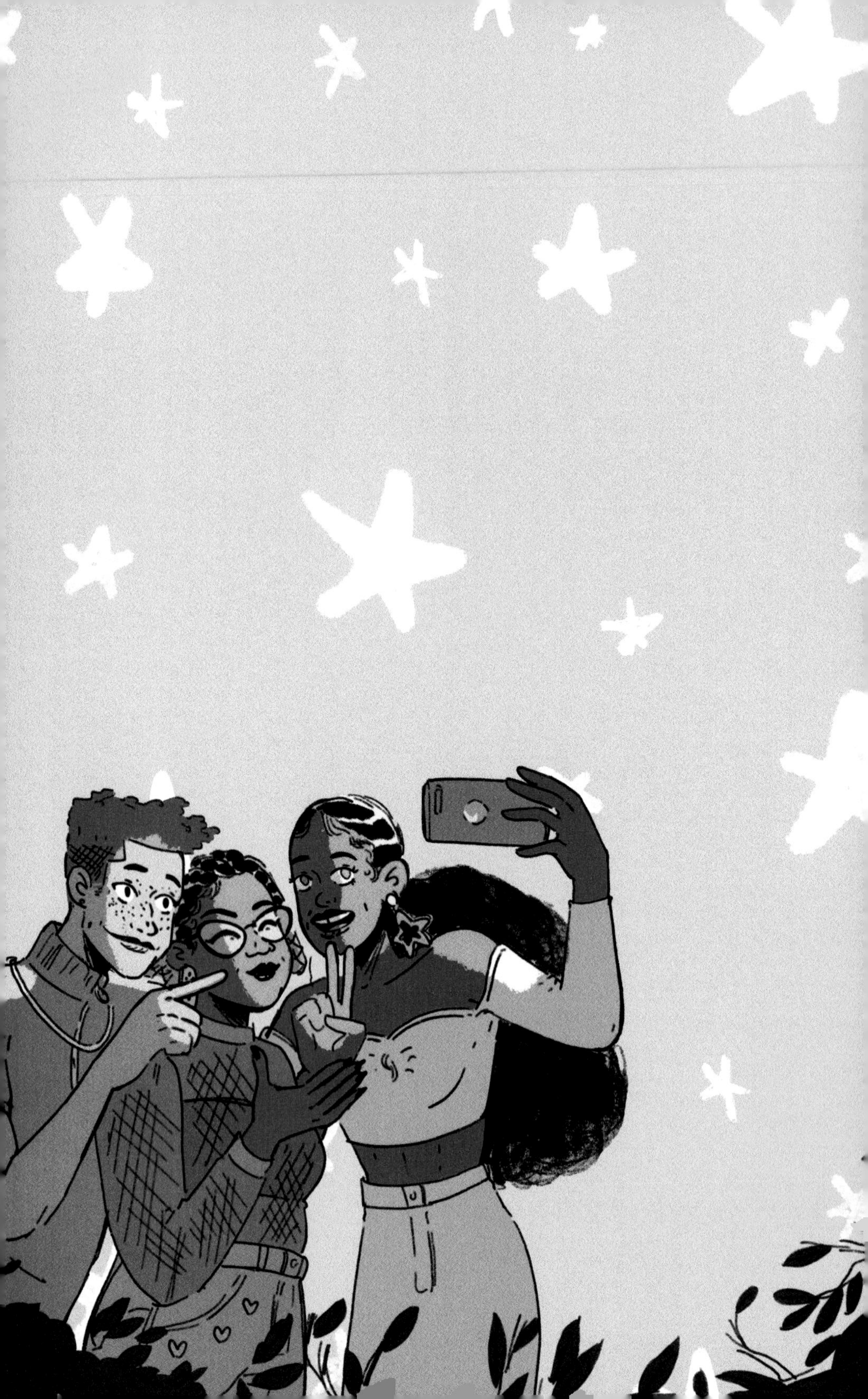

Acclaimed author **L.L. McKinney** and artist **Robyn Smith**
join forces to reimagine Nubia—Wonder Woman's
twin sister—in this #OwnVoices YA graphic novel about
equality, identity, and kicking it with your squad.

When Nubia's best friend, Quisha, is threatened by a
boy who thinks he owns the town, Nubia will risk it all—
her safety, her home, and her crush on that cute kid in
English class—to become the hero society tells her she isn't.
Keep reading for a sneak peek of *Nubia: Real One*.

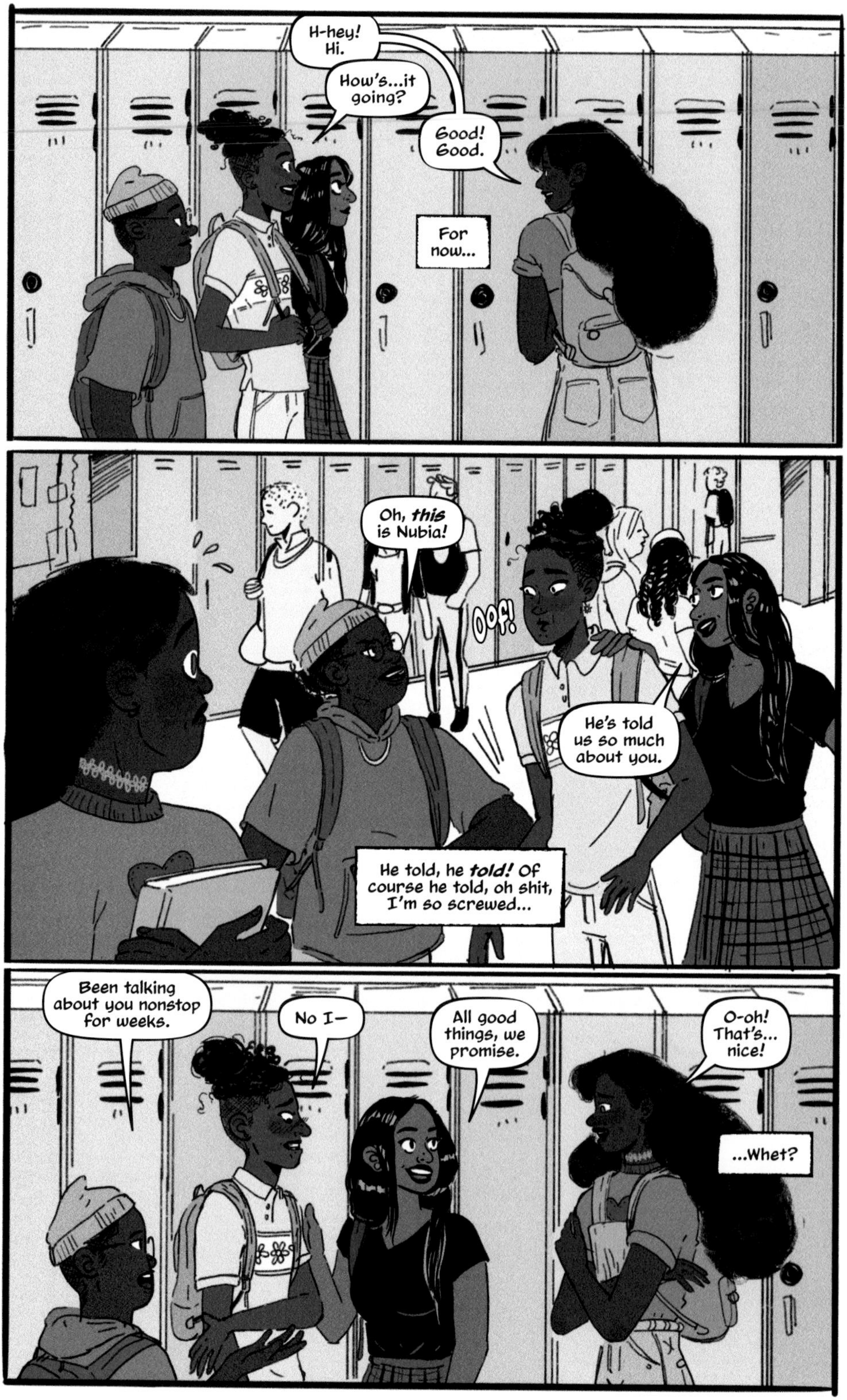
H-hey! Hi.
How's...it going?
Good! Good.
For now...
Oh, *this* is Nubia!
OOF!
He's told us so much about you.
He told, he *told!* Of course he told, oh shit, I'm so screwed...
Been talking about you nonstop for weeks.
No I—
All good things, we promise.
O-oh! That's... nice!
...Whet?

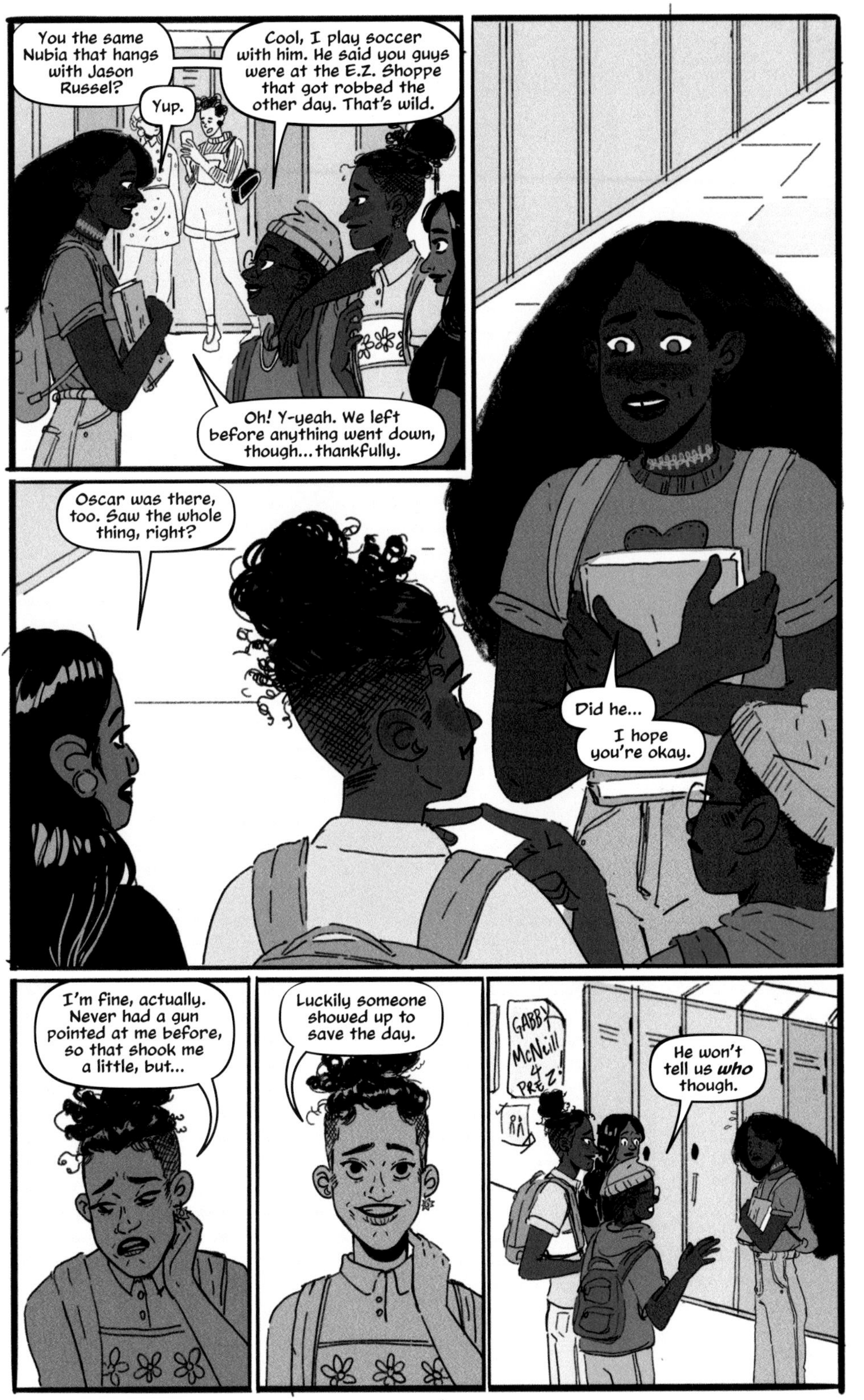
You the same Nubia that hangs with Jason Russel?
Yup.
Cool, I play soccer with him. He said you guys were at the E.Z. Shoppe that got robbed the other day. That's wild.
Oh! Y-yeah. We left before anything went down, though... thankfully.
Oscar was there, too. Saw the whole thing, right?
Did he...
I hope you're okay.
I'm fine, actually. Never had a gun pointed at me before, so that shook me a little, but...
Luckily someone showed up to save the day.
GABBY McNEILL 4 PREZ!
He won't tell us *who* though.

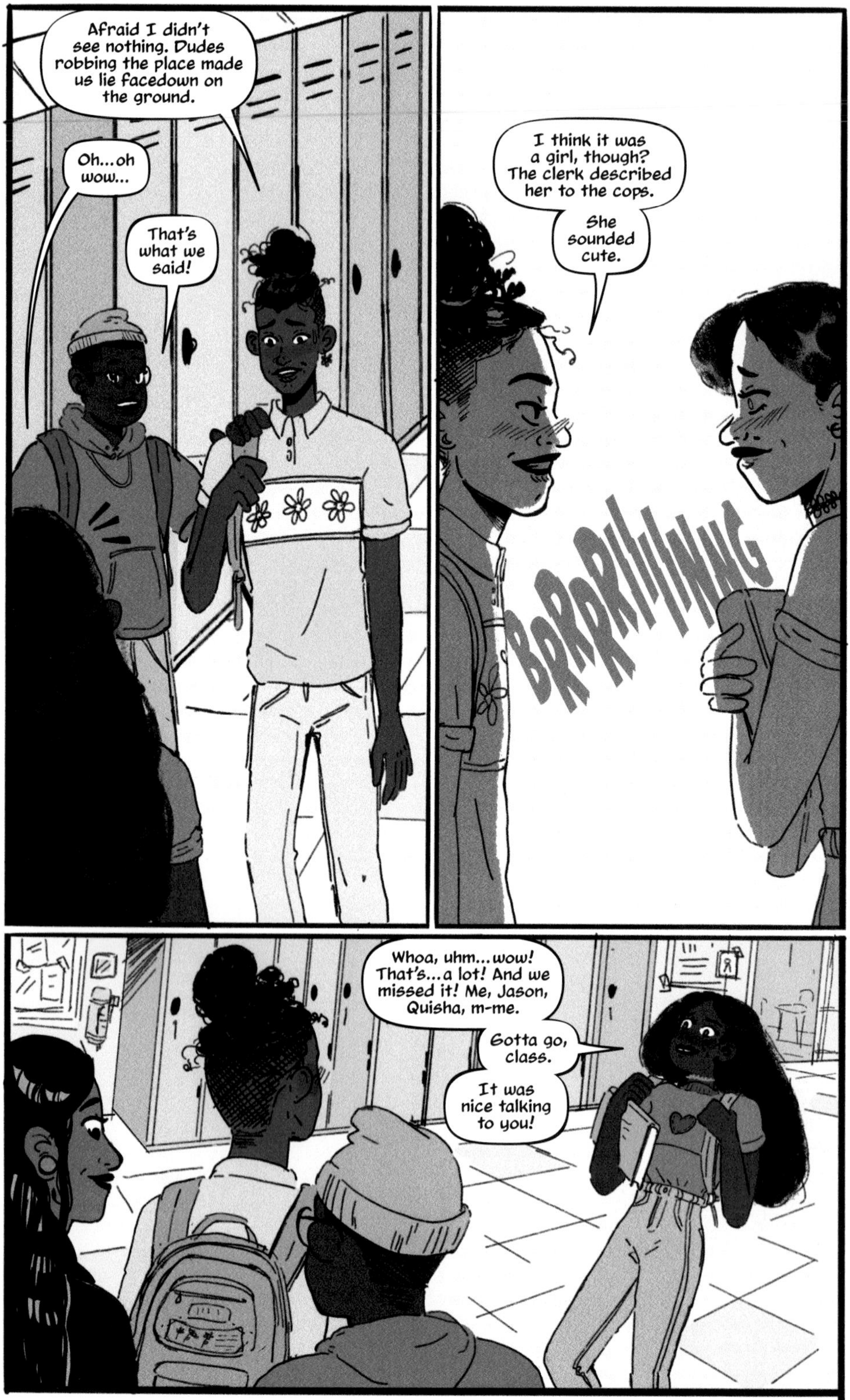
Afraid I didn't see nothing. Dudes robbing the place made us lie facedown on the ground.
Oh...oh wow...
That's what we said!
I think it was a girl, though? The clerk described her to the cops.
She sounded cute.
BRRRIIIIINNG
Whoa, uhm...wow! That's...a lot! And we missed it! Me, Jason, Quisha, m-me.
Gotta go, class.
It was nice talking to you!

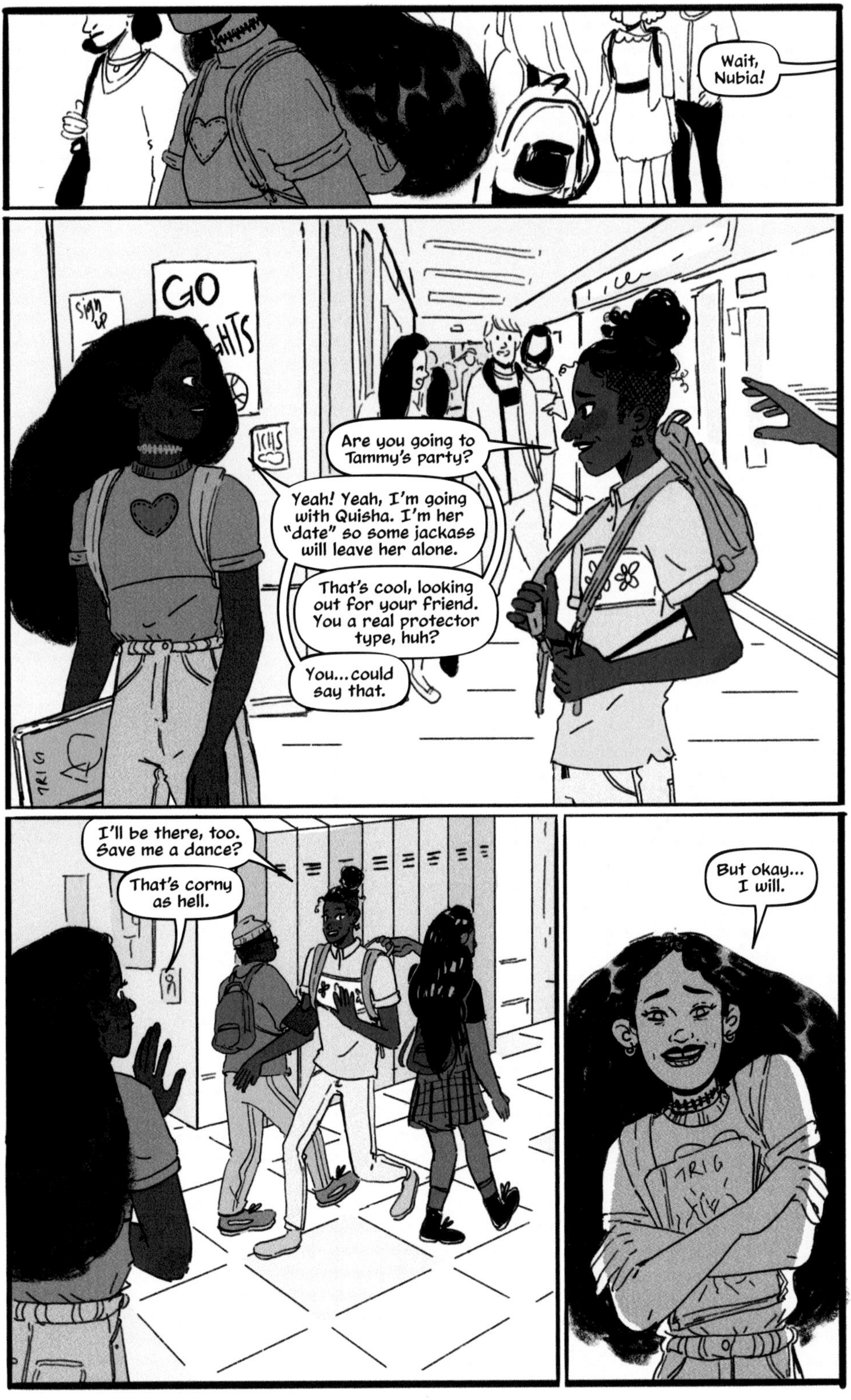
Wait, Nubia!
GO
sign up
ICHS
Are you going to Tammy's party?
Yeah! Yeah, I'm going with Quisha. I'm her "date" so some jackass will leave her alone.
That's cool, looking out for your friend. You a real protector type, huh?
You...could say that.
TRIG
I'll be there, too. Save me a dance?
That's corny as hell.
But okay... I will.
TRIG

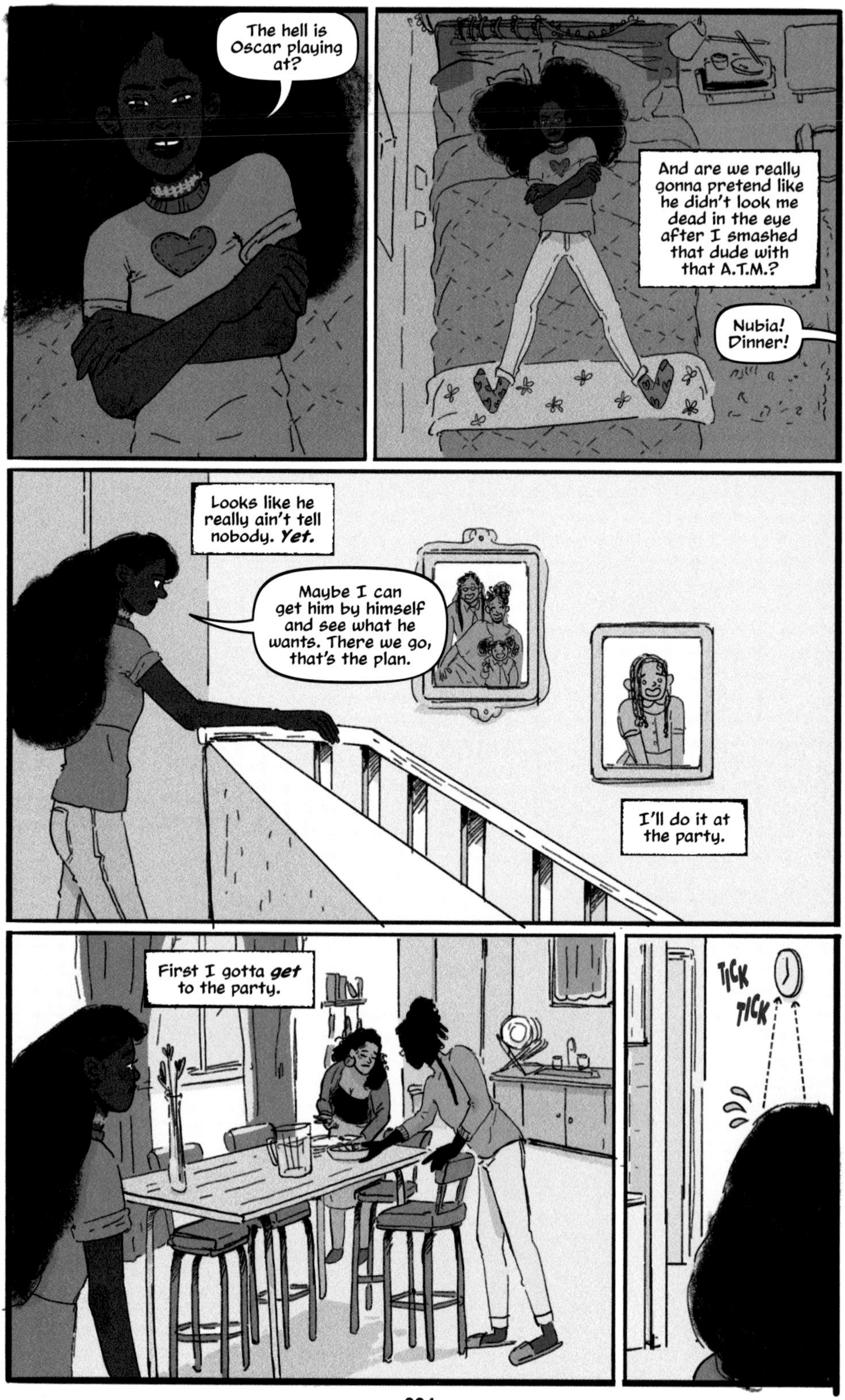

The hell is Oscar playing at?
And are we really gonna pretend like he didn't look me dead in the eye after I smashed that dude with that A.T.M.?
Nubia! Dinner!
Looks like he really ain't tell nobody. *Yet.*
Maybe I can get him by himself and see what he wants. There we go, that's the plan.
I'll do it at the party.
First I gotta *get* to the party.
TICK
TICK

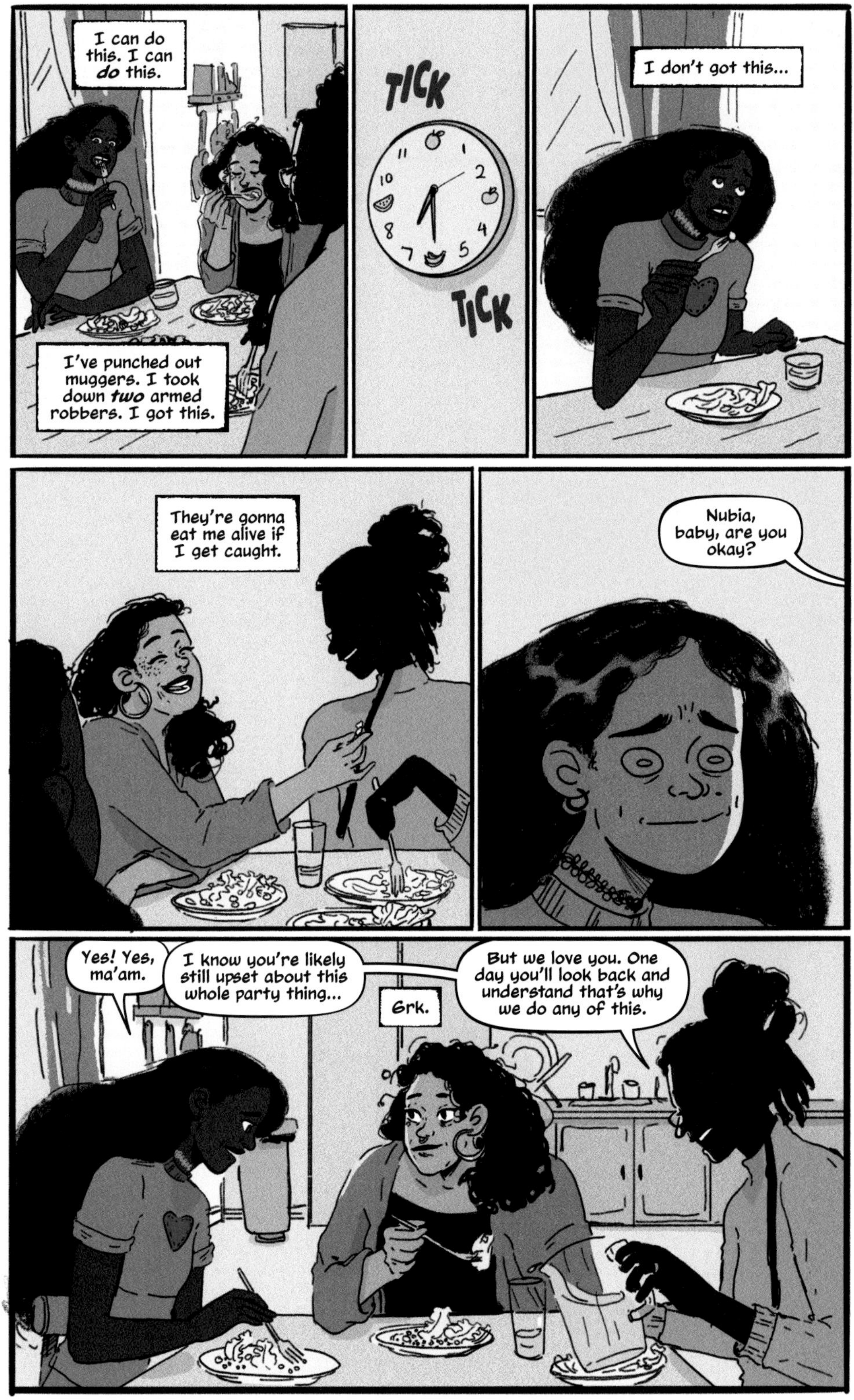
I can do this. I can *do* this.
I've punched out muggers. I took down *two* armed robbers. I got this.
TICK
TICK
I don't got this...
They're gonna eat me alive if I get caught.
Nubia, baby, are you okay?
Yes! Yes, ma'am.
I know you're likely still upset about this whole party thing...
Grk.
But we love you. One day you'll look back and understand that's why we do any of this.

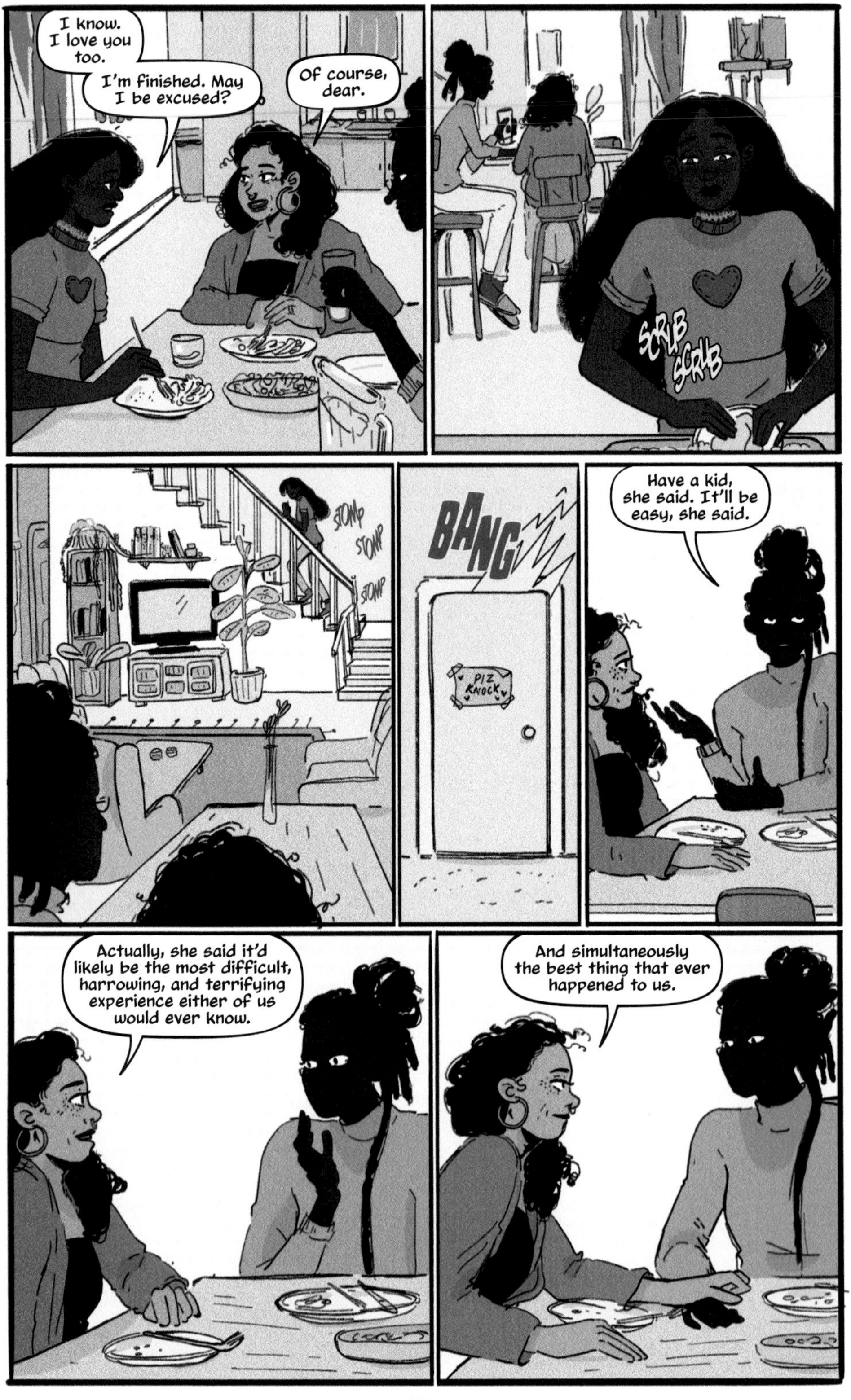
I know. I love you too.
I'm finished. May I be excused?
Of course, dear.
SCRUB SCRUB
STOMP STOMP STOMP
BANG
PLZ KNOCK
Have a kid, she said. It'll be easy, she said.
Actually, she said it'd likely be the most difficult, harrowing, and terrifying experience either of us would ever know.
And simultaneously the best thing that ever happened to us.

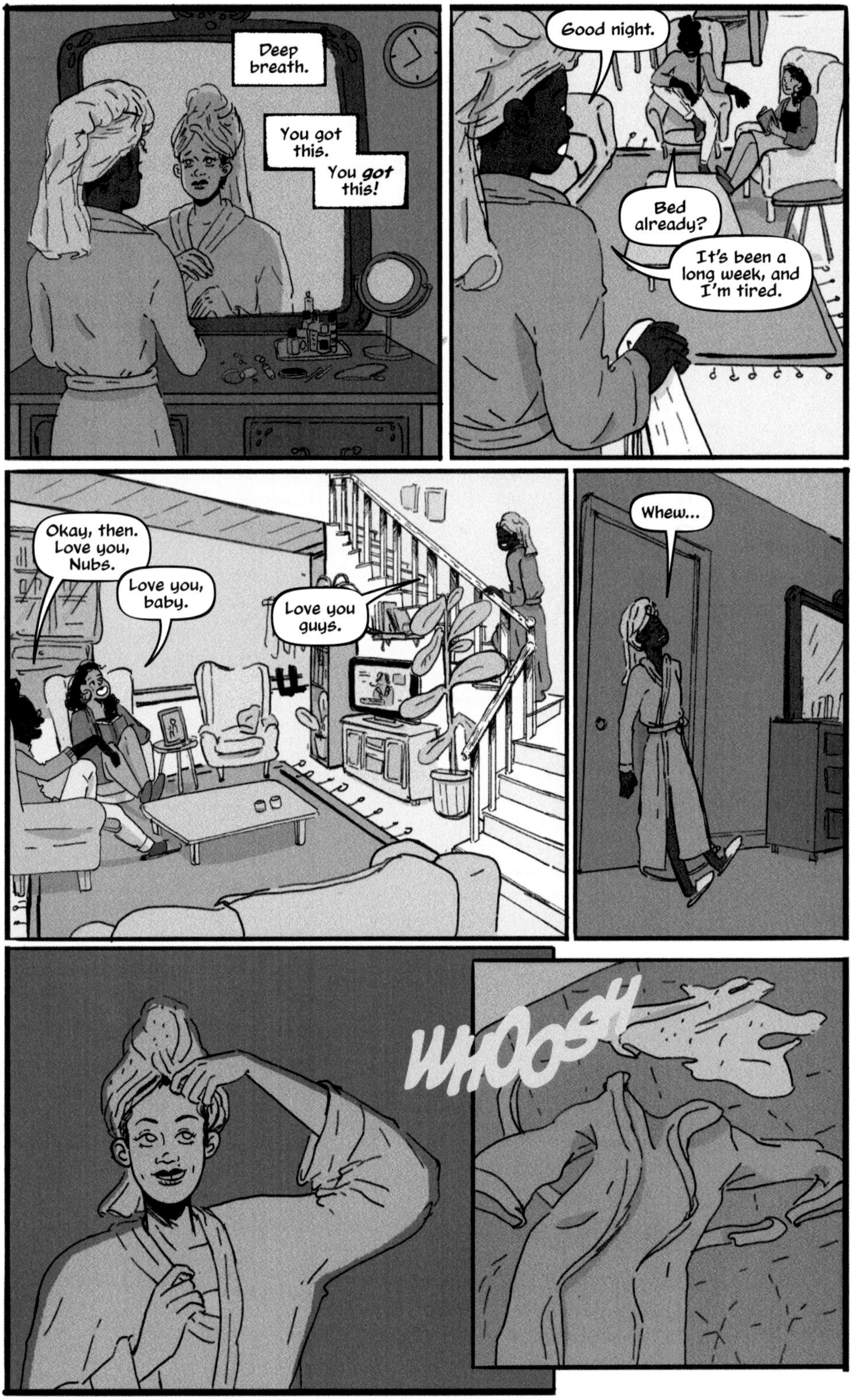
Deep breath.
You got this.
You *got* this!
Good night.
Bed already?
It's been a long week, and I'm tired.
Okay, then. Love you, Nubs.
Love you, baby.
Love you guys.
Whew...
WHOOSH

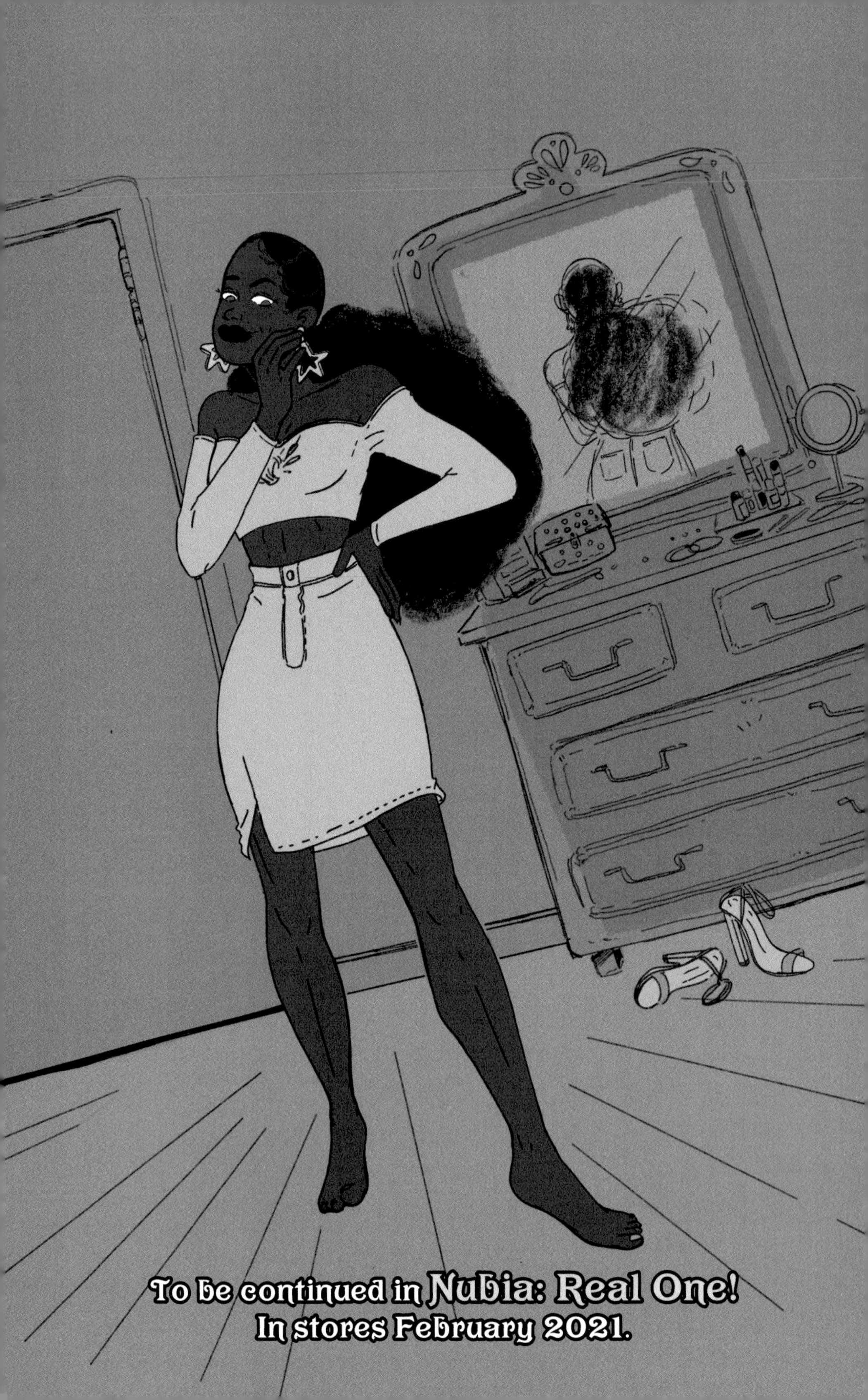

To be continued in Nubia: Real One!
In stores February 2021.